One Sour Grape

by

Jaclyn Tracey

One Sour Grape

Cover Art by *Jennifer Greeff*

The Wild Rose Press, Inc.
PO Box 708
Adams Basin, NY 14410-0708
Visit us at www.thewildrosepress.com

Publishing History
First Edition, 2023
Trade Paperback ISBN 978-1-5092-5124-7
Digital ISBN 978-1-5092-5125-4

Published in the United States of America

Looking around for her dad, Ava spotted still cuffed. She didn't see the gun-toting babysitter. Maybe they took her to mental hospital. And the little crop-duster pixy flew off too. Ava sat up and snuggled into her blanky. When something sparkly caught her eye, her head jerked in the direction of it and there like a nightlight at the end of the couch sat her jewelry box. Did she open it again? Would her gross talking doll still be in there asking her to kiss him? Yick, hence the reason she cut the heads from dolls. Useless.

So, if anyone bothered to ask her what happened this time, did she go for the truth? Tell them, a little pixy farted sprinkles on Harper and made her pass out, or she had her very own Jack in the box? Even Ava had a hard time believing it. And then there was Zeus. A god. With wings that only she seemed to be able to see. Everyone saw the man, not the otherworldly features he possessed, which in the eyes of the law made him look flat out crazy. And if Zeus were bonkers where did this leave Ava? She clamped her eyes closed praying when she opened them the box would be gone, she'd be back home in bed being tucked in by both her parents, and her brother would be hiding under her bed kicking her mattress trying to annoy her.

Dedication

For my Grandees ~ Noah, Ethan, Hadley and Logan.
My four musketeers, thank you for keeping me young
at heart, smiling, dreaming and on my toes. I love you
guys more.
To my Editor, Callie Lynn Wolfe~ You are my own
personal version of Spellcheck, the Copyright Police,
and one woman I value as my sister from another
mother. Thank you for being you and allowing me and
my muses to keep you awake nights.

Chapter One

Looking Up at The Clouds

The Solar Eclipse earlier in the afternoon left Ava Gabriel awestruck, as in jaw dropped, eyes wide, stars exploding within them. For this special event her mom went all out preparing a picnic for the family in the meadow. She even used the good linen, so this had to be a big deal. Ava wasn't sure who was more excited, her mom or her. Ava's dad passed out solar filtering sunglasses to view Selene and Helios tango through the sky. And dance they did, the moon with the sun and Ava with her family. The power of the universe spilled over Ava in spine-tingling euphoria. Cows wouldn't be the only creatures jumping over the moon tonight.

Today topped her charts in the *best day ever* category. She hadn't had this much energy in months. Her hair took on a life of its own as it floated in the air without static electricity. Her little brother, Ayden, pointed and laughed at her.

"Aves, you look wild."

Ava tapped his head, giggling. "You think you look any better?" Hearing that he gingerly touched his head and fled for the house with a shocked look on his face. Ava's mom always said, 'Doesn't matter the size of a god. Vanity will always be bigger.' He proved her point.

Once the total blackout passed the vistas' wavy

patterns afterwards reminded Ava of ribbon candy, the fragile Christmas treat that the moment your teeth crunched into it, a wicked mess ensued. For her, this occurrence, the eclipse, toppled Christmas, even more so once she found out Santa was nothing more than a poser.

Biggest letdown ever.

He could, *ho, ho, ho* all the way to you know where for all she cared.

How could her parents lie to her? About someone so important? What other fake stories had they knowingly filled her mind with? Was the tooth fairy about to get yanked out of the line up? Or Cupid pierced by his own arrow come Valentine's Day? Was true love doomed? She couldn't think that far ahead. Boys! She wouldn't mind pinging Ayden with an arrow or two.

After dinner Ava jumped into her jammies, slid on her pink and yellow polka dotted galoshes, and proceeded to drag her sleeping bag and pillow outside through the tall grass into the field. She'd promised to be on her best behavior tomorrow if she could lay outside tonight to watch a meteor shower. The sky seemed limitless this week between the eclipse and meteor show.

Sprawled out on her sleeping bag watching the lightning bugs brighten everything and listening to crickets chirping, Ava had one wish, that her parents and brother would come out and keep her company. It was sort of spooky out here all alone and other than today, arguing seemed to be the only activity her parents did together. On the cusp of turning six, Ava noticed everything, like more and more the babysitter seemed to always be here and her mom, not so much.

Stargazing, planetariums, constellations, Ava lived for it. The stars carried her wishes farther than any seedling from a dandelion could ever drift. It's how she skirted around reality, to be a kid and dream instead of having nightmares chasing her through the day, listening to her mother's muffled cries in the shower begging the gods to save Ava. That pretty much freaked her out because no one was telling her anything about her situation. Not knowing things made her nuts.

Her father was her rock. He encouraged Ava's enthusiasm for knowledge. He bought books on all the constellations and every night they read one together. It was their thing. Ava knew the history behind every deity and how the constellations got their names. Draco had to be her favorite because honestly who didn't love the little pyromaniacs. Dragons—she wanted one but the closest she ever got to a dragon was dodging dragonflies in the hay field. Not something she could boast about when she went into first grade while the other kids would be crowing about their summer travels. Maybe she could tame a squadron of them or maybe she'd watched too much television…the thought made her laugh until reality set in. Ava's only excursion out of her hometown happened to be a trip to the hospital. Not exactly bragging rights.

She'd been waiting for the eclipse and meteor show ever since her last trip to the infirmary. Covered in bruises, with no rhythm or reason, she had to spend a few nights in the smelly building for tests. Her dad spent the nights hogging the bed to keep her company. One morning, busy getting poked, Ava focused on the meteorologist on television telling her to mark tonight on the calendar for the astral show of the century and so she did, instead of all the blood draining from her arm. Her dad? Smelling salts were being stuffed under his nose after he passed out.

Tonight, the moon illuminated the world from Ava's vantage. The horizon bustled with brilliance, and she was more than ready for some razzle-dazzle. One good thing to look forward to because tomorrow there were more needles to try to find out why she was still getting giant purple blotches all over her and why she woke up tired and seemingly in a different spot each time after falling asleep exhausted. Her dad always kidded around telling her she had teleportation powers getting her from the couch to her bed, even though Ava knew it was her dad lugging her up the stairs because he'd accidentally wacked her head on the door frame a few times jarring her from her slumber.

Tomorrow also marked Ava's sixth birthday. Some birthday. A short sigh fizzled out to space. Tomorrow there would be no party. There would be no clowns. She wanted them to scare her brother. God knew she owed him.

And the absolute worst part of tomorrow, there would be no cake, which sadly meant no frosting, the best part of the entire day.

Instead, there would be a long, hot car ride to the hospital jammed in the back seat of the car with Ayden. At least she wouldn't get stuck with the babysitter tomorrow. The girl creeped her out, always had a sideways stink eye aimed at her, or a malign whisper in her irritable voice taunting, 'Boarding school', whatever that meant. Her brother's life goals were eating, making loud farts, burping the alphabet, and playing magic tricks. His favorite? Hiding a frog in her bed, hence the need for clowns.

Once at the hospital, there would be a ward full of

little kids all fighting for their lives, with bags of medicine hung on poles following them better than their shadows, that is, when they were strong enough to get out of bed and hit the hallways. Birthdays. She needed to celebrate this one like a goddess in case it ended up being her last.

****

From my pedestal

Stood at the altar, one leg bouncing, palms slick with sweat, I took in a deep breath hoping to take the pre-wedding jitters down a notch while I waited for the first glimpse of my beloved as she took her sweet time promenading down the aisle.

The rising cadence one would expect at the chariot races rose from the crowd as my lady entered the arena. Music filled the void as my blood pooled in my feet. Problem being, it, my blood, wasn't coming back up. Lightheadedness and chest pain followed.

Some twit, that would be my son, Hymenaeus-God of weddings, and the original wedding hymn, switched the tunes. We were now subject to the funeral march instead of the wedding trek. My neck snapped to my left. As if on some unforeseen cue all my groomsmen donned sunglasses at the exact same time.

"Tell me this is a joke," I demanded.

One of the men mumbled, "The joke brother, is on you if you go through with this."

I raised my voice above the music, "I'm changing my will, son."

"Love you too, Dad!" The stinking kid played on with more enthusiasm.

My neck craned to get a better view of my lady, whispers and jeers filled my head. Unfortunately, for me, my height did not match that of my family and friends, so I remained clueless as to why. Each man in my wedding party resembled great red oaks, me a sapling. With the guests all stood vying to catch a glimpse of my bride, I had the perfect view of everyone's backsides, not that I mind. Some are rather sexy. "I cannot see her," sounded rather desperate. I gave the best puppy-eyed plea to my best man, my dearest friend, who by fate, would also be my half-brother, Apollo. He nudged the next man in line, Thor, my wingman—literally, and beloved comrade in shenanigans.

"Give him a lift so he can see what he's getting himself into." Apollo's tone sounded more suited for a divorce instead of matrimony.

Thor gave a very subtle shake of his head no, so shrewd in fact, I nearly missed it. Sunglasses slid down his nose. Thor's ridiculous blue eyes widened when he knew I noticed.

"Really," Thor whispered, "I'm doing you a favor." His sunglasses were shoved back into place, his shoulders went back, and his chest shoved forward showing off his physique. I sucked in my gut. Didn't really help.

"You look ridiculous, Thor."

"Thor doesn't look anywhere near as ridiculous as the bride," my half-sister Artemis bellowed from the opposite side of the alter. She rolled her eyes and shook her head.

My voice as tendered as I could, I growled, "What don't I want to see?"

Another of my groomsmen, and another half-brother, Hercules, scratched his ear and then with uneasy fingers played with his overgrown mustache-goatee. The sides being so long he could have braided them. Full of brawn and balls, the eight-foot giant looks silly. He grew the peach-fuzz for today. Tomorrow we will be cropping it out of all photos, probably from the neck up.

The hulky man leaned into me, budging Thor and Apollo back a step. "Think Earth's version of Lady Godiva, yet not quite eye-candy. More radioactive."

I demanded, "Pick me up!" Thor obliged. Aghast, my voice rose. "Apollo! What in heavens did you do to her?"

"She stated she wanted to outshine the sun for you this day, dear brother. I granted her this boon. Be careful what you wish for."

As if I've never been told this before.

Hermes flit to me, removed his shades, gawked a second, before quickly donning the glasses back on his face and remarking, "She looks like a cross between the golden egg the goose dumped and a true vampire's ill-fated demise."

I shot back, "And what are you supposed to look like, Fly-boy? Nice hair." Hermes wore the opposite of a Mohawk. Bald straight down the center of his knobby skull, with a red frizzy ponytail sticking out each side. Even his nose was red. I have the original clown posse beside me. No one other than me is taking this ceremony seriously.

On the opposite side of the isle, Artemis conspired with my beloved's other attendants, my half-sister, Athena and beside her, Aphrodite, mother to my kid I just cut from my will. Her loser ex-husband, Hephaestus, watched her the way a serial killer scoped out his next victim. The man totally unnerves me. His eyes are bloodshot, he is teeming with perspiration and flies are swarming him. Our wedding guests have removed themselves from his personal space. After Aphrodite removed her sunglasses, her silvery eyes appeared as if she'd captured a few twinkling stars. The goddess would always outshine my bride no matter how much gold dust the princess caked on but looks aren't everything. Integrity, compassion, honesty, and a sense of humor are what any man wishes for. Looks would be the icing on the cake.

I love icing. Pity there will be none.

As I dangled from Thor's mighty grasp, jaw clenched, I squinted as our gazes met. My bride is blindingly burnished. I now get the shades. I've never seen her like this, and dare I say I never wish to again. A scowl crept onto my mug. I fought it. Piss poor poker player here.

She saw my first reaction—the one all brides base the rest of their eternal years of bliss upon. If they see us gush, we have a chance. If they see us gag, as I might have, chances are good I'll be in the doghouse with Cerberus tonight, who at this very moment is very busy sniffing and growling at her.

There's a tune in my head from days of old, something about *not touching this*, as the artist flits across the dance floor in genie pants. I'm silently cracking up. I have a vague suspicion today isn't going to go as planned.

"Stop laughing, Dion. She'll kill you later, if there is a later," Apollo whispered. Apparently, I am not as stealthy as I imagined.

The bride's silky locks have been woven into what I can only describe as a bramble nest. Not the look I expected. Arrowheads, made from sprigs of asteroids pop out from different angles throughout the updo. The contrast is probably lethal. She looks as if she is prepared to do battle. My brow wiggles in anticipation. I should pace myself for tonight. Maybe cut back on the wine a bit.

Pfft! Let us not forget who I am. God of grapes and good times followed by memory lapses and hangovers.

We, the bride and I, are opposites to the end of the galaxy. We both know how to turn heads—people follow her and look in the opposite direction when I enter a room.

"Seen enough?" Thor asked, not even straining a muscle to keep me held above the crowd.

"Never!" I lied, while my eyes pleaded with Thor to drop me. And drop me he did. Apollo caught me before I toppled over sideways. Guests would assume I'd had too much wine. I don't believe I've had enough!

I lowered my voice and elbowed my half-brother's side. "What did you slather all over her, Apollo? Will Cerberus be okay? One of his thick heads just licked her leg. Her flesh is erupting faster than it takes you to satisfy yourself."

"The fact you care more of the dog than your bride says volumes of your truest desires," he mumbled through a snicker. "Never mind that, look." Apollo pointed to my head. "Brother, your crown. Your grapes are literally shriveling up the closer she gets to you. We told you this union would have consequences."

My line of vision went to the ground. Raisins were hastily being carted off by tiny scorpion-like scavengers. I despise those things—raisins that is. They are the culmination of waste and ruin.

Thor added his two cents, "Can you say bad omen?"

I glared at him sideways.

"What? I'm stating the obvious, Dion."

Apollo added, "Your lady will be miserable before nightfall. You'll spend your first night scratching her instead of sating your itch. And what is up with the headpiece? She nicks you with that, Dionysus, it could be the kiss of death." Apollo fidgeted with his muttonchops he had so thoughtfully grown for this day. He saw me staring at them and commented, "You are just jealous."

Hercules interrupted, "Bigger problem, brother."

There we stood, with our heads cocked at an odd angle as my lady neared, her gait clumsy.

Hermes floated above us and asked, "Do you see what I see?"

"A sing-along. Splendid." Apollo went into an excited golf clap and began to belt out a children's song from decades past. Me thinks my brother has had more wine than I have today.

I grabbed his jaw and pointed his face in the direction of my bride's tootsies. "Focus! Please? Is her father grandstanding again?" Apollo slapped my hand away.

"When doesn't the king?" Hermes added. A collective bobble-head nod went down the line of groomsmen.

Laughter erupted from the guests watching the bride's father being dragged down the path as he clung in desperation to my bride's ankle sobbing. This could very well be the highlight of the day. "Unbelievable." I looked at my bride. Her face strained in an agonized portrait, she simply tossed her red-scalded hands in the air, palms up, her expression glowering, unknowing whether to console the insolent man or shake him off her. I turned to one of my groomsmen. "Hercules, you're up."

Without further ado, my colossus half-brother clomped down the lane. He greeted my beloved bride with a cordial, "You're going to be insanely miserable later. Don't make my boy the same," as he bent over to pry her father from her leg.

"I already am, Hercules," she answered scoring marks into her skin with bloodied fingernails.

"Justified!" Hercules gave an all-out tug on the back of my soon to be father-in-law's robe. The motion sent my bride and Hercules sideways. Hercules caught both their balances and then crushed the king's wrist under his foot until the father of the bride yelped. "King Minos, let go."

"Father, do it. Let go," my goddess begged while her mother, Pasiphae, helped steady her daughter, cursing things I've never heard a women say aloud. After a futile struggle the King hung over Hercules' shoulder. He pleaded, "Ariadne, no! Please daughter, do not go forth with this alliance."

Perfect! Her family is against us as well. And here I thought the man adored me.

I gave my index finger a discrete waggle towards a huge black hole where one can see into other galaxies. We call this phenomenon Heaven's Gate. Those not so fortunate call it walking the plank even though there isn't an actual plank. Hercules and the ankle-biter vanished. Not a moment passed before a dwindling, "*Nooo,*" echoed from the great beyond. Hercules returned wearing a smile broader than his massive shoulders.

If asked what just went down, I'm rather certain the answer is the King, but I shall not inquire any further, for ignorance is bliss.

Within a few awkward moments we, the golden goose—my bride, and myself, two love-struck kids, stood beneath a magnificent structure of marble and moonstone blended of what others now call Medieval Gothic and Victorian design, where two high peaked columns disappear into the stars. The half-brother I have no feelings for other than contempt, Mister perspiration himself, Hephaestus, designed the elaborate building. His head swells when people compare him to DaVinci. I wish one day it would explode. Each intricately carved column is a tower built with a thousand steps where a bridged arch connects the two structures in the center. There is a small room midway that holds our version of the Hubble Telescope, except ours is light years ahead of Earths'. We can see into people's lives, galaxies far beyond a human's comprehension. Voyeurs yes, but it keeps us apprised of our surroundings.

As we waited for the arrival of our divine elder to arrive my blushing bride looks to have ants in her pants, if she'd worn any. She has not stopped scratching since she arrived by my side.

"Ariadne?" I too rubbed my head because watching her squirm seems to have a trickle-down effect.

Ariadne glared at my half-brother. "Allergic reaction to the gold dust."

If looks could kill I believe Apollo would be missing out on the rest of the day. Good thing she isn't a Gorgon girl. Speaking of, Medusa is stood quietly alone near the exit of the grove. Guess Poseidon had more urgent matters ten leagues below the sea than to keep his lady company and come to see his nephew finally get hitched. Medusa has a new look. She's wearing sunglasses so she doesn't stone anyone accidentally, and a coiffure covering her head. This is a blessing because I for one, run like a banshee from snakes. I took a second to see if Athena and Hercules noticed her. The three do not play nicely in the sand box. I feel a war coming for them.

I nudged my half-brother. "Apollo, there must be a salve to counteract this irritant my bride slathered all over?"

Apollo shoved his glasses back on his head with his middle finger saluting the bride to be, taking away stray blond curls from his face. With an immoral gleam in his eye, he smiled and gave a little jiggle of his head no. "Has to wear off on its own time. Not sorry."

My lady moaned, "I'll be fine," as she bounced from one leg to the other.

"Will you make it through the ceremony?" I felt horrible for her. I wanted to scratch all her itchy parts, but at the same time my aversion to anything resembling poisoned sap coiled within me.

Seeing her agonize brought back memories, bad memories, of the time I'd been drawn and quartered for someone's giggles and… I made a promise I would not curse for a while. We'll see how long that lasts, anyway whilst I lay subject to torture, those who delighted in my suffering decided to add insult to injury by including the sap of ivy to my body. As if looking like a jigsaw puzzle whilst vultures nibbled upon open wounds wasn't bad enough, let's put an itch, oh say, right there out of reach.

I have waited for this, my wedding day, for more than a millennium and to see her so uncomfortable is arduous. I'd love to help her, but I am no healer. The true healer on the team is fighting back tears of laughter and losing. I stomped on Apollo's toes to let him know how distasteful his attempt to halt my union is.

Through taut swollen lips, Ariadne scanned the guests. "Where is your father?"

She sounded anxious, but not the same anxious I felt. The anxious thrumming through me wanted to marry the love of my life. She wanted to get this over with and move on. If I resembled roiling magma, I do suppose my motives may be in alignment with hers.

"Here," Zeus responded as he sifted down from thin air, his iridescent wings shimmering in the sun, his balance slightly off. His first reaction seeing my bride mirrored mine. Like father like son.

"Oh. My. God!" My father swallowed hard as he tapped his fists to his chest, his signature move. "It is better to enjoy the view of the golden rays of Helios than to try to emulate them, Ariadne. Senseless girl. Dionysus, last chance son to walk away a free man. Take it."

"Father!" I snapped. Disappointment weighed my tone.

Apollo clasped his hand on my shoulder in a tight grip. "For once in your life think before speaking, Dion. Use your head instead of your heart."

Zeus gave a humored nod to my half-brother. "Apollo? I'm guessing you are the mastermind behind this metallic muddle?"

Unrepentant, Apollo boasted, "You bet your moonbeams I did. I am not a fan of this fusion. Look at her. She is one juicy abscess with or without the paint. Have fun with that Dionysus."

Ariadne spoke up, "Can we please wrap this up?"

"Nothing spells out true love with more endearing words!" Please note my sarcasm as it nudges its way between the bride and me.

Zeus leaned to me, placed his lips to my ear and whispered, "Dionysus? Honestly, are you certain?"

I tossed my hands up and looked down at my feet in disappointment. I couldn't look at my father. I needed him to be on my side, happy for me, trusting my decisions, celebrating his son marrying the love of his life, not being his usual all-judgmental self. "Not you as well, Father?"

"An answer," the god demanded.

Frustrated, I tugged my fingers through my unruly curls and straightened my crown. Two more grapes shriveled and fell to my feet. I looked down at the dried-up fruit and then to my bride. A bolt of panic abraded every nerve in my body. What would my life be without my crown? It's all I am. My entire life has evolved around my grapes, wine, parties, and beautiful women. My bottom lip twitched before answering. "Ninety-nine-point-nine percent." Hearing gripes and grumbles from my guests, I turned to face them. I surmised, "Is anyone ever truly one hundred percent?" Noting Ariadne's entire demeanor stiffen, that one line would forever go down in history as the one that painted me the fool. I looked out to the crowd and saw many a heads bob while money changed hands.

Nice. Really nice.

When my father said, "Do you Ariadne, daughter of the late King Minos of Create, take my son, Dionysus, son of the greatest god ever, to be your lover, your confidant, your one true friend, probably only friend, the keeper of your heart as your husband," I didn't dare move a muscle, not even to spare a glance left or right.

The late king Minos? Plausible deniability wearing

thin if I move a muscle.

In constant motion squirming, the bride seemed to miss that line.

My heart plummeted when she answered with a miserable outburst, "Oh I can't do this right now!"

I staggered backwards into Apollo's arms. He steadied me with his arm over my shoulder and across my chest. He pulled me close and whispered, "It is for the best. Trust me, brother,"

Breaking free from him I got right in Ariadne's face. "You mean you can't get married right now? Or ever?" I had to know.

"I am about to burst, Dionysus."

Did I need to point out the unmistakable? Probably not, but Captain Obvious giddy-on-upped and blurted, "You already have."

Through puffy, red eyelids the woman's glower gave me goose bumps. Fabulous, any second now we would match in attire.

"Must it always be about you?" Pretty certain she doesn't want my answer. I stifled a chuckle. Ariadne twisted from me frantically pointing over her shoulder to her back. "Scratch right there. I can't take it another second."

Hand gestures amuck, I yelled, "Oh ladies in waiting? My bride needs you. This instant!"

A healthy dose of, "No way," and, "your bride, your blisters," echoed through the grove. Guess I didn't pay the ladies enough to stand up for her.

Her voice drenched with hostility Ariadne exploded, "Just scratch it now, Dionysus."

I gave my groomsmen an agonized glance. Each of them shook their heads no. "I have been instructed not to touch that. I am sorry. While we wait for this to resolve why don't we just get on with the I-dos?" I had to turn my head away while a few blisters splattered, some hitting my cheeks.

Apollo reached into his pocket and pulled out a pair of swimmer's goggles and dangled them in my face. "Protective eyewear."

"Very funny," I muttered as I strapped them on.

Unable to contain his delight, Apollo touted, "I thought so too." God bless the man even though the moron created this mess.

A quashed grunt escaped my father when he noticed the goggles. He rubbed the smirk from his lips and cleared his voice. "Ariadne? Answer yes or no to my question. Will you commit to loving my son?"

Loud enough for everyone to hear, Hercules whispered to Thor, "Or, just commit her?" Chuckles rose from the wedding guests seated on my side.

My shoulders slumped. My heart ached for my bride. Today should have been epic, not an epic disaster. I think my father had a change of heart seeing me defeated. Zeus's conviction changed. He now donned a choleric mask about him. He is the one person you don't keep waiting. Ever. He grabbed my hand and squeezed it to the point I almost cried *uncle*. "Regardless of the outcome, it will be fine, son."

The bride spun to me, looking worse by the seconds. I've never seen gold dust turn someone inside out. I'll have to remember this.

With a scathing, "Oh for the love of all things evil, yes," I was officially married. All that was left to do was kiss the bride. I went to pucker up and then thought better of it and backed away.

Maybe later. Her bottom lip is split wide open and bleeding profusely.

Regardless of my endeavors to remain free of poisonous body fluids, my wife planted what I can only describe as the opposite of true love's kiss on my lips, nicking my forehead with an arrow popping out of her veil. No romance behind the gesture. No loving, lingering gaze into my eyes. No, "I love you." No, "oops," or, "sorry," came as she turned tail and bolted into our wedding chamber, just a shallow grumble to sum up our true love, "All good things come to those who wait. Don't hold your breath."

Well, that was fun.

All in all, I'd say the shindig came off without so much as a hitch, and… I won a wager or two. Betting against your own ceremony—good times!

I may have performed the Shuffle Dance or as others call it, the Bacchic Jig, quite well if I do say so. Thor calls it the Bacchic Jiggles because of my eight-pack abs. He believes he is the funniest god ever. Someday, some woman will put him in his place. I hope.

All the female guests joined me on the dance floor. Their companions did not seem to enjoy the show. No accounting for taste these days. From the floor, I hear a few hecklers. Not certain whether this pertains to the blistering bride, coupled with the awkward father-daughter moment, or my mad dance moves. My hubris steers me to believe they speak of the little misses. I am a god on the dance floor. I've got moves. If you ask me, I am the personification of divine perfection without need for intervention. Just don't take a general poll until the wine is gone. Speaking of… I held my hand out and within a blink of an eye my favored cherub swooped in with a new goblet.

Chapter Two

Hopeful

The chunky cherub hovered in front of me, his wings flapping so fast I couldn't detect movement. "I do not know whether congratulations or condolences are in order, Dionysus, but either way, opa." The cherub then smashed the goblet of wine.

For the record, he is no longer my favored cherub. Who does that? Smashes a perfectly delicious goblet of wine on purpose? I am baffled. "You have thirty seconds to replace that, or I replace you." The cherub zipped off to the barrel and returned with a replacement. Goblet in hand, I chugged the way teenagers do their first beer, with reckless abandonment. A second cup went faster than the first.

Noise in the background amplified as my squad whooped it up as only drunken deities can. Apollo is the only one missing. I asked him to tend to my wife. My wife! Flutters filled my chest. This could also be due to Apollo slamming his fist into my heart after I begged him to look in on her.

I have loved my bride from the moment I caught my first glimpse of her. I'm one of those who believe in love at first sight. The moment your gazes connect, your body burns with desire, your mouth goes bone dry and you've lost your breath because she's stolen it. In a twisted manner I have been told this phenomenon is reminiscent of a witch tied to a stake as she stares into the eyes of the person tossing the lit match onto her pyre. For a single moment their lives connect, their bodies infernos, hers from being roasted, his from being hexed. I believe this is the epitome of a heated gaze. Some tried to warn me this would be my future. Phooey to them all. Me? I am the embodiment of a hopeful romantic. The new bride thinks she is funny always calling me a hopeless romantic. Her intentions I believe are not meant with malice. She married me. She must love me. I still can't believe it. I married the most beautiful woman in the cosmos. The mother to four, maybe five of my sons. Rumors abound one, maybe two aren't mine, but I am raising them as such and believing in our union. Like I said, ignorance is bliss.

Stood there, chest heaving, I attempted to catch my breath. Easier said than done. Misting lightly, I swiped beads of sweat from my forehead while I took in everyone enjoying the festivities. Something niggled my senses. By all rights, I should have looked like my cake topper, statuesque, sporting a ridiculous, white-blocky toothed grin, sugarcoated up to my nuggets in frosting, blissfully mounted on top of the world. Mounted by the bride would be idyllic, alas the little minx basically told me good things come to those who wait...

Tick tock, tick tock.

Physically I stood there, at the universe's summit, yet a part of me felt detached. Really not feeling so great. My stomach has a mounting rumble to it. Mounting... used to be my favorite word. I roll my eyes. I know it isn't food poisoning. Haven't eaten a bite all day. Feel as if I am about to be snuffed out. Breaking out in a despicable sweat now. Now I know what Hephaestus feels like. Uncomfortable does not do the word justice. Just how badly did someone want to win this bet? Something is genuinely off because the only time I ever sweat is well, never.

Too much wine. Too much sun. No food. Drinking on a hot day. Poison… Dumb-dumb-dumb. Not entertaining that thought.

I pray, *please don't let me face plant.*

Yes, there's a wager or two on this as well.

Speaking of down… This insidious sensation has me bent at the waist drooling and tooting simultaneously.

It is not pretty. Embarrassing however, exemplifies the moment.

And not a second later something warm and wet assaults my feet.

I did not puke on my feet.

Oh, for the love of God… Apparently the joke is on me.

Lost in my own chaos a heavy hand pads my shoulder. Startles the you know what out of me. I bounced and spun, one whisker away from shifting into my favorite form then tearing out someone's throat. Catching a glint of humor in his oh-so spectacular blue orbs I am barely able to contain the beast within.

I never heard Thor approach. "What is wrong with me? Rhetorical question. Don't even entertain answering it."

"Many things, old friend. Your nose is too big, your personal jewels not worth their weight in gold. I almost won the face plant bet."

"What happened to the not answering me part?" I manage a wan smirk. Both of my hands inadvertently go to aforementioned body parts. I find my nose without a problem. It is big enough! I believe prominent is a good description. "My nose, thank you, is just fine."

"No comeback on the royal jewels comment?"

I give my groin a final pat down. "I think they were heisted." I hissed a piteous sigh.

Thor's humor is evident with deep laugh lines around his eyes and plump lips. He shakes his head, and those long golden locks form soft curls around his face. He's too pretty to be so tough. He finishes with, "Really, are you all right, my friend?"

"The bride trotted down the aisle faster than a shooting star. Tell me, would you be fine in my shoes?"

Thor rubbed a grin from his lips before speaking. "I would never have walked that path, Dion. The route you strolled today is a one-way road to Hades' home."

My inner kitty snarled.

Hands flailing, I shooed him away. His eyebrow arched followed by a grin sure to win the hearts of countless women. I think he realizes I am sizing him up. His fingers reach to his mustache, then goatee to smooth the unruly hairs into submission. I am positive countless numbers of women have succumbed to those fingers' ministrations of his as well. This is followed by a snuffle.

Thor, the quintessential unadulterated man. This god before me is the embodiment of what all men strive to be when they look at their reflection in the mirror and ultimately fall short. Freaking Norse God.

Both of his hands on my shoulders, he bends and locks his sights on me. "If you need anything, Apollo will be free shortly. I believe he is conspiring with one of your most favorite people." His hands tighten around my shoulders, his idea of a hug, before he departs.

"Wait!" I shout as he tries to leave. "Get back here. Who is Apollo with? I thought he was tending to my bride." I hit my tippy toes, scanning the crowd.

"I will not pick your lard butt up again." The hulk laughs, but he stops moving. "You'll see who soon enough. I must go. I have a rendezvous with a beautiful lady."

"Of course you do. Why wouldn't you? Everyone seems to, but me, and I'm the freaking groom." I whined. I know, it's hard to believe, but even hearing my voice I couldn't dispute the pitch perfect gist of a teenage goddess. Those young ladies give the Sirens a run for their money. My lips thinned, and my head fell is defeat.

Nailed it.

The ground trembling with each step, Thor stomped back, got right in my face a second time, and head butt me.

There will be a new lump in the center of my forehead any second now. Ten…nine…ah, there it is…

His calloused index finger goes straight to the growing formation while my eyes cross watching him draw near. He has the audacity to poke the blooming crater dead center, and snicker. "Someone will need to crop that out of any upcoming pictures. Now you and your bride have something in common. Go get her, Dion, and don't ever sound like that again. The dance was bad enough."

My lips took a downward turn. "Really?"

"Did you ever take lessons?"

I shook my head no.

"It shows." His voice softer, he asked, "Are you okay?" This time he is completely sincere.

"Was I ever?" I wink, trying to laugh off the

nervous, awkward feelings fermenting better than my spirits are. "She really looks awful."

"Oh, Dion, her appearance has never been appetizing to anyone other than you... and Theseus. Today she showed her true self."

"Dionysus, besotted fool, son of the greatest god *EVER*!"

Both Thor and I drew our attention to Zeus. Kind of hard not to when his voice is echoing off the mountain tops. He tossed the emphasis on *ever*, as if we all weren't already aware of his awesomeness. Not a day passes he doesn't remind us. He finished up his spiel with, "Your father, Zeus,"—He always taps his chest with fisted knuckles after saying this...tap, tap—"commands you to get your assets over here. I'm parched, Son." He tossed me a smile saturated in sanctimony and confidence. The royal scepter thumped into the ground. A loud crackle followed. "Don't make me tap out three." The man wiggled his eyebrows in jest and smiled.

With an intent gaze Thor tapped his hammer. "Dion, if she hurts you, it will be my turn to return the favor."

Just once I wish a woman wouldn't find him the least bit attractive. It would take an all-out miracle. He strode off, his hammer swinging at his side. He never leaves home without the two-ton clump of metal. I never leave home without my crown. It's a heck of a lot lighter. The hammer and the crown both have the ability to end disputes. Thor's has a bloodier abrupt end to clashes. My crown produces drunken stupors, orgasmic hangovers, and leaves those lucky enough to taste its power, powerless.

"Dionysus!"

I turned in the direction of his holy voice only to get

jabbed in the eye with something sharp.

Instincts intact, I jerk backward, and inevitably curse all things feminine. What is it with crowns and veils today? This fiasco is a mad hatter's derby.

"Oh sweetheart!" Hera lies through pale, purple smudged lipstick. She slowly rolled her eyes up the length of me and slightly bared her teeth. Shivers invaded my soul.

My heart to the woman is bittersweet. Trust me: She wants it plucked out as I watch, skewered, sautéed or shredded. "I'm sorry," is uttered with venom as she gives a curt bow of her head toward my father. Her lips draw taut to let me know this apology holds not an ounce of sincerity. May she choke upon her words.

A ruby of unequivocal size dangles from the front center of her coronet giving her the illusion of a third bloodshot eye. Beneath her crown a lace veil covers her face with more diamonds and rubies sewn into the edges of the material than glasses of wine I've consumed this year. Needless to point out the numbers are staggering, for both. I wish it covered the remainder of her features, mainly her neck, with a tight twist knot. Purposefully she is trying to upstage my bride. I think the late father-in-law and Apollo's itchy paint beat her to the quick. She laughs and high-fives Hephaestus as she skulks past me.

Stepmothers: the reason for so many tragic tales. Mine is no different. She reminds me of Ursula, the beastly sea hag, with a shark's sneer containing the chum of expendable children jammed between her teeth. Enough about her. Today is my day.

Hours have passed since my little nymph's lips bristled me leaving me so hard my body still aches. Maybe the jewels weren't pinched after all. Eyebrow waggle, pinching sounds pleasant. Is she trying to prove absence makes the heart grow fonder? I ran a finger across my lip where my bride marked me better than a vampire does his dessert. The area continues to tingle. Fascinating. I could only imagine what potion she had on her lips to electrify my skin.

Out of nowhere like an untimely festive pimple on the tip of my brilliant red nose, my inner voice of reason is about to bark up the wrong tree. Why would Apollo go to such endeavors to stop this union? He has never liked Ariadne. Never trusted her love for me. None of my family has. This became blindingly obvious today. The patch of skin on my forehead where Ariadne's veil-arrowhead nicked me with is beginning to prickle. My lips feel slightly puckered without me doing the puckering. There is no way. I shan't even entertain the notion she… Nope. Not going down that road.

Poisoned me? There it is again.

Look at me, hopping, jumping and skipping down that boulevard.

Unease pounded at my gate. The brain's rusty cogs churned. A sobering process. One I loathe. I ponder, worry slaying my festal state with more ease than Medusa could stop someone's aging process with a mere *peek-a-boo*!

Squeals of endearments snag my attention to some guests fawning over Apollo. The fool flit his way through the gathering with a song in his heart, carting a goblet of wine in each hand with two women secured to each side of him. With not a care to the world the maestro of music gallivanted about making certain his bells got chimed.

Again, me over here feeling a tad out of sorts.

The original music man and his entourage stopped in front of me. He split a glance between the ladies and asked, "Please care for my goblets and later I'll care for you?"

I hacked up a hairball. My inner kitty knows BS when it hears it. Apollo has a knack for making the cheesiest of comments sound more like a decadent soufflé. This I envied. I stray from speaking some idiotic line with fear of immediately getting called out. Him? The infamous, "What's your sign?" is his pick-up line. Women can be so naïve.

I took in Apollo. He and I are more opposite than feast and famine. With his golden blond dreads piled high on his head, knotted and shaped into a girl's bow, Apollo's tall slender frame makes me look downright stout. There are a good five to six inches between us before his girly up-do. I shan't mention him with his anorexic waist, whilst mine has a slight bounce with each breath I take. Mischief glistened in my half-brother's light green eyes better than leprechauns give away those three all-glorious wishes, which always twist the dream-filled desire into a Shakespearean tragedy. Life's little secrets are all about the fine print.

If the new bride saw me dilly-dallying with strange women, it could cost me. Well, no more. I am a happily married man.

Maybe.

Nothing about today had gone well. My left eyebrow shot up in frustration. Controlling the bushy thing, I have deemed impossible.

Apollo played his lyre like none other. The music caressed my skin. At least something was. With this thought the right eyebrow now matched the left.

Weddings: Tell me again why I married this wench? My challis remains empty too.

"You see how nimble those fingers are?" One of the women asked the other pointing to Apollo.

I piped in, "Mine are just as flexible."

"Did you just say something, Dionysus?" The other woman mumbled, her gaze never flinching from Apollo.

Could Apollo just take them somewhere and end this all ready? Don't know how much more I can take. My feelings of inadequacy are mounting. Mounting, there's that word again. Where is the blistering bride?

Apollo finished up telling me, "Love you, dear brother. Time to man-up. Go take control of the wedding suite. You know the saying, 'She may have gotten you today, but you're going to get yours tonight.'"

Optimism as missing as the bride, I shrugged my shoulders. "Really? Is that your best, best man speech?"

"It is the nicest thing I can say." With a graceful sweep of his hand Apollo departed, bells clamoring.

Chapter Three

From My Pedestal

More determined than ever to one, make certain my lady is comfortable and two, possibly consummate my marriage, I trotted to my wedding chamber. Soft laughter filters out. Sounds as if someone is feeling better.

About to push aside a thick lace panel blocking the entrance and get this party started, a small being, a freaking elf, stopped me before I got a filthy foot inside. Skeletal in appearance, one might believe these imps to be harmless. Until they find out the exact opposite. Her silvery-white hairline began at her eyebrows and was drawn back to a tight ponytail. Fuzzy ears flopped out to the sides the way a puppy's ears do before gaining strength to stand at full attention. She had natural muttonchops over her lower jaw. Apollo would be envious. Her nearly see-through turquoise pallor accentuated reedy red lips. Twiggy legs stood apart, while gaunt arms crossed beneath a frail rib cage. From a protracted bony nose, bright yellow eyes glared up at me. Her entirety made her rather unpleasant to look at. And yet I stare. To put a perspective on this she is still not as bad as the bride was earlier.

"Please return later, my Grace," she hissed. Her gritty voice left me feeling like I'd been sanded with steel wool. "She is not quite ready, but she is most anxious for this evening. The gold dust has taken a toll on her flesh. I am caring for her. Go enjoy your guests."

"Is that Dionysus? He's still here?" The bride sounds perplexed. Or disappointed.

My frustration shoved the words forward, "Yes! Let me in. She is my concern. Not yours. I thought Apollo helped her."

The elf placed a frail hand on my arm and released a current of power equal to my father's scepter. I got blown about twenty feet backwards landing none-to-eloquently on my backside a little further back from where I started in the first place.

With the exception of the sloughing bride and the effin' elf, my entire demeanor is out of sorts.

I believe a tantrum is in order.

Silencing me, the mini nuisance added, "She does not want you to see her like this. Please, respect her wishes."

I stood in haste, brushed the moss and flower petals I'd spread around here earlier from my garb while the elf waited, unrepentant with regards to my health. I believe she could have killed me and not lost an ounce of sleep.

"I'll be back." Famous last words if ever.

To cool my jets, I trudged to the River Lethe, closed my baby blues, and listened to the water trickle over rocks. Most people think of the river in Hades, but it begins here and then filters down into the ultimate inferno.

All except me were partaking in the festivities I'd set in motion for this day. Impatience amped up her nagging rituals to a level of discomfort I was well, uncomfortable with. I am not known for being long-suffering. Given my upbringing I realize this is a lame excuse for my lack of self-control, but when your father is king of the world, all his children have to do is bat an eyelash or worst-case scenario lift a finger to get their heart's desires... not that I have ever stooped so low, but I'm contemplating it as I waste away.

The river's waterway circles half of the grove before being parted by three thick columns of an arched stone bridge. Benches were incorporated into both sides of the structure so one could idle their time losing themselves in thought, metaphorically speaking. If one were foolish enough to jump into the river...instant amnesia. Everyone knew the risk and still they leapt. Some to rid the pain of loss, some in hopes of fresh beginnings.

Some may have been shoved in.

Ah, good times. The first true smirk of the day found my lips.

And people blamed my wine for hallucinations or bouts of memory lapses. A butt-load of my spirits couldn't equate to one drop of the river's potency. The poppies lining the riverbed may have a hand in the amnesia as well. We, the gods, created an antidote to the river's magic just in case one of us wound up soggy.

Other flowering trees are dispersed along the river. They are a mystical cross between Angel Trumpets and Myrtle Trees. Large blooms, light pink and magenta bell-shaped buds hang from moss-covered limbs. The flower's sap guarantees true lust.

Hence the exact reason my wedding chamber resembles a floral shop. Petals cover the bed, bouquets line the path to the chamber, and I even infused my newest batch of wine with the delicious nectar. All angles covered. Foreplay, life is all about anticipation. I believe, *Carly* wrote a song about just that after I met her early 70's. Let J.T. have his delusions.

Not that I need it, an aphrodisiac, but one would take nothing for granted. Heck, for all I know maybe the scent consumed the new bride, and she'd found someone else to pleasure her in my stead. My optimism plummeted to an all-time low.

The ugly elf.

There's no way.

I laugh at the absurdness of my imagination while my heart shrivels one size.

Just a few yards past the water's edge lay Heaven's Gate where I think my father-in-law ventured off earlier?

Heaven's Gate is truly one of the most beautiful sights in the galaxy, as long as you aren't flicked overboard. For humans it would be like standing on the edge of Niagara Falls except the falls are bottomless and frozen with ice-blue stalagmites reaching for the heavens. Surrounding the ice sculpture, billions of dynamic-colored stars float. The abyss is one of the most magnificent sights in space. The deeper and longer you peer into its void you see a tiny ball of blue, white, and green and realize Earth sits far, far below you. I would give anything to toast with my bride here, to make a wish that someday we could take the plunge and travel Earth together, but I am beginning to believe she has no intention of the two of us doing anything together.

I wandered to the brink of the chasm contemplating taking the plunge alone because seriously, it has been that kind of day. Bending at the waist, I hold my crown in place in one hand, with my goblet secure in the other. To lose either, well one would sour my day and the other my life.

I'm miserable, not suicidal.

Those faint of heart should never venture this close to the edge for fear of tumbling head over heels for years before finding solid ground with no cushion.

Gravity loves to prove she has the upper hand when someone accidentally does a header.

Or again, is shoved. My inner kitty wiggles his butt playfully.

Hearing a gasp, I glanced back to note the blood drain from my father's face.

And now my smile is gone. My dear father is not so handsome when he worries. Come to think of it, he is not handsome. He is more of a pioneer. Rugged. Weathered. Fossilized might be pushing the limit, but it does get the point across. He still gets the ladies. Women love powerful, confident men. He is the proverbial angel atop a Christmas tree. He may even enjoy the bristled stick up his…

"Son, ge–ge–get back from there, you fool. And stop dancing."

The great and mighty Zeus afraid of heights? Hard to imagine, but the man's knees mimic cymbals being slammed together in a parade whenever he gets a foot off the cloud and seeing his favorite son so close to toppling over, the background noise feels like a marching band is trooping forth.

Zeus placed his hand to his ear with his head jut in my direction. "Dionysus!" The tenor of Zeus's voice stilled the celebration. I think my cheeks flushed. Warmth spreads like hot honey over my body.

Oh, I wish it were due to the honey. People are pointing.

I seem to be having one of those days where everything goes epically wrong. "Your Grace, if I should unexpectedly tumble through time, you can have all my casks of wine."

"Push the imbecile," roared from the man. My jaw dropped. No one dared move, especially me. One step in the wrong direction and he would get my wine. Heads toggled between my father and myself. Was Zeus serious? Wasn't he always somewhat serious, even when he jested? Isn't truth always coveted in sarcasm or jokes? Makes the ugliest of accusations easier to digest. It wasn't until Zeus bent at the waist engulfed in his own mirth others joined in.

Me? Goblet wedged between my blanched fingers, hand on my hip, eyebrow arched, my smile as absent as my beloved bride.

Zeus included everyone when he added, "People take me so literally. No need to push him. The fool will probably stumble off anyway."

To my chagrin, more money began to exchange hands.

"Seriously?" Again, I was ignored.

"Apollo," Zeus directed, "continue to regale me with your bedtime paeans, second favored son."

And the band played on.

Chapter Four

Free Falling

Me on the other hand? Purple sparkles engulfed me. This kaleidoscope of crap is blinding. More sparkles invade the insides of my nares. Sneezing ensues. My balance is blown backward, and with that it is all downhill.

Literally.

Laughing one minute, freefalling the next.

There it is, or was, the silver lining I just belly-flopped through.

The word, "Crap," escapes me. I censored out my potty-mouthed glossary just in case anyone heard me. I will not go down in history as anything other than a true gentleman.

There is a first time for everything. And from the looks of it, possibly a last.

Don't know how it happened, but it did. I am in the process of being greeted by Gaia's quintessence. Please note the sarcasm swirling through my brain since I am rather occupied screaming, "Crap!" My body twists, writhes in attempts to recapture my balance but there are forces greater than I weighing me down, my lard-butt being one of them. My one hand reaches, fingers fully extended trying to grab anything solid. Physics one-o-one, hot air is not solid while my dear lard butt is.

This party took a drastic turn for the worse if I do say so myself.

Humor? Check!

I remain able to catch glimpses of both the world I departed and the world I am about to make a smashing entrance to...

Sarcasm? Check!

Faces linger along the edges of the gateway. I see my father reaching for me yelling, "You dumb twit!" Apollo, Hercules, Thor, Eros, each wear the ugliest masks of fear I have ever witnessed, but no wife peering over the edge wondering what happened to her beloved husband. Hera is laughing and dancing. I can so dance better than her.

I see father shove two individuals off the edge, pointing at me, commanding things I can no longer hear, but I can understand. The man wants me back. I love him. I should probably tell him more often. It is a guy thing. Really stupid guy thing if you ask me. Sentiment is more lethal than Achilles's fragile little heel. Enemies look for weakness and showing love is an open door to kissing someone's tush good-bye. Is this why I am currently doing a header through time and space?

I read once it takes nine days and nine nights to fall from my home to earth. Unless time truly speeds up the way it has here, I believe someone used Common Core for mathematics.

A skyscraper with a lightning rod deflector, shiny, pointy, ruinous, threatens my cushy landing.

This is really going to hurt. Even more than the absentee wife. At least one pain should cancel out the other.

"Jelly belly! Look up!" And yet another nickname

that gets spread around due to my love of all things grape. Out of the corner of my eye I see my younger half-brother streaming towards me, his helmet and ankle's wings propelling him with more gusto than NASA could ever dream of having in their entire taskforce of spaceships.

Hermes, my savior. I reach for him… and miss.

I should probably lose a pound or two.

Not looking too good for me. Within what I guesstimate to be a half-centimeter of being a body on a spiked tower, something Vlad would have appreciated, a burning grip sears into my flesh around my ankle, and I find myself catapulted skyward like a bungee cord that hit the end and snapped, all the inertia now riveted in a new direction. Thor latches onto me and flips me upward through the air into the hands of Hermes.

I will need more wine if I am to survive this.

Sensibility still intact?

Did I ever have it? With a quick glance my crown is secured within bulging white knuckles, the gold embedded into my flesh.

Thor sidles up beside us with the devilish grin he owns. "You did not have to prove your father correct by falling."

"I love you guys," I huffed, still breathing way too hard. I won't tell him someone dusted me with magic sparkles. It sounds ludicrous even thinking it, yet someone wanted me off my high horse.

With a soft landing I am placed in front of my father. A rare scene unfolds. His eyes are filled with unshed tears. His arms latch onto me, drawing me close. He feels safe. Smells like the wildness of the horses running free. I don't think he has ever hugged me like this. It's comforting.

"You dumb twit," he mutters as he grabs the back of my head, cradles it, gazes into my eyes, his smile tight lipped, before crushing my face into his huge, solid shoulder. He finishes, "You really dumb twit."

Sentiment. Comes in all forms. He slaps my back a few times and then holds me out in front of him, I guess to check me over.

"If you'd just gotten me the glass of wine I asked for an hour ago, this wouldn't have happened."

"Love you too, father." I turn to see all the guests. Relief prevails. Well, all but one. Zeus placed a hard kiss on my forehead and walked away, the lilt usually found in his step, now as absent as you know who.

With his arm strung around my shoulder Apollo muttered in my ear, "Who's the moron now?" I love that man too. "She could have come out by now, Dion. I gave her salve hours ago to relieve the allergic reaction. She is as good as new. She is stalling." Apollo released me and shrugged his shoulders adding, "I am sorry," and truly meaning it. Thor handed me a challis of wine.

"Thank you for looking out for me. I owe you one."

"Find me a woman." Thor's grin is ridiculous.

"Deal. Just not today. And there will be no complaints when I hand her over to you. I cannot guarantee her response." I laughed at my own joke.

Thor held his cup out. "Blood does not make brothers. Friends you trust with your life does." Thor and I clinked our challises. The day's tension drained away in the same fashion my goblet of wine did as the last drops slipped easily down my throat. The old ticker fluttered once more. An eyebrow arched as I eyed the empty challis. Even went as far to twirl the pewter container in my fingers high, waving the glass like a white flag so those serving could take notice. Surely someone would recognize my distress over the void that filled my cup instead of my beloved brew.

And there she was, headed my way, challis in hand, a mischievous smirk on her sensual lips, my favorite wedding crasher.

Said no one with a functioning brain.

Thor bowed out laughing. "Nothing can save you now."

Chapter Five

Wedding Crasher

Surrounded in a falsetto of grandeur, the one woman, and I use the word loosely, the one I'd been avoiding like a well-placed arrow most of her life stood but a few feet from me. Her gown presented a lady who knew exactly what and who she wanted and how she would ascertain them. That would be me. Truly, she is the culmination of all godly beauty. Today even moreso: Perfect pink shades of lipstick accentuate lush full lips. The same color with darker shades of magenta draws your gaze to her ice blue eyes and unfortunately leaves you with a bad case of freezer burn in your mouth. To look at her one would think angel. To know her, people take a cautious step back. Others turn and run. I should be doing this right now. She is the ultimate devil in disguise. Her headdress is silver armor done in elegance. Pink sapphires are strewn throughout the cap outlining her delicate features. Her gown is a sheer sheath of diamonds and more pink sapphires. Beneath this is the body we created for her. If nothing else comes from our imaginations, we did create the perfect female. Earth's version would be Eve, but we added all the magic.

My wide-eyed gaze combined with the gaping jaw didn't win me any favors. God or no god, I am a man. Married man, I remind myself. She knew I watched her, but could she hear my heart thudding away with undo stress?

The lady of the hour looked around and then settled her frosty gaze on me. "What is that annoying ticking I hear? Did someone bring a time bomb?"

To me, myself, and I, I mumbled, "That would be you. Please do not detonate." To the universe I sent out a distress call. "Zeus!" Pretty certain she heard that as well along with all my guests.

With long, swift strides I reached father. "Who invited *you know who*?" I gave a subtle nod to my right where *she* pandered about. "Don't lo—"

Zeus's head snapped in the direction, yelling, "Who?" regardless of my request. He finished with, "Oh lordy me. Your day just took a turn a turn for the worse, Dionysus, if that is possible." His steel-grey eyes went wide. He raised the gold scepter and pointed, "You there!"

Behind the boisterous roar I'm positive earth's rotation tilted a degree or two. My father and thunder had more of a relationship than mortals do with sex and selfies. Trying not to make any more of a spectacle of myself, I snatched the rod and brought it to the ground— gently. "*You there* has a name and now she knows we are on to her."

The lady in question held her gaze. The longer she stared at me the more I felt caught up in the sights of the mares of Thrace. Horses foaming at the mouth, fur hackled, nares contracting, back hooves digging into the earth just as a bull does before storming after its prey. I despise those horses. Been hounded by them more than once, barely escaping. There is a reason the step-monster owns flesh-eating horses. Hera is the original man eater and so why shouldn't her mares take after their master? And why does my father put up with her?

My wedding crasher remained poised, not a hair out of place, a beautiful illusion. What this woman before me could make you think you see, or feel is completely unnerving. She is the ultimate mind player. She raised a hand and waved, her smile more polished than a politician's.

I. Am. Toast.

"Did you feel that father?" I had to know. "Her powers have grown."

"No, son," Zeus answered shaking his head, the long white curls on his scalp and chin followed suit. "It is good she knows. Maybe she'll be a good little goddess and try not to wreak havoc." Zeus's bushy brows wiggled as a devilish smirk crept over his carved face. "Hera said this ceremony would be a bore. Love proving her wrong."

Trying for nonchalant, my eyes shifted *her* way. "I believe havoc is her middle name." With a subtle finger I pointed to the containers my unwelcome guest carted around. With a dissatisfied moue, my top lip scrunched, and my shoulders sagged. A heady sigh flowed from the nostrils sounding an alarm. In my next life I want a smaller nose. "She is the douter waiting to snuff out the life of the flame."

"For the time being we can use your schnozzle."

My father is back up to a full chuckle again. "In all likelihood Eros allowed her passage. The pretty boy can't pass up anyone these days."

I nod in agreement.

Looking rather languorous, his hair tussled, his chunky cheeks ruddy, eyes glassy, Eros shouted back,

"You silly, silly god. I can hear you. Quite well. I believe the lady in question and all others heard you as well, my Grace. Not even I am so inclined or insane as to allow passage to a viper. A vixen indeed." With both hands Eros ran his fingers through two of the lady's locks and winked. "Excellent celebration, Dion. Let's bloody well hope it remains this way." And with that declaration the man wasted not another breath on me. Can't blame him.

I needed to retain some semblance of control. If I went ballistic now, she'd be all over me the way vultures love rotted flesh. My handsome mug all wrinkled in angst I shook my fists in vain. "All it takes is one sour grape to ruin everything. How did she get in?" I demanded answers. Zeus placed one hand on each of my shoulders, balancing a wine glass in one at the same time. I glanced between him and the glass.

"Don't even think about it," He said shaking his head sideways. "Breathe, son. She can't hurt you."

Hearing Apollo's mirth gravitate my way I believe there in lay my answer as to who let in the uninvited wedding crasher.

"Guilty as charged, you purple-footed fool." Apollo pointed to my tainted tootsies with a look of disdain.

Embarrassed, I tried rooting my feet in the soft moss as I stood there.

"*You know who* said she had a gift for you. I can only imagine what…"

"And your loathing of my bride," I added. "One disaster after another. Both no thanks to you."

The green-eyed god and Zeus clinked glasses. Conspirators till the end.

I shoved my empty challis at Apollo to hold. Hand gestures went amuck with my lame attempts at a game of charades to explain exactly what the woman carried and where. I crooked one arm close to my side then pretended to carry a parcel and skip around. Not only do I suck at poker, but charades too.

"Poor babe in the woods!" Apollo shouted.

"She is a babe!" Zeus added. Glasses clinked again.

I couldn't let it go. "Did you happen to see them?"

"Bosom? Hard to miss."

Drool all but dripped from my father's lips. All the history books are correct where his philandering and sojourns are concerned. I have more half-siblings than anyone. The six degrees of everything bacon started here.

I snatched the other glass of wine Apollo held leaving him with my empty one. If he noticed, he smartly never acknowledged it.

"So, she crashed your wedding, brother. She didn't wreck it."

"Yet. Once my bride sees her, or she pops open the pyxis, well I'll have some kissing of the—"

With his next sour breath my father latched onto my wrists, and he held my arms in front of him. "We won't let anything happen. I mean, what else could happen? You have already beaten death once today. Dumb twit!"

Most likely twice. I kept the poisoned and shoved off the edge of the cliff theory to myself.

Maybe stress has gotten the better of me. If my father didn't sense an inkling of trouble, why should I? So far, the pandering woman wielding the power to flip my life inside out seemed amicably content beside her husband. Maybe weddings really did bring out the matrimonial bliss in people. Well, everyone's bliss but mine.

Chapter Six

Praying For the End of Time

Anxious, hopeful, terrified, yes even men—ah—gods worry how or if a woman will accept them. My gut in turmoil, I sidestepped the woman of the hour and made my way to the wedding chamber again where I planted my filthy feet beside the entrance more silent than Thanatos. With a slight lean, my ear cozied up to the opening in the curtains. Way too quiet in there, then a conversation sifted out.

"I should make my way out to the party."

Wonders never cease.

"This is going to be monumental," my wife continued. Her voice alone solidified every cell in my body. Rock hard went straight to cement. There would be no beating this bad boy down for a week or more. I almost felt sorry for her.

Not really. I will make certain she enjoys every second.

Another voice, the effin' elf asked, "Are you going to miss your old life?"

"I've been waiting for this moment for a long time. I am more than ready."

Wow! I had no idea her feelings for me were so deep. My personal scepter wasn't the only thing to lift. My spirits were making a grand entrance. I am married.

My bride loves me. May sound trite, but the craters everyone blamed for the death and destruction of the dinosaurs on earth might have been the result of one our little spats. Mudslinging, temper tantrums here have a bit more flair to them.

Little bad history needed to clear up before today. Love at first sight, I believe in. The wife, I shake my head no. I have no idea how she missed my wily charms when we first met. She had given her heart to another years ago, but the puny excuse of a man broke not only her heart but her spirit, and somehow I got blamed. It has been a long journey for the two of us. Finding trust and faith a second time after you've been broken should be declared an absolute miracle. She is mine.

"Your surprise will be killer." They both laughed.

Curiosity piqued, I wanted my surprise now. I tried to peek inside, but immediately got called out. "Trinkler!" The elf bared her pointed, stained teeth. My inner kitten coiled and hissed.

Clearing my voice, I answered, "Not spying, my Queen. Just making certain you've not fallen asleep, grown cold feet or found another in my stead."

From across the room a foot lifted from steaming bath water. Toes wiggled. Water droplets cascaded down a long, full leg. A hand rose from the water with a finger crooking me in her direction.

A sign from God. Finally! My body pounced into forward motion with the grace and ease of my puddy. Down I went and knelt at the side of the wading pool. Awestruck by her beauty I turned away. She did that to me. Left me senseless. "Good day, or now evening, my Queen." My voice trembled. I feel like a pubescent boy on his first date.

My bride's fingers reached up to tangle with mine. She'd clearly been soaking a long time. Her skin appeared clammy, waterlogged, like someone floating belly-up in the sea for a week. Little more unease nudged its way under my skin. Lifting her hand to my mouth, I placed a kiss in the center of her wet palm even though it skeeved me out. "Are you being treated royally? Anything I can help with? A towel, my little raisin?" *God how I despise raisins.* "Blisters all better? That was quite the entrance you made this morning. A pure ray of sunshine." What I didn't say was I have never seen anything so disturbing, until now.

"Hello lover." Those sinful eyes of hers were her saving grace. "More wine. We're almost out." Her mouth looked swollen, her lips pink and full as if she'd been kissing someone all day. What the heck is one more thorn in my side? At least the split in her lip healed and she no longer had blood dripping down her chin.

It was a start.

She puckered and blew me a kiss. I turned and lifted my chiton, so the kiss landed squarely on my nice tubby tush. I spun back to face her, my grin genuine thinking we were finally sharing a moment, meant just for the two of us, oh, and the elf making more steam in the corner than the pool my bride expanded in. The imp gave an inpatient glare and wiggled an empty wine glass in my face.

"Really? That all I am good for?" I forced my lips to remain in an upright stance. Chances are good I appeared idiotic. I certainly feel it.

"I'll have your answer to that on the morrow, husband, but first..." With the snap of the fingers the bride's new sidekick scurried over and handed me an empty pewter pitcher.

With a robust shove towards the exit and order of, "Hurry up. Be off with you," she'd blasted me towards the door with her energy.

"Who are you, tiny gremlin?" I asked shaking off the pain.

"My bodyguard. Get used to her, husband."

"Why would you need a bodyguard? You have me now."

"Exactly."

I rubbed my butt as I stood. My heart? I would not give her the satisfaction of knowing she'd landed a crushing blow.

The bride stared me down. No quick comeback of, 'Only kidding, I know you will keep me safe,' came.

With a heady sigh I grabbed the pitcher and headed for the first cask I could drain. For me.

"Husband!"

I stopped on her command. When did I turn into a ragdoll getting kicked around? My short leash met its end. Her angelic voice tickled my fancy, whatever it means I like it. A slight shift in my chiton gave away any illusions I suffered from any erectile dysfunction. I should show Thor. At least someone would be pleased to see my... but then again... Thor has no use for my jewels. The shoulders drooped. I'm not even certain I do...

My heart stilled on her next word. Hopeful, not quite desperate, but rapidly approaching the state, I spun on a spot of sparkling purple pixy dust.

Interesting. Wasn't I lambasted with sparkles earlier, or was I just seeing stars because I'd been poisoned? I'd come back to this later. Right now, my lady required my full attention.

"Yes, my Queen?" Maybe the time had come.

"Oh this bath is delicious. The water caresses my curves in ways no man can."

And... maybe I am the village idiot. "I beg to differ your last statement, my love."

"A little something to nibble on as well would please me."

"I guess you missed the whole *I beg to differ part*."

"No, I heard you, but right now we are famished."

"And thirsty. Anything else?" My ugly tight-lipped, brows-pinched mug resurfaced.

She pointed to the exit. Clearly, she could have cared less. The effin' elf came to the side of the pool, sat and plunked her bony protuberances in the water. With a graceful bob of my queen's head, I'd been dismissed. Banished. Twice now in less than a minute.

"Oh, trust me, my Queen, I've got something you can nibble on, but it's not little. Not at all." My free hand yanked up my garb. With purpose I thrust my hips forward giving old mister blue suede shoes a run for his money. The vengeance roiling within me bubbled out in a sneer.

I stepped away and began a retreat from the room backwards.

Tired of my emotions being played worse than Apollo could sing, let her stew over the new arrangement a bit. I yanked the curtains closed and walked away with what little dignity remained stuck to me better than cat hair.

Outside, the cooler air filled my lungs and helped clear my thoughts. Never imagined my wedding day might turn into my divorce in the same setting sun. I passed the pitcher to one of the attendants.

"I am parched." The way the servant's eyes went wide and zoned in my throat, I am rather certain every neck vein, muscle and tendon pulsed with anger. The poor lad fled to the nearest cask.

Well, after this encounter with the new bride, falling off a cloud didn't sound so dreadful.

Beginning to believe my beloved has morphed into the original bridezilla, as those below the clouds now called premarital women. The expression fit better than those ruby slippers that caused the ultimate divide between good and bad witches.

Red happens to be the most powerful hue of the rainbow. It represents the heart, life, and love, figuratively speaking. The innocence of a women's lost virginity is colored this. For this reason alone red might be my favorite color. When this fiasco began, I'd hoped to be stained this color by nightfall. I should redefine this statement to not be so literal. I too have watched many vampire series. Vampires come in all shapes and sizes, euphoric to draw the very essence of life from people, willingly or not. Look at the wife, draining me slowly. I miss the movies. The wife, not so much.

With a slight tip, I straightened the crown, plucked off a handful of dead grapes and thrashed them into the nearby woods. This cannot be happening. I found a healthy grape and popped the juicy tidbit in my mouth and chomped. Visions of her heart danced through my head.

I'll repeat myself again: Love. My. Crown.

Looking out beyond the garden, the skyline caught my attention; the rainbow I'd summoned held lingering hues of violets spooned against deep pinks as Selene and

Helios finished their exchange of positions. The only thing I'd be spooning tonight was food into my mouth. "Bring us more wine," she'd demanded. Us?

Brakes applied, my forward momentum halted with a jerk. I spun and stomped back to the opening of my suite. Fear of exposing an ugly truth made my mouth dry. Courage mounting, oh I need a new word, rising—not much better…all thoughts lead to an abstinent night from my shoes—ah feet. I stepped inside holding my breath. On the opposite side of the room my dearest finally emerged dripping wet from the pool. The imp had draped herself better than a robe over my wife's naked shell, whispering in her ear words I could not make out nor did I want to know. They shared a lover's laugh before I turned away, my heart thoroughly shattered. I couldn't get out fast enough. Upon exiting I tripped. Scrambling to stay vertical I grasped at a table, only tilting it, and sending a vase of flowers to their second death.

"Dionysus!"

I spun to see the bride fumble for a robe. The elf remained glued to my wife wearing a vicious sneer.

"Yes, my love?" Infused in the question, tenderness missed out. Betrayal? Hurt? One seriously pissed off man? All-inclusive.

"What are you doing?" She had the audacity to sound upset.

"I believe I could ask the same of you." The soft rose color of her cheeks deepened. "Have I interrupted something? Starting without me? Well, by all means, do not let me stop you!" I headed back to the door, my stomach ready to rumble a second time today.

She yelled, her voice so loud and angry it would make other planets rethink invading us. "Do not be so vile."

I turned back, my stiff fingers tapping my chest I asked, "Me vile?" I forced a haughty laugh. It made my throat hurt. "Just pointing out the obvious, dearie." The perfect nose wrinkled. Somewhere in the back of my imaginative brain a little thorn prickled away like a bug stuck under my chiton. Just enough to leave the gate cracked and allow unease in swinging a machete hitting all its targets.

She wouldn't. Would she? Why would she marry me only to have an affair with another? An elf no less. Foolishness. She loves me. She loves me not. Am I honestly picking apart weeds?

Her head bowed, her voice a wolves' ventriloquisting as a sheep. "I was instructed this helps me prepare for our joining since I have never…"

"Never?" I roared, laughter of a hysterical nature following. "You are not a virgin."

"It's been years husband since I have, you know…"

"What am I missing here? Pretty certain we did the deed last week, or don't you remember?"

She looked away from me, but not soon enough. Her expression mirrored the one I had this morning seeing her walk down the aisle. She appeared disgusted at the very notion we shared intimacy.

Either I am truly the greatest inconsiderate idiot in the solar system or the most gullible. Time shall tell my fate.

"Could we have a moment of privacy?" I directed my question to the third wheel in the room.

My beloved tramp snapped, "Her name is Gwendolyn."

"Gwen… get out. Now!" I pointed to the exit of the

chamber since if I needed to ask again I might not, but instead grab the elf's long, silvery-white ponytail and drag her from my wedding loft, feet scuffing along the gravel.

She cupped my bride's cheeks in her hands and brushed her hair back. "My lady, I will remain outside, right next to the door. If you have need, just call to me." She placed a soft kiss on my wife's mouth, turned and glowered at me from over her shoulder.

Brows pinched, her sight narrowed, Ariadne asked, "Have I done anything to bring about such distrust?"

"You tell me, darlin'. We were wed hours past and since that fateful moment you have not stepped foot from here. Old rumors abound. Distrust weighs thicker in the air than a day of Hecate messing up every single spell she has ever cast."

Ariadne would not meet my gaze. Instead, she looked at my forehead. Well to be fair, there is a bull's-eye stamped on it thanks to Thor's imprint earlier. I rubbed my jawline, frustration mounting. Really despise the word now. I have no use for it. What have I gotten myself into?

Might as well finish tearing my bed apart. "If you had concerns about our joining you should have come to me, not some—" anger twisted my gut. I couldn't even say the word. My hands became knotted white knuckles— "Elf." The word burned like acid on my tongue. "Did our vows mean nothing? I took them seriously. I want to be the one making love to you. Exploring. Finding out what you like or don't. Me. Not some imp."

"Gwendolyn! Her name is Gwendolyn!" A second vase of flowers went soaring past my head.

Glory be to me, I finally got eye contact from the wench. Her index finger on her left hand has directed me to the exit. Her middle finger on her right hand has a more direct route to my uncle Hades' casa.

I need air. Time. Distance. All the things I didn't want when I first walked in here. All I'd ever wanted was this woman beside me, in my arms, in my space, breathing me in as I did her, loving me as much as I loved her. My feet took the lead.

"You're leaving me?"

"Psycho! They all tried to warn me. And you're no freaking virgin. We had sex last week. So many positions, none flattering to you. Have you forgotten the children we have or you and you know who share?" I stopped with my hand clasped over my lips. Those words would have been better locked in my head. Screw it. I continued, "Did you or didn't you order me out?"

She reiterated louder, "You're walking out on me too?"

I snagged a bauble filled with massage oil from the table beside the wading pool and threw it into the fireplace. Embers and sparks exploded, but the fire never matched my heated core. "Tell me you are not speaking of Theseus on our wedding night."

"Why not, Dionysus? You're about to walk out on me the same way he did. And you brought up the children."

"Is it not bad enough you have a woman in here fondling you, but now you bring another man in? I'm the man who stood beside you today. I didn't run off without a so much as, 'Kiss my tush. See you later, you senseless tart,' the way Theseus did, although I'm beginning to understand why he did. No, I'm the man who took vows to honor, cherish and love you through eternity." My head tossed back I looked up to the gods. *Why, I ask myself?* "I swore I'd love you till the end of time." My fists pound my head in frustration.

A grunt escaped her throat. "You love someone? Don't. Make. Me. Laugh. You have no clue what the word entails. The only thing you love is your stupid crown. It's all you've ever given didly squat over. I'd just be another conquest. Something to place in a bottle and occasionally uncork when your need arose. Give me the crown as a gift. A truce offering."

I caressed my headpiece. "And there it is." The real reason she married me: The crown jewel, not jewels... "Not. In. This. Lifetime. No one will ever don this other than me." Exit stage left. I'm done. Done! *And now, how I pray for the end of time.*

"Zeus!" My voice bellowed as I stormed out of the chamber, "I want an annulment this bloody second." Leprechauns and wishes—bad juju.

I, along with all my guests heard my father's answer, "So be it. Praise god." The three chest taps followed.

And just like that I was no longer a married man.

Chapter Seven

One Pyxis Too Many

Whilst I consoled the nagging inner voice with another goblet of divinely fermented grapes, convincing myself nothing really bad had happened yet, with the one slight, *oops I'm falling and can't get up moment, or I in all likelihood had been poisoned or the conversation to end all conversations, I am no longer married,* the bottom of my cup appeared. I've officially hit rock bottom.

Before I could ask for a refill my wedding crasher tiptoed my way.

This day just keeps getting better and better.

Ever notice a woman's entire demeanor changes when she realizes she has a man's attentions who both admires and abhors what he sees. The shoulders draw back, the breasts surge forward, the nipples come out of hiding, the tongue wets the lips, the hair gets tussled to the side and light fills her eyes as confidence steps out, roaring, "See me. Hear me. Feel me." The latter of the three is the easiest of the trio. My half-smirk has re-emerged. She is after all drop-dead gorgeous. I have the upper hand on this knowledge since I came very close minutes past of dropping dead.

Her huge almond-shaped eyes drew me in with the same enthusiasm the Venus flytrap caged its next meal.

Yes, given the chance, she would eat me alive from my shoes, if I wore them. My legs went weak. Defenses kicking in I flashed her the pearly whites in hopes of staying in good standings.

She approached, a new goblet filled to the brim. Her head bowed, she barely whispered, "Your Grace," as she offered me the drink with a slight curtsy behind it.

That bow from the back had Apollo pointing and lip syncing, "Holy Mother of God."

That had Zeus following with, "What is it now?" Apollo grabbed dad's shoulders and spun him in our direction. Zeus's thumb shot up. Hera had his digit wretched backwards before his next breath.

Subtly, the one gene we all lack. With a nonchalant shake of my head, I stared Apollo down. The moron gave me two thumbs up. I can't win! I took the lady's hand to help her stand. "My lady, thank you. Please, pay no heed to those imbeciles." I wasn't trying for cordial. My hopes were more aligned with saving my tush. *By the grace of the gods please don't let my ex-wife see me. Then again...*

This woman didn't look at me. She stared me down the way the devil did waiting for someone's soul to rise from a withered husk. Her ravenous eyes overflowed with carnal lust.

Tired of all things BS related I cut to the chase. "Why are you really here?"

"Came to see if the wedding actually happened. I had money it would not. Or was hoping."

She must have seen the disappointment in my heart. One treacherous tear leaked out of my eye.

She-devil—one.

Dionysus—still looking for his little royal nuggets.

As she told me, "I am sorry today has not bode well for you," she wiped the drop of water from my cheek. "Cheers to a better ending."

Every muscle in this body tensed. I'd become a sheet of thin ice being jumped on. Stress lines were etching their way through me, splintering one cell then the next.

With a casual glance I sought help. Certainly someone would rush to my rescue. My guess is everyone is too petrified to approach me right now in the wake of my wedded bliss unraveling.

"I take it everyone knows our business."

She leaned toward me and whispered, "If someone missed the show it won't be long until they hear of it. Hera, along with the cherubs are in the thralls of a gossipgasm right now."

"Nice word. Gossipgasm?"

"Dion, you more than anyone knows Hera's love of smut powers her ego. I'm betting the fight you and Ariadne had outdid any sex your monster-in-law has ever had."

Her sincerity almost sounded, well sincere.

"Glad someone is enjoying this." My head dropped. "Is nothing sacred?"

"Not on this mountain, Dion."

From the corner of my eye, I studied her. Staring down the Hydra has fewer consequences.

Instead, I arched my back, stretched my muscle-clad arms wide, titled my head back and prayed if I feigned disinterest long enough maybe she would simply move on to the next man in line.

"Dionysus!"

My heart startled. Gruff, I barked, "What is it you

seek, Pandora? I've had a crappy day so far. I'm beyond exhausted and tired of games." I shuddered. The voice sounded whiney.

"You married the wrong woman then. And you sound horrid."

"So I've been told, on both counts." This time I looked her over, frustration chiseled into my facial lines with more detail than Moses did the Ten Commandments. Gods help me she still has the cursed plain black pyxis she had been instructed never to open and under her other arm she has a rare pink, jewel-encrusted sarcophagus. Could the floofy pink box be my gift? Returning the favor? I see re-gifting in someone's future.

I straightened my stance, rolled the noggin to get the kinks out of the neck then gave her a sideways glance, eyebrows arched. I call this my tough as nails façade. Hopefully one of us bought it. Like I said earlier, piss poor poker player.

Pandora stepped closer, placed her frigid hand on my arm. Couldn't help the flinch. She is, after all cold-blooded. Squeamishness shows its true colors at the most inopportune of times. I may as well be a box of crayons.

She continued. "Your pleasures tonight are mine to give, Dionysus. I offer myself freely to you as my gift. Your blushing bride isn't up to the task. All she knows is how to kill relationships. Why do you think Theseus bolted away from her the first chance he had?"

My temper spiked. Why did I feel the need to defend the honor of the ex-bride who clearly has no feelings for me? Because no matter what, I am as she so aptly names me, a hopeless romantic.

I can see my headstone so clearly: Naive Dumb

Twit!

Time to tread lightly. Insulting a woman with the gift capable of mass destruction never goes well.

"Pandora, you are most generous, but tonight," I licked my dry lips and took in a breath. "My beauty, it isn't all about you. I know this is a hard truth to swallow for a woman of your mindset…"

"Mindset?" Her words slapped my face. Okay, maybe she really hit me.

Lady's got a mean left hook.

"Has no one schooled you on how to converse with a person? That is like starting a sentence with, 'Now don't be upset.' Half-wit!"

Pandora two!

I attempted to break the tension and offered, "You do see who my mentors are, do you not?"

We both spared a glance toward Hera and Zeus and I for one wished I hadn't. All I saw was Zeus embracing her with his lips attached to her throat, with her sneer directed towards me.

Pandora elbowed my side. "We could be doing that right now if only you would open your heart to me." Literally, her huge eyes twinkled with hopeful lust.

"How many times can I say I love another until it sinks into your thick clay skull?" Hindsight, dear lord I wish I had it. Or a filter on the gaping hole I call a mouth. Thick clay skull holds about the same magnitude of an insult like thunder thighs. I called a female satyr that one day.

Naïve. Dumb. Twit barely survived the aftermath.

If it was possible, Pandora's body began to glow red in the same manner a piece of ceramic does cooking. Coincidence? I thought not. Some of us were born from a womb, others strapped to their father's thigh, and others, I looked at Pandora... cooked in a kiln. Spontaneous combustion seemed imminent. My feet smartly budged me back, just in case. For the record, this basking in red I spoke of earlier... not what I had in mind.

"If I must explain it, you wouldn't understand. It's about the woman I vowed to treasure for all eternity."

She scoffed, "You and eternity? Don't make me laugh. Your idea of eternity goes from your goblet being empty to being filled."

Fingers to my head, I dug in and scratched before offering, "I'll give you that," while she waved to her husband. Odd, that the woman is tossing herself at my icky feet yet trying to capture her better half's attention. "Pandora, I have changed." Like my father, I tapped my fist to my chest. A hollow resonance sounded.

"You sound like the Tin Man, Dion."

"You heard that?" We both spared a glance at my aching chest.

Nose scrunched, she shrugged her shoulders.

"Crap." Rather certain my self-esteem tossed itself into the River Lethe. I may follow.

Pandora waved not one but both sarcophaguses in the air, attempting to flag down her spouse. Epimetheus seemed rather smitten speaking to Venus. If he weren't careful he'd get his head snapped off by one of the two ladies. Pandora's voice dropped as she admitted, "Love is blind, Dion. Men do not change. Especially Gods. Doesn't matter the size of the god, vanity will always be bigger. Arrogant lot of fools. Every single one of you believes you're better than the next. Mark my words, you'll come to me one day, lonely, broken or in one of your stupors everyone finds so delightfully"—she rolled her eyes at me. At me of all people and said, "cute," like it was a fate worse than death.

She straightened her shoulders, and with one fluid spin headed back to her husband's side.

From the corner of my eye a white flag waved from the matrimonial slammer.

Ariadne. What could the psycho possibly want this time?

"Dionysus, can we start over?"

I. Will. Behave.

The heart wanted to do leaps and bounds to her. The head wanted me to steal my father's trusty scepter and blast her into the neighboring galaxy. That idea I really liked. The feet wanted to River Dance a path to the land where no one gives a rat's patootie. I've followed the feet a few times today only to end up knee-deep in centaur manure.

Screw the consequences. Screw the fight we just had. Screw the fact she might have had an affair right under my perfectly straight nose. Screw the fact I had the marriage annulled. Screw tomorrow if I lived to tell of it. Just screw her and get on with the party. An overwhelming kinship to the honey badger warmed me. Bully for me my rant curtailed each cuss word I thought about making.

Goblet to the lips, I took a hearty sip and by hearty I mean I drained the cup dry. Which body part would win this battle of wills?

One leap of faith later the butt wiggled the same way my cat does just before attacking an object of desire. Not sure if my puddy wanted to tease or torture her. We will see.

She purred, "Hello, my lover. I am ready for you now."

My ex-bride's soft giggle hardened me where only a man could fully appreciate. Unless I shared the hardened state with a woman. My new catch phrase, "It's a win-win situation," would someday become as famous as me. Now all I need is Thor's trusty hammer. Conk!

About to tear into her, something on the outermost part of the grove caught my eye. Pixies, flitting around in the thicket of lush moss, watching me watching them. Voyeuristic. I liked them already.

"I'll be right back. Don't miss me too much." I tried to make light of this, but neither of us laughed. Somehow deep down, I already knew this to be the final good-bye. In my heart I knew today should never have happened, but dreams die hard. When I knelt and my lips brushed hers, I can almost say I heard the angels singing.

Nope: Apollo and the troubadours hamming it up. I knew better.

"Such drama, Dionysus. I haven't missed you all day."

And there it was, the harsh truth sugar-coated in jest. "Touché!" I feigned a smile as I headed toward the thick edge of the forest and the humming of wings.

Chapter Eight

Make a Wish

Snuggled in her sleeping bag, Ava lay anxious to see the first falling star. In the bushes by her house the constant chirping of the crickets relaxed her. She pretended each bug played a violin for her alone.

Beside her, she had a bowl of popcorn and a thermos of hot cocoa. In the not so far distance, her owl sat high on the barn's cupola watching her, silent as the night. Alone.

"You can come sit by me, Atty. I promise to keep you safe." Ava whistled to the bird. Atty was short for Athena. Ava thought Athena to be the most beautiful goddess in the universe. And her pet happened to be an owl, so Ava decided she sort of had a pet owl. She didn't tell anyone she'd been feeding the bird either. Didn't want to get in trouble for making a wild animal tame, but Ava believed the animal understood her. Was sent to her by angels. She'd heard stories of such things, when people were sick or sad animals came to their aid and since she wasn't well, an angel came to her. A dog would have been easier to explain, but the owl was seriously cool.

"Ava, move over." Ayden dropped his pillow on his sister's face and laughed until Ava swatted him with it and knocked him over. "Hey, mom said I could watch the sky fall with you. Is that popcorn? Can I have some? Ooh, look up there, Aves." Ayden pointed to the owl. "Your owl is watching you. Probably wants some popcorn. Give it some. Here birdy." Ayden grabbed a handful of kernels and tossed them into the air. Before one hit the ground the bird swooped down and snatched the fluffy kernel and flew right over their heads so close, they felt the breeze and the power of the bird's wings flapping. Ayden arched his head so far backwards his body fell again. He propped himself up laughing. "Did you see that, Aves? Wow!"

"Ayden, it's not my bird, but that was cool the way she caught the corn. Don't tell mom, okay?" Ayden nodded okay, but Ava knew the second he went back inside he wouldn't be able to keep their secret. He never could. "Why are you out here?" The little skeptic gave her brother her most serious face while she scooted over and made room for him in the sleeping bag.

"Coz tomorrow's your birthday and I feel bad you don't have any friends over tonight on account of the doctor tomorrow. And mom and dad are fighting again. Can I stay with you? Please?" Ayden made his best fool face, eyes squinted shut, all teeth, minus his two top front ones, grin look. It had never failed him.

With a nod Ava pat a spot next to her. "Here are the rules, Ayden. No farting." Ayden burst out laughing.

"Too late. Just kidding. Mom always says that too when I try to climb in bed with her."

"Promise me. And you have to be quiet now, okay? I wanna watch the stars fall and make wishes."

"Aves, what would you wish for? You can tell me."

Ava rolled to her side to look at Ayden. She popped a piece of popcorn in his mouth and giggled. "You quiet."

"I'll need more than that." He giggled.

She obliged stuffing another kernel in his open mouth. "Wishes are secrets, Ayden. Falling stars get the same respect as blowing out birthday candles. Everyone knows that. They're magic waiting to happen, and if you tell someone it won't come true."

His hands went out to his sides, palms up. "Well, Aves, if you don't tell anyone, how's anybody 'spose to know what to get you?" He pointed at her. "I'd wish for a new glove, Aves, so I could play baseball better."

With all her wisdom, Ava answered, "Last year was your first time playing. You'll be better this year."

"Really?" The young boy tried to sit up fast, but the sleeping bag didn't have rumble room.

"I promise. Now shoosh."

"Aves, for you I'd wish the moon and stars."

"I love you too, Ayden." Ava hugged her brother just before jamming another kernel of popcorn in his mouth.

Chapter Nine

A Bird's Eye View

I dropped down to one knee, my hand outstretched, gesturing for the pixies to come join the festivities. Squeamish and inching backward further into the dead hollowed log, not a one budged.

Can't blame them. Sightings of the tiny pests always turned into a free-for-all. Pixy nets, tall jars with holey lids to trap them, and then watching them wither in captivity. Humans do it to butterflies and lightning bugs; we do it to pixies. We learn by example. I do suppose we have not set the best paradigm for learning.

"Have it your way then, but there is honey-Myrtle wine on that table." I shot my thumb behind me towards the table where pitchers of my famous concoctions waited. Before my next breath, wings revved up with a swarm of tiny beings cruising past me with high-pitched giggles. Glittery dust, like the purple sparkles in my wedding chamber, coated the ground like freshly fallen snow. One of the pixies clipped me in passing, setting me on my butt.

I'd heard a pixies' love of both honey and wine went above and beyond my love for women and sex, incomprehensible to fathom, yet seeing their behavior, I concur this to be true.

In the short amount of time it took them to land, dive

in face-first, gulp and savor, three of the winged critters lay belly up, out cold with their tiny lips stained yellow from the wine.

The only pixy left standing, well sitting with her back against a candelabrum, sat a beautiful miniature version of a goddess only winged like an angel. Her annexes shined as the North Star does. She wore a diadem of intricate sculpture. Ornate gold flowers, gold leaves, gold vines all flowed into a circular cap with the top of her feminine crown holding an exact replica of her, an ethereal gold pixy. It is truly lavish.

Made my wreath lack wealth and glory even though I would never go hungry or thirsty as long as I had it. Bet hers didn't fuel her fire unless she hit the gold exchange. I bit back the charming grin I was so known for. On second thought, the full Monty gleamed. She gave me a blank stare.

Her gown matched the exact color of her eyes. Shimmering blue. In her delicate hand she held a folded rose petal as a makeshift cup with a small amount of the honey-Myrtle infused wine inside it.

"Thank you." The winged royal raised the rose petal to me. "Cheers. May good fortune always find you."

"The honor is mine—" I waited for her to give her name.

Petal to her mouth, she drank the last drop. After making a fist and jabbing it into her abdomen a few times a tiny belch squeaked past her stained yellow lips. "Ooh, good stuff." Then in a pleasant tone she added, "Tia for short. Queen Titania."

On her left bicep she displayed a gold filigree cuff with a silvery-blue bright star in the center. The Night's jewel. Myths went whoever had the arm band controlled the pixies. Betting she felt the same way about her cuff as I do my crown.

The little pixy went to stand but instead slid back to a seated position, her feet stretched out in front of her.

With the gentlest of intent, I held an index finger beneath her hand and touched her. A surge of her magic tickled my entire being. So tiny, so fragile in appearance, yet these miniature divinities wielded colossal magic. "What brings you today? Come to meet me perhaps?"

"Perhaps. Haven't decided if you would be worth more to me vertical or horizontal. I only came for the wine."

"I've been told I'm quite useful in either position."

With intent she brushed back a long strand of hair behind her pointed ear and flashed me the same devil may care grin I afforded her, except her teeth had a nasty, serrated bite to them. "Your reputation does you justice, Dionysus."

I admired her. "Hop on my shoulder and I'll bring you around and introduce you to everyone."

Tia reached behind her and grasped the stem of the goblet close by. Getting her feet under her, she pulled herself up. With a few wiggles and shakes her glittery wings enveloped and lay folded flat against her sides the same way a hand-held fan closed. After she fluffed her gown, she looked at me wielding a knowing smile from under thick white lashes. "You mean show me off."

"Aye, that as well."

"Are we safe here?"

I promised, "You have my word."

I watched the queen's slender eyebrow angle upward, making a crinkle in her flawless mien. From a sideways glance she quipped, "My army could topple all of you before you blabbed your first command," but I knew she hadn't meant it as a joke. I had the feeling the woman rarely joked.

"I enjoy a woman who makes me laugh." About to show her around a stone-cold hand on my shoulder sent a chill through me. "And then there's those whose overzealous nature I find a total buzz-kill. Please forgive me," I said all too hushed and hurried. Before the pixy had the sense to protest, I snatched her from the table praying I didn't tear her wings or snap any bones. I brought her through a slit in my chiton to hide the pugnacious little royal. With an abrupt spin I faced my first pottery project. "What can I do for you this time, my lady?"

"My offer still stands. You have nettled my curiosity, and some say this is not a good thing." Pandora tapped a finger to her box. "Who were you talking with? I saw your lips moving."

"Myself. Who better to make me laugh?"

"You have every one of your family and friends here and yet you entertain yourself. What do you covet in your other hand?"

"A secret gift for my ex-wife."

The instant I muttered those words I felt as if a bleeding lightning bolt slammed through me. Tia had bitten me. How could something so miniscule cause something so gargantuan? It was David and Goliath all over again. I am a goner. My eyes clamped shut. Tears leaked out regardless. I swallowed a scream. Teeth grit, I counted to ten. Eleven, sort of drifted off taking with it my sensibilities.

"Are you ill?" Pandora reached out to brush curls from my eyes. I backed away. Sickness spread through my veins.

"Fine, my Lady," I lied. "Must have been stung by one of the bumbles. Earlier, I had picked some flowers for Ariadne. One must have slipped inside my cloak."

"Let me see foolish man. Death does not become you."

"Aye, but how it follows me around this day."

Pandora began to tear away my clothes. Panicked, if she found the pixy it could lead to catastrophic events for them. Gods and Goddesses are beyond anal with superstition. Most believed if you find a pixy you enslave it and good fortune would be yours for the taking. With Tia fighting me, she must have thought the worst as well.

I disagreed with their ill logic. How would enslaving another produce good fortune or good will? Hatred yes. Centuries of bad luck, definitely. Throbbing phalanges most assuredly. After inhaling a few times and trying to suppress the mounting urge to break down in tears like someone stole my crown, I glanced over to the table where all the wine carafes rested. No longer passed out, the other pixies now zigzagged through the air, buzzing my guests, causing quite the ruckus.

"Pixies!" Artemis chanted in sheer delight. "Pixies. Catch them!"

Seems Chaos showed his ugly face at my celebration after all.

Pandora's expression turned choleric. "Pixies? You stupid, dumb twit."

"Like I have never heard that before."

With her next breath, her hands bunched around my cloak, Pandora tugged again trying to get the pixy. I clung to Tia for her life. If Pandora got her hands on her...

Well pandemonium would ensue. So it seemed, she had been aptly named. With a swift glance across the garden all my guests were busy chasing pixies, nets and all. My beautiful wedding, my gift to my bride, run amuck as everyone ran into someone else not watching where they were going. Tables were flipped. Food flew. There would be no five-second rule. My wedding cake had been reduced to crumbs. The cake topper of the happy couple? Ironically the groom's head lay at the base of the bride's feet. The newest batch of grapes smashed too. The ground saturated the color of pollen. My tears soaked into the loam along with the wine. Bloody batch was perfect.

Froth bubbled from Pandora's mouth. Just then I got a glimpse of the woman and realized we'd fashioned a true monster. Each of the gods and goddesses contributed something to create Pandora's life, but no one gave her love or a soul. Didn't really reflect well on us.

Tia broke my tangent when she yelled as loud as her little voice could carry. "Let me go, numb nuts!"

Beyond the capacity to remain civil I answered, "My nuts are not numb." For one slice in eternity, one I knew I would forever regret all eyes landed on me. Most days being the center of attention made me happy. Today not so much. Even more so once Tia sunk her tiny, serrated teeth into this host's personal scepter, what I called the giggle maker.

Tonight, no one would be in the thralls of laughter, especially me. The pain of being bitten had me doubled over, fighting the urge to vomit.

"Numb yet?" Tia snarled.

"Not nice," I sputtered.

The pixy's jaw had the power and strength of a Cyclopes coupled with the venomous bite of the drakon. My entire groin burned. My thighs started to shake and for a moment consciousness teetered in the making, until a new pain bit into my scalp and dragged my thoughts of dark bliss away from my dear gammy penis shriveling up and falling off.

Pandora threaded her fingers through my curly locks and ripped me backwards, off balance, jutting her stiletto'd foot out so I went down hard, hitting the noggin on a rock. For the record, not as thick as everyone makes it out to be. A warm, sticky patch of blood leaked through my hair, dripped down the side of my face.

Red. For the record, *ixnay* on the whole it's my favorite color.

The pixies stayed just out of reach, dowsing my family and friends with glittery purple dust as they flew over. One by one deities dropped. Apollo and even the almighty Zeus lay face down, immobile. Even Medusa was out cold, her sunglasses crooked over her eyes and nose. Someone would need to straighten them out fast before she wakes. Can't be too cautious where she is concerned. We gave her the shades so she could socialize. So far, it's worked like a charm. I watched the little pixies buzz one another as each member of the wedding party shook the ground with a solid thud. The winged nuisances zoomed right up to another one doing belly-slams midair.

With her robe barely secured, the absentee ex-wife finally made her grand entrance to the festivities. With calculated steps Ariadne reached me, stopping short when she saw *you know who* groping me. Did I call this or what?

"Pandora? Dionysus?" I watched her face go from all out concern to absolute indignation.

Above, pixies aligned their attack on both Pandora and me. When Pandora refused to acknowledge her, Ariadne tapped her on the shoulder hard, swatting and dodging the small creatures at the same time.

"Get your fingers off my husband, Pandora."

Pandora rebutted, "Ex-husband wench. You don't deserve him. Everyone knows you still love Theseus."

I'm beginning to feel like the proverbial third wheel.

Pandora's hand slipped beneath my chiton while Ariadne fought her. I played a regretful game of fumble fingers trying to keep the pixy intact. If we both survived this hopefully, she would appreciate the gesture.

"Are you senseless?" Adriane got in Pandora's face. Seeing the other woman's eyes glow demon red, I yelled, "Take a swing at her," in hopes of knocking the possessed woman from me. If I didn't have pixy poison thrumming through my veins I would have tried.

With deliberate motions Pandora turned towards Ariadne and with the vilest of intent she molested everything on me, but the pixy queen. "The statues below the clouds gave him more credit than he was due."

"Not true," I yelled to whomever still had their wits about them. With hopelessness plastered on my mug I looked at Ariadne. "Not true," I mouthed, as if I still stood a chance in Hades of the two of us ever doing anything again other than fight.

Ariadne gripped Pandora's hair and she yanked with every ounce of her strength. In the next breath Pandora went sailing and landed flat on her back. Ariadne jumped, straddling the other woman. She proceeded to slam Pandora's head into the ground. With Pandora a little out of sorts Ariadne stood and slammed her foot atop of Pandora's chest, pinning her to the ground while Pandora groaned words I've vowed not to air.

Ariadne pressed her heel a little harder into the smooth concave hollow of Pandora's throat. "Any last words?"

Before Ariadne had the chance to crush Pandora's throat Epimetheus tore her off Pandora with her writhing like a captured mermaid on a huge fishhook. My loathing of sea creatures remains steadfast. That I placed the wife in this category does not bode well for her. Or us.

Ariadne scathed, "Why Epimetheus? Why would you protect Pandora? She doesn't love you. She lacks a true heart. She has it in her head she loves him."

The wife pointed to *him*, ah—me, sitting here wearing a woeful veneer. She could have at least said my name.

Epimetheus answered, "For love, Ariadne. Love, no matter how misguided."

Ariadne mumbled, "Your compass is skewered."

Pandora got her feet beneath her, stood, straightened her gown and stormed off, never thanking her husband from saving her from a certain death. The moment Epimetheus let Ariadne free she dove on top of me. Seriously, I didn't see it coming, but then like I'd said all day, my game ended before kickoff.

"Everyone needs to step back and away from me," I snapped. This included the ex-wife. With a slight shove, I sent the spouse scrambling for her balance. I needed a moment to catch my wits. Pixies hovered, armed with bows, poisoned arrows drawn.

"We want our queen and king," one of the mini militias screeched. He shot a warning arrow just missing

Pandora's head. "The next won't miss."

"I wish that one hadn't," I muttered. "I do not know where she is." Then his words sunk in. "Wait, your king is missing too?"

"Do not act so surprised." The same pixy responded as he seemingly stood on air, his wings moving with such brilliance they made concentrating difficult. Or possibly it was the second batch of venom flowing through my veins. "You didn't really think we came here for your wedding, did you?"

With a ginger hand I scratched at the back of my head where the blood continued to trickle. "Yeah." So what have I proven today? I am the stupidest deity alive.

Rewrapping the cloth around her body, the ex-bride asked, "What happened?"

All too happy to give her version, Pandora clomped back over and accused, "Your spouse is a pixy lover."

With a few wiggles I managed to free my arms to my sides and push the old body into a sitting position. How, I do not know. My gut has bile sloshing around in it. The searing pain from Tia's bite equated to an electrical storm raging inside me. Head to toe, my nerves were live wires with the current amped up to the point I would soon sizzle. My legs were numb and tingling. I lifted one shaking arm and barely pointed to the other pixies. "I don't know where they are." I wasn't lying. Tia's little body no longer laid in my lap or in my grasp. Hopefully I didn't flatten her. I couldn't stand to find out and I wasn't about to ask for help and let everyone know I was at a total disadvantage. "Things got out of hand."

Pandora's glowering gaze met mine head on. "You mean me, Dionysus. I got out of hand."

I gave a tick of my head with my brows raised. My

look said what I smartly did not.

"Do not be so quick to judge me. I am the complete culmination of all that you are, every flagrant one of you."

"You are correct," I agreed, my tone softer praying to calm the woman. It took more energy than I speculated. "Yes, we made you. We also gave you free will. Choose wisely, Pandora. Your immediate actions will shape your future or curse your existence." *And the rest of us.*

"Nice twist, Dion." Her sarcasm could have knocked me on the butt if I weren't already here. In a fluid spin Pandora took in everyone, her posture stiffer than Zeus's scepter. "Well, if I fail in this life, you can all rack it to an experiment gone awry."

"Epimetheus, talk some sense to her," I pleaded on deaf ears. The man seems to want nothing to do with his wife. He is more conflicted in the heart than I am. Was I the only who could see where this was headed?

Pandora's hand shot out. "Epimetheus, do not take one step towards me if you value your life. You, husband have forsaken me at every turn. I am naught more than a worthless possession, like these." Pandora reached behind her and pulled out both the containers she'd brought to the wedding. She held her wedding gift high, the one she'd been instructed too *never* open. "I think it is about time we find out what you all thought of me to bestow such a cursed gift. Shall we?"

Saturated fats and cholesterol didn't have anything on the dread clogging my arteries. I attempted to jump to my feet, but that ended before it began. "Crap!" I still couldn't feel my legs. Couldn't walk. Couldn't stand, but I would be damned before letting Pandora open the gift to end all gifts. At the same time, I started a pathetic crawl towards Pandora, my legs dragging in the grass behind, Epimetheus reached for his wife. "Do not remove the lid," we yelled in unison. With a quick push of my upper torso, I managed to get into a kneeling position. I took in the scene, where everyone was. Pandora straight ahead, the black sarcophagus held out in front of her. Epimetheus stood less than a foot to my right and the perturbed ex-wife slightly back to my left. Everyone else: Various states of unconscious uselessness. I wasn't far behind.

"Pandora. Put. The. Container. Down." The moment I said this I evolved into Joel's mother in that movie where she's begging him to get off the babysitter. Like I said, I keep an eye on Earth… for the movies. To Pandy I added, "You'd be the laughingstock of the millennium. You don't want that."

"I have been the laughingstock of heaven and hell since the day I broke the mold. I believe it's time to pay the piper." Jug in one hand, her fingers splayed the lid.

Bloodied tears filling her eyes, Pandora jut the box out toward both her husband and I. The edges of the pyxis peeled back.

"Dear God, help us!" I peeked at Pops. Not this time. Survival instincts taking over, I ducked my head into my arm and shielded my eyes.

From the outer edge of the woods, fallen tree branches cracked. Twigs snapped, and the moan of a man came as clearly as the trouble Pandora reined. I looked.

Curiosity hasn't killed this kitten. Yet!

Theseus, my ever-loving nemesis, crawled out on his hands and knees panting, bloodied, resembling what

I can only describe as an unwilling canvas for someone's finger paintings, both eyes black, teeth missing. He went to point at me, but one of his arms lacked the phalanges to finish the deal. Instead, raw bones were exposed. He had been beaten to an inch of his life.

"You will pay for this," came out garbled. Theseus attempted to stand up, but in his weakened state he remained grounded on all fours like an abused animal. We had more than one thing in common at this point. Both grounded. Both hopelessly in love with the same demented demon-damsel-ex.

"I rue the day you came here. I have defeated the peerless Minotaur with honor—"

"Oh, shut up," I interrupted, "How many times must you bore us with the same old fable?"

He ignored me and continued his tale of woe, "You do not have the guts to face me as a man and definitely lack the balls to do so as a god, Dionysus."

"What is it with my balls?" I thrust my chiton up and peeked downward to make sure I still had the suckers. Really wish I hadn't. Swollen, purple, bluish and blistered. Apparently, everyone else thought the same thing seeing people cover their mouths and turning away in disgust. "Ouch."

Theseus's swollen gaze zoned in on my groin and he continued to rant, "Worried I would come for our girl, and she'd choose me over the drunken life of the party boy?" Except for Pandora's ill-fated sniggers a lull blanketed the arena.

One of us thoroughly enjoyed the show.

"Once you're finished with your outburst you might want to duck, Theseus. Pandy unleashed Hell's wrath." I waggled all my phalanges mustering the most malevolent grin I could muster towards the man missing his then shot my thumb to Pandora who looked just as surprised as Ariadne to see Theseus.

"How could you? Dionysus?" Rage turned Ariadne's cheeks bright red.

"What?" I gawked at the ex-wife. She thinks I am responsible for the mess? Wish I could claim responsibility. "Kudos to whomever beat me to it."

"How? Was it not enough that I agreed to marry you? You told me you loved me."

"I did." Crap! "Do!" That one line would go down in the history books for future fights. By now she must have an encyclopedia set of my rantings.

"You made me think he left me and that my only choice at love and happiness now fell in your arms."

"I did not make you do anything. What is it with women forgetting all about free will?" The desperation I felt clogged my throat. Even air seemed to be avoiding me. Everything got blurry. Pure outrage threatened to blind me and make me out to be the biggest fool. At this juncture there was little room to dispute it. I reached for Ariadne. "I loved you with every ounce of my soul. Believe this."

"Loved?" She pulled away. "You are soulless."

"Could you please allow me the benefit of the doubt before Pandora vanquishes us all into oblivion?"

Ariadne sat there stewing, no loving concern, just a loathing I'd never comprehend. "Sometimes love is not enough, Dionysus."

"Sometimes it's all one has to offer." I turned to Theseus. "I did not do this to you."

"Lies! You have everything to gain by doing this. You wed my betrothed. You and your cronies ambushed me, cut my hand off and left me to die beneath the new moon. The only reason I survived is to claim revenge."

"Well then, by all means, gather your evidence. Any DNA under your fingernails to prove it was me?" A small spiteful grin erupted. "Ah, scratch the last one. No hand. No nails. No DNA. No scratching. Perfect. I am being set up."

"Or so you want us to believe."

The ex-wife got her feet beneath her, resnuggled the robe and went to Theseus's side and then knelt beside him. Over her shoulder she shot me the evil stink eye. "Thank the gods the consummation of our blasphemous union never happened, and it shall never be spoken of again. Your name and mine shall never be spoken of with synchronicity again."

I yanked a few grapes from my wreath and devoured them, giving me just a wee bit of time to think and catch my breath before the next round started. Even boxers get a time out in between rounds. "I attempted to make an honest woman out of you, but there must be purity of heart in the first place. Or a heart." With a shrug of the shoulders and a sigh, I watched, destitute as my perfect festival went epically, disastrously, unequivocally wrong.

Chapter Ten

Every End Has a Beginning

With the seal to the pyxis no longer intact, scant bursts of light filtered upward. Concerts had similar effects for stage shows, awing crowds, drawing them in, the moth to the flame. Energy crackled then leached onto one person then the next with a charged boost that didn't stop until every guest at my wedding had been encased in an electrical sheath getting your basic tase. My legs would never be the same. The surrounding temperature plummeted. Helios flipped the switch and vanished into the dark side of the moon for a second time. The warmth, laughter, smiles of my special day all melted, except for the ice sculptures of Ariadne and myself.

The universe continued to mock me.

Wispy puffs of breath disintegrated with each exhalation. The deep, rich loam of my garden iced over with broken shards of frost. I can only imagine walking on it had the same effects as being barefoot and finding broken glass the hard way. The surrounding foliage withered the second the frigid splinters came in contact. In the blink of an eye my grove with all its glory had been freeze dried. Storm clouds lined up to flood our existence into the next phase of evolution.

My only remark, "Nice job, wedding wrecker."

"I'm pretty sure your popularity is lower than mine

right now." Pandora jeered before she peeked inside at her wedding present. Her eyes grew. She swat tears away and looked directly at me. "You can't save the world, Dion. Choose one. Me or her or, maybe Theseus will choose for you." Pandora wound up her arm and flung the box towards Ariadne. Reflexes working a heck of a lot better than mine, Ariadne caught the open box.

"Do not peer into the box, Ariadne," I pleaded, but my words bounced off spited ears.

The box croaked. I didn't have to look at it, the box made a sound just like Jeremiah. Ariadne's first expression showed the softer side I fell in love with: beauty, compassion, curiosity, but second by second her expression hardened. Her once perfect posture now left her hunched over, unable to straighten her stance. Her legs bowed, bones broke and remodeled in the same manner werewolves switch lives. Warts formed over her face, arms and chest. Her flesh turned a putrid shade of green. When she went to scream a long, thin tongue shot out and she lassoed a nearby pixy. Before anyone could stop her, she swallowed the screaming creature whole. Horrified didn't cut it.

My bride had morphed into Jerimiah's version of a good time. When her change ended her body was about the size a well-fed grass stained cipactli; part frog, part fish, part crocodile—one I wouldn't be seeing later if I could help it. She is the culmination of leftover parts in an assembly line with stout knobby legs and arms, betokening thickened yellow claws and did I mention she has two horns jutting out from her crocodile-like jaw? I might be flabbergasted.

With my world spinning out of control, don't ask me how I managed to get my feet under me. The head wound still dictated my lack of balance. The bites secured no consummation of any marriage. Not tonight or worst case ever, I feared. The latter I would reevaluate with the new dawn, if one came.

I began to laugh. The point of ridiculous had passed. I've never seen anything like it. I wonder if she could now shift as I can? Wonder if the spell will require a prince to fall in love with her to change her back to a woman. Like I said earlier, Jerimiah is going to be hopping tonight.

Theseus grappled his way to Ariadne's side, gaping at the warthog in disbelief. I am still laughing. I no longer give a hoot if I look bonkers or not. I am.

Whilst mayhem brewed, lightning bolts blazed conduits through the skies with more precision than Moses parted the Red Sea. The thermal penetration jarred everything in the vicinity. The ground, along with my confidence shook. Remaining pixies retreated into the nearby cove. No more arrogant belly-slams, just a bunch of goblins vying to get into the safety the first hollow log offered, and as far away from our little warthog as possible. Being second wouldn't win anyone a silver medal tonight.

Before I could comprehend the severity of the situation one dismal cloud swooped down and covered the entire garden the same way a saturated moldy blanket coveted the dead in shallow graves.

My little warthog croaked again. The look a woman or a frog could drop with the blink of an eye never ceased to amaze me. She nailed the death-by-glare look.

Still laughing.

The sad, pathetic thing is, even if she hated me, I would love her forever. Love makes zero sense in some instances, this being one.

I do love bacon... I now have the hiccups from laughing.

Epimetheus, however, did not run to Pandora the way Theseus and I had Ariadne. In fact, Epimetheus turned tail and ran the opposite direction toward the river. The bitter pain of betrayal Pandora's eyes held left crimson streaks down her cheeks. For a moment apathy poked my hardened heart. It was no wonder she sought comfort in another man's arms. Or maybe Epimetheus had taken all he could of Pandora's nonsense, and he no longer cared what her future held or who she held.

Ariadne turned to Theseus and groused, "I'm so sorry this happened to you. All of it." Her tongue shot out to lob a bead of sweat from his upper lip.

"Me? Look at you." Theseus cajoled.

In all honesty, I'd rather not. And did she slobber all over another man while she still held the hilt and thrust the proverbial dagger into my chest twisting the blade deeper? If I could've looked over my shoulder I'd see the tip of the blade protruding out of my back drenched in my blood. The pain from the head injury, Pandora's Armageddon, the Pixy Queen's little love-bite—sarcasm gaining momentum, my new pet warthog—none of these combined rivaled the intense agony ravishing this body seeing the brand-new ex-bride, the love of my life, oinking over another man.

"Oh rose nose—" my least favorite nickname after I'd consumed too many spirits came from my least favorite person. "—Look over here, lover." Pandora held up her arm and, in her grasp—the pink, jeweled sarcophagus. "This is my wedding gift to you."

"I think you've given us more than enough,

Pandora," Ariadne squealed. Her new voice is kind of sexy, not quite Demi, but maybe with a lot of practice… And a paper bag over her head.

From the tip of her tongue, she turned and began to rip a few insects currently munching on me.

Wonders never cease. "Second thoughts, or hungry?"

Her tongue snagged one of the scorpion ants carting away a grape that had fallen from my wreath. I ticked my head and shrugged a shoulder. "So, hungry it is. I didn't do anything," I concluded.

Her warty green face contorted as she yelped, "Bull."

"Frog!" Cracking up at my own jokes one second, the next, scrambling to hold onto something solid, rooted in the earth since I am not. Mt. Olympus seemed to be adding her two cents. Even Earth would feel this one. My home away from home may have begun atop this mountain, but there is a portal, a stairway to heaven, more or less, which allows us gods to ascend or descend to visit. This remains the reason for our mystique, the reason our homes and lives are not displayed like all those listed in Hollywood's maps of the stars. We value our privacy.

Deep into our current surroundings a deafening burst of grey ash mushroomed into the atmosphere shaking the very ground to which I am dearly clinging.

The Gods were indeed miffed.

Thick smoke steeped with chunks of debris darkened the skies in endless streams as the volcano purged every cancerous grain of earth. To my left a funnel formed and grew wide, the contiguous air volatile. Objects rattled and migrated towards the conduit as if the hole were a hungry magnet. Uprooted trees sped past us like massive arrows. The cyclone devoured everything. The Cyclopes, most of the guests who'd remained unconscious all became victims of the mistral, one body after another disappeared into the void. I watched in horror as my father, brothers and friends vanished. All I could think of was a huge vacuum cleaning house. With one silent hiccup Ariadne grasped my hand as the vortex attempted to claim her.

Now she wants me...

"Ariadne! Hang on." Every ounce of strength I could muster poured into a fight for her, but some things wielded even more power than even gods. The thrumming of blood in my ears deafened all other sound. Every muscle I'd neglected as of late, my arms, back, thighs, expanded, agonized me. If we lived to tell the tale I'd start working out. I ripped the remnants of my cloak off and attempted to tie it to her waist to get a better handle on her, but the funnel consumed it. Theseus too, extended his stump to her. Her webbed claws latched on to anchor her to us. We stood side-by-side trying to save our piglet.

Pitiful turn of events.

One last plea, "Pandora, make it stop. Close the sarcophagus. Save her. Take me!"

Instead, Pandora hit me again with what she claimed to be my gift, the pink floofy box. My footing slipped and I lost my hold on Ariadne.

Her other hand secured to Theseus, Ariadne yelled one last thing. "Find me. In this life or the next. Our love will survive."

Pretty sure I already knew the answer, but what the heck. In my best Travis Bickle voice, I asked, "You talkin' to me?"

Ariadne gave me a blank stare. Seriously, I wanted to give her the benefit of the doubt. Maybe she never saw the movie about the deranged taxi driver. If I am nothing, I'm an optimistic fool. I took her silence as, 'of course it is you, ex-husband.' She is of course preoccupied with trying to stay alive.

I shall die of laughter later. Sadly, looks like later is budging the line and closing in fast.

One blink later my ex took the plunge without me.

The storm plucked her from us the same way I plucked a grape from my crown and savored it.

Theseus turned to face me. For a split second we were comrades. We'd both lost someone dear to us. With a total look of despondency, he uttered one last thing, "See you in Tartarus rose-nose," before he did a header in to the conduit after my ex-wife.

Comrades for a second, my mortal enemy throughout eternity.

I rubbed my jaw. Did Theseus follow his heart? If I didn't do the same thing what did that say for my love of the woman I'd married and divorced in a few hours' time?

As if that didn't exactly say it all?

Pandora glared in my direction, her forehead wrinkled, her striking blue eyes filled with unhealthy curiosity. "Go ahead, rose-nose," she taunted, "prove me wrong."

There was no way in heaven I would take such a leap of faith into a giant toilet bowl only to get flushed to parts unknown after Ariadne had already been unfaithful.

I gave a slight shrug of my shoulders and shook my head no.

The giant maelstrom expanded. Oddly the hole in the atmosphere remained open as if it hadn't fully been sated. Screams sifted through the turmoil.

Still not jumping.

Pandora plunked her bottom on the ground and crossed her legs. Did she have lead in her butt? Why wasn't she being jerked around like the rest of us marionettes?

Clung to a nearby branch I inched my way back and made a move towards Pandora. I stopped in my tracks when she held up the ugly pink, floofy container again.

She glanced down at me from the tip of the turned-up nose and proclaimed, "I win."

"Win what?"

"You, for what you're worth. What you and I wish for appears to be on opposite spectrums of the sidhe, Dionysus. I want your love. You say sharing flesh is not a form of a relationship, or a commitment, only physical satisfaction. I say you are the world's largest hypocrite. There is not a woman here you have not shared your bedside manner with."

My index finger aimed at her. "Except you, Pandora."

I need a new tactic. Plan B, ready or not. "Love has an odd way of twisting fate. How you deal with love is how in return it deals with you."

"Is this karma you speak of? Dionysus, there's so much more going on here than you can see from the tip of your perfect schnozzle. Ariadne loves Theseus. The only thing my poor husband, Epimetheus, loves is gazing at his reflection in the mirror. I love you, and you love your wine, and not a one of us is going to get our happily ever after."

I bet I do. I tore a grape off my crown and popped the succulent tidbit in my mouth.

She gave me about two seconds to allow that to sink in before she concluded, "You live in a nice magical place where all your troubles are either swallowed, forgotten or slain."

She jiggled the pink jewel-crusted box again.

"Pandy, I cannot return what I do not feel. You do not control my soul, nor shall you ever control me." There! I told her.

"But I do, my love."

Epimetheus's head popped up from out of nowhere when he heard his wife's confession of love to me.

Timing! This would not end well.

And why should it?

The madman came directly towards me with the power and speed of a well-fed Calydonian boar. I couldn't get out of my way fast enough let alone his. Blame the wine, blame the bites, blame the two head bonks in the past few minutes, or just a lack of physical finesse from spending my days and nights drinking, I'd lost my edge.

"Dionysus!" Epimetheus shouted as he charged towards me. "How could you?"

"I—ah did not."

From what seemed thin air he produced a dagger. Kind of sort of looked like the one I used to wear strapped to my once muscular calf. That's it. I'm serious this time. Decision made. If I live through this, I will start working out again. Chariot races are a great way to spend muscles if I were the one running behind the chariot for my life instead of the fool driving the buggy.

It's good to be a god.

Snorting at my sarcasm, I dropped to one knee a second before Epimetheus attempted to sink the knife into my chest. I'd like to say shrewd thinking on my part thwarted the hit, but truth be known, sheer exhaustion triumphed. I reached out and latched on to Epimetheus's forearms. In one fluid drop backwards I brought the man's body down with mine while I positioned my legs between us. In a continuum backwards, I used the momentum and kicked the hefty rhino with my last prayer. The man summersaulted over my head into the vortex. Darn good aim if I do say so. I glanced over my shoulder, chest heaving. Other than tossing King Minos into oblivion, I hadn't planned on sending another in the same direction, even if it did work to my advantage. Hearing a branch snap I looked back towards the woman who in her own right earned the title as Dora the Destroyer.

She smiled. "Back to you, my boy-toy."

"Please," I yelled, "I am so not a boy-toy."

A snigger made her body jerk. "You keep thinking that, Dion. I want you to think about me every day of your lonely existence as other woman toy with you. I want you to realize what you could have had yet lost due to illogical ideations. I want you to experience this love you believe in from its infantile stages until death. Hers, not ours, Dionysus. We won't die. We're immortal. Remember this. You'll come back to me. On your knees, begging. So, winey wobbler, you up for a challenge?"

I laughed aloud. She'd asked if I were up for a challenge. One grape too many I answered, "Bring. It. On." Like a boss!

And then I sat there.

Unable to move. She'd somehow bewitched me.

Pandora opened the gaudy pink porcelain box. Inside, the sarcophagus sat empty. Not for long I feared.

"Dionysus, get in the box."

I did the head to feet show with my hand. "How much wine have you had?"

"Get in the box if you ever wish to see Ariadne again."

"Nope. I do believe that ship already sailed."

An angry jab sent me rolling backward toward the box.

At a most unfair advantage I looked up at her. "Unless you are blind, I am too big for a box meant for trinkets."

"Close your sinful blue eyes."

As I reached for her in hopes of grabbing the jewelry box and tossing it into the vortex, two things happened, or didn't. My arms weren't working and then she stepped back and squatted. Before I could protest, she scooped a handful of pixy dust up and she blew the substance in my face. The grit burned my eyes and made my face flush, as if the wine didn't do the trick. My world spun just as the portal did, in revolting, dynamic circles. I clamped the eyes closed praying when I opened them this would all be one huge prank.

"Now." With a hypnotic snap of her fingers my eyes snapped open and there I sat in all my glory, now the size of child's toy.

Absolute horror converged. My screams hit notes Apollo would envy. It took everything I had to get the octaves audible. "How? Who gave you the power to change a living being into something entirely different?"

"You and your cronies. Daddy dearest holds the power to separate lives in half, so you must search for your soul mate. Zeus gave me the power and idea. I embellished upon it. Each of you made me from a clay cast, adding your powers, hopes, dreams, fears, delusions, and hatred. I made you small like your pecker—oops pixy. Now stop your moaning. You sound more like a bug in the far-off distance I might feed to your bride."

"Ex, please!" My heart pistoning at rocket speed I watched Pandora reach, her greedy fingers headed right for me. I scooted backed up and hit a wall. Nowhere to go. Nowhere to run. With my next breath I dangled before her lackluster eyes. I now have first-hand knowledge of the fear and rage Tia encompassed earlier, now being able to walk in her shoes. Literally and physically. Speaking of said pixy, where is Tia? Wonder if she can dust me back to my manly state?

Pandora plunked me inside the jeweled box.

"Once again, Pandora, you've gone too far."

The faux goddess reached over and began to close the box while I attempted with vehemence to climb over the edge to flee. With a slight plink of her finger me and all my miniatureness slammed into the back of the box. I hit the back wall and slid to the floor, holding my crownless head. Oh crap! I needed to maintain some level of semblance whilst I crawled to the edge of the box and pulled my dizzy starry-eyed self to a standing position. She would not see the fear mounting inside me. She would not trap me in this state, and may the heavens have mercy if she shut the lid before I got my crown back.

"By the gods, Pandora, was one box not enough to sate the immoral siren. I beg of thee, do not close the lid. At least allow me crown. A king deserves to go down with his dignity. If you truly love me, please?"

Pandora toed the crown around in the dirt seemingly deciding whether to grant my one last wish.

Freaking leprechauns and their wishes. She bent over and picked up my wreath and chucked it in my cell. "So, here's the deal Dion; you need one woman to fall madly, passionately, in love with you. She must profess her undying amour to you in this itsy-bitsy state of yours. Oh, and might I add no one other than your true love will be able to see you? It's not what happens once the lid is closed where the problems lay, but you should worry more what the ramifications are once it is open." She jabbed a small crystal sword into my side.

"Ouch!"

"This is the lock to the box. Once latched in place, your fate is sealed."

"With my last breath you will regret this."

Pandora tossed her head back and shook out her locks. "Looking forward to some peace and quiet."

She lift the hem to her gown and began to sing and dance in circles around my cell. A little breathy, she tiptoed back over to the original black box she'd been instructed never to open. "Re-gifting. I like it."

"Bad idea, Pandy. Do not do—"

"Shush." Her foul gaze settled over me the way Argus observed his prey from over one hundred different views. Cyclopes get one eye; Argus gets one hundred. It is all or nothing up here. With the flip of her wrist, she tossed the black pyxis over her shoulder into the vortex. Pretty certain she just sent the universe a warhead of unequivocal size. If given the opportunity I will apologize. With a dip she scooped the jeweled box and me off the ground. Still dancing and twirling with a frenzied passion Pandora slipped. Here we teetered on the edge of the abyss. This doesn't get any easier the second time around.

Trust me.

The lid to my freedom slammed shut. The scraping of the sword along the latch made the hair on my neck and arms bristle. My entire world went black.

The last thing I recall is laughing until I lost my breath.

Be invisible they said. It'll be fun they said.

There's a furball lodged in my throat for the genius who coined this. I say, "Be ever so chary of your desires. To be seen by others for who you are and accepted regardless, is a gift like none other."

I always imagined what people did behind closed doors. Who doesn't, right? What others thought of me. If they thought of me. How many times my name accidentally filtered into the universe during someone's moments of tantric ecstasy, say instead of the current lover doing all the manual labor upon their object of desire. The odds are incalculably in my favor.

Let's face it, I am a God. Not trying to be arrogant or narcissistic or even Gaston. I am much higher in the rankings. Or was!

My current situation has thoroughly shined the almighty light on me, well not me per say, since I am utterly invisible sitting in utter darkness, but my outlook of life. I learned an ugly truth today: all this time Pandora has been hidden in plain sight, wishing to be seen even though her beauty shone brighter than Helios on his hottest of days. Everyone saw her, not for herself, but due to the illogical judgments we'd forsaken her with; the beastly burden we'd gifted her. We'd placed her high on a pedestal, an object of desire, something to be looked at but never touched, or loved or befriended. We waved from afar, smiled in passing and unintentionally treated her as if she were that one neighbor you tried to avoid at all costs. You know the one; you're in the market and you see them coming down the aisle toward you and suddenly you feel trapped. There's no room to run, not enough air to fill your lungs, not enough patience to deal with their soliloquy filled with boorish malarky you know they'll waylay you with until you're bluer than a bull's balls post-rodeo. Options are, you either turn quick and torpedo to the opposite end of the store or pray to be invisible.

I never wish to be invisible again. I'll take one for the team until my ears bleed.

In the end Pandora became more of a statue to us than the Michelangelo could whip up on a whim.

We believed she would be the keeper of our world, not become the ultimate destroyer. Boy did we get this one wrong.

Chapter Eleven

Wish Upon a Star

"Aves, Aves, there," Ayden's excited little hand pointed to a shooting star streaming across the sky. "We saw one, Sissy."

"Make a wish. You saw it first." Ava's voice couldn't contain her disappointment knowing her brother saw the first star falling. What if it was the only one? Tonight was her night. She felt it in her bones. Magic made her skin tingle. It hadn't stopped tingling since the eclipse. Her heart raced and if it didn't happen, what then? Tomorrow she'd be a silly six-year-old girl going to the doctor to find out if she had the 'C' word.

His head cocked to the side, Ayden squashed Ava's cheeks together. "I'm sorry, Aves. You can have that one."

Ava hugged her brother. For some reason tonight the little stinker was being so nice. "It's yours, Ayden. It's okay. Really."

Out of the blue Ayden started crying. His big green eyes were lost behind tears. "What's cancer, Aves? I heard mommy saying something about it tonight and she started crying then daddy got mad at her and started hollering for her to never say the bad word again and then she left."

Ava threw her arms around her brother and hugged

him. "I don't know what it is, other than not good, but tomorrow we'll find out. So, for tonight let's just count the falling stars. First one to ten gets out of chores tomorrow, okay?"

Through a few sobs and sniffles Ayden answered, "I was going to do your stuff for you tomorrow for your present anyway."

"Ya know, Ayden, I love you even when you make me crazy."

"Which is always." Ayden sniffled. "It's what brothers are 'spose to do, right?"

"You're supposed to protect your sister, silly."

"I will, Aves. Cross my heart and hope to die."

"Don't ever hope to die, Ayden. Promise me."

Ayden snuggled in closer to his sister and whispered, "For you I would, Sissy," just before he fell asleep.

For the next hour or so, Ava lost track of time and lost count of how many times her jaw dropped watching the stars crash to earth, some it seemed directly in front of her. This was the best night of her life. Hearing steps come up behind her she cranked her head backwards. Her dad was on his way out to the pasture carrying something large.

Index finger to her lips she mouthed, "Shhh, Daddy. Ayden's asleep."

He nodded and then set his large object down and wiggled his finger at her. "Come here. Got an early birthday present for you."

Joy and anticipation of what he got her had her out of the sleeping bag and sprinting towards him before he finished saying, 'present'.

"Daddy, holy cow." Ava put a gentle finger on her

new telescope and then turned around and threw herself in his arms. She hugged him with everything she had. "Daddy, thank you. I love it. How did you know?"

"Ava, my precious little goddess, daddies always know what their baby girl wants. I have another surprise for you."

"Another one?" she babbled. "Wow! This is better than Christmas. Oh, I know you're Santa, but I didn't tell Ayden."

Christian let go of his daughter and stood up. He fidgeted with the telescope turning the lens a few different directions before he said, "You're such a good big sister, Ava. Now come over here and look through the scope at this exact constellation I have centered in the middle."

Ava put her eye to the scope and closed the other eye to focus better. And there she saw it. "The Crown." She'd seen the constellation Corona in the planetarium so many times and had always wanted to see it in person.

"Daddy, how did you find it?"

"I'm just that good." He laughed and tussled her hair. "That's your crown up there, baby. No one can take that from you."

"Daddy, stars don't belong to people."

"This time they do. Your mom bought you the star in the center of the constellation for your birthday. Did you know you could buy stars and have them named after you?"

Ava started back towards the house.

"Where are you going, Ava?"

"To thank Mommy."

"She'll be home in a little while. I'm going to go back inside. Got some work to finish up. Have fun stargazing my little goddess. Love you more."

"Daddy don't go inside yet. Wait till you see a star an make a wish just for you."

When a star dropped right in front of them Christian started to say, "I wish for you to always be my—"

"Daddy, shush! Wishes are secrets."

"My little girl. Don't grow up too fast, Ava."

"Daddy!" Ava whined.

"I saw it too, Aves," Ayden mumbled, his voice sleepy. "Super cool. I think it hit the ground, Daddy."

"It only looked like it did, kids. Stars rarely touch the ground, but I'll go snoop. Good night you two. Love you."

Not two minutes later Ava had a canopy of flickering stars falling. Ayden hogged up most of the sleeping bag and both pillows snoring.

At the blue moon's brightest peak, Ava had made over twenty wishes. The no-cancer wish was a no-brainer. From her far left she watched the brightest shooting star she'd seen all night cut the darkness of the skyline in half. She swore there was gold dust in its wake. Fireworks would never again compare. The air vibrated around her the closer the star came, and it sounded like a train careening right at her.

And didn't stop coming. From behind her Atty, her almost pet owl, swooped down and clipped her shoulder. With a hard thump Ava looked behind her just as the star slammed into the ground not even fifty feet from her. The entire ground rumbled. Stunned, Ava didn't know what to do. Scared, she looked at the owl, the animal's wings spread wide, her gold eyes going between Ava and the fallen star.

Arms out in front of her, Ava got to her knees then

stood up and brushed off the dewy grass from her jammies. "You saved me, Atty. The star would have hit me." The owl winked. Yes winked. Scanning the field, there was something bright in the ground. Reminded her of the necklaces they always sold on the 4th of July that glowed for about a day and then got lost in a junk drawer. Taking curious steps closer, the glob appeared scorching hot. The surrounding soil had turned to what looked like brown tar, like the earth literally melted around it. She knew better than to touch the object, but she could definitely stare at it all night until the glow faded and then all bets were off.

"Heaven gave me a present too." Ava shrugged her small shoulders. A smile filled her heart. She toyed with the idea of waking Ayden up, but for once her brother was quiet, she let him be. Besides, this night was hers. This gift hers.

When the horizon started to turn a light shade of raspberry the rooster set off his morning alarm. Alone, Ava crawled out of the sleeping bag. At some point Ayden must have ditched her for a warmer bed. She made her way over to the spot where her star crashed. The giant orb hadn't gone anywhere. Still afraid to touch it, Ava ran back to the barn and grabbed a spade. Once she got back to the fallen star, she got her nerve up and touched the crystalized blob with the tip of the shovel. It didn't crack, or chip, or explode, or suck her inside it, which given all the sci-fi films she'd watch seemed a very real possibility. The big clump of asteroid did nothing. Other than spark her imagination. Still uncertain if she should touch it, she touched the surrounding soil to see if the earth still held warmth. The ground had a spongy feel to it, the way moss felt.

Well, she had to do something with the crystal. She couldn't leave it here. What if someone else found her present and stole it? She glanced around. Any minute now her mom would be coming out to tell her she had to take a bath and get ready to go. The sun was coming up fast today. Time marched on. Her mom always told her the older you get the faster time goes, but jeepers, she didn't feel any different from yesterday. And there it was, the creaking of the back screen door. The end of her perfectly good morning.

"Ava, come on birthday girl. We have a three-hour ride. Got to leave soon."

"What happened to pancakes for your birthday, Aves?" She mumbled. "Be in, in a sec, Mommy." Her swift mind thinking, she decided to scoop up her star onto the shovel and hide it in the barn until she got home tonight. She had the perfect spot too. With the shovel all the way out in front of her she held on to the handle and managed to balance the hefty rock and slide the barn door open by wedging her foot inside and then sliding her knee up and nudging the door open.

Passing the horse stalls each one of her pets came and peeked over their gates. Long silky noses greeted her. "Sorry Halo, not breakfast yet. Lolly, same goes to you. Whizz, your stall stinks like you know what. Daddy will be in to feed you guys in a little bit." Halo tried to sniff the end of the shovel as Ava walked past her and when that didn't work the brown horse tried to lick her. "Not now, pretty girl." On a mission, Ava kept going. This balancing act reminded her of Easter, when she had an egg on the end of a spoon and had to race other kids at the Bunny Hop Festival except then the prize was a humongous chocolate piñata filled with candy that her dentist tried to buy back from her when she crossed the finish line first. Silly man should have known buying his own candy would have been easier!

Outside the last empty stall, a giant leather trunk rested at the base of an old post. Weathered, cracked leather straps held greenish brass buckles in place. The paint on the trunk chipped in some spots and faded in others. Nothing ever got put in or taken out of the box because Ava had the key to the lock. Tucked under her shirt Ava wore a charm necklace her father bought her for Christmas a few years ago. Every year for her birthday or holiday he added a new charm to it. The key to the trunk was also on there and no one ever seemed to notice. Hiding in plain sight.

Very gently she set the shovel down and fished the chain out from under her jammie top. With a little wiggle and twist of the key, the lock snapped open, and she removed the clunky, gritty, metal bolt. She flipped the rusted clasp up and pushed the rounded trunk's lid up and rested it against the splintered beam.

A strong musty odor whiffed up her nose. Light squeezing in through a crack in the siding caught dust particles floating in the barn. One sniff had her eyes watering and Ava sneezing. Inside, the trunk looked like a mass burial ground. Little bodies, some headless, some legless, some missing arms, butt-naked, lay in twisted, mangled piles.

Dolls.

Ava was not a procurer of dolls, even if she was stashing them. Every time she got one, it got tossed in the trunk with the rest of them. For burial purposes she threw a handful of dirt over them then closed the lid. Dolls were pointless. They didn't talk or play back or do anything other than take up space. To buy them fancy clothes when her parents could be buying her pretty clothes? Again, pointless. Yes, for a young lady, Ava had her priorities. And what was the big boobs all about? Ava didn't like them and didn't want to play with a doll that flaunted them. Flaunted happened to be a word the babysitter taught her on the rare occasion she acknowledged her existence. Ava had caught the babysitter flaunting her boobs one too many times on her phone talking to one of her many boyfriends.

"Ava!"

Her mom's voice made her jerk just as she had the star over the opening in the trunk. The crystal cluster rolled off the edge of the shovel and bounced off plastic boobs and bodies until it settled in.

With a quick tug the lid slammed shut, the lock got put back on and Ava made her way to the horses. "Halo, Lolly, Whizz," Ava put her index finger to her lips and mouthed, "Shoosh! It's our secret." With a quick pat on each of their soft noses and a good scratch behind their ears she told them she loved them and scooted out of the barn running back through the field to the house.

"Happy birthday, little girl," her mother, Greer, wished her. With her arms wide-open Ava made her way into them. There was nothing better than her mom's hugs, well except her dad's. "Did you have fun sleeping outdoors all night? Did your brother keep you awake?"

Ava backed up and looked around. "No, Mommy. Ayden wasn't with me when I woke up. Where is he?" Worried, Ava turned and headed for the stairs.

"I'm here, Aves," Ayden answered as he came in the back door carrying a basket of fresh eggs and tried gently to set them on the counter. Regardless, one popped out of the basket and rolled to its death, shattering all over the tiled floor. "Oops!" Wasting no time Ayden grabbed a wad of paper towels and began wiping the egg up. "Gross! I had to feed the chicks."

"In the barn?" The question came out more like an accusation.

His hands on both his hips, and head cocked to the side with a silly face Ava got her answer.

A chunk of panic about the size of the star went off in Ava's belly. Was Ayden in the barn when she was? Did he see her secret hiding place? "Did you see me with Halo and Lolly and Whizz?"

A bigger grin materialized on her brother's face.

"It's ok, Aves. It's like birthday candles. Cross my heart."

Her finger shot up for him to stop speaking.

Even though she understood his reasoning she didn't like it. When she got back from the hospital, she would have to find a new hiding spot.

"What's like birthday candles, Ayden?" Their mother asked.

"Shooting stars, Mama. They're special. Like Ava."

Ava's mom walked over to her son and hugged him. "You are so sweet. You really do love your big sister."

Ayden wormed his way from his mother's grasp. "Mama!" His cheeks flushed.

Ava got him off the hook. "Mommy, I saw my present last night. It's so pretty. Someday I'll fly up to see it."

"What did you get, Aves? I didn't see any presents. Were you hiding another doll? Even I know you don't like them."

Both Ava and her mom chuckled. "Yup. The

babysitter got me one."

"Ahhh!" He nodded, hands still firm on his hips. "She's not so smart."

That he could reason. Her secret was safe. "Mommy bought me a star. I'll show you tonight."

"Way cool. Can I have one too? How do you play with it?"

"You don't. You just look at it and watch it twinkle. Like mommy's diamond ring."

Ayden's bottom lip flopped over. Through a slight sigh he said. "Never mind. Stars sound like your dolls, dumb. I still want my glove." After he said that his eyes went wide and his hand covered his mouth trying to get his words back.

His mom ruffled his hair. "Your kindergarten entrance party is coming soon, Ayden. We'll see."

Walking past his sister, Ayden got in her face and whispered, "I'm getting one. That's why ya tell people your wishes, Aves."

"Birthday goddess, shower. Pronto." Ava's mom tapped her on the behind in passing. "When you come down, pancakes and then we're off." Her mother shot her thumb over her shoulder pointing to the bathroom. "Move it cupcake, or there won't be any later on."

"Hey, Aves? I found a present for you this morning. It's not the prettiest, but I want you to have it. I gotta wrap it first, ok?"

"Your wrapping looks like a toilette paper roll rewound after the cats scattered it." Ava smirked.

"Tonight, Ayden. When we get home. I'll help you," their mother offered.

Through giggles, Ayden whispered, "Works every time. Learnt that from daddy."

Chapter Twelve

Crossing Bridges

Pulling into the parking garage of the hospital, Ava's belly gurgled. Ayden shot her a curious glance and scooted into the corner of his seat. She didn't feel so hot. Did the not knowing what ailed her make it easier to digest or harder? Would finding out ease her fears or worsen them? She did not appreciate unanswered questions. Were her parents going to fight even more if the "C" word became her reality? Walking through the parking lot, nerves took over and her leg began to shake. Her mom hugged her then slipped her hand in Ava's as if she knew Ava was petrified. Her mom's hand was wet and slippery. She had an idea her mom might be scared too. Ayden grabbed her other hand and squeezed hard. Right this second, she loved him more than anyone would ever know.

Once checked in, they had to wait in a room painted with colorful butterflies with children chasing them with butterfly nets. Another wall had a swing set with little kids in various stages of reaching for the stars. The ceiling had clouds covering it and cherubs peeking over the edges of them. It didn't matter how lovely everything appeared, Ava couldn't get past the aromas of the hospital. Even Whizz's stall smelled better on his worst days. She hated this place. Deep down she knew a lot of little kid's dreams died here.

When the nurse came in wearing pajamas with stars and moons all over them Ava smiled and pointed. Her mother quickly grabbed her hand. "It's not polite to point, Ava."

"But, Mommy, look at her jammies."

The nurse laughed. "It's fine, Mrs. Gabriel. Ava, I wore these for you because I remembered how much you loved the stars when you spent a few nights with us before, and I know today is a very big day for you. And as much as I wish these were jammies, they're called scrubs." The nurse pointed to the chair by the window and pat the seat. "Come here birthday queen."

Ayden piped in, "Scrubs? You have to clean too?"

"There isn't much I don't do, Ayden."

The chair, Ava looked at it and thought quicksand. It would swallow her whole, but she remembered she promised her mom she would be on her best behavior today and she was a big girl now. Six-year-olds didn't cry. She climbed in and sat in the blue plastic recliner while her leg continued to bounce. She couldn't help it and couldn't stop it, but she didn't cry, even when she saw the needle coming.

"It's okay, Ava," the nurse cajoled. "This is the smallest needle I have. It's called a butterfly. See it even looks like one of those on the wall." The nurse showed her the needle. "It has little blue wings probably like the ones in your belly. Am I right?"

Ava nodded and even managed to muster a smile, but she turned her head away. She didn't want to look. Ayden on the other hand had his nose buried right in there watching. "Aves, your blood is so dark it looks black. Isn't it 'spose to be red?"

The nurse answered, "Everyone's blood is a different shade of red. Inside your body it's blue. Hold your hand up and look at the veins in your hand, Ayden. Pretty cool huh?"

Ayden nodded. "Does it hurt, Aves?" He rubbed her shaking leg.

"It's okay. Not as bad as I thought," Ava lied through chattering teeth.

"When we're done here, Ava, one of the staff is going to come take you down for a picture of your chest and belly."

Ayden cut in, "Why not her face? She's prettier than most the girls I know."

Half of Ava's face scrunched sideways. "Most?" Everyone laughed, but her.

"Yes, she is, Ayden, but we need to peek inside her body to make sure she's just as beautiful on the inside. It won't take long and then, Ava, I hear you made some presents for some of the children here?"

Ava nodded and pointed to the bag her mom carried in. "I colored pictures for my friends."

"Perfect. I'm certain they'll love them. Okay, you sit tight for a few minutes and then one of the ladies will come get you."

Inside the x-ray room where Ava had to get an MRI, those butterflies in her belly were acting more like vultures. When they put the headphones over Ava's ears tears started rolling. She knew she promised to not cry but going inside a tube strapped down, closed in, petrified her. "Mommy please don't let them lock me in a box..."

"Mommy," Ayden asked, "Can I lie on it with her to keep her company? Brothers are 'spose to protect sisters." He flashed such a heartfelt grin at Ava more tears fell. Ava's mom looked at the technician. The technician shrugged his shoulders, looked around and came back carrying a hefty blue lead-lined blanket along with another headset.

"This keeps the x-rays from getting you, Ayden. Crawl up, but there are rules, little man. You can't move, and you can't touch her, and most importantly you can't fart."

Once again laughter roared through the room.

"I can promise everything but that," Ayden answered as he climbed up on the cold hard table with her. Once he had headphones on and was covered by the hefty lead blanket the technician told them both to give a thumb's up if everything was ok, or a thumb's down if not. Two thumbs wiggled up and they slowly vanished inside the tube.

The loud pounding the machine made didn't compare to Ava's heart. She hated being in confined spaces. She couldn't imagine being trapped in a box like this her entire life. It was torture.

"Ayden, you gave me the best present ever. Thank you."

"But I didn't wrap it yet."

"No, silly. Being with me in this thing."

"Oh, you'd do the same for me."

If Ava hadn't been told not to move a muscle, she would have hugged him.

"Aves, can you promise to keep a secret?"

About to nod, Ava remembered the vow of not moving a muscle thingy. "Yup."

"That star I saw fall to the ground last night was all burnt and black and kinda looked like a jar mama puts applesauce in. I went and got a bucket of water and poured it over the rock. That's where I was when you woke up. Now you have a real star to play with. I just gotta wash the chicken poop off it."

"Did you open it to see if anything was in it?"

"No. Daddy took it before I could get a peek. The babysitter saw it too."

"Harper was at the house?"

"Yup. I don't like her."

"Me either."

After the test ended the nurse came down and greeted them. "Ava, do you want to go see your friends and pass out their gifts?"

Eager to get out of this noisy chamber Ava hurried for the door towing Ayden behind her. "Mommy, can I have my bag?" Greer handed her the gift bag. "Thanks. Come on Ayden." Feeling a little prouder, Ava skipped down the hall to the great room where all the kids played together that were allowed to be in open areas with other kids. Some of the kids weren't so lucky. There were pictures for them as well.

A giant banner strung across the doorway that read: Happy 6th Birthday Ava, made all her earlier woes vanish.

She looked in the room and there was a cake with candles, and some presents on the table all decorated with sparkly papers and bows. Her head snapped back to her mom. Greer walked over to her and hugged her.

The nurse told Ava, "Your friends found out and did this for you. Birthdays mean everything in this ward."

Ava gave a meek smile and shrugged her shoulders. "Wow!"

It took all of two seconds for Ava to be mobbed by

seven of her friends she'd met when she stayed here a few weeks ago.

It took even less time for Ayden to help himself to the frosting on the cake. Index finger swipe, he came back with a glob of the confection and with eager eyes popped his finger in his mouth and made little yummy sounds.

Even with the party and surrounded by her friends, Ava kept a close eye on her mom. The doctor had come in and asked her to step out in the hallway. Secrets weren't good. Adult secrets were the worst. Especially when they revolved around her. After a few minutes of watching her mom's head bob up and down and her arms hug herself, her mom came back in to join the party not looking herself. Her skin had gone white, and her eyes held red streaks. Her smile vanished faster than Ayden ate his cake. About to ask her if she was all right, the loudspeaker went off, and a woman's voice blared, "Code grey to the ED. Code grey. STAT!"

All the kids, Ava included rushed for the exit to see what the commotion was all about, but the doors to the children's wing had already been closed and secured. Ava stopped running and looked at the pile up of kids with each of them vying for the window spot to get a glimpse of whatever was going on just beyond the lockdown.

"What did that mean? Are the children safe?" Greer asked the nurse headed for her children. "Ayden, back away from the door. Ava, grab him." Panic laced Greer's voice.

"They're safe, Mrs. Gabriel. Nothing or no one gets through those doors unless we want them to. We treasure our children." Shaking her head as she peered out the hallway, the nurse continued, "We've had an influx of vagrants last night. Full moons and meteor showers always bring out the crazies. They're memories are shot, probably high on whatever street drug is most popular today. Blood-alcohol levels through the roof. I've never seen anything like it. Not a one of them has a clue how they wound up in little old Black Hills, South Dakota. It's sad, but funny. One claims he is Zeus. Another claims to be Apollo, singing like he inhaled helium. He's totally dreadful."

Greer elbowed the nurse's side, adding, "Absolute shame it wasn't Thor," just before giving up a coy grin.

Ayden threw his mom under the bus. "Mama's favorite actor is him. We watched Thor five times so far and I got popcorn every time."

"He's mine too, Ayden. There's one in the psych unit right now claiming to be him. Our hallways will look like it's the Academy Awards waiting for a glimpse of the god if word gets out."

Ava noticed her mom's hands shaking. "Mommy?"

Even Ayden noticed. "Mama?"

"I'm fine. Just need water. I'm parched."

"Ayden, go grab mommy a juice bottle from the table."

Glancing down the tip of his perfectly straight nose, Ayden shot her a look. "Magic word?"

"Please?" Ava bat her long strawberry blonde eyelashes a few times as she shoved him forward.

"Thank you!" Ayden flew off and came back with a pouch of lemonade.

Greer grabbed the drink and nodded a silent thank you to her son. "It's just the long drive. I'll be fine," she added trying to comfort the children.

"Honest?" Ava asked, not buying it.

Greer managed a small smile. "Honest as Abe."

"Whatever that means. Then can I meet him, the Zeus dude?" Ava pleaded with her hands clasped in front of her.

"And I wanna meet Thor," Ayden butt in.

The nurse gave a stout, "No! The last thing delusional people need is an inquisitive six-year-old and four-year-old—"

"—Almost five," Ayden adamantly corrected.

"My apologies young man, almost five-year old, playing right along with them and feeding them more make-believe."

"How do you know it's make-believe? Mommy?" Ava asked, getting annoyed. "Maybe they fell from heaven. Aliens are real. Daddy's always saying things about the illegal ones. And with the meteor shower maybe they fell off a cloud."

The nurse ruffled Ava's strawberry blonde hair. "I bet your mom taught you to never talk to strangers?"

A giant moue replaced Ava's smile. She knew where this was going and didn't like it one iota. "Yes, Ma'am," came out in a defeated tone.

Greer slid her finger under her daughter's chin and tilted her head up to look at her. "The nurse is right. Look, baby, we need to get home. We still have a long ride ahead of us. Go finish passing out your pictures and then we can scoot out the back door. Can we do that?" Greer looked to confirmation from the nurse.

The nurse squat down in front of Ava and held her arms open waiting for a hug. Ava jumped right in along with Ayden. "You two are so precious. Ava, what a big girl you were today and Ayden, I wish my brother loved me half as much as you love your sister." The nurse looked directly at Greer. "Mrs. Gabriel, don't think about the tests today, okay? Go celebrate your special day. Let me know when you're ready to leave."

Ava told the nurse, "Everyone here made it more special than I dreamt of."

"And the cake was really good," Ayden added.

Once Ava's artwork had been distributed and hung in each of her friend's rooms, the nurse hit a buzzer and the back door opened. Greer, Ayden and Ava went down a few flights of stairs and then walked through a long corridor of rooms that looked nothing like the floor they just left. The walls were dull. The paint chipped. The air smelled like bleach. Ava's eyes watered. Ayden plugged his nose and gagged. The floor had brownish-red stains smeared all over them and doors to rooms had tiny windows in the center of each with metal bars, nose art decorating each. Big padlocks like the one Ava used to hide her dolls and the star in, hung on the outside trapping people in.

Ayden said exactly what Ava was thinking. "I think we took a wrong turn, Mama. I don't think we were 'spose to come all the way to the dungeon."

About to turn around since they must have been in an area that should have been cordoned off to everyone, patients included, a loud boom bellowed down the opposite end of the hallway blocking their exit. Shivers prickled Ava's leg, but these were different. Fearing needles invading her space versus whatever made the floor vibrate were two different beasts.

A heavy metal door with multiple ding marks crashed into the wall. Ava, Ayden and her mom stopped dead in the center of the hallway. Three men busted through the opening, arms and legs all jumbled with copious amounts of swear words coming from all of them. Two of the men donned officer uniforms. A third man wore silver bracelets and shackles around his wrists and ankles. From the wall of padlocked doors faces appeared and pressed against the windows. Each person looked worse than the previous. Their mouths moved, yet silence prevailed. Before she had a chance to say anything, her mother had Ava and Ayden tucked under each arm like baby chicks, and the three of them crouched to the floor while the armed guards dragged an elderly man past them kicking and screaming, "Judgment Day, boys. Armageddon! Ring any bells?"

His white hair and beard fell in choppy, uneven layers. In all honesty, Ava thought Ayden could've done a better job cutting off the hair. He'd done hers once. A trip to the Curl Up and Dye boutique immediately ensued. Another reason for the clowns.

The elderly man's hand stretched for Ava, his skin wrinkled, his fingers crooked with reddish angry looking knobs popping off every knuckle. Brown spots decorated his skin better than a Dalmatian displayed freckles. Kind of looked like all the marks appearing all over Ava. Hers started out purple and slowly faded to brown. Maybe he had the same disease she did and that's why he was in the hospital, but in isolation? Locked up? Is this where she'd wind up if they had the same thing?

"Momma, I want to go home. Now!"

"My evening star, you're here. Thank God, well me, we found you. Let the others know I am here."

"Others?" The crack in Ava's voice projected her fear, but for a reason she couldn't comprehend, she reached out to the man. The tips of his fingers brushed hers. He tried to latch onto her, but one of the guards placed his body firmly between the two of them and got his grip free of Ava's.

Even the short contact sent a gust of energy through her body. She'd never felt this much of a power rush even after sticking a bobby pin in an outlet once when she was little.

And stupid.

"Get her away from here, Miss," one of the guards advised.

"He's just an old man. Be nice to him," Ava shouted. "He's sick too."

"That he is, little one. Your nice old man just put two of my men in the emergency room. Now get out of here."

"You can't treat me like this. I am a god. Tell them, my evening star, tell them who I am."

The old man's stormy grey eyes foretold the future. There were clouds roiling, lightening shooting from one eye and illuminating the other eye, with all his blood vessels pulsing brilliant orange. The strength and power the man emanated gave her the feeling she'd been dropped inside a static electric bubble and sealed shut.

"Did you see that?" Barely a whisper slipped out. "Did you feel it?" An anxious glance between her mother and brother said she'd been the only one to witness the man's supremacy.

"He's fruity-tootie. He doesn't even know your name, Aves." Ayden tried to drag her away from the old man, but to no avail, she didn't budge.

Then her mom stepped in, picked her up and tossed her over her shoulder.

"Not fair!" Ava kicked and screamed just like the

old man. "No! Mommy, he's real."

"I know you too," The old man pointed a long knobby finger to Greer. "My comrades and I met you when we came down below to check on earth. You were very hospitable. Very! And I know your little boy too."

Chapter Thirteen

Irony At Its Worst

Once in the car Ava's mom barely spoke. Clearly, the old man had shaken her.

About an hour into the ride, Ava broke her silence and asked, "Did you know him, Mommy? Or did he fib?"

Her mom shook her head no.

"But he said he knew you."

"He is an old man in need of help. They have him in the right place. The hospital is a good start. He'll get the treatment he deserves."

"He could have been a real god. He could have had a ride on one of the falling stars last night. What if he really is God and people ignore him? Or don't believe him? The pastor at church says God will come back some day. What if no one believes him and we miss our miracle?"

"Impossible, kiddo. You give hope too much of a wide berth."

"You told me hope is the only thing we have left. Hope is fearless."

"Little girl, you are fearless. When did you get so smart?"

Very matter-of-factly with a little bob of her head, Ava avowed, "Kindergarten was pretty tough."

Her mother smiled into the rearview mirror, and

then continued to drive, peculiarly quiet. Usually, her mom had heavy metal tunes blaring for the long ride and singing along with them. Ava thought right now she was driven more by fear. Her long slender fingers had a better grip on the steering wheel than daddy did his remote to the television. Maybe she didn't have the music going because Ayden fell asleep.

"How much longer we got?"

"A few hours, baby. Close those giant emeralds and relax."

With her pillow propped up against the window she looked outside and between the engine's lull and the scenery as it wisped past, Ava's nerves calmed. For the ride home her mom decided to take the Spearfish Canyon Scenic Byway route to break up the monotony. Hand's down she loved this countryside. This area held one of her favorite spots, Bridal Veil Falls. On sunny days like this she could see mountain goats on rocky jut-outs of the side of the mountain defying the laws of gravity. In the summer rock climbers could be spotted all over the surface, but in the springtime with all the rain the falls looked like a wedding veil.

As they passed Belle Fourche, Ava's mom whispered to her, "You are now in the center of the United States, Ava. You are halfway to wherever you want to go."

"Home?" Ava perked up.

"Not quite," Greer chuckled.

Her shoulders slouched, she cozied into her spot and snuggled the blankets around her and Ayden. Buffalo grazed the countryside in small herds. The bison stumped her. Ava couldn't figure out why the humongous animals didn't tip over, they were so top-heavy, a lot like her eyelids, but she fought sleep. Teepees along the rode let her know they were approaching a few casinos and tourist spots. As her mom had mentioned on other trips this area had horseback riding, chasing tumble weeds races, and some of the 'mighty-finest cowboys' to be seen. She also told her the night skyline of the Badlands could lead her to a path in other galaxies. She alleged, 'It was the stairway to heaven.' Maybe someday Ava would see it for herself.

A little further into the ride an occasional prairie dog popped their head out of a ground hole and then disappear and then another one would appear a foot or two over. Hawks and turkey vultures never seemed to be too far off.

With Ayden up against her, his head flopped on her shoulder out cold she went back and thought of the delusional old fart. Could the old man really be Zeus? The hospital had him locked in a cell. Her reasoning kicked in and she decided her mom was right. Zeus would have super-duper powers and would have escaped. There! Problem solved. He was a nutter. Solving all the world's problems for the day her tired eyes finally closed…

Until the car's forward momentum came to a screeching halt. Both Ayden and she were lifted from the seat, projected forward and then snapped back to their seats with the same tenacity a slingshot fired a rock into the atmosphere and then decided to snatch it back.

"The brakes on the vehicle aren't working," Greer yelled, as the car began a sideways spin. Ava grabbed Ayden and hugged him for all she was worth. Trying to regain control of the car, her mom's hands were crisscrossing left, then right then left again on the steering wheel.

"What the heck is that lady doing in the middle of the bridge?" A mere second passed. "Why is she wearing a crown and wings? Hold on!" Greer screamed, "We're going over."

"Over what," Ava yelled back and then she saw it. And wished she hadn't.

The bridge crossing the Cheyenne River.

The entire driver's side of the car careened into the water first. Ayden's head slammed into hers then hers met the window with a nauseating force. Glass cracked and in an instant the outside pressure of the river shattered the window sending shards inward. Water flooded the car. Every time she went to yell water rushed into her mouth or up her nose or blindsided her. She saw stars and if anyone ever tried to tell her they weren't real she had a bona fide bone to pick with them. "Mommy!" The name flowed from Ava's little body better than water pouring into the car. She took in her brother's petrified faced and she was certain hers didn't look any better. Even the frigid temperature of the water couldn't numb her. "Don't cry, Ayden. I got you. It'll be okay. Keep your head up so the water doesn't get up your nose. Mommy! Get us out!" Ava fumbled, her fingers shaking so badly she didn't think she'd ever get Ayden's seatbelt undone, let alone hers.

"Aves," Ayden screamed, "let go. I got this, Sissy," as he got them out of their seats.

****

"What happened?" Christian pleaded, begged, demanded repeatedly to anyone, the police, the search and rescue divers, anyone with a pulse, people on the opposite shore watching in horror, but no one answered him while his frantic legs paced him up and down the long expanse of the bridge. Cars crawled by the accident at a snail's pace.

Ava saw everyone. There wasn't a face she couldn't recall that ogled, stared, pointed, or turned away refusing to meet her destitute eyes. Sat on the edge of the ambulance's bumper with a blanket wrapped around her soaked body, she shook, completely numb. Not because she was cold but because she couldn't grasp the events that led to this.

"Mommy said a lady landed in the road. Said she swooped down with giant black wings wearing a gold crown. Mommy swerved to miss her and then yelled the brakes didn't work."

Without ever taking his eyes off the river, Christian answered, "Your mother's traumatized."

Ava tapped her father's arm. "Daddy, where's Ayden? Before you and the police got here, Mommy said the lady hissed at her and stole him."

Arms locked tight across his chest, Christian snapped his attention to Ava. "Did you see a woman? A woman with black wings wearing a freaking crown fly off with Ayden?"

"No. I was trying to get Mommy out of the car. Where's Ayden?" Ava raised her voice this time while tears welled in her eyes.

Her father sat down on the edge of the bumper beside her and threw his arm around her shoulder and hugged her to him.

Ava wiggled free of her father's embrace. Louder she asked, "Daddy, where's Ayden?"

He bent over, brought his hands up and raked his fingers through his hair. "The police, divers, and water patrol, they're all searching for him. They think he was swept away with the current."

Ava slid off the back of the ambulance and ditched the blanket. She raced to the embankment, her eyes weary from both crying and the strain to find her brother in the dark murky water. She turned her head back to her father, her soaked strawberry blonde locks whipping in the wind coming up from the river. "Daddy, I had him in my arms. And then he hollered, 'Let go.' But I didn't. I swear I didn't." With an impatient hand she swiped her hair behind her ear only to have it escape a second later.

"I believe you, Aves." Christian looked at the mangled mess of a car being secured to the tow truck. "It is a miracle you lived." Water drained out of every possible inch of the wreckage. "How did you get out, Ava?"

Ava shook her head. "I don't know."

"Ayden didn't just vanish in thin air, Aves. It's impossible. Maybe someone took him from the road. A lady with a funny hat and a black cloak that looked like wings? A car? Someone's got my son." Christian grabbed one of the cops headed his way by the man's jacket lapels. With pure desperation and fear conveyed in his voice he begged, "Please, he's not in the water. Maybe someone brought him to the hospital? Did anyone check?"

"He hasn't been admitted. We've checked," the cop answered.

Christian shouted, "Then he's been abducted. Look for cameras, footage." His hand shot out and he pointed under the bridge. Two cameras were visible along the main cables of the bridge's structure. Then he shot his finger up to the center tower that also held a camera and spotlight. From where he stood now, two more cameras were visible on the deck of the bridge, both aimed towards the water to monitor boats. "The bridge has to have this now after 9-11, doesn't it?"

The officer gently placed his hands on top of Christian's and pried them from him. "We pulled the footage off the cameras, Mr. Gabriel. Blank! Like it had been erased. Not even the car going over is on it. The guard rails are severed in half, the car is demolished and it's a miracle you have your wife and daughter and I swear to you Mr. Gabriel, we will find your boy. If it's the last thing I ever do, I'll find your son."

"What about the other missing boys from our hometown? Jimmy Fields and Brady Wells? They've been missing a year now with no trace. You gonna promise to find them too? Their dads are waiting too. Useless words." Christian turned away from Ava and the officer. Heavy sobs cut through the chatter of radios, the loud voices of the divers, and the blare of the horns as cars continued past. The cop put his arm around Christian's shoulder and suggested, "Go be with your wife at the hospital. She needs you." Christian gave a solemn nod, but stood there shivering, staring into a void.

Tears cascaded down Ava's cheeks. "Daddy, I want Ayden back. He's gotta be so scared." With his arm stretched out Christian wiggled his fingers to Ava. She came running and grabbed his hand. Once in his grip he wrapped his arms around his daughter and held her. With a gentle tug he swung her into his arms and onto his hip then made his way back to one of the police cruisers.

"Have you heard word on my wife? How is she?" Christian asked the officer, his tone a bit softer.

The officer answered, "The ambulance shipped her

to the same hospital you all spent the morning at."

Irony at its worst her father had proclaimed. Ava agreed to look up the word *irony* when she got home.

Her first day being six, Ava decided getting older had no redeeming qualities.

One cop told them, "We'll resume the search in the morning. There's nothing you can do here. Mrs. Gabriel will need you both."

"My son needs me. I'm not leaving. Can one of you take my daughter to the hospital to be with my wife?"

Ava grabbed her father's face and yelled, "No, Daddy, don't leave me."

Christian set Ava down and knelt to her height. "Ava, you're my big girl. You'll be fine. I need you to take care of Mommy for us. Can you do that until I find Ayden? Please?" Christian crushed Ava to him. With a gentle kiss on her cheek, he released her and began to walk away. "I love you, baby. Forever."

"I got her," The officer who earlier had told Christian he'd find Ayden offered. "I'll make certain she's safe."

Both hands on the backseat window Ava pressed her face hard against the glass, watching petrified as her world unraveled. With each passing second her father got smaller and smaller until she no longer saw him.

Chapter Fourteen

Little White Lies

Day three of being in the infirmary, Ava considered herself orphaned. Her dad literally dropped off the planet with as much ease as Ayden had. He hadn't come back. He hadn't called. He hadn't left any messages. Her mother went through bouts of either being lucid one moment, or a raging lunatic the next. It was fun.

She rolled her eyes. Being blindfolded on a rollercoaster equated to the situation. There were peaks, there were troughs, she wanted to scream throughout the entire ordeal, yet Ava remained too numb. Ava missed her home. She missed her family. She missed her life. She missed her horses. She missed Ayden. He had to be so scared. This should have happened to her, not him. She was supposed to take care of her baby brother and she failed. He saved her somehow, she was certain of it.

Curled around her mother in the hospital bed, Ava laced her fingers through her mom's swollen ones. Her mom's usual warm touch felt foreign. Cold regardless of how hot she was. Distant even though they shared a lumpy twin bed. Doctors, dentist, nurses, and technicians bombarded the room in a vicious game of follow the leader, each with an agenda, poke, prod, pound on her chest…

IV poles like the ones her friends had in the pediatric

cancer unit hung beside the bed. Three different bags dangled from one pole, two more from a second pole. One bag had blood in it. Morphine also hung in one of them connected to some sort of blue contraption that doled out doses of the med in tiny increments. The nurse told Ava the medication killed pain. Ava had asked if she could have it too. Her heart hurt. She got pudding.

Her mom wasn't doing well. They'd listed her condition as critical, due to the head trauma her mother endured in the accident. Both her eyes were swollen and black. She looked like a vampire on Halloween minus fangs because she'd also lost all her teeth.

Ava heard the doctors talking outside the door in hushed whispers. They'd all look in at her mother then their intent gazes would fall on Ava filled with pity. If she heard the words, "Poor kid," one more time she might end up with the Zeus guy locked away.

The fact that her mom didn't wake up when she spoke to her was the worst, but the nurse told her all the meds would make her sleepy. To talk to her would have alleviated some of Ava's fears because right now they grew faster than the weeds in her fields.

When her dad finally walked into the hospital room, he didn't look any better than her mom. His eyes were red, puffy, his hair greasy and his clothes were the same ones he had on the night of the accident. And if things couldn't get worse, the babysitter waltzed in behind him.

Ava whispered, "Hi," to her dad. To Harper, diddly squat.

"How's your mother doing?"

"Have they found Ayden?" Ava didn't answer his question. If he were blind then yes, maybe she'd answer, but anyone could see her mom had seen better days. Her mom lay right here under his nose. Ayden? She stared at him until he answered.

"No word." Christian sat on the foot of the bed and wiggled Ava's toes. She tugged her foot away from him. Harper made herself invisible by wedging her body into an empty nook between the bathroom and the tiny closet. "I'm so sorry, baby. Tell me about your mom."

"She's supposed to rest. No talking. And no visitors that aren't family." That she directed to Harper.

No sooner did Ava finish giving her father the riot act Greer opened her eyes and tried to mumble, "Where's my boy?"

Christian made his way to the head of the bed. He leaned in close to Greer and whispered something Ava couldn't hear. More secrets.

Whatever he said agitated Greer because the alarms above the bed began to blare. Greer placed her hands over her ears and with a grimaced, red face she squeezed her eyes shut and groaned. A second later a nurse came running in.

"Everyone needs to leave. Now!"

"Why?" Ava asked not budging. "What did you say to her, Daddy? She was okay."

"Her pressure spiked honey," the nurse paused for a moment as she cleaned off a port in the IV line with a tiny swab and then pushed a medication into the tubing. "This will bring the pressure down. Quite honestly, I can't believe they don't have you in an induced coma." The nurse jabbed her stethoscope at Christian. "You need to maintain some semblance of control before you are asked to leave. And if you do leave, you might want to take your daughter with you." The nurse documented some information into a lap top computer and before she walked out added, "I mean it. I am done babysitting."

Once more Greer went to speak, but her words came out more like someone trying to win a world record for stuffing marshmallows in their mouth. Frustration evident, her mom's hands knotted into fists. Greer jerked her body into a sitting position, groaning with each move.

"Ava, tell them. A lady swooped down from the sky with huge wings. She is real." Her words were barely audible.

"Mommy, I didn't see anyone."

"There was a woman, Christian. I swear."

The worst babysitter ever added her useless two cents, "That's the funniest thing I've ever heard."

All heads turned to the girl who had a wad of gum wedged between her front teeth stretching the substance out in front of her. She looked at Ava, Christian and Greer and snickered. "Well it is," she snidely added lacking an ounce of empathy or concern.

His voice contemptuous, Christian lashed out, "I agree with Harper. A woman dropped down from the sky and disappeared with our son. You are insane, Greer. What did you do to Ayden?"

Ava craned her neck, her head snapping towards her father. "Daddy!" Contempt coated his name. She threw her arms around her mother's neck and nuzzled into her. "It's all right, Mommy. He didn't mean it." She peeked out from her mother's hold. "Tell her, Daddy. Tell her sorry."

Christian's lips stretched thin, pressed tight together. He shook his head no. "I can't, baby."

"I hate you, Daddy. Mommy would never hurt Ayden. Never. I want to go home. And I want my brother."

Christian leaned right in Ava's face and said, "Lose the *tude* tootsie, or else."

Ava watched her dad's index finger orchestrating a silent battle.

Terse words filled the void. "I didn't think it could, but this day just got worse." He inhaled sharply and finished with, "I spoke with the doctor about your daughter. Did you hear me, *your* daughter, Greer?"

If it were possible her mom's color went one shade away from translucent. Air had more color. Ava didn't understand.

"What did the doctor say, Daddy?"

"Ava, your test results are back. You have a blood disorder called Hemophilia. You'll be fine. Not cancer. We must set up some treatments, but you'll be okay with meds and caution. Ya see the funny thing is, and honestly, it's not funny, I gave blood when I spent the night here for donor purposes in case you needed it. Ava, my blood came back fine. Your mom did the same thing, but her blood has a glitch. The same issue yours has, Aves. She's what you call a carrier of the disease you have, but this is the part you need to pay attention to Greer. Ya listening?" Christian grabbed her arm and leaned over Ava into Greer's face. "In order for *your* daughter"—once more he enunciated the word harshly—"to have hemophilia, both parents have to have the gene, which can only mean one thing."

He lost Ava. "What, daddy?"

Christian looked at Ava, tears flooding his eyes. "God forgive me, Aves. I love you. I love Ayden. I wish none of this ever happened, but it did. Ignorance is truly bliss. Greer, you," he pointed to her and then tapped his chest, "me, we're so done. So over. You've lied to me. To Ava, to our family. To put it in words Ava, you can understand, she lied to us, Aves. The worst lies a mommy could ever tell someone." He looked back at Greer and choked on his words. "Is Ayden even mine?"

"Mommy?" Looking between her parents, Ava had no idea what was going on. Her dad made no sense.

Harper mumbled, "This is way better than reality television."

Both Christian and Greer yelled in unison, "Shut up, Harper."

Greer didn't look at anyone when she shook her head *no*, answering Christian's question.

"Ava, I love you. I may not be your biological daddy, but that doesn't make my love any less real." Without looking back Christian headed for the door, as dear sweet, bubble gum chomping, Harper waddled behind him better than a baby duck who'd imprinted on him.

Ava fled to her dad's side and threw her arms around him. "I'm sorry I said I hated you. I don't. Please Daddy don't leave me again. Take me with you so I can help find Ayden. Please?" Tears and sniffles overtook her. He took a few steps forward, away. She fell grappling onto his ankle.

Gently Christian peeled Ava's hands from him. "I need time, baby. I just, I need some time." He kissed the top of her head and walked out, leaving her alone.

"Daddy, please? No. Don't leave. I love you." Ava liquefied onto the floor in hysterics until the nurse coaxed her up into her arms.

"You can't leave her!" The nurse yelled after Christian, "It's abandonment. We've held off calling the authorities for the past three days under the circumstances, but this is it!" The woman's words never caught up to Christian. He'd already disappeared into the elevator.

The rest of her afternoon Ava occupied her time in the atrium alone. She didn't want company. No friends. No one. Not even her mom. Especially her mom. Her mom forever preached to her about telling the truth. Ava decided the entire line her mom always spewed, "Do as I say, not as I do," really fit her mom. The words she'd said to her mom after her dad left her weren't nice. Calling someone, your mommy, a liar and cheater wasn't nice, but then her mom wasn't nice for doing those things. Telling her mom that she wished she vanished instead of Ayden felt good at the time, but now not so much. But she wouldn't say sorry. Her mom needed to first.

And when her dad came back for her, she wasn't going to talk to him either. She'd been betrayed by her mom and abandoned by her dad. Could her birthday week get any worse?

No amount of frosting could make this better.

"Ava," The nurse who'd been taking care of her mom walked into the atrium and sat down beside her. "Do you have your dad's cell phone number? It's pretty important. I need to talk to him."

"Why? I don't want to talk to him."

"Because your mommy's not feeling so good, and she wants to talk to him."

Ava stood up to go to her mother's room, but the nurse put a hand on her shoulder. "The doctors are with her right now, honey. Let them help her."

"What's wrong with her?" Ava yanked her shoulder

free from the nurse's grasp and bolted down the hallway to find a crowd of medical personnel stood around her mother's bed. One man was pumping up and down on her chest and someone else was yelling the word, "Clear!" Once he yelled that Greer's body jolted a good two feet off the bed. Ava knew enough to look up at the monitor in the corner of the room even if she didn't understand what she saw. She had an idea a flat line wasn't good. Heartbeats had little hills and valleys; life's ups and downs as one nurse described them. Alarms blared. One of the doctors looked at Ava and then one of the nurses and nodded to her. In her next breath Ava was being escorted back to the atrium, kicking and screaming, "I want to see my mommy. Let me see her!"

"Let the doctors help her. Right now you can help me by giving me your dad's cell number. Do you know it?"

"Of course I know it," Ava screamed. "I'm not a baby!" Ava picked up a crayon, wrote the number on a piece of paper, and threw it at the nurse then crossed her arms over her chest. Crying. She was over it. Not one tear escaped.

Chapter Fifteen

Courage

Once the nurse disappeared, Ava walked out of the atrium, down the hallway, down the stairs and down the long, scary, grey corridor where she saw the crazy god being hidden. There wasn't a nurse, doctor or police officer in sight. The area felt like a library, eerie, quiet. With a tap on the window, she waited. When a mass of white hair and murky grey eyes hogged the window Ava jumped back and landed flatly against the opposite side of the hall, her back pressed tight to the cold bricks, her eyes huge. The man's hair had already grown. It was longer than hers and hers touched the top of her tush. A giant smile went across the man's face. Then a finger pointed down to the lock on her side of the door. He was mouthing something, but she couldn't hear him even if she knew what he wanted. Ava would want the same thing. No one needed to be locked in a cell with no one to speak to. It's how she felt right now in the hospital. Trapped. Alone.

Fingers to her chest she fished out her charm necklace and looked at the key to her padlock and then the bolt on the outside of this guy's door. Pinched between her thumb and index finger she wiggled the key at the man. His smile grew even bigger.

Ava liked his smile. His teeth were perfect. Every

picture she'd ever seen of homeless people had them looking poor with dirty clothes, worn out holey shoes, if they had any on, and missing teeth. Or maybe she had it all wrong. Maybe homeless people had nice teeth. Once had nice clothes. A family. A roof over their head. People that loved them. Maybe something horrible happened to them and that's why they needed help. Not to be passed over, made fun of, or bullied. Her mind swam. If a puppy sat on the street someone would snag it and help it. Why didn't they do the same for those less fortunate? Ava studied this man on the opposite side of the lock and knew he wasn't homeless. Just lost. And he needed her. Or maybe she needed him more.

"Here goes nothing." The key fit into the padlock and after a jiggle or two Ava felt a clunk and the lock give way. When one end snapped free Ava glanced up from under nervous lids to the man.

So now her little voice or reason spoke up? Nice timing. The little nagging voice asked, "Is this really a good idea, Ava? You don't know this guy. He could be a nutter. Your mom could be right."

And that's when she loosened the lock and freed the could-be nutter, crazy looking could-be God.

Once again, she found herself with her back against the wall while the door slid open, and the man peered out into the hallway.

Just in case.

"Is it safe?" He looked both left and right from the door jam. "Those two men zapped me with an instrument wielding the power of my scepter. It was most unpleasant."

Afraid to speak, let alone move an inch, Ava looked out of the corner of her left eye and then her right before

137

she gave the tiniest nod yes when she didn't see anyone.

Once he stepped out into the hallway the crazy god seemed to engulf the entire space. He had to be a giant. He was taller than her dad and her dad was mammoth. This guy was seven or eight feet tall. His outfit wasn't anything a respectable god would wear. No crown. No gold bling. Only hospital garb: light blue jammie bottoms with a string barely tied around his rock-solid waist. The leg length didn't reach his knobbed calves. He knelt to her and held his hand out.

"Thank you, my evening star. I owe you my mortal life."

"Your what? Are you really a god? And why do you keep calling me a star? I'm Ava. If you were God you would know that."

"Maybe that is why I am calling you a star, Ava."

Head cocked to one side and her lips scrunched she added, "And, I'm not touching you again. You zapped me too. I'm just a little girl. You are wrong." She tucked her hands behind her back on the off chance he tried to grab her.

A loud gasp came from Zeus. "I am never wrong."

"Well, my mommy says men are wrong all the time."

"I am not a man. I am a god." The giant grew a little taller trying to show off.

"God. Man. Same difference. Do you have a penis?" Ava's bottom lip jut out and her green eyes grew enormous waiting for him to stop laughing.

"How old are you again?" Zeus dug his fingers into his wild locks and scratched.

"Six."

"Well, with logic as this I cannot dispute, I am

indeed a man."

Ava butt right in, "Then you're wrong. I'm just a little girl named Ava having a super crappy day and I don't know you. I think I would remember meeting a giant. Mommy says you're a crazy old man, not a god. I said if you were a god you wouldn't be stuck here."

Zeus gave a smile with a gracious nod. He slipped his hand under Ava's chin and tickled her. "I don't want to give away secrets, Ava."

"Who am I gonna tell? My brother is missing. My mom is in the bed upstairs and my dad left me. Where did you come from? If you are truly a god, can you find my brother? Can you make my mom better?"

The huge man smoothed his tangled beard in thought. "Missing? That's not good. Tell me what happened. For some odd reason my powers aren't working right."

Ava slid down the wall and hugged her knees to her chest. She giggled when Zeus did the same. She really laughed when she heard his pajama bottom split under the stress of his enormous thighs. Zeus only shrugged his shoulders and winked.

Ava poured her heart out to the giant who held the sincerest smile she'd ever seen. For some reason she felt safe with him. After telling Zeus all the details of her worst birthday ever Zeus thanked her for sharing such intimate information with him.

"I'm sorry I don't know where Ayden is, but I promise if we find him, I'll bring him back to you. As for my home? It would be easier for me to show you. Would you like to go outside? By the way, what year is it, my evening star?"

"Name. Is. Ava!" Came out a little ticked off.

"Really? You're a god and you don't know the date? Can't you read? Gods can do anything no matter where they are. Ya just gotta believe."

"That is what I love about you, little goddess: Your optimism."

"You're kinda scaring me." This guy kept infusing mumbo-jumbo into her head. Junk she didn't have room for. Way too much on her plate as it was. Without realizing it Ava's feet were scooting her up and away from the man she just set free. That little voice was giving her more grief, yelling, "Run Ava run," and not with the same tone the young Jenny had when she was egging on, *Forrest*.

"Mister Zeus, I gotta go. My mom is upstairs and she's not feeling good. Don't kill anybody, okay? I don't want to be a compass."

"I think you mean accomplice, my evening star."

"Yeah, that. And stop calling me that. My name is Ava."

"As you wish, Ava. Before I leave have any other of my brethren shown up in the area?"

A giant huff of frustration blew out Ava's little nose. She wanted to get back to her mother's side. Now. "I heard a nurse tell Mommy another god, Thor might be in the area. Oh, and some horrid singer, Apollo."

Zeus's laughter bellowed down the hall and then echoed like he was still laughing even though his lips were shut. "Odin is a god. Thor, his son, is a toddler comparatively speaking."

"Clearly you don't watch all the good movies then. Thor is my mom's favorite God."

"I'm certain he is. Many women have found him enjoyable company."

The look on the giant gave Ava's belly more rumbles. She kept getting the idea he held many secrets from her. "I really gotta go. Bye." Ava sidestepped the hulk, and with a faster pace headed back towards her mother.

Zeus's voice chased after Ava, "I owe you for my freedom. Thank you. I'll be easy to find if you need me."

Brakes on, Ava stopped and turned around. Fear, that too she was done with. "What's your name? Your real name, Mister?"

"Zeus."

Hand on her hip and her head cocked she said it louder. "I said your real name."

Hands on his hips mimicking her stance he answered, "I do believe I just told you."

"Well Zeus, from what I learnt at bible study, don't go telling people you're truly a god. People get scared at stuff they don't understand, and when they get scared, they either lock them up," Ava pointed to the cell, "or they kill them." Then Ava pulled up her charm necklace up in front of her and showed Zeus a crucifix with Jesus.

"Yes, that. Not one of humanities finer moments in history."

Eyes narrowed, Ava asked, "If you're a god and Jesus was God's son, are you related?"

"Different planets, different galaxies, little twinkler. Each planetary system has their own god. I am not from Earth."

Sarcasm laced, Ava added, "Of course you aren't," followed by, "how come you don't use magic if you're a god?"

A grin spread across the huge guy's face before he broke out in song and dance. "I'm trying to stay incognito. Lay low. Go with the flow. Be in the know. See how things go…"

Giggling at a god, Ava covered her mouth. "That might not a been nice. Sorry for laughing at you. You dance funny like my daddy. Stop rapping. Gods don't rap. Do they?"

Zeus chuckled. "Gods, little girl, can do whatever they want. If you need me, call."

"Except get out of locked boxes." Ava made her famous half-scrunched, *ya think-face*. Before her disbelieving eyes Zeus disappeared. Gone. Ava's breath caught in her throat. No one would believe her except… "Oh my god, Mommy!"

Ava almost fell backwards trying not to plow right into him when Zeus reappeared in front of her.

With a tap to his chest he asked, "That was awfully quick. What do you need?"

"Don't do that," she scolded the giant. "You'll scare people. We just had this conversation, remember?"

"I said if you need me call. You called."

"I said oh God, not oh Zeus. There's a difference."

Zeus bent over to the Ava and kissed her on the top of her head. "Not where I come from, Ava. You got spunk little one."

Her fingers to her head, she massaged the tingly part where he kissed her and grumbled, "Ewh!"

With a spin the huge man turned and headed down the hallway to the exit. His back had a giant tattoo of wings. They were beautiful with deep periwinkle swirls mixed with silvery ovals that seemed to float and travel over his skin with his muscle movements. They reminded her of butterfly's wings.

"They're real, Ava. I can fly. I just don't usually."

"Let me see." A real god or a real good fibber she'd find out one way or another his claim to fame.

When his feet lifted off the floor and he went horizontal like a superhero, his tattooed wings stretched so wide their span width almost hit each side of the hall. His knees, however, began to shake and he plummeted to the floor.

"I am a tad out of shape," Zeus confessed. He did one push-up and stood.

"You're scared of heights!" Ava pointed at him. "Gods aren't spose to be scared of heights."

"Everyone has one thing they fear, Ava. Tell me yours?"

"Never seeing my mom and brother again."

"Then you need to go be with her. Now Ava. Go. Run."

His face, when he told Ava to run, it said something more. It said he knew things that she would never understand no matter how old she was. His stormy grey eyes transformed to an ice blue and frost covered his body better than the hayfields after a cold November rain. Seeing this, Ava bolted as fast as her feet carried her yelling down the hallway, "Mommy, I believe you about the lady falling from the sky." When she got outside her mother's room words failed her. "I'm sor—" never finished making it out. Her feet skidded to a halt seeing the same mob of people still around her mother's bedside. Buzzers hurt her ears, but her mom didn't seem to care. She lay there content. "Mommy?" After running up flights of stairs Ava's chest heaved for air. Her mom's chest lay stagnant.

Ava's dad rushed to her side and got down on one knee, with his hand out for her. She crossed her arms tight over her chest.

"Where were you? We've been searching all over for you. Don't ever scare me like that again." Christian tried to hug her. Still very upset with him, Ava pushed him away.

"Where were you, Daddy? I was scared too." Ava brushed past her father and budged through people to get to her mother's bedside. "Mommy!" She looked around the room, at the nurses who weren't looking at her. Avoiding her all together actually. It was the babysitter all over again. She glanced back at her dad. Tears rolled down his cheeks. He was the second person she'd been mean too and made cry. He deserved it. She didn't care.

The monitors. The nurses were busy turning them off and silencing the alarms. Her mom lay there with her eyes closed, peaceful. She looked like she'd been placed under a spell.

"Mommy, wake up." Ava shook her mother's arm. A growing bubble of fear blossomed in her stomach. "Stop," Ava screamed at the nurse, "stop unplugging stuff. She can't live without it." Ava bolted towards one of the monitors and plugged it back in and with fury thrumming through her veins she began punching all the buttons trying to make her mom's heart monitor work.

"Ava, stop!" Her father's tone was soft.

"No, Daddy. She needs help!"

"Something happened, Aves."

"No, don't you say it. Don't you dare. I'll hate you forever." Ava grabbed her mom's cool flaccid hand and tugged hard. "Mommy!" Her voice cracked. It seemed to be an ongoing thing lately. When her mother didn't respond Ava screamed, "Mommy, wake up. Please wake up and talk to me." Little gasps rushed in and out making her chest raise in short rigid bursts. She fought the truth. "Mommy, no!" She whispered, "Mommy please, I'm sorry. I didn't mean what I said. Don't leave me. I'm sorry." Ava hadn't realized she'd crawled up on the bed and lay down beside her mom. She tugged her mother's hand to her cheek and laid it there, trying to pat her cheek the way her mother used to, to comfort her whenever she was scared or upset. Underneath, the tips of her mother's fingers were purple, squishy, cold. "Mommy, talk to me. Please?" Little whimpers filled a silent room.

Christian wrapped his hands around Ava's tummy and pulled her up to a standing position. The festering bubble popped. Ava's disbelieving eyes understood more than a little girl should. "No, Daddy. No!" Tears covered her flushed, angry face. "Mommy, I love you, please? You said you'd never leave me. You lied." Ava's knees gave way and she landed beside her mom again. She cupped her mother's cheeks and squashed them together. "Please look at me." She collapsed on top of her mother, her fingers gently running through her mom's hair.

"Could we have some time, please?" Christian asked the staff in the room to leave. "Aves, I acted irresponsibly these past days, but I was in shock. We had so much to deal with and no time to understand it. Your mommy is in heaven now."

"*NO!*" Rebellious, Ava screamed like someone a hundred times older.

"Aves, she loved you. You were her little goddess. She called you that from the day we found out we were pregnant. She always said Ayden was a god too. Aves, we need to go home and call your grandparents. Don't get mad at me, but—"

145

Harper cut Christian off, "Hey, Squirt. Thought you could use a big sister for a few days so I'm going to stay with you and your dad till you know—"

The shot Ava gave her dad could rightfully have placed him in the same grave as her mom. "Know what? Daddy, no! I don't need a big sister. Especially her. Please? I just want mommy to come home. Please don't make her stay with me."

Christian pleaded, "Ava, I need help too."

Ava pleaded, "I can help you."

"Just for a few days."

Ava wiped her nose on her sleeve and turned her back on her father and the babysitter and bent over and kissed her mother's cheek. "Take care of Ayden, Mommy. Love you more forever." With her head down Ava slid off the hospital bed and walked out of the room.

Chapter Sixteen

Starting Over

Weeks passed, but to Ava the time seemed more like she'd been trapped in an hourglass full of shards of broken glass being constantly flipped over just after she'd gotten the last sliver of glass out of her only to start all over again. Mornings started before sunrise and the only thing evenings were good for were restless dreams. Her grandparents came and went. They begged Ava to stay with them for the rest of the summer, but Ava couldn't leave her dad like this. He wasn't himself. Right about the time her grandparents left the steady stream of other people coming with food slowed down too. Thankfully this also ended the uninvited hugs, kisses, cheeks being pinched, and all the whispers. Ava despised secrets while the adults seemed to bask in them. Every time Ava walked into a room people's heads would automatically snap up to see who came in and once they saw her silence would fill the room better than the radio on full blast. The moment she walked back out of the room tiny voices started up again.

Ava had enough. She'd resigned to the idea her life would be her dad and her. Oh, and the babysitter. Harper had all but moved into the spare room. Why she was there came as a complete mystery because as far as Ava could see, the girl did diddly squat. Didn't cook, but she did eat whatever Ava put in front of her. Her specialties included, cereal, scrambled eggs—shells included, burnt toast and her favorite, pizza. The babysitter didn't clean, but she made a bigger mess than Ayden ever did. Didn't do any chores at all. But she did follow her dad around better than his shadow. Pathetic.

As for Ayden, it was as if he never existed. In a drunken rage one night, her father went through the home with more accuracy than a forensic pathologist. He bagged everything Ayden owned: clothes, shoes, toiletries, toys, video games, pictures, even his bedroom furniture got tossed into the back of the pick-up truck and hauled away. Ava fought for every trace of her brother's life she could spare but, in the end, only ended up with his superhero turtle pillow along with the new glove he never got to play with. The pillow smelled of Ayden: grass, mud, hay, horses, and maple syrup.

The police had not one lead or clue. Ava grouped the police in the same pathetic category as Harper, useless.

Her father did nothing other than drink, sit on the couch and stare at the television. Sometimes it wasn't even on. There was a question in Ava's mind if her father had turned everything off in his brain as well. While he spent time doing nothing with Harper, Ava did all the chores, fed the animals, milked the cows, and attempted the laundry. Some of her dad's tidy whities were now a pretty pink. Ava liked the color. Her dad didn't even notice.

Wide-awake anyway, with rainstorms threatening to hang around for a few days, Ava got a jump on feeding the horses. Out of bed, she slipped on her galoshes and wiggled into a purple hoodie making her hair come alive with static electricity. Bent at the waist she wrangled the long locks into a ponytail and then she tucked her jammies into the boots so they wouldn't get mucked up. Headed down the steps, the second one from the bottom always squeaked when someone landed on it. In the darkness, mad at the world, and wanting her father's attention she didn't just step on the step, she jumped up and down on it. Loud creaks climbed to the second floor, but no one stirred. Not her dad. Not Harper. Not even the mouse. "No wonder everyone in Whoville lost all their presents." With a huge snort, scrunched lips, and her attitude much larger than she, she stomped through the kitchen, opened the screen door, walked out, and with as much oomph as she could muster, she slammed the door shut.

In Whizz's stall, with the shovel she used to transport the *star*, her head shaking no, she changed that thought to *the worthless star*, Ava scooped up the horse's leftovers and made her way past *the trunk* and went out the back door to the compost pile. She repeated the process through Halo's quarters. About to get Lolly's space spiffy, Ava heard tires snapping on the uneven rocks of the driveway. She ran to the sliding gate at the end of the barn and peeked out.

Two men in suits got out of two dusty SUV's. Both men headed for the front door. Maybe they found Ayden. Knowing the doorbell would wake her dad up and get him in a bad mood she tossed the shovel aside and charged for the front porch before the two men pressed the panic button.

Breathless and praying for good news, Ava yelled, "Did you find my brother?" With reckless abandonment Ava careered around the men and got to the door, blocking the entrance.

"Hi, Ava. I'm Detective Bradshaw. And you know Harper's dad, Detective Noyse. I need to see your dad. Is he here?"

Ava nodded. "Asleep. He's always asleep. Even when he's awake."

"I feel like that too sometimes," the detective responded.

"Did your mommy die too?"

"Ah, no honey." Visibly uncomfortable, the man cleared his throat. "I only meant, ah, can I talk to your dad?"

Impatient, Ava pointed to the chairs on the porch. "Have a seat. Did you find my brother?" She asked again, louder.

Both men shook their heads no.

"Yup. Useless." Barely on the opposite side of the door more whispers floated in behind her.

"Poor kid," she heard Harper's dad say. She liked Harper's dad even less than his daughter.

"Did you hear her father's not the biological one?"

"Heard many things about their relationship. Heard it was on the edge of ending. Now we know why. The test on the car brakes is in. Tampered with."

Swallowing a gulp of anger not only ruined her appetite for breakfast, but she was certain her entire day.

Up the stairs again she went making certain to pounce on the second step once more. Just because. With her hand on the knob Ava heard more chatter and muted voices coming from her parent's room. Hope filled her heart. Her mom had come back after all. Maybe Zeus saved her. With a flick of her wrist Ava shoved the door open needing a miracle. "Mommy?" She bolted in and in a fraction of a split second her hope turned to despair.

Her dad sat up and tugged the covers over his body and yelled, "Get out! Now!"

Too stunned to move Ava froze looking back and forth at her dad and then, "Harper?"

"It's not what you think, Squirt."

"Stop calling me that. Daddy why is she in here? This is mommy's room."

He didn't look at her when he said, "Get out," again. "Ava. We'll talk in a bit."

"Me get out? Daddy, make her get out. This is mommy's room." Hand on her hip, she raised her voice, "We don't need to talk, Daddy, but you might want to put some clothes on. The police are downstairs, and they are more than willing to talk to you. I am not. Harper, how old are you? Your daddy's on my porch." She spun for the door.

"Ava, no!" Both Christian and Harper yelled, "Don't let them in."

Stomping did not do justice to her exodus from the room. Down the stairs, one brash thump at a time she marched past the police. She spun at the last second, her hand secure on her hip. "Your daughter is playing naked Twister in my dad's bedroom." She turned again and didn't look back even when she heard the squeak of the front door bust open and slam into the frame. Yelling, screaming and objects being broken followed.

Inside the barn, Ava fished out her charm necklace and went for the key. Once she had the trunk open and her fallen star in her hand, she threw it as hard as she could into the cement wall of the silo. "I hate you." She ran over to the giant crystal, picked up the pristine object and threw it again. "You're such a liar." The crystal bounced off the wall and landed at her feet, not a nick or scratch to be seen. "Wishes are spose to come true when you see a falling star. You made nightmares. I hate you." With both her hands solid around the cluster Ava drove the rock into the ground over and over until her arms shook and tears blinded her vision.

*****

"What in Tartarus is going on?" My voice echoed, and my ears popped. Stuck in a continuum of rolls, spins, bumps, I toppled head over heels, unable to stop my body from careening into all the sides of my prison. Time is oblique. I've lost track of how long I've been trapped in this Rubik's cube, but forever sums up what I feel. The ride to say the very least has been turbulent. One minute ice slicked the walls and floors. The frigid temperature causing all the sensation in my extremities to become as nonexistent as I seemed to be. Freezer burn has a new meaning in my life. Hands out in front of me, my flesh has a slight bluish hue coated beneath icy crystals. Imprisoned inside a glacier until the next spin… then the container burned like lava. The frost on my body, my eyelashes, my freaking nose hairs disintegrated in a puff of smoke and left me with the perception I'd become the main course at a BBQ gone awry; very awry! I can say honestly, I am the embodiment of the term mummified. Slightly dehydrated with the worst case of dandruff in the history of the universe. In my mind I can visualize old dandruff commercials as the man brushes white flakes from his shoulders and all the girls are stepping away from him repulsed. This is what happens to a mostly good mind when it's shrunk, the body is compacted into a state of something smaller than a turd you produced and flushed a few hours earlier and bounced infinitely through space for an undisclosed timeframe… My crown, however, still produces giant, juicy grapes. My saving grace. I can remain toasted the remainder of my flight. Bully for me.

When the capsule's propulsion through time and space slowed, my heart raced in anticipation this roller coaster ride would end soon. The brief respite allowed my equilibrium to return. But for how long? Space had some fickle nuances about her. She sides more with Chaos than Gaia. One loved dynamic upheaval and the other strived for tranquility. Opposites to the very end.

With caution, wobbly, and sore beyond compare, I made it to a vertical stance. On my feet, sharp pains bore into my butt. Throbbed as if a chimera had sunk its fangs deep. Did Pandora slip the slimy little serpent in the box as a going away gift? At this point I wouldn't put it past her. Hands behind me, I pat down my sore aching glutes. Finding something that shouldn't be there panic roared its ugliness. Something was lodged in the narrow confines of my glutes. With a tug the object tore free. A brilliant flash of light illuminated the small dark cell and nearly blinded me. Something made a guttural squeal. Squinting to make out the object I rubbed my eyes with my free hand. Tears would have been a blessing, but alas the orbs were as dry as my skin. I strained to focus. The crown on the squirming entity seemed to radiate the power of the sun. Well, one age old question got answered, 'Where in the world did the pixy disappear to?' Voilà, Queen Titania. Flattened. Scowl, top lip peeled back bearing pointy teeth. Not smelling so sweet.

"You!"

Pissed.

Can't blame her. Good chance a toot or two escaped

during this voyage.

In utter amazement I watched as the tiny entity blossomed before me. She grew to my size and stared me in the eyes, seemingly as surprised by the current situation as I. Index finger to my lips, I opened the trap to say something, anything, to smooth over the awkwardness of our current togetherness, but seriously, what could you say to someone you just pulled out of your tush? "I got more moves than David Copperfield." I blew a hunk of what I hoped was lint from her hair.

A combination of angst tussled with curiosity while I watched the pixy maneuver into a series of stretches followed by fluffing her once elegant gown. Only God knew what the little diva had raging through her mind. And then the mystery came to a brash end. Words flew from her angry, taught lips with the precision of a true archer, with yours truly the target.

"You, grape gobbler, are no magician. You are a giant ass. I can say that because I have been where no man has ever been."

I raised my brows and shrugged my scrawny shoulders in jest. "Hold that thought."

After one long drawn snort she followed with, "Why does this not surprise me? Some secrets are better locked away."

"Locked away like us?" A slight sigh slipped out showing how much this current situation truly irked me. I hadn't had the luxury of pondering the situation until this rocket landed. It's one thing to be able to see your enemy face to face, to be able to plan a defense, but I couldn't wrap my thoughts around the reasoning behind Pandora's hateful actions. "Doesn't pay to lie, Queen Tia. Or covet secrets. This one we bestowed on Pandora has definitely come full circle to bite me in the…"

"That was me, fool. Soon you'll realize the difference. Believe me when I say if I ever see the porcelain princess again the bite I give her will leave her wishing she'd tangled with Stheno instead. The Gorgon would impose a much swifter fate than one I can foresee." The Queen's brows drew close and her scowl promised vengeance.

I offered a simple nod understanding her wicked desires. The fire in her gaze heated the pithos a few degrees and gave away how serious her threat was. "Anyway, are you all right?"

"Define all right, Dionysus. We've been traveling at the speed of light for what might be years. We're locked in a capsule with no way out and we have no food. And my accommodations have not been five star."

Her tiny bare foot stomped down. "What the heck happened?" Tia took her crown off and bent at the waist and ran her fingers through her tangled, matted down locks.

"That crown of yours has some pointy edges." I rubbed my butt.

From an upside-down position Tia gave me a look of disgust. "That wasn't my crown." The evil sneer showing all those pointed teeth she gave sent a shudder through my ragged remains.

She added, "A rain shower would be most welcome."

"You do have a certain bouquet about you."

The look. I'd recognized it from other women when their moods dictated the end of days. She didn't find me humorous. Pity. From the looks of things, she would be stuck with me quite a while.

Hoping to lighten her mood, and mine I added, "At least I have wine. We won't go hungry."

"This isn't a beautiful island and you're not Captain Sparrow."

She piqued my curiosity. "You've visited the land down under as well?"

"A few times," she conceded. "My sister, Tinker, lives in Hollywood and my sister, Bell, lives in Orlando. So do we know where we are?"

About to answer, a slight rumble sent us spiraling again.

"Hang on!" With reflexes that surprised even me, I snagged the pixy in one gentle grasp and held her close so the possibility of crushing her as we careened into the six sides of our cube were removed from the equation.

"There isn't enough wine to make me rethink dusting you again if we survive this."

"You're welcome."

The saying, the older you get the faster times go by, someone got astronomically wrong. I have no idea how old I am but being trapped in this time continuum seems to have stalled. Forever didn't begin to express how it feels to be entombed in a jewelry box soaring through interstellar molecules with a pissed off pixy. When the golden crown she wore pierced my palm I added queen. PO'd pixy queen.

"Ouch! You're crushing me!" The pixy yelped. "Let me go and stop touching me."

"Ugh!" I moaned. "I am trying to save you from certain death. I mean no harm. I'd squash you better than my grapes."

"Have you had a good look at your physique?" Tia laughed at me when the capsule slowed momentarily. All right so maybe my ego remained larger than life whilst the rest of me shriveled up.

"Remove your calloused fingers from my bosom."

And there went my happy thoughts. I'd roll my eyes if I didn't fear they'd get stuck. Back to frustration filling every atom of available space. "Just once could you say thank you?"

"When we land you and I are finished with this touchy-feely game. Got it? We are dividing this plot in half." Tia poked her nail into my chest to prove her point.

"Stop touching me then. First you bit me, now you poke me. If I didn't know better, I'd be led to believe you like me. You're like a little kid that keeps pestering another to get their attention. Lest not forget you came to my wedding, little royal pain in my tush."

A raucous grunt filled the void. To be honest, I'm not certain which end of her it came from, but I will remain a true gentleman, keep my manners in check because there isn't a man alive stupid enough to call out a lady on a gas leak.

"I wouldn't touch you even if you were the last man in this galaxy." She poked me again.

"You tooted and you're trying to distract me." I poked her back. Manners-schmanners!

"Ignoramus. Release me. Now!"

"Fine! You're on your own. I shan't apologize if I topple you as we break the speed of sound. One would think being trapped with a woman for nothing short of eternity you'd draw a truce, not a line down the center of the box declaring war. Women!"

This minikin made me nuts. Made my blood boil. Was tenacious as the day is long. Not my fault she wound up lodged where the sun didn't shine. In a way my tush saved her. And I ended up being the one with a bug up mine. We went to our respective corners like the dueling boxers we'd become and sat in silence, she steaming, me brooding. It seems to be what I do best.

From the corner of my eye, I glanced her way and received *the look* again. She has mastered it. The look makes someone rethink all past actions and conversations, analyze exactly how much trouble they were in. Your neck? Your eyeballs? Over your head? Drowning in poop? With a quick look at my feet this point seemed past moot. This prison lacked the amenities of a modern home.

A bony index finger with what could only be described as lethal talons pointed to me. Her thinned wine-stained lips drew to one side. The veins in her neck appeared so taut they could snap any moment. As if her mental status hadn't already?

"What did you do to my king?"

"Nothing. I'm being set up."

"I do not believe you. You also claimed innocence as far as Theseus's ill-health."

"Again, not by my hand. What have I to gain by doing something to Theseus or your better half?"

"I am his better half."

My one brow shot up along with a minor curl to my lip. Body language can be so much more trouble than words. "She's about to dust me again," I said to no one who gave a hoot. Number one rule; never piss off a pixy. "Seriously? That's the other thing I don't understand. You never run out of…"

Chapter Seventeen

Be Careful What You Wish For

Making the sign of the cross over her chest, Ava closed her eyes in despair. She then gave the fallen star one final kick, her big toe taking the brunt force. Hopping around yelping, "Pickles," did nothing to alleviate the pain shimmying up her leg. The force hurled the rock into the silo's wall again. Something other than her toe cracked, or at least she hoped it was something else. Curiosity trumped pain and silence beget the air.

With quick lopsided strides she hobbled to the edge of the wall praying the cement didn't chip. Her dad had recently replaced the silo, and it cost them what he claimed to be his first-born child. Maybe he meant his second child since Ayden vanished.

Something pink peeped through a long crack in the star. The bigger question popped into her thoughts. Touch it? What if it had alien poison coating? That's what Ayden would have thought. She bent over and picked up the object and walked to the tool bench where her dad kept all his farrier instruments to shoe the horses. A hoof pick used for cleaning out the gunk in the horseshoes would work nicely to pry the crystal shell off whatever was trapped inside. She knew she had to be gentle. She didn't want to break anything. Archeologist always looked so dainty in sand pits when they unearthed treasures. After getting nowhere painstakingly picking and prying the star, Ava decided to treat the rock like a hardboiled egg and give it one more whack since plan A of being overly cautious backfired. Plan B in effect, she placed the crystal in a clear spot and grabbed a sledgehammer. The hammer had to weigh as much as she did. With a bit of oomph behind her, she hit the star head on.

Ava gave a little fist pump. The outer shell collapsed faster than a sandcastle being swept away during high tide. When she went to pick up her treasure, she scratched her head. How did a pink jewelry box get stuck inside all the crud? To open it or not to open it? What would Ayden do? A smile found her lips. She knew darned well he'd have opened the box long before now.

Background noise outside the barn intensified. She'd almost forgotten the ugliness ensuing. Wishing she could forget all together wouldn't happen either. It was one thing to walk in on your parents when they were busy playing hide-n-seek, but seeing Harper naked? Bile rose in her throat. She hoped Harper's dad grounded her. At her own home.

"Squirt?"

Ava grabbed the box and headed for the barn door. With a quick turn, she told Halo, "Be right back." About to walk out a subtle fluttering of wings distracted her. A soft swoosh brushed over the top of her head making her crouch fast and nearly topple over backwards. Her owl landed between her and the exit. "Hi, Atty." Down on one knee, Ava held her hand to the bird. The bird didn't move.

"Ava?" That was her dad. Not talking to him today.

"Where are you Squirt? Got a present for you."

"Harper?" Ava questioned. To the bird and horses, she babbled, "I think Harper got in trouble you guys. And quite frankly I hope she gets a whooping." The owl slowly turned its head sideways, its huge gold eyes wide. Halo whinnied. Ava pushed herself into standing position and headed for the door. The owl spread her wings wide blocking Ava. "Atty, I'll be right back. Move over, silly bird."

Instead of moving out of her way the bird ran straight for her and knocked her down just as a blast of buckshot went sailing over Ava's head. Chunks of wood tore away the backside of the barn leaving gaping holes. Petrified, Ava did what she did best... she screamed. Back on her knees and hands with her box in her grasp she crawled through hay, mud, and well she hoped it was mud, back into Halo's stall where she hid behind the door. Around her, restless horses paced and snorted. "Atty," she whispered, "come here. Get out of the way." She prayed the bird understood. When she looked up the bird was back on the rafters hidden.

"Don't be scared, Squirt. I won't hurt you."

Then why are you shooting at me? The door to the barn creaked and another shot rang out. "Ava?" Her dad screamed again, "Ava, where are you?"

"Harper, put the gun down." Harper's dad, Detective Noyse ordered.

Yup, whooping time neared.

Another blast ripped through the barn drilling a hole in a rain barrel that had been placed directly under a tiny hole in the ceiling. A steady stream turned into what her mother would have called a 'freaking mess'.

"We're running out of time ya rotten little tattletale."

Fear teemed from Ava's skin like she'd just gone

through the ice into the pond on a frigid winter's day. She'd seen enough scary movies to stay put and remain as quiet as possible. She wasn't some little kid about to get dowsed with ketchup and act scared. Right here and now she'd earned the Oscar.

Looking for a way out or a weapon to defend herself she hid the pink box inside the bib in her overalls. With the horses still making all kinds of noise Ava managed to crawl under the gate and get a good grip on the sledgehammer without being heard and drag it back into the stall. She held the handle really close to the base of the instrument, and with all her might heaved it up onto a barrel of oats in the corner. *That dumb God, Thor made it look so easy*, she thought as her breath came out in a huff. If anyone came into Halo's stall, she planned to bean them, if she didn't drop the ten-ton hunk of steel on her feet in the process.

"Ava?" Detective Bradshaw's voice vibrated off the walls.

"Father, get your hands off me." Definitely Harper again. Good. Maybe the gunshots would stop.

"Arrest the SOB, Bradshaw. She's underage." Harper's dad, Detective Noyse demanded. He sounded plenty mad.

Yes! A smile found Ava's lips for a moment.

Harper's enraged voice filled the barn. "Father! Did you forget I turned twenty last month? I'm not a baby anymore. And Christian is only twenty-five."

Then another chunk of Ava's world chipped away hearing, "You can't arrest me. What's going to happen to Ava? She's all I have left."

He probably should have thought about this before now. Ava didn't run out to see what the commotion was.

Couldn't stand up and yell for help coz then she'd give her position away. What if dear old Annie Oakley's ill-begotten clone still had control of the gun?

With everything Ava had going on right now, her dad outside getting new silver bracelets and anklets, Harper taking potluck shots at her, Ava took another moment to pray. Prayed for all she was worth that this star fell to the ground for a reason. For a good reason because right now she needed a miracle. She couldn't live through another crummy thing happening to her. With a balancing act between the sledgehammer, she tugged the box from her overalls. A glimmering little sword locked the container. She jerked the small crystal sword back through the clasp of the box and held it out in front of her. The tiny sword-shaped crystal looked exactly like a diamond. The tiny grommet went into her pocket on the off chance she found a real jewel.

Please be a miracle. Once the box opened, a bright light flashed the barn. An odor from inside the container seeped out and Ava gagged. This smelled so much worse than Whizz's stall ever did. Through teary eyes and a runny nose, she saw something move in the box.

She wiped her eyes. And again. There was just no way. Her eyes and brain were playing tricks on her. "Holy cow! Aliens?"

Something blew past her faster than the bullets Harper shot at her.

The tiny creature buzzed her with the tenacity of an angry bee. Both hands occupied she couldn't even shoo it away. Couldn't do anything other than jerk her head from side to side and front to back like a busted bobble head doll. "*Elf?*"

"Bite your tongue, kid." The tiny creature scorned,

"It's pixy. Pixy Queen Tia to be precise, little girl."

Still shuffling side to side and vying for a good look at it, Ava whispered, "Me little? I think you have that backwards."

Queen Tia hovered within an inch of Ava's nose and made a "Shoosh!" sound.

It worked. Her mind turned into an electrical junction box. An influx of information trying to be processed and distributed overloaded her circuits. She had a storm of people she needed to tell this to. People she could show this imp to. People who would believe her. Her heart sank. The only people she wanted to share this with were either dead, missing, or being fitted for an orange jumpsuit. The pixy remained eyelevel to her, her wings going so fast Ava couldn't detect movement.

"Ava?"

"Hide," Ava managed to whisper to the pixy.

The pixy didn't have to be told twice. The little creature looked like a bottle rocket landing on the wood beam right next to the owl. Atty immediately pecked at her probably thinking lunch arrived. If hearing the pixy say, "Athena, we will finish this once home," didn't freak Ava out something from the jewelry box touched Ava's fingers. The box got tossed in the air while another scream got muffled. Where was the spider that touched Ava's hand? She glanced around seeing nothing and then picked up the box again, scratching her hand to alleviate the tingle. When she looked in the box again Ava felt her eyes nearly pop out of her head.

"Can you see me?" The doll-sized man pleaded.

Pretty certain words would fail her, under her breath she whispered, "Shut up." This could not be happening. She'd lost her mind for sure.

The man's voice bellowed while his arms raised, and little fists balled in angry knots. "This is the biggest punk of the millennium!"

Ava got her face right next to the box and whispered, "I'm thinking the same thing."

The man continued to babble, "I'm officially screwed. My life is now in the hands of a toddler."

"I'm six and stop whining. You sound like the babysitter."

"How dare you. I do not whine."

The look. Ava stared the mini man down. "You nailed it, Major Nelson. Did your genie shrink you down because you sound like a sissy?"

"You are not funny, tiny human. Release me this instant."

"Hush!" Ava gave the little man her jut out jaw, tight-lipped look. "Tiny human? What is it with you two? The doctors told me some strange stuff could happen to me between the new medicine and my mom's death and brother's disappearance, but this? This takes the cake. Kids are known for really bizarre imaginations, but I can't even make sense of me anymore. I've. Gone. Bonkers." Her fist clenched to the point her knuckles were white just like his, one by one tears slipped past the strong façade she'd held onto the past weeks.

"Release me? Please? Just give me a quick kiss, tell me those three infamous little words everyone longs to hear, you love me, and set me free. It's all I ask. We'll call it a day. I'll give you anything you want."

"Ewh, you are so gross," Ava groused.

"Not exactly the catch phrase I need, kid."

Laughter bellowed. Ava went from crying to hysterics in the matter of a heartbeat. The stress of her caustic life finally eroded her thin grasp on reality.

Eyeballs peered over the top of the stall. "I *see* you. Today seems to be my lucky day." Harper crowed.

"Well, I'm glad one of us is having a lucky day. You," Ava directed to the man in the box, "I said shut up. I can't believe I got a kid's toy. A freaking whiney Jack in The Box? Sorry Mom for swearing. Really? I'm six, not three." The lid got slammed shut and the box dropped in the pile of hay. Ava reclaimed a stranglehold on the hammer and swung with all her might yelling, "Assassin. Assassin," as her assailant opened the gate. In all honesty Ava didn't know what was worse: Harper with a gun all but shoved up her nose or the little doll asking her to kiss him… or her mind now the equivalent of a bag of marshmallow atop sweet potatoes left forgotten only to be reduced to ashes in the oven: Her mom's signature dish.

The hefty hammer took a direct dive down and landed on the soon to be ex-babysitter's foot. Harper dropped the shotgun shrieking. For the briefest of moments Ava thought about apologizing to the little genie in the box about his whining. Harper had the pitch perfected. In Ava's next breath the pixy torpedoed the foul-mouthed girl with the precision of William Tells's arrow and then hiked up her blue glittery gown and lambasted glittery stuff all over Harper. The babysitter went cross-eyed and fell. Detective Bradshaw blasted in the barn with his gun drawn, one foot in front of the other for balance, one hand under his other supporting his firearm.

The detective fired off a stream of questions. "Ava? Are you okay? What happened? Have you been shot? Did she hurt you?" He pointed to Harper, as he holstered his firearm. "Do I want to know?"

Beyond stunned, Ava looked at the Harper then slowly cranked her attention to the officer. "I don't think you'd believe me if I told you." Not a second after she answered the detective the pixy dove from the rafter and circled in behind Ava and whispered, "It's our secret."

The detective asked, "Did you hit her with the sledgehammer?"

"I think someone hit me with one." Ava's knees buckled and down she went.

Chapter Eighteen

Finding Friendship

Subdued noises came and went in the same fashion when Ayden fidgeted with the volume on the television, up one minute, down the next. Voices changed, some shouted, while other demanded lawyers. That one sounded like her dad. With a giant grunt of, "Oh God, this can't be happening," Ava opened her weary eyes.

Someone was kind enough to supply her with her pillow and her blanky though.

With her hands wound around the edges she pulled the soft, snuggly cotton up tight around her neck, and begrudgingly attempted to lift her head to see where she landed this time. For the moment, she rested on a scratched-up, mostly deflated leather couch in a back office clustered with magazines of guns, a book titled, *Idiots Guide to the Dumbest Criminals*, stacks of yellowed papers smelling of dust, and a rubbish can overflowing with styrofoam containers, pop cans and candy bar wrappers. A box of half-eaten donuts sat open on a table beside the couch. Flies skulked around the box to get crumbs. A few were stuck in a frosted donut. A wall of glass complete with fingerprints and nose art overlooked the main station. Officers busied themselves, some behind desks gnawing on half chewed pencils, some yelling into phones, others streaming from one spot to the next. One guy sat handcuffed to the chair, his ankles chained to the floor. He caught her staring at him and stuck his tongue out at her then made a lizard movement with it. Ava returned the gesture. Seriously, kids could pull off goofy faces way better than old people and get away with the cuteness. This guy looked dumb. An officer passing by slapped the side of his head ordering, "Leave the kid alone."

Looking around for her dad, she spotted him still cuffed. The gun-toting babysitter? Nowhere to be seen. Maybe they took her to a mental hospital. And the little crop-duster pixy flew off too. Ava sat up, crossed her legs under her and re-snuggled into her blanky. When something super sparkly caught her eye, her head jerked in the direction of it and there like a nightlight at the end of the couch sat her jewelry box. The last thing she recalled was tossing it into a pile of hay. Did she open it again? Would her gross talking doll still be in there asking her to kiss him? Yick, hence, the reason she cut the heads from dolls. Useless. When she had a free minute, she'd find the battery in this one and yank the plug.

So, if anyone bothered to ask her what happened this time, did she go for the truth? Tell them, a little pixy farted sprinkles on Harper and made her pass out, or her owl, Atty, saved her from a bullet, or she had her very own Jack in the box? It was easier to swallow the gross, chalky tasting medicine she needed when she got sick, than this, whatever it was in front of her. And then there was Zeus. A god. With wings that only she seemed to be able to see. Everyone saw the man, not the otherworldly features he possessed, which in the eyes of the law made him look flat out crazy. And if Zeus were bonkers where did this leave Ava? She clamped her eyes closed praying when she opened them the box would be gone, she'd be back home in bed being tucked in by both her parents, and her brother would be hiding under her bed kicking her mattress trying to annoy her. More commotion in the entrance to the building made her give up the slim hope of normalcy and focus on the present conundrum.

Being carted in, still donning the same hospital jammies, ripped out backside included, when she saw him a few weeks ago, the crazy god winked at her. Her insanity level placed her on a thin tight rope, wobbling, safety net M.I.A. Was he following her? He searched the entire space until his eyes fixed on her again. He nodded since his hands were locked behind his back. Zeus's voice bellowed, "My evening star, hello little goddess. You called?"

Ava quick ducked back under the covers.

"You called! I heard you loud and clear." Zeus yelled.

Ava did a super-fast quick peek. It appeared the entire precinct heard as well with all heads aimed in her direction. "Stop that," she mouthed just before ducking under the blanket again just as fast.

"I see you."

"I'm not playing peek-a-boo with you."

"Shut up you crazy old fool." A cop beat Ava to the punch.

"I still haven't found your brother. I'll keep a look out."

With the mention of her brother Ava bounced off the couch, her blanky in tow. She grabbed the jewelry box and got within a few feet of Zeus, bent over, and stared him down. The arresting officer did the same thing to

Ava. The triad looked at one another before she finally spoke up.

A little on the snarky side Ava demanded, "Can we have a minute?"

The officer started to escort her back to the room she woke up in. "What can I do for you?"

Ava put the brakes on trying to stop the man from dragging her away from Zeus. "Not you. Him. I wanna talk to him." Ava pointed to the harmless old man with the white beard wearing torn pajama bottoms and bare feet. The wings went without mentioning. How could no one else see them?

"Not a good idea. He is going to spend some time in the mental health unit. We found him on top of a building getting ready to jump. Said he could fly."

"But he—" Ava shut up. No need in getting an adjoining suite with the crazy god.

"Maybe he had a parachute."

"Maybe he's just nuts," the cop argued. "Caught him just as he was taking that last dreaded step off the side of the building."

"Whatever." Eyes narrowed, Ava's attention hit the crazy god when he started talking again.

Raspy, Zeus muttered, "You are rather observant, little twinkler. Pretty pink box! Take great care of it. You hold my lifeline in the palm of your hands."

Ava's bottom lip rolled over into a pout. "Can I talk to my daddy?"

The policeman sounded sincere when he said, "Ava, you're getting a head start on picking all the wrong men in your life."

Shoulder jut out, hand on her hip, with her little flippant tone she asked, "What does that mean?"

"What it means, Ava," Detective Bradshaw interrupted the other cop, "Is that I've called your grandparents. They're on their way to get you. Your dad is in some trouble. He needs to fix a few things before he can go home. If he goes home."

"What did he do?"

"Naked twister with a minor is against the law, Ava."

"She said she was old. Twenty. When can I talk to him?"

"In a bit. He's in with his lawyer."

"Where's the babysitter?"

"She's been arraigned and left."

Head cocked she shouted, "But she tried to kill me. Oh, and did you know Harper is the last person to ever see Jimmy Fields and Brady Wells? Brady and Jimmy were my friends." Ava had nothing to lose at this point by throwing the babysitter under the bus. It just so happened to be the truth, but no one ever questioned Harper. Maybe now that Ayden disappeared someone would ask questions. "She babysat them the nights they vanished, and their moms died. That's what my mom said."

"Honey, you've had a lot of stress over the past few weeks. I think you need some rest. Go back in my office and watch some cartoons until your grandparents arrive."

"I don't watch cartoons." She stamped her foot down making everything on the detective's desk rattle. "I want to go home. Now!" Ava glanced over at Zeus to see what he was doing. The wrinkled old man wiggled his bushy brows at her.

"We'll go for a ride soon, Ava. I'll take you to the moon and back."

"My key doesn't work in the cell you're headed for this time, Zeus." She gave him an *oh-well* shrug of her shoulder.

"But the little sword you have with you does."

With that, Ava felt something in her chest flutter. How did he know she had the little diamond sword in her pocket? She'd forgotten all about it. She whipped her blanky around her shoulders with more accuracy than a superhero did his cape and plunked her behind on the chair across from Detective Bradshaw. With a slight groan she put her feet on his desk, her galoshes caked in dried manure with sprigs of hay jutting out. When she saw the detective eyeball her filthy feet, she winked at him.

"Fine, sit there. Just don't touch anything and don't talk to anyone in silver."

In a flippant tone she muttered, "They're not werewolves." From under those strawberry blonde lashes, she looked up and flashed him her little grin.

He glanced at her, his olive-green eyes intense. "You're cute, kid. I'll give you that. Now behave. Pretty jewelry box ya got there. What's with it?"

The detective went to grab it from her, but Ava jerked the box tight to her chest ready to fight the man.

He pulled back in haste, hands up like he was being arrested. "A little protective, aren't we?"

Her tone harsh, if her words possessed hands, they would have slapped him away. "It was a birthday present from my brother." She fibbed. He didn't need to know where the present came from. And speaking of which, she needed to go find the star her brother found. The detective gave her a funny look. "You wouldn't want me touching your gun, right?" He couldn't touch it, her box.

No one could. What if someone saw her little genie?

Then again, what if no one saw him?

Would that mean she was crazy like Zeus? She was beginning to feel it. Only one way to find out. She pulled the box in front of her and with caution peeled back the top. Her breath caught somewhere between her lungs and nose.

There he sat, legs crossed with his arms overlapped over his chest, blazing blue eyes glaring at her.

"Shall we start over?" The little Jack in the box asked.

Ava slammed the lid, worried the detective heard him. She gave a cautious glance the detective's way. The detective didn't look any different. Same olive-shaped green eyes with short black curly hair waiting patiently for her to decide if she trusted him or not.

Time to find out if she needed a shrink. Hesitantly she passed the box to the detective.

"Thank you for trusting me enough to see your special gift. I'm sorry about your brother, Ava." With gentle hands he picked the box up high and held it in front of him then turned it upside down and jiggled it.

"Be careful," rushed out of her before she had a chance to corral the thought. She didn't want the little Jack getting tossed around and hurt.

"Got something breakable inside?" He grinned.

He was being so nice to her. Why? Good cop, bad cop routine? Every station had one. Harper's dad had, *Bad To The Bone* tattooed on his arm with the picture of a K-9 Shepard chomping on a prisoner's leg wearing an old black and white striped jumpsuit. She liked the tattoo, not the man.

"Can I open it?" Detective Bradshaw asked.

"Yup." Her heart pounded so loud she could hear the blood rushing in her ears.

"It's very pretty and looks expensive. Shame it's empty. You need some jewelry to fill it."

With defeat controlling her voice she said, "The only jewelry I own is on my neck and it never comes off."

She had her answer. Insane. Ayden always called her crazy. Now she knew why. Hmmm. Now what? She didn't feel any different. Is this what insane people thought? They felt normal? Even though they saw imaginary miniature men stuffed into a jewelry box she got from a falling star, or pixies pooping magic dust to make babysitter's wielding guns to pass out, or owls that save people? Or gods trying to fly? Overload on the circuits again.

"I'm hungry. Can I have my box back? How long till my grampa gets here?"

"I got ya a pizza, kid. Should be here soon. Your grandparents will be here in about an hour."

Ava studied the detective. No wrinkles. Chunky cheeks. Huge greenish-grey eyes. Mustard on his shirt. Messy hair. Long eyelashes. Skinny. Light-up sneakers. She pointed and laughed. "For real? My brother has a pair just like them." Her laugh faded. "Had. He had a pair."

"Kid, I promise I will do everything I can to help find Ayden. My mom bought me the shoes. Not much I could say."

"You don't seem old enough to graduate high school, let alone be here or wear a gun. How old are you?"

"My parents claim I'm a medical prodigy. Finished

high school at fourteen, college at seventeen, police academy the next year and have been here for two years. Do the math, kid."

"You're twenty. You and Harper should play together instead her and my dad."

"You're rather proficient at math for being little."

"My mom said I am special too."

"I can see why she said it." The detective smiled. He leaned over his desk towards Ava and whispered, "Can you keep a secret?"

With a quick glance around the room, first to Zeus, then her box, Ava nodded. Not a problem. "Yup!"

"Harper's dad keeps getting her out of all kinds of messes. Guess being up the Chief's butt gives you privileges."

"Yup!" It was her favorite word and Harper was her least favorite subject to gossip over, look at, deal with, think of, period. Ava tossed her legs off the desk and stood up. When she reached for her box, the cop handed it to her. Once she had it in her grasp she turned and headed back for the couch. "I'm going to watch cartoons," she told him, but as she passed Zeus, she reached inside her pocket and plucked out the diamond sword and snuck it in Zeus's hand. "I want it back, crazy man."

"You're going to need it, lil goddess. I can't help you figure your problems out," he added in a soft tone, "only you can."

"Me problems?" She shook her head. "You, yes. My dad, most definitely. I'm getting pizza and watching cartoons in a police station. My mom died. My brother vanished. My dad likes girls almost my age and I see men that fly and little imaginary people, oh and pixies that poop pass-out dust on people. And they think you're crazy. I got a question for you, Zeus."

"Shoot, Ava."

Ava's index finger pressed her lips making a, shoosh, sign. "Don't say shoot so loud in here. Are you nuts?"

Zeus managed a look even she understood. "Misinterpreted, lil goddess, as always it seems. What's your question?"

"How come the cops arrested you when you tried to jump? I saw you fly. Or try too."

Zeus nodded to everyone in the precinct, "Perception is the key to life, lil goddess. Only you can see my magic."

"Ayden had every right to call me crazy!" Ava laughed all the way back to the couch. Wedged in a sinkhole in the old sofa, where countless others probably did their time, Ava waited to see what life tossed at her next. With the jewelry box in her lap, she flipped opened the lid. What else could happen? She's already given in to the fact she'd lost her marbles. If she found them, she'd store them in the box with her imaginary friend.

"Hi." She gave a tiny wave to the man in the box.

"Are you going to continue slamming the lid on me?"

"I did that so no one would hurt you."

The little guy sat up straighter.

"So then you have feelings for me?"

"Ewh! Stop saying stuff like that. You wanna get arrested too, like my daddy, and get put in jail?"

"Think someone already beat you to that punch line, tiny one." His hand flowed along the inside of his cell showing her what he meant.

Ava stuck her face really close to the container and whispered, "Are you a bad man? Is that why you're in this box? How come the cop didn't see you, but I can?"

"You wouldn't believe me if I told you and you'd accuse me of being gross again."

Ava's imaginary friend gave up a half worn out grin.

"You didn't happen to see a little pixy queen fly by, did you? Seem to have lost my traveling companion."

This time Ava perked right up. "No way! She is real?"

"As real as me."

A large gust of enthusiasm rushed from Ava's nose. "You're not helping me."

"I could say the same of you."

Walking by, Detective Bradshaw stuck his head in the office. "Who ya talking to kid?"

"Not you!"

"Okay," the cop drawled out slowly with a smirk and continued doing whatever twenty-year-old cops did.

"Who's that guy," The little gladiator-wanna-be asked.

"Some kid playing cops and robbers. What's your name?"

"Dionysus."

"Dinosaur?"

"No." He shook his head. "Dionysus."

"You're probably as old as one anyway."

"Older. Watched them evolve and expire. Seen a lot of things follow the same path. Don't call me dinosaur."

Index finger shot up, she exclaimed, "Then Jack."

Dionysus smiled. "How did you come up with that?"

"Easy, you're my Jack in the box."

"Hopefully I won't be forever."

"Looks like the pizza arrived. You hungry, Jack?"

"You have no idea."

"You still yapping with imaginary friends, Ava?" Detective Bradshaw asked as he set the pizza box on the dinged-up end table. "Soda or water?"

"I'm set. I've got wine," Dionysus popped a handful of grapes into his mouth. Ava snapped the lid shut and giggled when she heard him through the container, "That's not fair."

Very slowly, Ava inched the lid open and peeked in.

"He can't hear me or see me. Only you can."

"Perfect!" She watched Dionysus go so far as to get up and do a little jig around the box.

"I think you've had too many grapes. They make wine, right?"

"Kid there isn't enough wine to make me comfortable in this hole."

"And I think you've spent too much time in here alone," The young detective Bradshaw answered.

"I wasn't talking to you." Ava's hand flew over her mouth. Oops!

"Who then?" Detective Bradshaw stuck his head in the room and looked around.

"Me, myself, I… my imaginary bestie." Ava gave the detective her best winning grin.

"Needs practice, kid." The detective placed a bottle of flavored water on the table beside the pizza. "Plain or pepperoni?"

"Loaded. Thanks. Has my dad eaten?"

"Your dad? Forget him. I haven't eaten in like a billion light years." From down under Dionysus's arms waved to grab her attention. He had it, but she couldn't keep talking to him, with well, *him* about to pull up a spot on the couch beside her.

"Detective, do you have any napkins?" Ava piped in just as the guy's tush touched down. "I get messy when I eat, or at least that's what mom said."

"Be right back. You don't look like a messy kid. You act more grown-up than most six-year-olds."

"That's what everyone says about me until there's food in front of me." Ava jammed the end of a slice of pizza into her mouth and made a satisfied, Mmmm, sound. To Dionysus she broke a piece of pizza off and chucked it in the box. "You need to keep quiet. You're going to get me in trouble."

"Kid, I think trouble follows you better than your shadow."

"Me too." Ava's head bobbed up and down with her statement. It certainly felt like it. "Okay, he's back so please—"

"One more hunk of that. It is out of this world."

"No, that would be you."

Ava broke off a second piece of pizza and blew on it before she handed him the food and then carefully closed the lid. "It's hot. Be careful."

When ruckus in the way back of the station started Ava eyeballed her new friend, the detective, running full speed towards Zeus, her dad and Harper?

Not again. With reluctance she cast the pizza aside and sat upright in the couch, her restless little feet tapping on the floor. The detective had his gun drawn. Ava straightened her spine and sat on her hands to get a better view. For the moment anyway, Zeus had no cuffs holding him in place. That didn't surprise her, but when she heard the words, "You married them? Under what authority? Is it even legal?" shrieking from Harper's dad, the pit in Ava's stomach hardened into something that resembled a knot in her hair secured by a wad of bubble gum her brother so kindly assaulted her with one night. She tucked Jack and her box back inside her overall's then proceeded to stomp her way to her father's side. For the moment she became the center of attention.

With a hard tap on his shoulder, Ava asked, "Daddy, what just happened?"

Detective Noyse piped in with his face looking like a sun-dried tomato, "He married my daughter, Ava. Right here. Right under my bleedin' nose. Without my consent. By this hooligan no less." The detective shot an accusatory finger towards Zeus.

"Zeus?" Ava's voice cracked.

"Who?" Detective Bradshaw asked.

With her palm out she offered up, "Him," pointing at the smug looking sentinel.

Detective Bradshaw added, "He's no god, Ava. But he is a priest, or so says his ID card. Unfortunately, the marriage will stand. It is legally binding. Harper had the paperwork ready."

"I want to know who stood up for them?" Harper's dad yelled so loud Ava didn't think anyone would own up to it for fear of this guy, especially since the man had his gun drawn, pointed to the ceiling.

"I did." Some random prisoner conceded, also handcuffed to an iron bar cemented into the floor. "Least I could do in the name of true love. Isn't it romantic?"

"Moron." Ava yelled at the stranger and then with a swift left hook, she slapped her father so hard he fell over, the chair going with him.

"Holy cow, kid." Bradshaw yelled as he and Zeus grabbed Christian and picked him up.

"You are going to have one heck of a shiner," Bradshaw added. "Someone get some ice, please."

"I'll shoot anyone holding an ice cube." Detective Noyse waggled his gun making his point crystal clear.

"Christian!" Harper's irritating voice screeched.

Christian spewed, "I had to, Aves. I'm so sorry. It's not as it seems."

"Really, Daddy? You married the worst babysitter in the whole-wide world. Mommy's been gone a few weeks and you married her?" The look Ava produced said it all, flat out disgust and disapproval.

"One word Squirt, boarding school." Harper gave a nonchalant scratch of her nose with her middle finger as she smirked.

Without sparing Harper a glance Ava rebutted, "That's two words, idiot," and went at her father again. "What about me, Daddy? Don't you care about me anymore?" Ava gave a determined swipe at the tears trying to flee. "Am I not enough to spend time with? Am I not your family anymore? Your little goddess? You're the only person I have left and you don't want me. You're tossing me out like you did all of Ayden's stuff, like I'm something cluttering your life and stinking up the farm more than all the pooh in the barn. And you have the nerve to tell me it's not as it seems? Is anything?" Ava wrapped her arms around her stomach, caught her breath and continued, "Zeus? Why? After everything I told you?"

"How old is she?" Detective Bradshaw asked the universe.

"It's written in the stars, little twinkler, and I know you believe in them." Zeus handed Ava her little sword back just as the cuffs were being snapped back around his wrists.

"I hope all your stars fall to the earth and splatter like mine did."

"They already have, lil one. It's why I am here and why you hold the box."

Top lip all scrunched Ava bit out, "Don't believe you, Zeuster. That's short for Zeus imposter. I don't believe in anything anymore. Come on Jack. We're going home. To Gramma's." Her little feet plodded, making items on desktops rattle.

"The kid doesn't weigh enough to move dust. How does she do that? She's got to be the original lead-foot." Detective Bradshaw's comment again went unanswered.

Not much later Ava's grandparents walked into the station with open arms. Without another care, Ava fled to them and buried herself in their safety. She ignored her dad, the new stepmom and her crazy friend who she no longer considered her friend or anything other than crazy.

Chapter Nineteen

Pinky Swear

Tucked in the back seat of the truck with a video playing, Ava tapped the headrest her grandpa leaned on. "Grampa, can we stop at the farm? I gotta feed my horses. I think Daddy will be spending his honeymoon in jail." Ava didn't tell them everything. She wanted to find the star Ayden hid. He'd said something about chicken poop. Even missing he would always get the last laugh.

Standing in the barn staring down at the chicken coop Ava knew this wasn't going to be pretty. She had to get the hay wrapped up yet too. Fall would be here soon. When had life turned her into an adult? Six going on twenty-six?

"I won't be long," Ava yelled over her shoulder.

Ava's grandmother responded, "Okay. I'll pack some belongings. Anything in particular?"

"Nope. Bet I'm out before you are." Ava made it a game. A race. Her grandmother was all over it. The lady might have been in her forties, but Ava new fast and this lady made the Tasmanian devil look like he was dawdling.

The chicken poop! Even the giant rubber gloves she'd donned didn't help. Ayden—guardian angel or mini demon in disguise? Ava clearly believed the latter of the two. Clothes pin on her nose she went for it. "It's gotta be here. It's gotta." The texture reminded her of making meatballs, mushy. Slimy. With one last sweep through the mountain of manure, Ave's hand brushed something jagged. Her breath stilled. Her fingers groped a sharp bulky item. Crouched on her knees Ava tugged— hard. With a slight sucking noise and no warning, the article broke free of the muck and sent Ava rolling backwards feet over head to land on her belly with a giant hunk of what looked like a block of greasy coal.

She wiggled free from one glove to rub her nose and tuck a strand or two of hair behind her ears. Her grandmother's voice bellowed, "Come on, lovie. I want to get you settled…"

Seeing Ava emerge from the barn filthy her grandma stopped short. "Please tell me you're not covered in what it resembles or smells like?"

With a half shoulder shrug Ava fibbed again. "I slipped in the dark. Nice huh?"

Ava's grandma laughed. "You need a wash-off before we go any further."

Off to the well they headed. Bent over the side of the round brick structure Ava's grandma hoisted up a bucket filled with fresh rainwater. "Hold your hands out in front of you. You are messier than Ayden ever dreamed of getting. Good job."

Ava giggled. "Gram, you look just like mommy. I miss her." She watched her grandma turn her head for a second and gulp down a choking sound.

Barely able to respond her grandma whispered, "Me too, lovie. Me too. I should probably tell you how I met your mother. We didn't have a conventional introduction. She never told you this?"

Ava shook her head no.

"Well, I used to keep books for the church and one Sunday night after mass I was locking up and I heard crying. I wound up finding this beautiful rosy-cheeked little girl wrapped in a white blanket made of silk and lace. Her wild red curls never matched her personality. Long story short, I ended up adopting her. You look exactly like she did when your mom was your age. You, however, are more precocious that she ever was."

"What's that mean?"

"You can look it up tomorrow and tell me."

"You don't even know what it means and you said it?"

"Oh, Ava." Her grandma hugged her tightly and kissed the top of her head. "You seem to have a knack for getting into, well... loads of..."

Ava peeked sideways at her. "Don't say a bad word."

Her grandma laughed. "You know me well," she told her just before she dumped the rest of the water over Ava's head.

Shocked by her grandma's actions, Ava gasped. "Gotcha good, lovie," her grandma laughed as she headed back to the house.

Squeaky clean, the horses and chickens fed, and the star Ayden had found hidden safely, after Ava dropped it in the well, she climbed back into the truck, ready to go to her grandparents. A new chapter in her life. She didn't want to go. Everything she knew and loved was here, on this farm. Her animals. Her brother. What if Ayden came home and she wasn't here to greet him? He'd be alone. Scared. A lot like how she felt right now. Her memories. It's all she had left. Sadly, those she could pack up and take anywhere with her.

In the front cab, her grandparent's soft chatter comforted her. When an oldies channel on the radio played a song about not forgetting someone, or recognizing the person, Ava sang the song to Jack.

"I like this melody, Ava. Your voice soothes an old soul. Can you regale me with it again?"

"Re-what you? Are you back to being gross?"

"Sing to me. That's what it means."

Through an eruption of giggles Ava sang a few versus of the song again.

"You all right back there, kiddo?" Ava's grandpa asked.

"Yup. Just singing one of mommy's songs."

"I think you and I found our theme song, Ava. Don't you forget about me, lil goddess. Will you call my name? My real name? Promise not to forget about me." Dionysus held his little finger up to Ava. "Pinky swear with me."

The laughter continued. Ava thought this guy was too funny. "How do you know about pinky swears?"

"I invented them a long time ago." He gave her the brightest grin she'd ever seen and waggled his finger higher.

"No way!"

"Way!"

"You're a silly man, Jack." She tapped her finger to his regardless. "I promise to never forget you, Jack. Always infinitely."

"That's a long time, Ava. I hope you mean it."

"I do."

"I heard that once and it didn't quite work out as planned."

Jaclyn Tracey

"What happened?"

"Sorry. I think all the carbs you fed me has gone to my brain. I am babbling."

"Carbs? How about all the grapes you've been popping in your mouth? Where you keep getting them from anyway?" She peered closer in the box. Nothing in there but a line straight down the center.

"The grapes come from my crown. It is magic."

Hands tossed in the air, Ava finished, "And why wouldn't it be? I think I just turned into a kid in a fantasy movie. Everything I ever thought was make-believe is real and everything I thought was real is either missing, buried or locked up."

"Life's funny like that, lil goddess. Some things are never as they seem."

"My dad said that tonight too."

"He's a smart man to understand then."

"He's not my real dad."

"Does he love you? Does he take care of you? Does he care more for your life than his?"

"I always thought so. But everything changed the night the meteor shower happened."

"Trust me, little one, it changed from my angle too. Don't give up on your dad. Everyone has a bad period. His is now."

"Mine too." Ava nodded in agreement.

"I know. It will get better."

"Promise?" Her eyes grew wide with hope.

"Promise, Ava. What are you sipping?" Dionysus pointed to the flimsy pouch Ava held.

"Grape juice. Real grape juice. Not make-believe. Wanna sip?"

"If it is as good as pizza, then yes."

Ava trapped some of the liquid in her straw and brought it to Dionysus's lips.

With a giant gulp he swallowed. His lips puckered and his eyes clamped shut. "Bleck! These are the worst grapes I've ever had."

"What a baby face. Let me try your grapes."

"You're not old enough, lil goddess. A few more years maybe."

"Why?"

"My gift to the world is wine. Some people build things, some sing, some bring people together for peace. I consider my gift one along those lines. People gather and sip juice made from my grapes and laugh and enjoy life with each other."

"I wanna be happy and enjoy life again." One single tear slid down Ava's cheek. Out of nowhere Ava started whispering to Dionysus everything that had happened to her over the past few weeks. It felt good to have someone listen to her without treating her like a fragile snowflake about to disintegrate on the tip of someone's tongue. Truth be known, she felt more like an avalanche waiting for an acorn to fall from a tree and trigger her downfall.

"Lil goddess, your bravery remains steadfast. Your life will come around again. Everything happens for a reason."

"Then why are you in the box? What's your reason?"

"To meet you of course." Dionysus gave her his award-winning grin a second time.

"Nice try." Ava pointed telling him, "You have something stuck in your teeth." Ava laughed watching the mini man try to suck the obstacle out with his tongue. She ended up laughing so hard she cried. "Who put you in the box? A wizard? A wicked witch with ugly warts on her nose?"

"Pretty close. Definitely a wicked witch."

"Why?"

"Lil goddess, you ask an awful lot of questions."

"And you avoid the answers. Mommy used to say politicians did that."

"I like you, lil one. You're smart."

"How old are you? Are you truly a Geek god?"

"Greek, not geek. Age is irrelevant—"

Ava butted in, "Unless you're trying to eat grapes. And I meant geek. You dress funny." She went to pick a grape off his crown, but he gently nudged her hand away.

"You have a wild side." Dionysus teased.

Ava's hand flew to cover her mouth. "I am not wild, but I'm getting sleepy. Will you be here when I wake up?"

"You're stuck with me, angel. For better or worse."

"Good. I like you too. Do you want me to leave the lid open?"

"It's okay. Tuck me in and I'll see you on tomorrow's sun."

"Move your big butt over you hunk of dried fruit." The pixie's voice shocked both Ava and Dionysus. The miniature woman blew threw a cracked opening in the rear window of the truck, stopping right in front of Ava's nose. Her squeaky voice explained, "It may not be the nicest home, but it's all I've got for now."

"Holy cow, you're really real." Ava wound up in hysterics.

"Aren't you a cute little girl? Now go to sleep." Tia spun one hundred eight degrees, hiked up her gown, flashed Ava and dusted her right in the face. Boom! Out she went.

Chapter Twenty

One Sparkle Too Many

"Tia!" The amount of anger I infused into her name shocked both of us. "Why would you do this to a child? You don't have a maternal bone in your body."

The queen shook her head no. "Ah, so the god has feelings for his little goddess after all."

"She's a child who has lost everything."

"She'll be fine. She's in a restraint of some sort. I didn't want to draw attention to us back here. What's happened to her is our fault. We need to fix this mess."

I shook my head a resolute no. "Pandora's fault."

I glanced at the child now so peaceful in slumber. Her strawberry blonde locks were sifting in the air from the open window and her scent reminded me of a field of lavender. In the coming days all I could hope for was to bring no more turmoil to her life, but with Pandora and my brethren beneath the clouds? Anything seemed possible.

***

Scurrying about I gathered the leftover Gummy Bears, sunflower seeds and raisins Ava left back to my half of the box before the pixie queen joined me. The raisins? I looked upon the fruit horrified that others would purposefully let a good grape end up in such an appalling state. Ingrates! But maybe Tia would like them.

I have resigned to the fact this is my new home for the time being and I shall make the most of it. If and when I see Pandora again, I need to think of a fate worse than this befitting of her. Looking at the age of the kid I have been given to spend my days with, sadly, I have time to contemplate such retribution. With a graceful sweep of my hand, I welcomed Tia in. She appeared thankful since she'd been clinging to the seatbelt strap while she sat on the back ledge of the seat. "Majesty, I hope our new accommodations meet your expectations?"

She touched down with a curtsy. "Lose the formality, Dionysus. Or is it Jack these days? What a name to call someone. It's so metrosexual."

"So *what*?" I asked, thinking I need to catch up on some of the jargon used below the clouds these days.

Tia produced a half sneer. "It's not a compliment. In our day you were either a man or a woman, not a bit of both."

"Then what's Eros?"

"Ahead of his time." We laughed then both stopped abruptly when they realized they were getting along and agreed on something.

"Okay, that was awkward. Anyway, Dionysus, it appears only one of us has been condemned to this jewelry box. Dear God, I believe he's the only one who can help you. I can't. I'm sorry. I wouldn't wish this fate on anyone other than the person who cursed you."

"Funny, I was thinking the exact same thing moments passed. The little goddess you dusted is my key to freedom. When Pandora cursed me, her exact words were, 'Someone has to tell me they love me and seal it with true love's kiss.' How hard can that be?" I puckered up laughing.

Tia swatted me. "Fool. I wouldn't kiss you if you were the last man on earth." She shook her silvery-white hair out of her vision and wound the length into a bun, securing it with her crown. "Only you could find humor in this situation, Dionysus. It's as if you don't exist. She's the only one who can see you."

"Other than you. Why is that?"

"We are different species, you and I."

"You have my deepest apologies for dragging you down under. When we get home, I promise to help find your king."

Those eyes of hers zoned in on me, the silver in them looking more like roiling mercury. "So, you truly had no part in his disappearance?"

She still distrusts me. Not certain whether I should be upset or thankful she still has the sense to look out for herself. "I had nothing to do with your husband's absence."

"The Fates control us. I accept your word. So what have you learned since we touched down?"

"That I like pizza and that this lil goddess of mine will test my limits. How could Pandora have known I would meet my soulmate here? She blurted the spell out in hopes I would rot alone in here, never to be seen again."

"Horse before carriage, my lord. Do not underestimate Pandora. She conjured a spell out of thin air, and it worked better than any of Hecate's spells. This young girl needs us. Watch over her. And I'll watch over the both of you as best I can. I found your father."

"Yes, me too. The last I saw of him he was

handcuffed to a chair. Not exactly what he's used to. The cuffs definitely. The rest, not so much." I laughed.

"You're still laughing?"

"If I can't laugh then she wins, Tia and I'll die before I let the woman best me. So, from here on out we make the best of a dire situation. We can get you some better living quarters on the morrow's sun."

"I appreciate your concern, but I won't leave you. Your father, did he know you were in the precinct?"

"I believe he knows, yet is as helpless as I. There's some strange pulls of power going on down here. Do you feel it? Everything feels tainted. The girl's father for one. Not to mention the disappearance of her brother. She said a woman fell from the skies and then her brother vanished literally in thin air. Would a good samaritan take him? These humans still have affection for doing good. Maybe all is not lost yet down here."

"Look at the wreckage of these lands, Dion, war, famine, homelessness, disease, terrorism. This race too will succumb the same way all others have. Greed. Hatred. Indifference. Ignorance. Racism. You're a dreamer if you think otherwise."

"Hope is the one constant in life, Majesty. It is the one good thing we placed in Pandora's box. There was validity in this."

"Hope is but a sliver of light. Darkness always falls."

"Darkness overcame me until I found you wedged, well you know where." Head cocked, I'm pretty certain my impish smile lit up my face.

"Where the sun does not shine. I do believe that was the darkest, scariest place I've ever ventured." Tia blew me a kiss. She removed her crown and placed it in the corner of the box. "I have a question for you. Before we were removed from our reality is it true you were able to shape shift to a cat of your choice?"

I nodded yes since I was chomping down a Gummy Bear.

"Food for thought, shifting… it might get you out of these confines. Freedom could be as easy as puking in someone else's shoes instead of your own."

The little pixie went into a fit of hysterics pointing at my feet thinking she'd made the joke of the century. Okay so maybe one of us thought of it first. Wish it were me.

"My current size dictates I'd most likely end up an adorable kitten getting my nose rubbed in it. I'll try if the time presents itself. Nothing gained, nothing lost, right? Nice dream, freedom. My father is currently locked in silver and powerless and here I sit. I pray my brothers' fate is far different."

"Speaking of dreams, a queen needs her beauty sleep. You want a little dust? I know you haven't been sleeping because I haven't heard any snoring." Her one silvery-blonde brow arched. A half-satisfied smirk followed.

"You know me so well and yet I still live. Thank you." With a wholehearted smile and a half bow at my waist, I finished, "I'm good. Got my grapes. And I do not snore."

"Pfft!"

She gave me a cynical sideways glance. I don't think she believed me. I don't snore unless I've been drinking. Hmmm…

Ankles crossed I slid straight down to the floor, then straightened my legs out as the tush touched down, clasped my hands behind the noggin, laid back, and let heavy eyelids land with a sigh. Maybe tonight would be the first true night's sleep since being imprisoned. "Sweet dreams, ladies."

Tia said one last thing to me before closing her unique eyes. "She's not who you think she is, Dionysus. Tread lightly." I lay there for what felt like a million moons, running that through my thick skull. Well, if Ava isn't who I think she is then who in God's name is the little angel? She has to be or my stars alignment is one hundred percent out of whack. With a casual glance at my surroundings, I suppose this goes without saying.

Did the pixy make a wise observation with regard to my ability to shift? What good would it do if I wound up a kitten? Those tiny fur-balls are harmless, adorable cuddlers. If I sprouted into my full lion, chances are pretty good some dickless dentist would have my hide stuffed and mounted before I had the chance to nibble off a few heads.

Two grapes later, Hypnos pulled his magic act. Thank you, God of slumber.

***

"What in Hades? Tia, hang on!"

"What's happen—not again," Tia's words were sliced while she and I were shaken into a constant jackhammer marathon.

I foresee a headache. Make that a whopper; hold the special sauce.

Someone is attempting to congeal us like we are oil and vinegar. Pickle me purple if it isn't working. I fished around for Tia's hand and once in my grasp reeled her to my side. This time she didn't fight me. When the propulsion finally stopped a mixture of squashed grapes and glitter coated the walls, floor, ceiling and us.

Tia's silent sobs filled the void. "Are you hurt?" I asked as I brushed her long silky tendrils from her face. I didn't see any blood or scrapes, only a woman whose remarkable eyes were filled with not only tears but also frustration.

She shook her head no. "Just tired of being subjected to the whims of the world. Thank you for trying to protect me. I apologize for being a jerk this week."

I finagled my way to a stance and offered my hand to her. Then without warning I dove back on her when I heard Ava yelling, "Get your hands off my present, Harper."

This teenager proves to be more pestilent than any of the four horsemen. With the top open Tia squirmed from under me and jetted out going straight for the nosey troll, sending the giant backwards, off balance.

"What the heck is that?" Harper yelled while she took a few swings with her left hand, her right hand glued to my box, refusing to relinquish her grasp.

The pixy spun furious circles around Harper with her intent to dust the bejesus out of the wench.

Really not certain what to do, Ava and I watched as the pixy darted towards Harper from all different angles, but continually missed her target. Harper grabbed a bottle of cologne from the dresser and began squirting it at Tia. A musky scent overwhelmed my nose. A dash might be nice, but not the entire bottle. Harper's actions backfired because the teen immediately started sneezing and dropped the bottle.

Tia took advantage of this and whizzed up over her head, hovered, lifted her dress then made a frustrated face going aneurism red. She took a deep breath in and again she tried, grunting. Finally, a long-drawn-out breath followed by an, "Ah," filled the room when one lonely glittery flake appeared. It, the sparkly little turd, sifted through the air until Harper caught it on her tongue like a snowflake.

You can't fix stupid! I swear to God, yes, I tapped my chest like Pops. I've never seen anyone so daft. Who catches poop on their tongue?

Harper took up space on the end of the bed. Ava didn't waste a second and with a well-placed foot she shoved her off. Harper landed belly-up on the floor wearing the look of a drunken sailor. I know this look intimately.

Tia looked between Ava and I then with a shrug of her shoulders said, "Perfect timing, huh? I'm out of ammo. I need honey. She won't be out long." She buzzed upward struggling to make it to a shelf above the bed. Safely on the shelf she spun towards us, her appearance ghastly. "What did you do to these women?" She demanded, "Are they mummified? And here I thought you were a normal child, Ava. What other atrocities have you committed to my kind?"

I watched Ava produce a look that went light years farther than confusion.

"Huh?" Ava muttered. "They're dumb dolls. I didn't murder or shrink anyone. Grampa!"

Noting the troubled teen rubbing her eyes and yawning, Tia nestled between a few of the mummies on a shelf, each positioned differently, each wearing a different design of clothing.

Once Harper got her bearings there would be seconds left before the mutant would be up and running. I could almost read her mind, which as an afterthought,

I didn't find comforting. She made her way to a kneeling position and looked around for Tia.

"Little nuisance, I'll flatten you."

Tia struck a pose, blended in with the buxom mannequins better than rum did with pirates. "Hmmm," Harper murmured. "Must have been a dumb fly. What's the big deal with the piece of pink junk, Squirt? This thing is nothing more than an empty jumble box with fake crystals. Looks like something you made your mom in kindergarten."

"So what if I did? Give me it!" Ava kicked Harper's leg then stomped on her toes with all of her sixty pounds.

"Jeepers, Squirt. Is that anyway to treat your stepmom?" Harper fell onto the bed and pulled her leg up to rub her foot. Ava took full advantage of her change in focus and ripped the box from Harper's hands.

More yelling filled the small confines of space. "You are not my step anything."

Here I stood. Helpless. Useless. Invisible. What did I do to deserve this? I deem myself a failure. My little goddess needs me yet my hands are tied. I am unable to do a blasted thing to save the pint-sized damsel. A newborn baby holds more ability to manipulate a crowd than I do in this current state of utter ineptness. Stripped of my masculinity, pride and stature, my charmingly good looks, my honor barely remains intact. For how long though, is the question? Once my fingers are able to grasp Pandora's long smooth neck I will ring her head in circles until her eyes bulge, her lips go periwinkle, and the noggin drops to my purple-tainted tootsies. Having a plan calmed the inner beast until Ava's distress brought me back to my current state of uselessness.

Angry sobs roared from Ava's soul. "That's my

mom's ring. Take it off. Give it back to me now, you wicked witch."

"Mine now, Squirt. I'm not an Oz character. Trust me, there is no comparison. Your daddy gave me this. Maybe I'll take the jewelry box to keep it in." Harper reached out to reclaim the container.

"No!" Ava swung with all her might and clocked Harper in the side of her head with the box and me. The teenager toppled sideways into a dresser. For as much I wanted Ava to knock some sense into the teen, I'd have liked it a heck of a lot better if it hadn't been my current home when she did. A thin line of blood welled from Harper's temple before the fluid resembled melted wax dripping down her cheek.

Harper reached to the wound. Her fingers came away dotted red. "Oh my god, I'm dying!"

"I wish. How did you even get out of jail? Grandpa!" Ava's voice bellowed a second time.

My hands shot to my ears. The kid has a set of pipes on her. Could she be related to Euryale? The Gorgon's howls could turn stone to sand and crumble.

Huffing, Ava's grandpa entered the room holding his chest. "Ava? What is it?" Through grit teeth he reached out, and with his calloused fingers latched on to Harper's shirt. Ava and I watched Harper's body jerk into motion, her feet tear out from under her, kicking wildly at air. Her grandpa did it with such ease it made plucking dandelions from their roots look harder. He proceeded to drag the writhing teen down the stairs, one loud clunk at a time.

My poor little goddess. Tears overcame her innocent green eyes. The little trooper swiped her hand under each eye and brushed her hand off on her pants trying to be stoic. With her hands shaking Ava placed the jeweled box and me on the bed and left the lid open.

"I'm so sorry, Jack. You okay?"

"Go tend to your family, Ava."

Tia swooped down beside me. "I'll meet you there in a minute's time, kid."

"Tia, there is green tea with honey in my cup. You can have it." Ava nodded and headed out of the room leaving me behind.

"Did she say honey?"

I'm not even certain I blinked before the pixy had her body draped over the edge of the glass with her lips to the fluid.

Chapter Twenty-One

Cat's Out of The Box

"Get out. Both of you. Christian, I'll put the nail in your casket myself to keep Ava."

Even from my cell I could hear the scenes unfolding downstairs as if I had front row seats. Granted they would have been better, but I'll make do with my surroundings.

Harper must have continued to fight Ava's grandpa. "Sit!" he'd ordered. I heard the screeches of chair legs scrape against the floor and guessed he shoved the teen down with a bit of resistance on her part. Rage controlled his husky voice. "Don't open your mouth. Not a word or to blow a bubble."

Smart for the first time since I've met the bimbo or maybe too petrified to make any snarky comebacks, she remained silent. If I were a betting man, I'd give this vow of silence less than thirty seconds.

"Harper," Christian pressed, "please, I don't want any more of a scene."

"I'm your wife, Christian. You can't order me around. You're not my dad."

"No, but he's old enough to be." Ava's grandmother snipped.

Good jab, Grannie. I'd make one heck of a mediator. Humor returned; a smile cracked my lips. I heard the door creak. I'm guessing Ava's grandmother must have shown Harper the way out since I'm not privy to the action. Might I reiterate how badly my situation rots?

I hear Ava's grandmother yelling, "Get out of our home before I call the cops. Ava doesn't want to see you, Christian. And get the ring off your finger before I chop it off, Harper."

"My dad is a detective. You can't touch me."

"Harper?" Christian's voice matched the confused look my handsome face made. His voice topped Ava's grandmother's in pissed off octaves. I hear what sounds like a fist slam on a table followed by inaudible gabbles. Something shimmies and smashes to the floor. Didn't sound like a head. They tend to have more of a wet, sloppy thud with an abhorrent scream for a precursor. I shan't go into further detail.

"I never gave you the ring. How'd you get that?"

"But you were going to give me it. Right?" The teen whined.

Thank you, lord. My worst fears have been dismissed. I sound nothing at all like a whiney teen. The little home wrecker nailed it. I feel so much better. For me anyway. My little angel downstairs is going through hell. Wish I could find a way to sooth her soul. The child has somehow stolen my heart. She is a true fighter.

"Let me go, Gramps. Christian, make him let me go." Harper sounded horrified.

"Take the ring off, Harper," Christian demanded.

"No. I earned it," the little thief bawled.

Ava's grandmother shouted, "This should have gone to Ava, not you, you little sociopath. Take it off now before I do."

The grandmother is really starting to grow on me.

She is fearless. I see where Ava gets it.

"Put the hatchet down. Oh my god, you insane old hag, no!"

An insurmountable yelp from Harper coincided as a swooshing noise sliced through the air and sunk into something. The precursor I'd just mentioned before the inevitable thud... I know this sound intimately. Giving end thankfully, not receiving.

Barreling down the stairs two and even three at a time Ava launched herself towards Harper before her feet even hit the bottom two stairs. She landed on Harper's back with a choke hold on her neck, her legs secured to Harper's waist, riding her better than a cowboy on a pissed off bull. Pretty certain the kid missed the severed hand with blood squirting all over painting the kitchen, while Harper flailed in pain and shock. This time I had a bird's eye view. There's a saying life can change in a heartbeat. Sometimes it doesn't take that long.

"Don't you dare hurt my grandma." Hand under Harper's jaw, Ava yanked backwards going for the neck snap. Possibly there is validity between violence in movies and video games? Just an observation from an outsider.

Tia kept Ava's pace landing on her shoulder, but with so much struggling the pixy couldn't get a clear shot without hurting either Ava or her grandmother.

"Ava, get away from her," Ava's grandfather pleaded.

"Kid, you need to let go of her. Look around. Holy god, Dionysus!" The pixy's high voice pierced my eardrums. Purple glitter exploded beneath her.

Someone is happy to see me.

Seriously, I am rather impossible to miss.

Was it the pixy's plea, my appearance or both when everyone realized they had otherworldly guests with them? Ava's grandparents, Harper and Christian looked at Tia and then me, no one saying a word. The reaction I get once changed always amuses me. Momentarily the chaos stopped. Before them, sauntered in a svelte lynx with a silky greyish-black mane completely poofed out. Mufasa couldn't look this bad if he tried. Black whiskers stretched from the sides of my furry little nose to the outer edges of this silky mane. Their lethality outdid a porcupine's needles. The fur beneath my chin purred famous pirate. It split down the center to hang on both sides of my jowls. The only thing missing were little crystals and gold fobs entwined in the fur. I could get them later. My eyes couldn't have been any bluer. I'd caught a quick glimpse in a mirror on my way down. My smoky-grey coat held flecks of white underneath. Jet-black tufts of fur topped my satiny smooth ears.

What I really thought rocked the look and found sexy as hell is how my bottom two incisors jut out over my top lip showing off the under bite of the century. I'm kidding. There is nothing sexy about an under bite, but for some reason humans find it *cute*. I recall Pandora saying the word as if it were a fate far worse than death. She is jealous.

I haven't even got to the best part yet. My paws? Another thing earthlings always point out. 'Look at them paws.' Why not skip the innuendos and jam your face between my back legs. You'll get the answer. Without further ado, Big Foot's tracks pale in comparison. Squashed grapes my patootie.

My butt does its kitty wiggle since smiling isn't an

option for cats. Our snarls work so much better. My personal attributes impressed me. Lest not forget the claws. Razor sharp and ready to tear into whoever touched my little goddess or my queen. I have grown a serious affection for these two. The crown of grapes goes without saying. All cats believe they should be worshipped. Why should this god be any different?

I am back in business.

Wings blazing, Tia pushed off Ava's shoulder and gave a little fist pump of triumph as this puddy padded in. With a slight flitter Tia dropped down into Harper's sights, so close the troubled teen's eyes crossed making her head jerk backwards. With a subtle flick of her pinky, Tia plinked Harper on the tip of her nose, which made an absurd crack. Blood rushed from her nostrils. Rather pleased with the outcome Tia made a graceful spin and went back to Ava's shoulder and whispered, "Get off the wench's back before you get messy."

Gagging and more pleas for Harper's life filled the kitchen. It took Ava a second to then notice the hand on the table not connected to anyone. Ava back-flipped landing on her feet, Tia hanging on for the ride. Ava didn't scream as I thought the girl would, but she did walk over and slide the ring off the bloodied purple, twitching digit before she stuffed the ring in her pocket. I really admire this kid, although I see some sort of therapy in her future. She would do well with the company I keep. Harper didn't move. Her stump and nose continued to gush. Unfortunately for her no one seemed to notice her predicament since Tia and I entered.

"Well, I guess the cat's finally out of the bag, or should I say box?"

With an effortless pounce I landed on the counter

and plunked my behind down. Grandma gasped. I do believe she's not used to having felines in her kitchen.

"Did the cat just speak?"

Or, maybe she's not used to cats communicating. We talk all the time. There is this little thing called listening.

Knuckled-white fists in the air, Grandma roared, "You'll be the main course in a Chinese restaurant if you don't get your fur-ball butt off my counter."

I looked around. There was no way she meant me. I haven't even had time to set foot in a litter box. Of all the things to worry about right now she chooses a potential germ-fest? I mean for real, look around at this mess: She lobbed Harper's hand off. Right now, this room belonged in Hell's kitchen, the real one, and Grammy's worried about my furry little tush? Someone's priorities are messed up.

"I'm dying. I'm really dying. I'm going to bleed to death, pass out. Christian. Please?" Trying to get her feet under her, to flee this insane comedy of errors I am guessing, Harper didn't get farther than the floor.

Christian's pasty appearance I wouldn't call stellar either. He has his head between his legs hyperventilating.

"Anyone? Did the kitty just speak?" Ava's grandma, reiterated, louder. "The wild kitty? The one scooching across my damn counter?" She tossed a cookbook at me.

"I had an itch."

"Sweetheart," Ava's grandpa muttered, "I think someone switched my meds."

Still busy hand-talking grandma replied, "No one said anything about a crowned talking lynx or an elf."

"How presumptuous! I'm so not an elf, Grandma. I am a pixy. And if you missed the headpiece that would be queen pixy, thank you very much." Tia's little nose shot straight up in the air scathing at the indignance afforded her.

"Sorry?" A subtle shift of Ava's grandma's eyes to her husband followed by a slight brow hike showed her astonishment at the situation.

"Accepted." Tia nodded.

With the dynamics shifting faster than pit crews change tires, I took time to bask in the human ability to think, act, accept or deny, acknowledge or ignore, or go total berserker with the surroundings. We have a father and daughter who have lost everything including their relationship. Their wife, mother, now deceased. Their son, brother, MIA. We have the father who married the now handless tart on the floor who isn't much older than his daughter. We tossed in a pixy, and a magnificent talking cat, and not one person has noticed Harper face down on the ground bleeding out. But who am I to point out the obvious? Christian on the other hand is now staring at me as he gulps in too much oxygen. Kinda feeling slightly better about my failed marriage. A guttural instinct made me hiss with this thought.

Ava's dad sounded breathy speaking, like he might pass out any second. "There's a wild, talking cat in here wearing a freaking crown. A crown, Ava! It's speaking! And then there's a miniature lady with dragonfly wings on your shoulder. I don't feel so good."

With a grunt, Harper lifted her head and turned to face us. "You don't feel so good?" As if we didn't all hear her the first time, she yelled, "You don't feel so good?"

With a graceful swan dive from Ava's shoulders, Tia did a flyby over Harper and tooted. "This just makes things so simple. Aren't sparkles the best?" Harper's nose crinkled, her eyelashes fluttered, she sneezed once and her head hit the floor.

Thank you, universe, for shutting Harper down. Have I mentioned I love this little queen? She is freaking awesome. She smells seriously good too. Cotton candy and raspberries. She makes me hungry. One day maybe I'll tell her. When I'm having bouts of insomnia because the second I say anything that could be misconstrued the queen will dust me into the next galaxy.

Somehow Christian made a move towards his new bride. His skin is layered in mist and his mouth is watering. St. Bernards don't drool this much. My lips peeled back, I growled halting any further advances. Call me old fashioned but I want the brazen hussy out of the picture. She makes my fur poofy. She is a siren in kid's clothing.

"They're butterfly wings, Daddy. There's a difference ya know."

Tia shot me a worn-out look. "Isn't this how our last day in the grove ended? Dear god, what is it with you people. You act as if you've never seen a pixy before. I know you've all seen my sister, Tink? She claims she rules a planet called Hollywood? My other sister, Bell, lives in Disney? Anyone?" Tia spun a furious three hundred sixty degrees eyeballing each of them.

"They're cartoon characters." Christian offered. Uncertainty in his tone dictated his self-confidence didn't show up today.

Tia nodded laughing. "They're characters all right."

Christian opened his mouth to say something but must have thought better of it. Instead, his jaw kinda hung open with a dazed appearance covering his stupefied face.

Just to keep the guy on his toes I stretched, one of the more familiar moves where my butt aims for heaven, my back arches to make me look like a slide and when you reach the end you meet the claws. Ava's grandpa took a stance in front of his wife to protect her.

"Gramps, the kitty won't hurt you."

Christian added, "That's not a kitty, Aves. It's a wild talking animal thingy."

Claws clinking impatience on the tiled counter, I answered, "Please... I have evolved enough to communicate with you. I am not a thingy." I attempted my famous grin forgetting for the moment it would be lost in this form. Darn. The incisors aren't user-friendly. I probably look more like Dracula's familiar.

It's a good look.

I instructed, "Sit down before you fall down, Grandma. You look a little tipsy." The old lady lobs a hand off a girl and doesn't blink twice. She sees a talking kitty and you'd think the floor dropped from under her.

"Yes, I think I will." The ground came fast.

Tia swooped down to her level. "You okay?"

The older woman glanced up at the pixy with her wings fluttering to give a mini light show and she gave a nod clearly certain she had no idea what she nodded too.

Christian went for Ava, arms stretched as far as he could to grab her. "Please, Aves come home with us."

With an effortless bounce I had my front paws on Christian's shoulders, claws through the shirt, but not the skin. Yet. If compliance didn't follow through, my claws would. With one long, drawn out growl in his face I had Christian backed up against the kitchen wall. He slid down, me riding him to the floor.

I wouldn't hurt the man, but scaring the guy? Call me a bully, but I love seeing fear in morons that throw away everything dear to them. Ava approached us and reached down to rub behind my ears.

His hands spread to his sides, Christian pleaded, "Ava, don't touch the animal. It's probably rabid. Wild animals don't just strut into a house wearing a headpiece and act like a talking tabby. He's not Morris."

"Who?" Ava grunted.

Her grandpa answered, "He was a little before your time."

"I was beginning to think the cat had your tongue Grandpa." Ava giggled. "You've been so quiet."

I hissed in Christian's face one last time just because my mood dictated it. With a graceful twist I jumped off Christian headed for Ava where I weaved my furry body in and around her legs purring.

"And pixies don't usually fly in either, Daddy, but she's here, and oh, your wife is on the floor making a mess."

"Ava, I love you. Come home with us. I miss you."

"Nope! Remember what you said in the hospital? 'I'm not your real dad,' seconds before you left me." Ava's little lead foot met the floor with a resolute boom. "Left me! Alone."

I saw that one coming a mile away.

Ava's grandpa quickly changed the subject and piped in, "How did you get out of jail, Christian?"

"Harper's father didn't press charges since we were married."

"What a wuss." Ava's grandpa fired another question, "Okay, how did she get out of jail? She attempted to shoot Ava."

Christian mumbled, "She's out on bail."

Sarcasm laced, Ava's grandma added, "How inconceivably convenient," while a second cookbook slammed Christian in the chest. He didn't flinch. I have to wonder if this guy is comfortably numb, or a total nincompoop. I'm betting the latter. I really adore this grandma though. She's loaded with more chutzpah than I have testosterone thrumming through me. Almost impossible to fathom.

Christian gave Ava an anesthetized glance. When Ava wouldn't look at him, he struggled to get to his feet. His attempt to get past me backfired. He hit a brick wall.

"Daddy, you need to get your wife to the hospital. Don't forget her hand. I'll bag it in ice." She didn't hesitate, go squeamish, puke or make a face like her father did. Yep, he just tossed cookies all over the floor. Ava waltzed over to a drawer by the stove, opened it, grabbed a large plastic bag, slammed the drawer shut with her little bony hip, and made her way to the fridge. Next, she pulled out ice trays. With a few twists the cubes all popped from the plastic holder. A few fell on the floor, but all the rest went into a bag. Reflexes taking over, I may have chased one or two of the cubes and pawed them under the fridge.

Lest not forget for the moment I am a cat and cats can be...

Then came the hand. With outstretched fingers she latched onto the clump of flesh and plunked it in the ice, sealed the baggie and handed the hand off to her father. He bolted outside holding his stomach. No need to guess what came next.

"I'll have grandpa drive me over to see my horses." Ava ran her fingers through my fur. "Come on, Jack.

How long can you stay in the shape of a kitty? Can I take you to show and tell the first day of school?"

Looking through the screened door Christian called, "Aves?"

Head tossed over her shoulder she gave him her best *what now* look.

"I'm sorry."

"Yeah, Daddy me too. Sorry you married a wrench—"

Tia interrupted, "Wench, not wrench, dear."

"No, I meant wrench. Harper clamped onto my dad and choked the sense out of him. And sorry you walked out on me when I needed you more than ever. Bye. Don't forget the worst babysitter ever." Ava did an about-face and clomped up the stairs with Tia on her shoulder, and me all but tripping her up trying to race her to the top.

When we hit the spare room Tia asked, "Mind eraser?"

With a little vault I jumped on the bed circling a few times before wiggling my butt into a soft spot on the comforter.

"Yes. I'd imagine they're all lightweights. A couple grapes each should do it."

"What are you talking about, Jack?" Ava sat on the bed next to me and removed my crown. This is where on any other day in my existence I would have put on a freak show, but instead this ravenous calm stilled within me. Ava plunked my crown on top of her head, looked in the mirror and smiled. "I always wanted to be a goddess."

My heart stilled at her beauty. I had to catch my breath before I mustered, "You already are, Ava. You just need to grow into it." I've never seen anything more lovely.

Tia shot me a reprimanding warning.

Wish cats could roll their eyes. "All women are queens, Ava." I licked my balls just because I could, then preened my paws, gaze intent on the tiny tyrant. "Better?"

Disdained nose in the air, Tia gave a poignant nod, but nodded to the crown again. "See anything different?"

Astonished I somehow kept my shock contained, the crown held a completely different appearance atop Ava's head. Flowers with tiny buds bloomed. Magic in the making.

"You, my queen, are very astute. Game changer there. Ava, we can't let your dad and his zombified sidekick remember any of this. Or at least a talking cat and a pixy."

Tia tossed in, "Or grandma getting a little kooky with the cleaver."

"Exactly." I plopped my head in Ava's lap and did a sly roll-over for a belly rub. "Like I said little goddess, your world isn't ready for us yet. Heck, most days we aren't ready for our awesomeness."

Both Ava and Tia giggled at my humor. For the first time in forever I had a family.

"So how long can you stay like this? I like having a kitty that talks to me." Ava ran her fingers through my thick pelt and rooted in deep every now and then giving me a mini massage. God, this felt good after being cooped up in that trap.

"Shifting has limits. Only when my flight or fight senses kick in can I change."

"Or when he's had way too much wine." Tia told Ava.

"Okay! What's the fighting and flying thing?

Sounds like a superhero battle thing."

"I do suppose I fit the description."

Tia snorted at my joke. "It is your body's response to something, usually bad. Your adrenaline ignites your body the way a match does gasoline. And you have two choices…"

Ava finished with, "Either boogy or hammer someone?"

I love the way Ava takes everything at face value, no questions asked. Her logic is black or white, none of those grey shades everyone seems so fond of. Thor would get a kick out of the way she thinks too.

I watched the little girl perk right up. "Tia, my grandpa built me a doll house. It is in the attic. It's really a castle. It's got furniture, a bed and covers. The potty is fake, but you can have it if you want."

"I am touched, kid. You are most generous."

"Well, you two have been so good to me. It's the least I can do."

"Food?" I perked right up.

"More honey?" Tia added.

"Be back in a minute." With a gentle hand under my head to move me, Ava scooted off the bed and out the door.

"Well, my grace, whilst you feed your furry face, I'll go take care of our current problem. You are aware the kid ran off with your crown?"

"I'll share it with her. Bet I could win a few bucks there. No one in their right mind would ever expect me to share my headpiece. A few days ago, I most likely would have lost too. Here are enough grapes to make her dad and his underage bride have a serious hangover." I gathered a small stash of grapes I'd kept in one of the corners of my cell and stuffed them into a tiny backpack made for dolls. "Will you be able to track them? Plant a vivid picture of the idiot girl getting her hand sliced off while mowing the lawn? Seems humans never learn from this one or snowblowers."

"Puhleeze!" Hands on her hips, legs slightly spread, Tia tossed her head back in disgust before her glare marked me from the tip of her nose. "I am a thousand times more effective than a blood hound and way better than any demon at mind games. Besides, with the splatter trail the girl left, Hansel and Gretel could have found their way home."

"Do we tamper with the girl's grandparents?"

Tia shook her head no. "I think Ava gets her rational from them. They'll be fine. Shooting up to the attic. Be right back."

"Hey trouble," I called to Tia before she disappeared, "when you get back, I'll probably be back to being a kid's toy. I can feel the change coming."

With the words, "Got your back, as always," the pixy vanished.

Chapter Twenty-Two

Two Worlds Collide

In the garage, better known as Gramp's Grotto, Ava found the older man raiding an old icebox. There was also a fifty-inch television, a computer, a library up one side of the wall with a sliding ladder, a hammock swinging at the far end of the room in front of the window, and a reclining brown leather chair. Ayden and she had spent many summer nights out here listening to tall tales her grandpa entertained them with. Bet he never envisioned this story.

Grandpa had a bottle of beer in his hand. Not mincing words, she asked, "So Grandpa… have I turned into *that kid*?" Ava made quotation marks with her index fingers when she said *that kid*.

He smiled. It was one of his best qualities. Hand's down, the other was his hugs. He always made Ava feel safe and loved. Seeing the grin spread on his red lips made the corners of his green eyes crinkle. To Ava, he was the cutest old man on earth.

"Sweetheart, to me, you've always been 'that kid.'" His warm chuckle lifted her spirits. "What does that even mean, Aves? Come sit." Her grandpa walked out of the garage and headed for a picnic table under a huge whispering willow tree. He sat down then pat the spot next to him.

"You know what I mean. How many kids do you know have a pixy and a lynx fighting the new stepmom for a ring or your grandma whacking off her hand? Is Gram going to get arrested too?"

"Call me senile, but I have a feeling the pixy and your kitty are going to take care of the mess."

"Grandpa, why aren't you freaking out?"

The older gentleman reached over and tickled under her chin. "There is nothing tangible on this earth that states we, as humans are the only creatures able to drink a cold beer or a pop. I've always believed in magic, Aves. Without it life would be death." Her grandfather reached behind him and surprised her with a cold can of cream pop. When he pulled back the silver tab white frosty bubbles oozed out.

Ava's face lit up. "Before dinner?" Once in Ava's hands she put her lips to the can and sucked off the foam.

"It's our secret."

"So are the kitty and the pixy, right?"

"Absolutely." Ava's grandpa took a long drink from his bottle and when done wiped his mouth off with the back of his hand. "You got a mustache, goofball."

Ava giggled and did the same thing her grandpa did, wiped her mouth off.

Ava's grandma approached the table carrying a tray of hotdogs, macaroni salad and utensils to eat. "Dinner's up. Eat it while it's hot."

"Can I take a hotdog to the kitty?" Ava clasped her hands in front of her in a praying position. "Pretty please?" Her grandma ticked her head towards the house. Taking that as a yes, Ava stabbed a dog off the plate with a fork then proceeded to hack at the squiggly thing. "Gram, you made doing this to Harper's hand look easier."

"Can we not talk about that… ever again?" Ava's grandpa asked holding a hand over his stomach.

Ava's grandma shrugged her shoulders. "Not sorry."

When Ava finished quartering the hot dog into miniscule tidbits, she fled to the house yelling backwards, "Thank you. Save me one. Jack? Jack?"

Ava set the plate down on an old-fashioned roll top desk by her bed and waited. No response. She flew to the window only to peer out a gaping hole in the screen. Nothing there. She wanted her lynx back. Crossing the room in a flurry she grabbed the jewelry box, and with trembling hands opened the container chanting a little mantra, "Please be in there. Please be in there!"

Empty. Her heart sank. No tiny man she'd grown to like and trust. No pixy to hang on her shoulder. She was so much cooler than a parrot. No sparkly dust. No grapes. Empty. Just like her heart. Her voice cracked, "Jack, please don't tell me I made you up."

"Meow." Was she hearing a cat cry?

A muffled noise roared again. "Meow?"

"Jack?"

Ava crawled back over the bed to the window and looked down the rocky drive. Coming up the dusty road with something hanging limp in his mouth, Jack raced home being chased by a swarm of dragon flies and about twenty or so pixies. Ava bounced off the bed and charged down the stairs, through the kitchen and out the front door running full out down the gravel path. Skidding to a halt, with dust trailing her, she got on one knee and held her hand out. "What happened?" When the dragon flies and pixies saw Ava they dispersed into a thousand different directions.

Dionysus gently dropped Tia in Ava's hand. Her outfit looked like it went through a paper shredder. Her wings had tears in them rendering flying impossible.

"It's a war zone, kid." Tia scarcely answered, her voice frail. "Excuse my French, but poop has hit the fan."

"What happened?"

"I was bushwhacked by pixies. Pixies. Did you know they're all over your farm? Did you know they use dragonflies as protection? Better yet, did you know the dragon flies can spit fire? Look at my tush. They tried to incinerate me!"

A surprised 'O' formed on Ava's lips. She shook her head no. "No way!"

"Way! Look at me. They could have cared less I am a queen. They laughed and told me to go back to my own country."

With Tia in the palm of her hand Ava ran to the house. Once in the kitchen she turned the water on in the sink and made sure it wasn't too hot. "Hold your breath."

"Not a problem," Dionysus answered as he rubbed his paws over his watering eyes. "What is this stench?"

Ava's nose twitched followed by three consecutive sneezes.

"Bless you lil goddess."

"Thanks. It is ammonia or bleach or both mixed."

Tia started to choke. "I'm going to be sick."

"Gram cleaned the kitchen. I'll be quick. Hold your breath."

"Wha—" Tia ended up choking down water. Angling her head away from the flowing water Tia gurgled, "You trying to water-board me, kid?"

Ava struggled with the pixy. "I have no clue what

that means. Stop squirming. You're not a gremlin, or the wicked witch. You won't multiply or melt. Will you?" Ava quickly pulled Tia out of the water and looked to Dionysus for the answer. "Right, Jack?"

"Dowse her." A cup of water swooshed over Tia's body.

Quick to wipe her eyes and flap her flailing wings Tia's anger showed. "Kitty cat, I'm going to drop you off at a Chinese restaurant myself."

"Looking forward to it, Majesty. I am hungry." The lynx landed squarely on the counter next to the sink. "Clearly Ava, you have never been cooped up in an itty-bitty box for light years with the little she-devil."

Ava couldn't help but laugh at the scowl the pixy made. Then there was the constant joking between the two of them. They poked fun at one another all the time, but Ava could see through it. They liked each other, or at least respected each other. Her parents used to be like that. Something burned in her chest. Oh, how she missed her family.

"Kid," Tia yelled through splashes, "this is it. I'm soaked and look like a drown rat, or is that cat?" In a second her unique eyes turned into liquid silver. Before Ava could figure out what was happening Tia climbed on the back of the sink and grabbed the hose, aimed it in Dionysus's face and squeezed the handle spraying the lynx. The cat sneered, and then shook his coat covering everything in water.

"Good one, Majesty. Next time I cart your little tush around I might just chomp on it instead."

"I owed you that, your Grace." The three of them laughed. Tia finished, "But seriously, kid, I'm showing more skin than strippers do."

"I don't have a problem with it." The lynx swished a playful tail…

"I'm dusting you when I feel better."

"I'd expect nothing less." The lynx bobbed his head then wiggled his butt playfully. "Kid, the crown?" Dionysus stretched his neck towards Ava. A half-scrunched lip formed on her face as she begrudgingly settled the headpiece back on his head, taking care to tuck his ears on the outside. "Thank you."

Teeth chattering, Tia reminded the two of them, "Still flashing naughty bits here."

Dionysus looked around and spotted a roll of paper towels on the far end of the counter. Swagger intact, he sauntered to the roll and nudged it towards Ava. It tipped over. He pawed it a little closer. The paper roll went toppling off the counter allowing paper to stream across the sparkling clean floor.

"Nice move cat." Ava's grandma barked as she carried all the same things she went out with back inside.

Paw up, Dionysus started to defend himself, "I didn't—it wasn't—all right it was me, but I didn't do it on purpose."

"Said no cat ever when entertaining themselves by shoving items off counter tops. What is going on in here?" Ava's grandma asked. "Aves, you never came back to finish your dinner. I saved you some. So can I get a formal introduction?" Ava's grandma walked over to the window and yanked it open. Then she walked to her pantry and disappeared for a moment. When she emerged, she had a large stand-up fan, which she wasted no time plugging in by the window. "Little to aesthetic in here. Got to love bleach."

"Queen Titania here. Tia for short and not looking

so regal at the moment, Grandma." Tia curtsied while trying not to flash the grandmother or grandfather who walked in carrying flowers.

"Jack here." Dionysus raised a paw.

Grandma gave the cat a wide girth. "Allergic. Sorry. Call me Maggie. The spouse is Charlie. Ava, run upstairs and grab a few of your dolls off the shelf. Those clothes would probably fit your new friend." Ava's grandma gave her the little shoo-off finger. "And get the glue. Looks like we have some triaging to do."

Ava's face lit up. "Be right back. Maybe all the money you spent on doll clothes won't be wasted after all."

Maggie shook her head. "Never in a million years did I think they'd wind up used like this."

"Me either. Isn't it great?" Ava yelled back.

Within the hour, Tia was on the mend; her wings spread wide so the glue wouldn't bunch or scar the delicate flesh. After Dionysus changed back to his mini-self Ava had a few outfits for him too. The first one he wore would have any soldier standing at attention. Her fake soldier doll never looked this self-assured or cool. Ava knew this intimately. He lay headless in the chest in the barn with all the other mangled figurines. Unfortunately, her grandparents could not see or hear Dionysus until he'd shifted back to a cat.

After a few minutes of hysterical laughter coming from the jewelry box, Ava had been given the 'all clear' signal to open the box again. It was her turn to laugh until she cried. There Dionysus stood, dressed as a genie in black silk baggy-balloon pants with a wide metallic gold elastic waistband. He also wore a pink silk vest with nothing under it other than jiggly muscles. His unruly dark curls hung from under a matching gold turban, the crown flattened on top of the hat. For shoes he had somehow managed to tug on gold curly-toed slippers. Yes, he looked ludicrous, but Ava told him, "You look gallant."

"Nice fib. Surprised you know that word, gallant."

"Daddy reads," Ava's voice caught in her throat, she looked away from Dionysus, "read to me every night. He said it was the best way for kids to learn."

"Your father is a smart man. He'll come around lil goddess." Dionysus took off the crown and turban and gave her a sweeping bow. "I need a weapon. Something to protect myself with in case of say a rodent or bird sees me in here?"

"The queen and I are the only ones who can see you, but okay. You never know, right?" Wheels turning Ava headed for the laundry basket. "Oh gosh, I almost lost it." Tossing one item after another of clothing over her shoulder to form a new mountain of laundry Ava finally found her overalls and tucked deep in the pocket, her diamond sword. She handed it to him. "I want it back, Jack. When you get big and no longer need it. Deal?"

"My lady, you drive a hard bargain, but this one I look forward to fulfilling." Sword in hand, Dionysus slashed the glimmering blade through the air turning, crouching, jabbing as he went through his moves. His final act, he stabbed a grape, pulled it up from the floor of his box and popped the tip of the knife in his mouth and chomped away. "It is a real diamond if you're wondering. Nothing but the best."

"I'm so going to hide this later."

Charlie started calling Queen Tia, little black Dahlia, after she came down the stairs perched on Ava's shoulder wearing pleather pants cinched her waist and tapered down to the ankle. Ava curled her white hair into long ringlets then added hairspray to give the locks a little more volume than necessary. Next, Ava cut slots out of a black pleather jacket for Tia's wings. Beneath the jacket she wore a red sequined halter-top. Red patent-leather ankle boots with heels completed the look, until Tia tried walking in them. Then she slaughtered it. With each step she tripped, slipped, or toppled over.

Ava's summation, "You're a much better flier."

Discouraged, Tia huffed, "Ya think? I don't understand why this should be so difficult."

"Because, your gracelessness, you've been barefoot your entire life. Ava, guide her around till she can remain vertical."

"When you are all done playing dress-up come out to the television," Ava's grandpa hollered from the family room.

"Tia, you look out of this world," Dionysus told her. "I've never seen anything so small so sexy."

"If you're fishing for a compliment, I cannot reciprocate." Tia twittered with a tussle of her hair back off her shoulder. "You look more like a court jester."

Ava plopped on the floor a few feet from the television, her head propped, chin in hands on her elbows. On top of Ava's head the pixy nestled right in mimicking Ava's position. In front of them sat the open jewelry box.

With background music playing a song about *God being one of us,* the anchorman reported, "Two worlds have collided," as his struggles not to laugh deemed impossible to miss. His cheeks were brilliant red. Tears slid from the outer corners of his eyes. "Fantasy or fact.

Heaven meets Hell here in small Town U.S.A. We have people roaming the streets claiming to be gods and goddesses. A new theatre opened downtown this week. These actors must be drumming up business." The television screen went from the reporter's face to a video taken by an amateur camera phone.

"Tip the jewelry box up so I can see, Ava. Please?" She obliged.

"Your majesty, is that—"

Tia stood on top of Ava's head.

Ava fidgeted. "The heels are poking my scalp, Queen."

"Apologies!" Tia leapt, arms extended to her sides, her body grace in motion. About an inch before she crashed into the shag-piled orange carpet she pulled up and soared straight up and flew to the TV where she hovered smack dab in front of the screen. "The wings work. Yippee!" She spun in a circle and squealed. "Yes, it is. Apollo and Eros are together."

Dionysus raised his voice, "Can't see through your little femme fatale pixy behind. Move it."

Both Tia and Ava laughed. Tia answered, "We're now even for the metrosexual comment."

"It bothers me slightly," Maggie added, "that we are only getting one-sided conversation from you two. We can't hear whatever is in the empty jewelry box, Ava."

"Shame, Gram." Eyes glued to the tube she said, "You'd die if you could see my genie."

Dionysus gave a gentle shake of his head. "Life really is stranger than fiction or at least mine. Apollo is singing and people are poking fun at him. I told the moron he couldn't sing."

Maggie added her two cents. "They stand out better

than a Ninja in a delivery room."

Charlie followed with, "The entire purpose of Ninja's is not to stand out!"

Ava glanced at her grandpa. He shrugged his shoulders. "She's your grandmother." He gave Maggie a sideways smile before he took another gulp of beer.

The news switched to a video showing a flash mob surrounding a woman in the town's center wearing next to nothing. Cameras exploded to capture a glimpse of a woman so surreal, so compelling, men were falling on their knees before her on the sidewalk. Cars came to a screeching holt. Bumpers were smashed. Chaos erupted in the street.

Ava's grandpa grabbed his chest and took a deep breath.

"Charlie?" Ava's grandma rushed to his side. "What is it?"

Charlie slapped his cheek a couple times and sat back on his chair. "Wow! She is drop dead gorgeous."

In the crowd one bold man set a boom box down blaring *hip hop music*. He approached the woman, took her hand and began to dance like no one watched. His left hand in her right hand he held her out at a distance then spun her around and reeled her back to him, his face mere inches from hers. He winked. Then without notice he spun her in the opposite direction, her see-through jeweled gown flowing with her moves showing off more than her perfect dance form. He brought his other hand up to hers and turned her sideways. The two promenaded, crisscrossed their feet with each other's laughing as they made their way through the crowds. They reached a wall and turned back, sashaying, him leading her every step of the way. They faced one another, hands held in front of them and they leaned backwards while their feet busied themselves shuffling, jiving and their hips swinging in circles. The gorgeous woman smiled, delighted in the movements the man offered, even when he swung her around his back then did a quick change of hands and rolled her over him, so she flipped right over him and landed on her bare feet.

"Do it again," her angelic voice cried. "I adore this foreplay."

He stopped dancing. She kept right on going, her arms high, twirling in a circle around him while he turned to keep up with her. He looked her in the eye and said, "Lady, I'm shooting a dance video, not a porn movie."

"Not with me you're not." The woman grabbed his shirt and pulled him within a hair's distance of her mouth. "This is where the cameras need a close up. Look closely, Dion and Epimetheus."

"Oh, this isn't going to end well, Dionysus." Tia spun with a look of disbelief at him. "She is out for vengeance."

A wicked grin emerged as the woman looked directly in the camera and kissed the man dancing with her, pouring her power into his body, giving him a boost of energy that ramped up his feet. The soles of his shoes began to smoke. They danced faster, her body snug against his, her breasts taut against his chest, her hips grinding into his. Dirty dancers couldn't duplicate the heat this couple exuded.

Ava's grandma glanced at Charlie, with a longing in her eye. "We used to dance like this."

"We still can." Charlie gave a playful smile to Maggie.

"I see body-casts in our future." Maggie giggled.

"You guys are gross," Ava added holding her hands over her ears.

The couple on TV tangoed in endless spins until the song trailed off.

At the end, the surreal woman curtsied, stood straight, shoulders back, and whispered in his ear, "Never lead a woman to temptation and then deliver her from evil. Playing with one's emotions is a volatile game. Some say it turns one's heart to that of a pebble." She laid a gentle kiss on his cheek and then walked away. The man stood there like a stone statue. When he didn't move another person in the crowd approached and tapped his shoulder. The dancing fool cracked and then crumbled into a pile of dust. A few people in the crowd ran like rats for shelter. Others applauded.

"That is the worst acting I've ever seen. Really. Zombie movies have better special effects." Maggie looked around to Ava and then her husband with her mouth slightly ajar. "Oh, don't tell me you bought this act?"

Tia asked, "What was that? Have you ever seen anything like it? Dear lord!"

"Pandy." Dionysus whispered. "She survived the landing, and it seems has much more power than I ever imagined."

Tia's lips drew thin. "You constantly underestimate her. That is your downfall, Dionysus. And you mean fall," she corrected.

"No," he corrected, "landing. The fall makes you feel you're a bowl of gelatin in a microwave being torqued into an extinct organism. It is the landing that shows no mercy. I will never let her get the upper hand on me again." Fingers in his curls, Dionysus primped and tucked a few stray hairs behind his ear. "What are we going to do?"

"Zeus!" Ava blurted.

"Zeus can't fix this," Dionysus added sullenly.

"No! Zeus!" Ava bolted to the television her finger tapping fast and furiously on the screen. "He got out of jail. Do you see his wings, Grandpa? Aren't they beautiful?"

Her grandma shook her head. "No Aves, that is Woody, from Cheers."

"Nut-uh!" Ava disagreed shaking her head back and forth. "Zeus!"

From the television came, "We're here all week. The Apollo Theatre." Apollo took a gentlemanly bow and then grabbed a ruby red ribbon dangling between his legs and swung it in mad circles. A sinful smirk filled his face. "For you, Dion. We're coming for you."

The camera panned along with Zeus and caught him grabbing Apollo's ear then dragging him down the sidewalk, still singing. When they caught up to Pandora each man looped an arm through hers before they disappeared in the menagerie of fluid movement of bodies. Epimetheus trailed behind like a lost pup.

With a solemn face Charlie turned his big, sad eyes on Ava. "So the sky has fallen?"

"I wouldn't be here if it hadn't," Tia told him.

Dionysus chucked a grape at Tia. "Hey!"

The pixy huffed. "Sorry, we wouldn't be here. Better?"

Dionysus nodded. "Tell him a few stars fell, but that's all. Tell him everything will be fine."

"Grampa, Jack said not to worry."

Dionysus waggled a finger in her face. "That is not what I said."

"What? I said what you wanted, mostly." Ava grinned, nailing the cuteness factor. "Grandpa, Grandma, that's Zeus. He's the crazy god from the hospital I told you about. The one that married daddy and the ring thief."

Ava watched her grandparents look back and forth between one another. They looked like they had their quota of fairytales come true for the day and were going to go hide under the bed. She didn't blame them. Might even join them.

Charlie hesitated before answering Ava, but he had to tell her the truth. "I don't see any wings on him, Ava."

The queen of pixies scowled. "Kid, help me out of this jacket. Careful with the appendages. I don't want them to tear again after you got me back together so nicely."

Ava sat up so Tia could land in her lap. Very carefully she removed the jacket.

"Thanks, kid. Pandora has self-esteem issues. She wants to fit in, but everyone knows she's different."

"Aren't we all different? Isn't that what makes us eunuchs? That's what mommy used to tell me to keep me from putting Ayden up for adoption. That he was eunuch."

"Unique, kid. Big difference." A genuine smile formed on the pixies small angelic face. "Good point though."

Dionysus tapped his index finger to his lip a few times before an exhausted grumble emerged. "She wants retribution for the gift. I suppose turning my life upside down was not enough." Two grapes were plucked and popped into his mouth.

Tia attempted to wiggle her way out of the boots.

"Give me your foot. I'll help." Dionysus offered his hand.

"Are you guys boyfriend and girlfriend?" Ava asked.

"I'm married, Ava. My king and I were separated when your Jack and I fell to earth. Someone kidnapped him. Pretty certain he's up there worried as sick about me as I am him."

"Just like me with Ayden?"

"Exactly," Tia answered.

"Are you married, Jack?"

Dionysus's shoulders drooped as he glanced towards Tia. "Lil goddess, someday I'll tell you all about her, but right now we need to find a way to get me out of this tomb. Maybe my father can help me."

Ava butt in, "Jack, I have an easier way."

"You going to wiggle your nose like a witch?" Dionysus laughed.

"Duh! Excuse me." Ava stood, inhaled and let the vocal cords rip out, "Oh my God, Zeus!"

Tia buzzed into Ava's view in a flash, her wings revved up so fast they were virtually invisible. "Kid, are you alright?"

Ava put her index finger to her lips asking for silence. Didn't happen.

Charlie sprung from his recliner and her grandma jumped back, the two of them collided into one another both toppling back into the chair, arms and legs tangled.

"Ava!" Her grandma hollered, "What the dickens?"

Ava shot the same finger up waving it back and forth, asking without words for a moment. When nothing happened, her smile faded. "The crazy god no-showed."

"What was that all about?" Her grandpa asked.

"He told me all I had to do was to call him and he would come. He promised. He can fly here."

"Lovie, he looked a little busy with his friends. He really said all you had to do was call him? I didn't see wings."

The head bobbed. The moue solidified. "Yup. The detective said Zeus is a real priest, but I saw him fly. I'm not making it up. You saw Jack turn into a kitty and talk. I'm not fibbing." The sniffles were a telltale sign of Ava's distress. Her grandma rushed to her side once Charlie pushed her off him and got her to her feet. With her arms hugging Ava, her grandma suggested, "It's getting late, lovie. Maybe your god went to bed. We believe you. It is rather hard not to when we have a royal member of the pixies here with us. Go get cleaned up and get some zzz's. Tomorrow we'll take you to the farm to see the horses and get some clothes and personal items. School starts soon too so we need to go shopping. And I really didn't want to tell you, but we need to get you back to the doctor for a treatment in the afternoon." Ava's grandma leaned in close and squeezed Ava then kissed the top of her head. "Love you more."

Ava wiggled free. "I don't need any medicine, Gram, please. I feel fine. Cross my heart. Please don't make me go back to the hospital."

"I'll be by your side, lil goddess. You won't be alone." Dionysus gave up a lopsided smirk with a little jig in hopes of eliciting her sweet smile.

"Ava, you won't win this one. I'm sorry. I'm not going to lose you too. I can't." Before Maggie even finished her spiel tears welled in her eyes. "Go on up, lovie. I'll be up to tuck you in shortly."

Chapter Twenty-Three

Twisted

The scent of pink turtlehead flowers, white clematis, fuchsia-colored Mexican sage, and lavender monkshood blooms whiffed up Ava's nostrils, stirring her slumber. Her grandma called the mixture of scents a floralgasm. The term torpedoed over Ava's head. A single strand of hair wisped and tickled her nose. In no mood to be tickled ever again she let out a large huff and sent the strand backwards.

A lot of things bothered her lately. The only thing a first grader should have had to worry over was what outfit she would rock the look with on her first day back to school accompanied by of course, the perfect lunch box she would carry, not the rest of the drama she'd been subject to lately: Her mom dying. Her brother missing. Her father and the babysitter... she choked on anger at the thought of them together. And then there was the trip to the doctor. The last thing she wanted to worry about, her dumb disease and more needles... Emptiness seemed to have a direct route to Ava's heart. A frigid void filled her. All she wanted was her life back. Her mom. Her brother. Her dad, minus the muck stuck on his shoe.

Oh, the ring! Ava leant over the side of the bed and fished around for the piece of jewelry from her pant's pocket. The diamond sparkled just like her star. This ring she would never lose. It was a part of her mother. The only trinket she had left of her.

With outstretched fingers and going for stealth, Ava latched onto the pink-jeweled box and flipped the lid open. She fought a sudden outburst of giggles. Tia slept in the box with Jack, although she clearly ruled the space. Curled-up, jammed in the corner with his crown on, Jack looked about as comfortable as Ava had been all night. At least he was using the pillow and blanket Ava gave him from her dollhouse. Tia lay kitty-corner spread-eagled across the box wearing her crown as well. One of her wings lay draped over Jack's face. Every time he took a breath her wing rippled over him. It must have tickled because he wrinkled his nose and muttered inaudible sounds but didn't budge. His hand and the queens were entwined, fingers laced.

"Jack? You awake?"

With a slow response Dionysus went to stretch and then saw his hand in Tia's. He was very careful to slip out from under Tia's wing and grasp. Rubbing his eyes he whispered, "Good morning, lil Goddess. I take it you can't sleep either."

"I didn't mean to wake you," Ava whispered back.

"You didn't. I didn't want to wake up our queen bee. Been lying here waiting for you. You're up really early."

"My tummy has a knot in it. Been listening to the thunder. There's a storm coming. Sometimes they can be pretty scary and we have to go below ground for cover."

"Someday I'll take you to ride one out above the clouds. It's nowhere near as scary and quite beautiful. It's all about perspective."

"So I keep hearing." A grin found Ava's lips. "Jack, am I crazy? Are you and Tia real? And Zeus?"

"Well sweetheart, if I'm fake then so are you. Does that make sense?"

Ava gave a giant nod with a bigger smile. "Completely. We're both nuts. How come no one other than Tia and I can see you, really? Or how come I am the only one to see Zeus's wings?"

Dionysus had to think about it before speaking. He didn't want to scare the kid to death leading her to believe they'd be tied together through eternity if Pandora had her way, but he didn't want to lie to her either. The kid deserved the truth. She'd already had too much trauma to handle. "Some people call what you and I have serendipity Ava, that we were destined to meet. It is in the stars. Others say dumb luck. You might be thinking bad luck." He laughed alone.

"I like you. It's fine. That doesn't explain Zeus's wings." Ava wiggled and propped herself into crossed legs, setting her box in her lap. "How come I am the only one to see what he can do?"

"Again, lil goddess…" Dionysus scratched his head. "You have a special insight to a world others only dream of. You are truly special. To me."

Someone's throat cleared. Tia rolled to her side, one wing enveloping like an accordion. She propped her body up on an elbow, with her head in her hand. She piped in, "Dear lord you two are awake early. What's a queen gotta do to get some beauty sleep around here?"

"Majesty, didn't mean to wake you."

"It's fine. Kid, Jack is correct. You are special. To all of us." The queen pixy sat up, glared at Dionysus before brushing her hair from her face and realigning her crown. She licked her lips and finished, "Just because you see magic where others do not does not take away its true element. Some humans are so closed-minded they barely can see their own nose without questioning its purpose." Tia nudged Dionysus. "Dionysus isn't one those people." Tears leaked from the corners of the queen's eye. She looked at Dionysus. "Tell me that wasn't funny," she asked, wiping under her eyes.

Dionysus gave her a sideways glance fighting a smirk. Then he started singing, "I want a new nose. One that isn't too big. One that doesn't run all day. One that doesn't turn red. One that doesn't cost too much."

Ava cut him off. "I know that song, Jack, except you changed all the words. Mommy used to sing it all the time. Something about new drugs."

"Your mom taught you all the great music, Ava."

"You two, don't ever stop believing what your eyes sees or your heart feels. Miracles happen all around you all the time. People are too busy second-guessing life to experience it." Tia stood, stretched her arms, flexed her wings and lifted off. "My grace, please excuse me? I need at least a day's slumber. I'll be in the castle if you need me. Your snoring... It is a true miracle no one's killed you over it."

"Majesty," Dionysus rebuked, "That was all you. I never slept."

Tia started, "I do not—"

Dionysus shut her down, "I know, I know... Snore or fart. Yeah! Got it." He looked at Ava. "Are all women like this?"

Ava nodded. "Yup."

"Get some rest, kid. You have a huge day ahead."

"Will you guys be coming with me?"

"I am at your whim, lil goddess. Only you can decide." Dionysus shrugged his shoulders, his head leaning on his right shoulder.

"I'm doing some recon stuff, kid. Want to see if I can dig up the location of the others who fell. You'll miss me for sure." Tia winked. "Be safe."

"You too." Ava giggled as she closed the lid and tucked the box under the covers beside her. Even if she believed she'd gone totally cuckoo, she picked two of the best imaginary people to spend her time with.

***

Greyish-black clouds trundled above the farm making certain any scant trace of sun be devoured, the exception being brilliant streaks of light slamming into the terrain. Storms were about to have their way with the earth. Didn't matter. Ava couldn't wait to see her horses. She'd stay with them through the turmoil to keep them company.

One back road away from where she lived, trees were down, power lines tangled in branches better than her hair did ponytail holders. Convoys of emergency vehicles sped past them, all headed in the same direction of Ava and her grandparents. Gnarly roots started to develop in her belly when they turned onto the road she lived on. Firetrucks converged over her property, hoses blasting water into a charred shell of what used to be her home. EMT's rushed past, lights swirling, alarms blaring. The house she'd grown up in had been destroyed. Water oozed from holes in the siding as steam rose leaving only glowing embers. All of Ava's belongings were strewn across the property. Ava leapt from the truck before her grandpa had the vehicle in park, leaving Jack locked in his box wedged in the back seat.

"Ava, no!" Both her grandparents screamed in

tandem. Maggie pulled the same stunt Ava did, jumping out of a moving truck to give chase.

"You two will be the death of me," Charlie shouted while his foot slammed down on the brakes making the truck raise the back end completely off the ground and then bounce.

Headed for the barn Ava didn't stop running. She flew right past her father who was busy consoling his new wife.

"Aves," Christian brushed Harper aside when he noticed her and took off after her.

"Get the horses," Ava ordered.

Breathless, Christian yelled, "Ava, the storm is only just beginning. There's a tornado. It's headed right for us. Get in the storm shelter."

"Not without my horses." The foot stomp she produced made the earth vibrate. Both Ava's grandma and her father gave a, *what the heck was that* look.

They were ignored.

Out of nowhere a perfect circle opened in the center of grey saturated clouds. A brilliant, glowing magenta ring encased the opening looked like what appeared to be a whirlpool of fire, eddying, discharging flames and sparks. Lightning bolts pierced the ground around them. It was as if the heavens unleashed centuries of pent-up hatred in seconds. Trees split in two, causing more fires to ignite. The flames jumped from one tree limb to the next. A lethal game of fiery dominos entailed. Hail, the size of baseballs found targets no major league pitcher could ever hope to ascertain. The tin roof of the silo amplified the noise. Ava covered her ears while she made her way inside Halo's stall. The horse gave her a low nicker greeting. Ava got on her toes and kissed the horse's nose. "Hi, baby." She grabbed a bridle from a hook and coaxed the horse into it. Once Halo had her bridle on Ava ran to the next stall and did the same to Whizz.

Once she came out of Whizz's stall her temper reached boiling point. "A little help would be appreciated. Jeepers, Dad, did you do nothing while I was gone?" Ava's voice out amped the raging storm. In a panicked rage she ran to the last stall. "Where's Lolly?" She didn't see the horse anywhere. Fear thumped in her chest. In one fluid spin Ava was in her father's face screaming, "Where is Lolly? What did you do to Ayden's horse?"

"She broke a leg in the field when Harper rode her."

"No!" She knew exactly what his next words were. "Don't you dare say it, Daddy."

Christian wouldn't look at her. She turned to her grandma who was busy leading the two horses out of the barn.

"Grandma?" Tears fought for an exit and rushed her cheeks. Arms tight across her chest, Ava hugged herself while her legs shook.

Maggie met Ava halfway through the barn and brushed her hair from her face. "Come on, lovie. Let's get the carrier hooked up to the truck and get these guys to safety. Christian, someday you'll pay for the hell you're putting this child through."

"I don't understand any of what or why this is happening," Christian confessed as he followed them from the barn. "I am lost."

Not a foot outside of the barn her grandma turned back, rushing to get back in. "The hail, its treacherous. The horses will have to ride the storm out here, lovie.

Come on. Head for the shelter."

About to protest with her last breath Ava heard what she could only describe as a freight train coming straight for them. At the far end of the meadow a hungry funnel dropped out of the sky and touched down chewing up anything and everything in its path. In the distant meadow a whole house went in, splinters came out. A cornfield disappeared to leave bare husks scattered in its wake. The tornado's high pitch popped her eardrums. The walls in the barn began to expand and contract the way her mom's chest did when she was in the hospital fighting for her last breath.

Roof panels groaned, giving way to the driving fury. Rain poured in. Halo and Whizz reeled back on their hind legs, both kicking blindly. Their eyes were wild, huge. Their ears pinned to their heads, snorts of heartbreaking fear hit Ava. Whizz came down hard clipping Ava's father. Christian fell on his back and the horse stomped on him square in the chest. If Ava didn't know better she'd have thought the horse did it on purpose. Christian made no move to get up or out of the way. Without thinking Ava jumped and grabbed the reins to get the horse off him before he killed her dad, if it wasn't already too late.

"Daddy? Daddy, wake up. Please? Grandma get him up."

"I'll send your grandpa after him. Come on."

Her bottom lip quivering, Ava whimpered, "Grandma, I don't understand any of this." She bent down and kissed her father. "I'm so sorry. I do love you even if you don't love me anymore." He never responded. "I never told you or mommy. Please don't hate me too." Her face drenched, hard to tell if it was tears, rain or both.

Ava stood, feeling years older. The innocence of a young girl gone. She'd turned into a miniature version of an adult overnight. She pulled down on the reins, and in a very soft tone spoke to the horse. "Whizz, it'll be okay. I'm here now. It'll be okay." At that point Ava really wasn't sure she was trying to console the horse or herself, but the horse settled.

Her grandmother nudged her. "We got to get out of here, Aves or we'll all die."

The hefty wooden beams supporting the barn's second story cracked spooking Ava, her grandma, and the horses. A huge portion of the hayloft broke free, hanging by a prayer, spilling bales of hay and loose dirt to the lower level they were on. Another loud snap immediately brought the rest of the loft down, just missing Ava, but crushing Christian's legs. He never flinched.

"Daddy!" Dust made it almost impossible to see through. Ava fought to hold onto the reins with one hand and fiercely rubbed her eyes with her free hand. She couldn't get a breath without choking. Splinters bore through the barn like arrows and with a loud creak, the back gate to the structure sailed into the unknown. From behind her, Ava's grandpa grabbed her and pried her fingers free of the reins on Whizz. "You're coming with me, kiddo. You can hate me tomorrow, but at least I'll have that rather than regret." Charlie slapped the horse on his butt as hard as he could and yelled, "Run Whizz, and don't look back."

Maggie followed Charlie's lead. She let go of Halo and shoved the horse's butt towards open ground. "Run wild baby. Run."

Both horses fled, leaping the fence in the field as if it didn't exist, hooves kicking up muddy earth in their wake, nostrils flaring, tails in a straight line behind them, they ran in the exact opposite direction of the storm.

"Daddy, I'll come back for you. Promise." Ava screamed being carted out of the barn like a sack of potatoes under her grandfather's arm.

In the musty fallout shelter three firefighters sat on a cement bench, all jammed in thigh-to-thigh, caked in mud and stinking of smoke. Ava blamed the men's odor for her eyes tearing. If everyone would stop starring at her, maybe she could think straight. Claustrophobic, she despised being in confined spaces. How Jack had survived as long as he had amazed her. Then her heart screeched to a stop.

"Jack!" She stood. So did Charlie and without another word he pointed back to the bench. Ava sat knowing the storm shelter only had one way in and one way out.

Her grandparents sat like sentinels on the stairs blocking the opening. She'd never get past them.

She'd left Jack alone in the box, with the sword through the bolt. She'd been playing with it and forgot all about removing it when she saw her home in ruins. He was trapped, alone and probably scared. She needed to get to him.

Guilt ridden, she'd done the exact same thing to him some witch had when she'd promised him she would watch over him.

Missing from the menagerie in this mildewed, muddied pit of despair were Harper and her father. Harper? Well in the back of her mind, Ava hoped the wicked witch landed under a house. Her dad? He was already buried under the barn. With her knees to her chest, her arms secured around them, Ava rocked back and forth. One of the firefighters scooted next to her and tossed his arm around her shoulder. With a glance in the strange man's direction Ava rested her head on his shoulder. Apparently, he needed comforting too.

When the world around them quieted more sirens and alarms filled the eerie silence. Ava emerged from the shelter squeezing her grandfather's hand. Sunshine emanated. If Ava had just woke up, slept through the war-struck zone she'd have never known a tornado put what was left of her life into its final spin cycle. Unfortunately, she didn't just wake up. Looking out at the destruction, hopelessness loomed in the air.

More shredded memories to pick up the pieces too. The aftermath of the storm didn't compared to the horror of the reality. What the fire didn't demolish the tornado did. Mud and debris covered everything. A few chickens and roosters with ruffled feathers pecked around looking for food in the rubble of what used to be the barn. No sign of her horses.

"Be careful where you step, Ava. There might be live wires buried under the debris."

Ava paid no heed. She ran as fast as her legs carried her to the spot she'd last seen her dad.

"Ava!" Her grandfather gave chase, "Stop!" When he caught up to her, he wrapped her in his arms and clung to a struggling little girl. "I'll let go if you promise no more trying to rip my heart from my chest."

Through a series of heavy sobs Ava finally shook her head in agreement. "I'm sorry. Do you think daddy made it out? And where's the babysitter? I hope the wind took her far away."

"Me too, kiddo." Charlie once again had Ava's hand in his grasp as they carefully walked the barn's foundation, steering clear of the center where Christian had been trapped beneath wreckage.

Slabs of roof crushed posts and beams. Ava's innocent eyes looked at her grandpa's older wrinkled ones. The usual twinkle, as missing as her father.

Rusted, battered tin lay sheered into jagged edges. In her path Ava found the sledgehammer. Of all things. "Got to start somewhere, Grandpa." She picked up the handle, and with everything she had she swung. Busting her way through the debris, she sent hunks of posts over her head, her grandfather ducking and cursing right alongside her. She paid no heed and battled forward on a mission. With the roof broken into manageable pieces a few of the EMT's carted the remnants off.

"I've never seen anything like it in my life," one of the firemen said to everyone, in awe of Ava's unbelievable strength, will and determination.

"Adrenaline is a miracle drug," another added.

"That isn't adrenaline," Maggie said under her breath, "It is all Ava. It always has been. You haven't seen anything yet."

"Her father is under this mess. Let's help her instead of standing here," Charlie urged to those gawking as he continued to haul debris.

In her own little zone Ava continued to swing the hefty hammer. Her sole goal—finding her father. She might have been mad at him, hurt by his choices, but the idea of never seeing him again, and seeing him crushed beneath the roof and walls of the barn hurt as much as losing her mom and Ayden. When she hit the cement foundation her enthusiasm and gusto plummeted. Maybe she had the wrong location. After all, the place looked nothing like it did ten minutes ago. Bent over Ava picked up more junk, dragged boxes out, hauled soaking wet blankets out to the grass, rolled saturated bales of hay to the side, nothing. With her head slumped forward, her strawberry blonde locks matted in an ugly state, her waterlogged clothes adhered to her, Ava skulked past the firefighters and her grandparents.

"Where you headed, lovie?"

"Truck."

Her thighs burned before she came to a dead stop in her driveway. Her throat clogged. She rubbed her eyes. Her very last straw—her grandfather's truck had vanished in thin air. She scoured the meadows in search of the vehicle, or a wrecked clump of metal. Nothing. Gone.

Jack was gone. Ava's legs buckled. She did nothing to stop her fall. Face plant to the ground, she wept. Little sobs turned into wails. Ava found herself knee deep in tears and blood when she went to brush her hair from her eyes. She'd sliced her forehead open on a rock. Head wounds bleed enough on their own. Add Hemophilia to the mix and the area looked like a crime scene. Everything she'd ever loved had vanished. She couldn't catch her breath. She couldn't breathe. She didn't want too. "God, why?" With that question her world began to spin again with the same vengeance the tornado had until a blissful feeling of silence comforted her.

Chapter Twenty-Four

Nothing More Than a Hot Potato

I am one hundred percent certain I no longer am in Kansas, or any other place where I might find an ounce of comfort, never mind sanity. Right now, I am thankful my queen is not trapped in here with me. I believe my chauffeur, Charlie, has abandoned the vehicle. Quite possibly my lil goddess is now the one manning the controls which would explain the chaotic bumps, rolls, and non-stop momentum to which I am being subjected. The radio is blaring. It is country.

I. Am. Doomed.

Alarms and sirens are in a screeching match with the honky tonk music yet oddly someone is singing completely off key trying to drown out the other two. I wish I could say I recognized the voice as Apollo, but this sounds so tinny, so nasally, I know of only one other who could sound so vehemently atrocious. This collective muddle might make me appreciate country music more right now.

I snorted. Nah! Not a chance in Tartarus.

The engine dies on the truck, a door creaks in agony as it opens, and with what felt like a chariot coming to a dead stop after the wheels break off and forward momentum clueless of the change in inertia, my body went airborne only to have gravity laughing as she slammed me back to the ground.

Life lately is one giant adventure. If I ever again contemplate to utter the words 'I am bored,' shoot me. Please.

Voices haggle over my container. The dear stepmother, Harper, is bartering me off. There it is again, the reason I despise stepmothers. Ava's and mine anyway. I know there are people out in the universe who step up and love someone's children with their whole hearts and how fortunate are the children and the parents to have such love. To have a family. I am envious. I had one for a day. I want it back. I am naught more than a hot potato getting passed around.

Harper must be nervous since my box is shaking again and the pitch of her voice increasing. Staying true to her nature, her loud boisterous self, blared, "One hundred dollars. Not a cent less."

Another person calmly says, "Two bucks. Not a cent more."

Is this what my worth is? I think not.

Priceless for starters. I both hear and feel vibrations as the diamond sword scrapes free from the bolt. The roof to my imminent domain opens. From my perch I see the lovely one-handed Harper showing a woman my home the way a realtor would a dilapidated trailer she is attempting pawn off as one of the homes of the rich and famous. The woman interested in my cell is out of my view, busy tapping away numbers on a calculator, I can only presume by the sounds of the rat-a-tat-tat. I pray one of them sees me. Yes, even desperate enough now to have Harper acknowledge my existence.

Thank God, chest tap completed, I wore the tux today. My lil goddess said I looked dapper. Slightly wrinkled after being tussled about, but I clean up nicely. My heart is hammering. I can't believe neither woman has mentioned anything. I waved the tiny white hankie I found folded in my front pocket and yell, "Hello ladies," as I flash them my pearly grin. I straightened my crown, crossed my ankle over my other leg, hand on hip and show off my suave, debonair stance waiting for a response. Nothing. Neither one glanced my way.

"Fifty for the box?" Harper barks at the clerk. "Sorta in a hurry."

Be interesting to see how much an invisible shrunken, sometimes drunken deity, and a snazzy-jeweled box go for these days.

"Harper, I can't give you two bucks for this bedazzled chunk of clay."

"How do you know my name?" Harper asked.

"Well, unless you're wearing someone else bowling shirt you have a name embroidered on it."

Harper glanced down and muttered, "Oh!" like the light bulb finally flickered. "Come on, ten bucks."

"It is worthless... except for the tiny little doll's bracelet. The ring, I'm not touching."

"No, it is not empty. I am right here," I roar until my throat is raw. "Look right here." I'm jumping up and down, flailing the arms, the hankie—it is mostly clean for God's sake, as it sends out a distress signal. I even stoop so low as to pluck a grape or two from crown and chuck them at the ladies. Neither one blinked. What a waste. Note to self: No sharing.

"Fifteen bucks," Harper demands. "Not a cent less."

"Five." The woman finally caves and counters, probably to get her out of her sight.

"Sold." All I see is a wad of gauze and white tape

wrapping her stump, which solidified her current moronic standings. This box where I currently have my butt plunked is worth more than the Hope Diamond. Either the woman who just bought it knows nothing about jewels, or she made the deal of the century. And got a fantastic booby prize to boot.

That would be me.

My guess is Harper's next pit stop will be a drive thru with slim pickings off the dollar menu.

I watch the tyrant slam the engagement ring on the scratched-up glass countertop beside me. The ring the little thief lost her hand over cast a rainbow of colors under the store's lighting. "Seriously, how much can you give me for this? Just between you and me. No one needs to know. If you're worried about Christian wanting the ring back it ain't a problem. He's quite dead. Killed in the storm." Not an ounce of remorse cushioned her words. No tears. Her face didn't hold concern, loss, hope, but sociopath? She just might be related to my ex. I am thinking my new arrangement might be for the best.

Where in heaven is Ava? Please tell me she did not succumb to the storm? Or from Harper's evil hand.

The storekeeper's tone remains aloof. "I'm sorry for your loss. I don't want the ring."

I think I like this woman who will be my jailer for the next segment of my life. The fact she can't see me nor that I can escape does leave me with the slimmest of hopes Ava or Tia will find me, but at least I won't be subject to the whims of a dimwit.

"Five more bucks for the ring and I'll leave quietly. Please?"

The woman Harper basically gave me to turned around with a withered five-dollar bill jammed in her hooved-like, greenish, fingers. Warty fingers. My heart, the one pounding wildly is now skipping beats.

And the true dimwit takes a bow.

A grenade began to rumble in my gut. Strawberry-blonde locks cascaded over the counter and brushed my cell. The light green eyes looked directly through, and then past me. Pretty certain she yanked the metaphorical pin from the tiny explosive in my gut. I purged all the French toast I'd scarfed down this morning.

Missed the toes this time. Optimism: Eh!

Some call my predicament destiny... More like calamity. My fate is sealed. There Ariadne stood in all her glory, green, warty, horns jutting from her bottom jaw, not having an inkling I stood in front of her. Tia's bracelet and I have been bartered off from a two-bit whore for a five-dollar bill to my ex-wife. While Harper busies herself stuffing the money into her bra, which quite frankly I'm amazed she even has on, a bell jingled from the front of the store. I'm not even sure why I looked, but I did. I know better than to utter these words, but what else could go wrong?

Detectives Bradshaw and Noyse strut in, taking separate paths to approach Harper, trepidation noted in their stride. Harper's dad has that appearance you get when someone in your family dies; the grog-blossom nose, the red puffy eyes. He barely made eye contact with his daughter.

Can't wait to see his reaction when he sees my ex.

"Harper," His voice came out subdued, "You have to come with us. I can't get you out of this, this time, kiddo."

"Daddy, I didn't set the fire to the house. Lightning hit it. I swear. And the dang horse threw me. And don't even try pinning Jimmy Field's or Brady Wells's disappearances on me. I know everyone thinks it was me, and that I started the fires that killed their moms, but I didn't. I bet Ava blabbed some piss poor lie. The brat is so going to boarding school."

"Shut up Harper. For God's sake, shut the hell up." Her father placed the handcuffs on the struggling girl's right hand. Then he cuffed his hand to the opposite cuff.

Answered my question before I had a chance to think it; how do you handcuff a one-handed lunatic? Chaining an insane person to my side wouldn't have been my first option, although… I suppose I did the same thing with Ariadne.

"Harper," Detective Bradshaw walked around to her handless side. With a thorough grip around her bicep he said, "We never mentioned Brady or Jimmy, or the fires. But each time something has happened you have the uncanny ability of being there, and then coming here. We did a little research after a tip last week."

The girl's eyes were wild, her pupils nearly black, her vision darting back and forth between the two men while her feet tried taking her in reverse to get away from them. This I watched from a mirror high up by the entrance to the door, the one that alerted the clerks who came in or left.

How far did the little she-devil get?

Nowhere. She got nowhere! Detective Bradshaw yanked her back. She continued to prattle, "Wrong place, wrong time, Daddy. Daddy, you know me. I didn't do any of those things. I would never! Mother told me too."

"Harper!" Detective Noyse gasped. His brows met in the middle where a deep crease in his forehead appeared. "You desecrate your mother's memory?

Ungrateful excuse of a human, you are. Read her, her rights, Bradshaw. We should have left you in that church the day we found you. Adopting you sucked the happy from my life. We saw how happy Maggie and Charlie were adopting Greer and we had such high hopes good fortune would follow us, but instead you have been the bane of my existence."

Detective Bradshaw took in a good-sized breath and began. "Harper Noyse-Gabriel, I'm placing you under arrest for the attempted murder of your husband, Christian Gabriel—"

"—Whoa! Wait, you mean he's not dead?" The not quite widow paled.

"Sorry sweetheart. We found him in the field in critical condition. Not sure if he'll live to collaborate the undo misery you've placed on this family, but time shall tell. Now, allow me to finish your arrest, I mean Miranda Rights…the murder of Greer Gabriel, and Jimmy's mom Annabel Fields and Brady's mom, Maribeth Wells, attempted murder of Ava and Ayden Gabriel, arson on two counts, animal cruelty leading to its death, and felony possession of stolen property."

"Daddy!" Harper continued to struggle, yanking her one arm free from Detective Bradshaw's stronghold. "Daddy, Greer got in an accident. I promise I didn't do anything to the brakes. The stupid horse bit me the day I tried shooting Ava."

"Jesus, Harper, shut up."

Detective Bradshaw added, "We never said anything about the brakes, Harper." The younger cop continued, "I'm so sorry, Noyse." Harper's father turned his head toward me in shame. He'd gone a deathly shade of aneurism red.

When you continue to coddle a person and ultimately, they mess up their life and everyone's around them I believe this is defined as enabling. Vicious cycle. No one wins.

"Miss," Detective Bradshaw called to my once beautiful backstabbing bride to get her attention. When she tottered around to face him, instincts kicked in and the detective stepped back, his facial expression filled with both disbelief and aversion. His eyes widened, his nostrils flared, and the jaw dropped.

Saw that one coming too.

She truly is the carnage after a mad scientist totally bollixed an experiment of cloning species together. The detectives shared a glance. Together they shrugged their shoulders, trying to cognitively make sense of the quagmire before them. Unless you live in my world some things are simply unexplainable. Which begs to differ… why didn't Harper react to Ariadne's grotesque form? How many humans resemble a cipactli in this neck of the woods? I hope none.

Detective Bradshaw cleared his throat. One more time for prosperity. "Where is Trudy? This is Trudy's Trinkets Shop, and you are so not Trudy."

The ex's unibrow inched upward. "Distant cousin. She's a little under the weather today."

"Very distant cousin," Bradshaw replied with a head cocked sideways stance. I like this guy. He listens to his instincts. "We will need the ring."

"Absolutely." With a sly smirk on her crocked-little horny lips, Ariadne slid the ring to the detective who already had a plastic bag in his trembling grasp.

After doing a double take at the warthog, he slid the bag to her and asked her to place the ring in the bag. Once the diamond had been placed in the baggy, he zipped it shut, secured a strip of tape over the seal, jot down the word *evidence* on it in bold red marker, the date, and his initials, and then put the bag in his jacket pocket. The two men resumed a speedy exit, Harper in tow struggling with a last-ditch effort.

"What the hell is wrong with that lady?" Bradshaw murmured on his way out.

"I've never seen anything like it, her. It!" Noyse whispered. "I guess there's extreme people getting all sorts of implants and tattoos."

With the slamming of the door, Hell's bells jingled one last toll for me. I believe Ac/Dc just electrocuted me.

"You're forgetting something… Me!" I pleaded to the universe. "You got the ring Bradshaw but forgot me. Dear lord, don't leave me behind with her. She is Harper's evil twin!"

Like the bling in the baggie, my fate too had been sealed shut. I am now the proud property of my ex-wife who has no clue I'm in front of her. Another jingle alerts Ariadne a new customer has come in. Head swimming, I pop myself up on the edge of the box. It's Bradshaw again. He knows the box is here. He knows Ava will want it back. All he needs to do is walk over here and pick us up, the pink floofy box and me, and be on our merry way to the county jail to drop off the delinquent murderer, arsonist, animal abuser, psycho-babbling teen.

"Miss, your name please?"

He has to be kidding. He's asking for her name and number?

The conniver hesitated, twirling a strand of hair through the pudgy thick, yellowed keratinized claws. "Aerie Summers."

"Well Ms. Summers, don't leave town."

"Am I under arrest or suspicion as well?" Her bottom jaw snapped shut. Last time I saw that she'd devoured a pixy in one chomp.

"She's freaking guilty of something," I bellow.

To no one.

"No, Ma'am. We might need you to testify, that's all."

"And possibly try out those cuffs." Little Miss Piggy gave a playful grunt.

The detective swallowed hard and shook his head no.

Pleading to my half-sister, goddess of justice on a last-ditch attempt I dropped to my knees and bowed my head. "Dike, she needs a mud pit. Have mercy on me, not the wench."

The young detective bit his cheeks. His comeback, "Tying up appetizing ladies is one of my favorite games. You, however, make me appreciate being vegan."

Wicked comeback. Now just don't forget me. Faith in humanity is still restorable.

Just as he plucked a business card off the counter, pocketing the card instead of me his walkie-talkie blared, "Bradshaw, get out here now. She's trying to fly the coop. Literally." Both the ex and I swung towards the exit, our gazes locked on the storefront window and the show just beyond it. Bradshaw pounded the door open and leapt into action. Both men struggled with Harper trying to keep her grounded. Black wings flapped with the intent to break free. Harper no longer had human legs, but instead the twiggy appendages of a bird. Claws pierced her father's face. She lifted the man off the ground, his body dangling helpless. Bradshaw hung onto

Detective Noyse's ankle with one hand and squirmed around trying to get his gun out of his holster with his free arm. This seemed to be a vain effort to keep Noyse and the creature grounded. One shot exploded bringing the Harpy and both men down. If I hadn't seen it with my own two eyes, I wouldn't have believed it, but jeesh it made so much more sense.

Harper is a Harpy. Am I slow on the uptake or what? Now the storms made sense. She'd orchestrated them. Once upon a time Zeus controlled the Harpies. They beheld the power to make it rain, make it snow, or make it all blow away. Years back, Hera killed many of the harpies in a jealous rage. Rumors abound Hera still holds a few harpies prisoner to get the remaining harpies to do her dirty deeds, always promising those jailed freedom. Heard eons past Hera was attempting to round up all the offspring the gods created below the clouds. Another reason I despise the woman. Now, as for Ava's brother? Harpies are well known for kidnapping. Food for thought once I am free and home.

A crowd gathered in the street and sidewalks watching, some horrified, others laughing saying the special effects for someone's video weren't so special as Harper dragged her body down the walkway trying to flee.

I suppose that saying, 'truth is in the eyes of the beholder' is spot on.

Bradshaw put another round into her, but it seemed to only aggravate her more. Bloodshot eyes, snarling and clawing at anyone that came in her reach, Harper pecked her way up a utility pole to a stance, her one wing bloodied and lopsided, her other twitching. With an instinctual fevered will to live, Harper took the skies, struggling to get higher while Bradshaw took aim again. Noyse then came out of nowhere like a speeding bullet and toppled Bradshaw allowing Harper the chance to flee. One minute they had her. The next she pulled a Houdini. Detective Noyse, ever the enabler. Love is truly blind.

Chapter Twenty-Five

Blindsided

Before I had time to wrap my mind around how I might get out of this cluster and get a message to Ava, or to find her, I had been hauled into a back storage room. The space is crammed with boxes, antiquities of all sorts, cuckoo clocks, dust—so much dust, tattered furniture, dishes, some chipped, some with mold adhered to them. Musty, cluttered clothing racks. Hoarders would need new undies seeing this mess. Mothballs are the new air freshener. Shoes are stacked atop the racks, the previous owner's smelly feet still lingering. Hats of every fashion era hang on sporadically placed hooks along a pegboard on the sidewall. In the corner of the room buried beneath more items sit two caskets, simple by design. Pine, casket-shaped, narrower on one end, roomier on top. I hope they are empty, but by the aromas back here I'm guessing they're occupied. Thanatos had his work cut out for him.

My olfactory senses overload. The combination of mold, mildew, mothballs, toe cheese, dust and possibly a corpse or two played a vicious game of tickle my innards. Tickling the outer parts is a whole other ballgame. My eyes teared up for two reasons: I sincerely miss the tickle the outer parts and abhor tickling the innards. A series of boisterous sneezes followed by a hushed, "Gesundheit!"

Possibility I just dropped a present in my pants… it's possible I am not invisible.

I wiped my eyes and tried to focus. Of all the places in this world I never thought I'd wind up a second time today, I wound up. First the ex's greedy grip and now Pandora's lap. Not a cozy setting by any means. My estranged wifey-pooh has this look of sheer satisfaction plastered over her that only a deranged serial killer might understand. Right now, she is the scariest person in this solar system.

"So, you can see me after all," I direct the question to Ariadne.

With an almost nonexistent shake no, Pandora eyeballed me with a downward slanted glance. I nearly missed it. Beginning to believe everything I thought to be true is a total lie. Suddenly Ava and I have more in common than peanut butter and bologna.

With my senses slow to return I scan the room only to see the long end of a scepter, one brought down from my home, used to eradicate immortals, my thyrsus. How many times could I have used this as of late? The pinecone tip is resting on Pandora's throat, honey dripping down her neck from the weapon, the vines wound around the staff, all healthy. Not two seconds ago I'd have given my crown to see the scepter runneth through my captor, but now? Me thinks something is amiss. I misplaced this tool eons past, or thought I had. Ariadne must have pinched it from me one night. Now I'm rethinking that line the elf had said to the ex before I had the marriage annulled, 'This will be killer.' She planned on using my scepter against me.

Wheels in my head are turning mush to steam. On

the other end of the weapon is my dear old fingerless nemesis, Theseus. However, he seems to have used one of his wishes granted to him by Uncle Poseidon. He got his hand back. Regardless, the rest of him looks like a turd.

The turd speaks. "Did you get the bracelet, Aerie?"

Ariadne or now Aerie dangles Tia's arm cuff from two thickened yellow fingers. "We are golden, my love. When we get home the pixies will be ours. The Elves have aligned themselves with us as well. The pixies will think their queen dead."

Her posture stiff, her neck veins pulsing, Pandora added, "The pixies will revolt."

"Not if they want their king back."

At least I know these scoundrels have not found Tia. But this doesn't tell me where she or Ava are.

"Is he in there, Pandora? Is the dickless imp in the box?" The wart hog sounded fervent. Swine flu, perhaps?

Theseus peered over my home all but foaming at the mouth. "Yeah, is he in there? Dionysus? You arrogant fool! Come on say something."

"Death to you all," I yell. Chest puffed out, I told them off. Theseus poked his new finger in my home. "Missed me! Neh-neh. Neh-neh, neh!" I think Ava is rubbing off on this *dickless imp*. Seething here. The comment did not go unnoticed.

"Look for yourself. The box is empty. You got your treasure, now leave." Pandora's facial expression screamed professional poker player. Not once did she give away my presence.

Why? Why is this woman who clearly has it out for me trying to protect me now?

I hate women! Not a one makes sense. How can women become so jaded between the age of six and a thousand? She's probably older; I'm being a gentleman not going into detail.

Ariadne studied Pandora with the authority of a mongoose about to take on a cobra. The feral wench went a half circle, her slit crocky-eyes glued to my imprisoner tapping her hooved stub of a finger to her leathery lip. She jabbed Pandora. "Why is it only you can see him, Pandy? Did you really love him?"

I gasped. My sharp intake of surrounding oxygen did not go unnoticed. Pandora's eyebrow slowly rose causing the corner of her lip to curl. Women when silent are so much more a threat. I watched Ariadne, oh excuse me, Aerie, hunch in on herself, her already porcine lips stretched taught, her cheeks drawn back to resemble the Joker's. Sadly, the entire joke is on me. Does Pandora truly love me? Naïve, dumb twit has resurfaced.

Pandora's expression remains aloof. She would so whip my butt in poker.

Belligerent, the ex continues, her hooved fist slamming into a nearby cardboard box, "The pixy must be with him now. How can she see him? I thought only true love would make him visible, and how unlikely is it for him to find such a thing, because who could love a proverbially drunken, whiney, slobbering child every day?"

You did, ham hocks. You even gave me three, may be five kids before we were wed, unless Theseus is truly their dad. If this is the case, I'm going to send you to slaughter once I'm...

The conniving consort is on a roll. Best way to see who your true friends are, is to become invisible so no one can see the true you. It's a good thing really because I'm about to cry.

"Love comes in many forms, Ariadne. Just not your version. Dion is and has always been a gentleman. He is giving and caring, both of which you know nothing of the meaning." My captor gave the ex the evil stink eye.

"Pandora don't look at me like that. I heard you have the Gorgon's powers." Ariadne turned her head away. I looked. Cats and curiosity—synchronicity. One more reason we are considered a-holes. Pandora's pupils expanded to the entire width of her eyes. Pure Draculish. With that thought I peel my eyes away. I may be a naïve, dumb twit but I'm not stupid. There is a difference.

Theseus prodded Pandora with the edge of my scepter treating her as if she were a wild animal. Kudos to her, she didn't even flinch. "Pandora, how did you turn that peon to stone? None of us have had powers since we crash landed."

Ariadne exploded, "Way to go, Theseus! Now she knows we don't have any powers, and the scepter is useless. You wasted all that honey dipping the end of the pole in it. We could have trapped the pixy with it. Brilliant. You just may be stupider than Dionysus." Ariadne gave him two horns up with her monstrous profile. A long time ago, possibly yesterday, I thought it was endearing the way her little snout turned up. Today I'd prefer to see a red line of demarcation slicing one side of her throat to the other. Where's the executioner when ya need one? Theseus pulled back on the scepter but held onto it the way a child does a balloon. With. A. Death Grip.

"Dear Theseus, lean into me and allow me show you how I solidified the insolate fool's life." Lips puckered

Pandora blew my archenemy a raspberry.

"Yes, Theseus, please, do as she asks. Kiss the crazy pottery project," I yell, forgetting for the moment whose lap I squat in.

Middle finger extended she scratched her nose whilst gazing down upon me, mischief blazing in her brilliant eyes.

I had no idea she has a sense of humor. Must have inherited it from me. My gracious grin is displayed. "One can hope, Pandora." I end with a demure wink.

Hope... The last remaining thing we added to the pyxis. All is not lost.

Yet. Is the glass half full, half empty or refillable? One grape pops into my mouth. Answered my own question. I even tossed a few of my delectable tidbits into my jailer's mouth out of courtesy for not handing me over to the warthog.

Ariadne and Theseus go into a huddle, their voices trying to outdo the others as their conversation heats up. I think I smell bacon sizzling. Out of nowhere a flash of light catches my eye. I smile. An honest one, all teeth and gums and my heart flitters. Tia, my tiny queen has zipped in to save the day.

Tia hoovers in front of Pandy and I, just out of reach, until she notices Pandora is restricted in movement.

She swooped in close and whispered, "I told you I am better than a blood hound, Dionysus. Help is on the way. Hang tight."

Before I could thank her or ask about Ava, she'd flown the coop.

Pandora opened her mouth for a few more grapes. I obliged and pitched a few in there. Still have great aim.

"I have apologies to make, Dion," Pandora started

to whisper but the bell in the front of the store rattled. Theseus nudged the ex towards the door. "Go tend to whomever entered and hurry back. I want this charade over with."

When I hear off tune vocals belting out, "I'm too sexy for my pants, too sexy for *pretty much all my clothes and everyone,*" my vision gets all blurry. I'm not crying. Happy tears break the dam. The moron I know and love, and might I add, is butt-naked and barefoot has taken the song to the extreme. Apollo, my little ray of sunshine.

That's my boy.

Apollo and Ariadne struggle coming through the threshold of the back room, her head making a solid clunk on the doorframe. Both Pandora and I flinch in unison and then laugh. Last thing I expected to be sharing with this woman is grapes and laughter. Look at us taking a ride on the wild side.

Apollo has Ariadne by her mane dragging her, her hooves scuffing along the old wooden floorboards. Slung over his shoulder he wears an aluminum jazzed-up cross bow, arrows neatly aligned in a leather pouch within his grasp should he desire to spear someone…anyone, I am no longer fussy. If I were to guess, the tips of the blades could be more lethal than a microgram of cyanide. The man does love a good poisoning.

"Where's my boy, Theseus. If you've hurt him, you're a dead man."

I knew it… Fist pump time.

I watch my half-brother give a nonchalant glance to my current housing situation, and the woman's whose hands hold my life, literally.

"Randy Pandy. Well old girl, you do get around. Thought you dodged me in the city, didn't you?"

"A girls got to try. Glad you were able to follow the stone trail I left you." Pandora's hand shot to her lips and in between giggles she uttered a shameless, "Oopsie!"

I glance upward to her shocked. "Pandy, you didn't?"

Her answering grin spread across her face the way cancer invaded someone's lungs: nothing pretty about it. "Mount Rushmore will pale in comparison. I will be adding at least one more to the total." She winked at Theseus. Better him than me.

I see Apollo leaning in towards Pandora, Ariadne's locks still entwined in his grasp, grunting, and struggling to break free. "Actually, Pandora, I followed the pixie's path. Less carnage. Less reporters."

With a quick jerk of his wrist the piglet squeals, "Let me go, Apollo."

Apollo seems not to notice. He has other things on his mind apparently as he places a chaste kiss on my warden's lips. She appears as surprised by this as I am. Her head hits the back of the chair, her artic blue eyes frozen wide open, lips same position. His eyes widen and he reels back, blaring, "You taste exactly like—"

"—Coffee." Pandora answered like a lightning bolt stimulated her.

I know the feeling intimately. No need to elaborate.

"Like coffee," Pandora reiterated. "It is quite a delicacy in these parts. I'd offer you a cup, but Theseus is being rather anal about my movements, which is why I'm tied up in the chair."

Could Apollo taste the grapes I afforded her? So… he must know I am here.

I'm about to break out in song and dance, but shall remain clothed.

"Coffee?" Apollo shakes his head a fast no with a sly smirk pouring onto his face. "Delicious? Definitely. If I didn't know better…"

"You don't." One of Pandora's eyebrows hit her hairline, her expression ruinous.

"Apollo, release Ariadne," Theseus demands.

I roll my eyes. What an imbecile.

As Apollo yanks Ariadne's hair up and down like a yo-yo he says, "You tell me where my boy is and I'll be gentle with this one's demise." My ex sent a plethora of pain-filled sobs into the room. I feel nothing for her. How sad is that? We had a history together before the annulment. I say let history rewrite itself. I need a new ending. A happy one would be the icing I never got at my wedding.

Now would be an opportune time for a country song I seem to be perseverating over. "We had it all, until the night of the great fall. I loved her, but she loved him, and on a whim, Pandora pulled the pin on our little box of sins. Oh, that's what happened the night the sky fell. I'm now in Hell, trapped in a tiny cell, invisible to most; it's why I feel like crap on toast." This is why I despise country music. Not once does the ditty ever have a happy ending, but dang if it doesn't give the synopsis to my sad tale of woe.

Theseus cleared his throat and swallowed a lump of something—fear perhaps? "Dionysus must be with the pixy."

"Then where is Zeus?" Apollo asked, "And you have Dionysus's trusted staff?"

Pandora answered for Theseus. "Zeus, Hermes,

Eros, Athena and Aphrodite and Epimetheus headed to the Badlands to go home."

Apollo looked genuinely confused. "Without us? Father left without us? Something must have happened."

Pandora gazed directly in my eyes when she said, "I will tell you the circumstances after I am free."

This cannot be happening. Have I been stranded on this godforsaken planet? What does she know that I don't? "Is Ava okay?" She gives me a subtle shake of the head. I hate not knowing. Did I truly just say this? Me? He who believes ignorance is bliss? I'm the idiot these people keep referring to.

Straightening his stance and going for the overhead stretch Apollo must have realized my ex and he were still interwoven. With a loud *kerplunk* Ariadne's head hit the floor. She ran her warty, clubbed fingers through her rat's nest, sobbing.

Me? Still do not care. Misery loves company.

Apollo drew and pointed an arrow towards Theseus before the man considered moving an inch. He warned, "I wouldn't." Apollo wiggled his index finger, his grin malevolent. "This woman alone has caused more plague than Pandora's pyxis. She hurt my brother. That alone is just cause for punishment."

Theseus raged, "Your brother left me for dead. Mutilated me."

"Dion is a lover, not a killer, you idiot. That was all me. I knew he madly loved this…" A well-placed kick slammed into Ariadne's side followed by a hacking cough. He finished with, "And the only chance he had at happiness happened to be if you were out of the picture. Ariadne, this is for ruining Dionysus's wedding day not to mention his life."

Ariadne sniveled, "What about my life? My happiness?"

"Your happily ever after is about to take a dramatic turn." Apollo twisted the crank on the bow making the bowstring taught, stretching the string to a point of no return.

When Theseus straightened his shoulders, puffed out his chest, and took that first and last step toward them, the arrow sailed through his Adam's apple.

I knew things would go south fast.

The man's stunned face painted a rather poignant picture. Eyes bulging, a few gurgles, but no audible words formed. Voice box officially obliterated. Bloody saliva trickled out of his lips, down the side of his cheek, and out of the new tracheostomy he'd been given. Gurgling ensued.

The wildebeest scrabbled her way to Theseus's side. "You won't die, my love."

I wouldn't bet the farm on that. Apollo's arrows are killer. Pun intended.

Apollo reached behind him and fished around for another arrow, lifted the weapon with care, placed it in his crossbow, aimed and plugged my ex in her thick hide with a neurotoxin that rendered her immobile. Her stunned face made me once again believe in karma.

Pandora wiggled her hand around the rope securing her to the chair. The thick twine unraveled at her touch and fell to the floor in piles of dust. She set me and my box aside and stood. Rushing around gathering her belongings, Pandora grabbed Apollo's arm. "We need to get home. Zeus has Ava, Dion."

Busy dragging bodies to the caskets, Apollo stated, "The stairway to heaven is visible until nightfall,

Pandora. We must leave at once. Help me get rid of the trash."

"Who is the boy you seek, Apollo? I know it isn't Dion, because he is right here, and you knew that the second you lay eyes on us." Pandora waited.

Curiosity hit. "Yeah, who is he looking for? Tell him a harpy might have kidnapped the young girl's brother who found me. The creature has caused nothing but havoc. You and she might be kissing cousins, Pandora." My one brow waggles in ill-fated amusement.

Apollo asked, "Is he all right?"

Busy jamming items into a huge floral canvas bag she'd hoisted off the wall, Pandora replied, "Was he ever?" She cast a playful smile to Apollo. "He is fine."

"Dear God," I mutter minus the chest tap, "tell him I'm not okay. Far from okay. And tell him he doesn't need you to talk to me. Only I need you." With this omission two huge hopeful eyes peer into my dwelling.

"You are halfway there, Dionysus." A smile poured onto Pandora's face that I can only describe as hauntingly beautiful.

I ask, even though I know the answer, "What does that mean? Halfway there? Pandy, how did you know I would be here?" I have to know.

"Of the gifts bestowed in my creation your father gave me strength and wisdom. Aphrodite added her beauty, Athena her cunning edge, Apollo his love of apothecary, hence your shrinkage and invisibility issues, Mother Nature—she gave me life and death and you… you gave me your foresight, and one other tiny gift, hope. I told you before we toppled from the mountain top you would apologize to me and tell me you have love for me, and you would need me. Halfway there, Dion. I'm holding on to the hope portion."

"I apologize for anything I've ever done to wrong you, Pandora. Truly, but with your foresight you must realize I cannot offer what I do not hold."

"We have a deal you and I. Nothing about this has changed."

"Why are you holding me to this? If you truly have feelings for me free me of this curse. That saying humans love so much; If you love something/someone set it free. I'm that someone."

She said nothing. A silent woman is never a good thing.

Not certain which is worse, me in here rotting away, or Ariadne and Theseus being nailed into a casket. I believe the second casket is holding the under-the-weather storeowner, Trudy. Apollo is hysterical. The god has a warped side to him.

And there goes the light of day. Cell door shut. Darkness is my companion for the time being. Guessing Pandora had all she could take of me.

I raise my arms and wave my hands in the air like I don't care... but I do. Damn it.

Chapter Twenty-Six

Fessing Up

Eyelids fluttering, vision clouded, but nowhere near as murky as her current conditions, Ava moved her head slowly side to side trying to figure out if she died and went to heaven, or if she were trapped in a dreamscape. Clouds, she was cushioned in clouds. Stars dangled so close she could reach out and touch the glistening molecules. A misty spectrum of colors shimmered in the sun. She'd never witnessed anything so breathtaking. And then she realized why… and where her ultimate destination awaited. Did she look down? Ummm nope! This right here, being this close to heaven was enough.

Hand to her chest for a quick inspection her clothing felt soft, feathery. Oddly, peace blanketed her.

Or was that Zeus's wings? With a slow lean backward, Ava's eye widened taking in her view.

"Good afternoon, my evening star. How are you?" Zeus sounded somewhat exhausted.

His hot, stale breath hit Ava in the face. Her nose crinkled in disgust.

"I was beginning to worry you wouldn't wake."

With a subtle eye shift, and a few blinks a white curly beard came into view followed by intense stormy grey eyes gazing down at her, concern obvious. Ava went to sit up, but quickly realized Zeus had her in his arms with one wing curled around her protectively.

"Better question, where are we?" Ava shot back, her voice verging on a tremble.

"Look around, little one. Take in the beauty of this world from an angle not many have the opportunity to see. We are climbing the stairway to heaven."

"Crapola, I died?" Ava really began to fidget. Zeus wrangled her in tighter.

Quick to reassure her, Zeus cajoled, "Shush, my little twinkler, you are as alive as I am."

Ava poked the god's rock-solid shoulder. "Not reassuring me, Zeus. Not at all. Stairway To Heaven, that's a song, not the real thing."

"And yet here you are, ascending your way to God's Golden Gates. Open your eyes little goddess, take in your surroundings. And in all honesty, this is more like an escalator to my home. I like to get my exercise and climb as we ascend. This thing is pretty snappy."

"All right, so if I'm not quite dead, why am I going to heaven? Is my mom here? My brother? Did you find Ayden?"

"I need you to see our healer. The head wound you have is significant. You would have died had I not gotten to you in time. Not many can mend such a thing. Not even I. It seems you have one of the few diseases of a deity, which comes as no surprise to me, but you on the other hand have just been given some substantial information I wish for you to digest rather rapidly."

"Are you my real dad?"

Choking down a snort Zeus replied, "No. Rather quick thinking on your behalf. I am impressed."

Matter-of-factly she replied, "Six-year-olds are pretty smart these days. Who is my dad? Thor?"

Stumbling and shifting Ava from one arm to the other not to topple over from laughing he answered, "I hope not. You are more mature than he."

"Is Jack? Is he ok?"

"Ah, my invisible boy in the box? I've been informed he is in good hands. I'm not even certain your mother knows who your father is. She had a knack for being what humans call, *a groupie*. And might I add, she had some royal blood in her veins."

Ava snapped, "That's an awful thing to say about my mom."

"It is not awful, Ava, to love more than one person at a time. I have been practicing this phenomenon since the dawn of time. Your mother was a beautiful, passionate woman. She had many suitors. Dionysus, if you're curious has had many too. Do not judge him. He has years of wisdom behind him and youth in front of him to guide him farther."

Waving her hand back and forth for the man to shut up and stop talking, Ava's words jumbled, "I, ah, yeah, that is just too much for me right now. Maybe in ten years. Maybe never." Ava flopped backwards into Zeus's arms and settled in. She looked around trying to decide if she had wound up in a dream that outdid Dorothy's and Alice's combined.

"About the ten years or never Ava…" Zeus went on to explain time warps, wormholes, black holes, Father Time, and the one hole in time Ava would soon visit.

****

Day ten billion of my captivity, okay, maybe two at the most but the tidbits and morsels of nourishment I once received have dwindled to the point my stomach actually growled. 'Tis most disconcerting. I miss the gummy bears and the company that came with them. As I lie in wait plotting my escape, a rule to live by flits through my mangled mind; never ever tell a crazy inbred goddess the truth. They can't handle the truth. Lie to her face and live with it. Deal with the consequences when and only if you must. I'm not one for lying, but in this instance, I say, "Wear that Pinocchio schnozzle with pride." It may also double as a weapon—poking out an eye or shoving the thing up someone's...

Once I've untangled my unruly beard and mustache, I pop a grape or two in my mouth with hopes of going back to a time where time had no meaning. All this revenge plotting has simply drained me.

Not a soul has inquired of my whereabouts, come for me, or visited since Apollo left me stranded. Did something happen to him as well? For his sake I hope so. I hope someone staked the moron to a bed of nails and daily jabs icepicks in his eyes because if he's not enduring the same sort of living hell I am, and he left me here to rot like fallen grapes I'll follow through with these ideas.

More plotting—more grapes.

I have come to the realization I will never see Ava again. Hope her father has man-upped and got his head out of his butt. Which oddly makes me laugh thinking of the pixy. Poor old girl. My tush is not a friendly place to be... especially as of late. My pixy queen said her ability to find someone outweighed a bloodhound's.

Pfft! A sale on honey perhaps, but not a drunken deity stuffed in a trinket box engulfed by mothballs and molded fruit—my balls. I'm talking about the shriveled up, useless gems I once flaunted with pride. I honestly thought we were friends. Naïve. Dumb. Twit. N.D.T.

How? How did this happen. N.D.T. that is how. Because I am a trusting, hopeful romantic, give your heart and soul to a gal who obviously wants to rake it across hot coals kind of guy. Again, N.D.T.

I remained sober for an undisclosed amount of time. Pretty certain it was the worst five minutes of my life.

If the lid to this tomb ever opens Jack is going to need some oil from the Tin Man's stash because I can't even stand up.

I have yet to beg. I will not ask Pandora for mercy. Ever.

My surroundings are squalor. Filth, excrement, and lest not forget pity engulfs me bit by bit. I am the California coastline being eaten away in waves of despair, loathing, futility, and those are my good days. My bad days I am worse than Loki crying his poor woe-is-me's because Thor is Thor and he's not. In this, I do feel Loki's pain. No one looks good standing next to Thor.

I'm having a beautiful dream. The sun, like I have never experienced Helios in all his grandeur. I used to think he was no more than a hot ball of ash and attitude: *Mr. Over The Top Without Me You'd Freeze Your Kahunas Off...* To be perfectly clear, I still believe this about him, but right this second I miss the hot head.

So bright, I had to squint as to not go blind. One of the most stunning sights in the Milky Way and you aren't allowed to peek at it without burning your orbs out. Just shows you how arrogant Helios is.

There is music infiltrating into the background of my dream. It sounds so much like Apollo attempting a song, I even dream I have leakage from my eyes. My shredded heart aches. I do not want to open the bloodshed slits only to be so beyond disappointed I would not make it back sanely, although this point might be well past moot.

A scrumptious, mouthwatering aroma whiffs up my perfectly straight schnozzle. A temptress. It. Is. Working. Food! Someone offered me food! I imagine a giant hunk of meat, rare, blood still saturating the flesh. Pandora's for all intents and purposes. My stomach growls again. This dream continues to taunt me.

"Is he alive?" Sounds like my little matchmaker, Eros. Now I know I'm dreaming.

Then Pandora's grisly voice chisels through my eardrums. "Wakey-wakey!"

Noooo, you wretched woman. Is it not enough you stole my life, now you steal my dreams? I attempt to slam my fists into the floor of my cube, yet my strength has waned to the point I can barely tap it.

Brilliant blue hues canopy the entire ceiling. I inhale, still hoping for the beef on a grill to fill my lungs first, then my stomach, instead freshly cut grass tickles the nostrils. I find this scent refreshing. Sure as heck beats the stench to which I've been thrown away in.

"Come on Dion, wake up." Pandora's impatience blazes an unwelcome jolt through my core.

"Dionysus? Can you hear me? We are headed home, brother."

This is too good to be true. Squinting, I shield my eyes with a trembling hand. When my vision clears, I see Thor looking at me, but still not seeing me. Eros pokes around my cave, hitting me. I flinch in pain, but he pulls his hand away unknowing I am here. I have the same ghostly properties as Casper. Fabulous. I'd roll my eyes if it didn't hurt just keeping them open. I am outside. The sun really did blind me. I've never been happier.

"What needs to be done to get him back, Pandora? This charade has gone on long enough. Is he in there? Is he alive?" Thor has backed my captor against the wall. If this were a movie the only thing passersby on the sidewalk would see would be a tall man in a romantic embrace with the devil in disguise. Thor has concealed his angered body language with his cape. He has her flat against the wall of a building.

I scream, or attempt to, "Don't touch her. She holds the Gorgon's curse." Thor does not heed my warning.

He's a dolt. Well, to be fair, he can't hear me but he is still a dolt.

Pandora's head swung in my direction, her snarl as vindictive as I feel. She goes in for the kill.

"I love you," I barely whisper, each word feeling like a nail in my coffin as they reach her. I hadn't intended ever to give her this, ever, but I have not the energy needed to shift into my puddy and shred her to pieces. I will die before I ever allow her to harm my family or friends. Her motions towards Thor quell. Then I receive the full-blown stare-down.

"Louder," comes from a skeptical Pandora.

"I need you. You have saved me from a truly loveless existence." This has so many double connotations. Yes, she has saved me from Ariadne, but she also stripped me of any relationship I could ever hope for. Stripped me of my manhood. My pride. My dignity. My freedom. My life.

As if he is naught more than a bug, she flicks Thor away with a dismissive plink of her delicate little finger. By his facial expressions I believe he is more astonished than I. With her gaze intent on me, she sidled up to the table on which I subsist. My friend is currently flat on his back, his legs up against the wall, his eyes crossed.

Her face comes so very close to my container if I had the oomph to spit, well... I don't so why bother fantasizing.

Her head tilts towards me. "Say it again. This time without choking."

And here I thought I was so suave...

"I need you." Baby steps. Let me practice this one a few times before going for the gold. Her eyebrows elevate causing her forehead to get those nasty crinkles no one likes other than plastic surgeons. "I need you." I have found my new source of entertainment. Fibbing on a gargantuan scale.

"Why? Why now, Dion?"

"Because trapped in here I have come to realize how truly precious time is and spending it alone is a sin. As is spending it with the wrong person, to which you saved me from, and I am eternally grateful for. I've learned life does not revolve around me." You on the other hand have yet to learn this phenomenon.

"What else?" She asks, caution weighing her words. She's squinting now, eyes narrowed. Looks rather serpentine. If her tongue slithers out and does its slurpy-slurpy motion I'm a goner.

She does not trust me. Can't say I blame her. I don't trust me right now. "I love you for having my best interest at heart." In the most sardonic, freaking, mentally unstable, agonizing way possible. You insane... My fists in knots shaking, I pray.

Why? Nothing else in my life has worked.

I manage a smile. I'm beyond exhausted.

Long slender fingers, nails like mine when I am in

my kitty form, painted black with diamonds on the tips, creep towards me. I like the look. Maybe Ava will paint mine someday.

And there it is, *hope*. The thing I'd all but lost. Renewed strength, a little fresh air, seeing two of my best friends here to save the day, the only thing I needed now was a body people could see, back to my larger-than-life status… and this woman's head on one side of a guillotine and neck the opposite.

It took every last iota of strength I could muster to stand. Muscles atrophied to the point I can't hold my weight, I leaned over the wall of the box, my arms planted firm along the sill, my head plopped atop of entwined fingers holding on for dear life. Tears continued to spill from the depth of my bowels. What a cluster I have become. "I. Love. You." I looked right at Thor when I said it. I won't ever tell him this. Did it so I didn't lie to her face. "I. Need. You." To set me free once and for all. That too was directed to my friend.

Her tone softened, the beautiful, jeweled eyes widened. I despise the fact her beauty still tugs at my heart. There was a time we were friends.

"What happens if I release the curse?"

I get out of here and happy dance my way home… after I slaughter you. "What happens if you don't?"

"Dion, I have misjudged you so horribly. I thought you would cave, give in, cried wolf a thousand times over by now for your freedom yet you remained so proud. Honorable. I believed you to be childish, impetuous, incapable of patience. Loveless. Self-absorbed. If I set you free will you go to her?"

"Do not believe your list could have gotten much longer."

"Oh it could have," Pandora responded in a softer almost playful tone.

Gotta say I really didn't see this conversation ever seeing the light of day, but then I'd given up on that, the light of day, as well. Up until my captivity, she'd been spot on about all her accusations. "Well," I concluded saying truths I had never considered, "possibly this time-out is exactly what I needed to realign my realm. Possibly I should thank you instead of holding hatred." The odd thing is I meant it. All of it. I don't hate this witch, all right maybe I still hold *some* resentment, but I don't want her dead anymore. "Go back to Ariadne? This implies there was something there in the first place to go back to." I shake what used to be soft manageable curls a staunch no.

Pandora's head dropped and what looked like red tears stain her cheeks. You've got to be kidding me—she cries tears of blood?

"It seems my overzealousness is instigating more havoc than the gift to end all gifts." With a slight turn Pandora reached into her pocket and pulled out a stained hanky. "My heart has been thoroughly broken. I thought I had this all figured out. Your future, mine..." She mumbled more to herself than us, "All he had to do was say he loved me. And mean it. He never even came searching for me."

"What? Wait? Hold up!" My nasally voice bellows. "I told you I loved you. I'm right here." Me, now waving a stained hanky myself offering myself up like a virgin on her wedding night.

"This was truly never about you, Dion. Well, yes it was but so much more. You were a pawn. Remember you gave me foresight. I needed to find out what kind of man you are or have the potential to be. My granddaughter's life depends on it. You! You of all the people in the universe. The gods picked you for her keeper. Her protector." Pandora had her arms raised, hands fisted shaking at the heavens. "I'll never understand their choice."

I am almost speechless. She can't possibly be referring to Ava. Can she? "What? Who is your granddaughter? Wait! You had kids? When?"

"When I first devised this plan all I wanted my husband to take notice of me again. Figured if he got jealous enough he might find it in his heart to love me, but then this godforsaken vision hit me about my grandchild. I needed to make sure you were the right man for her. I never would have let you lay a hand or any other body part on me, and if you did, which you did not, thank you, I would never have gone through with the rest of my actions. I would have brought her here to meet you but then you had to go insult me and I lost my temper— go figure, and the rest is history…" Her voice trailed off as sobs got louder.

"So, you unleashed hell on Earth. You tortured our brother and now the pyxis is MIA? Bloody hell. That is what it'll be. Bloody hell!" Thor swung his hammer through a nearby window.

Needless to say, "Don't go barefooted for a bit."

Piping mad, my throat cracked screaming. "All this was done so you could see if Epimetheus loved you? He jumped in the river before I booted him to oblivion. He probably has no idea who you are. And for the last time, who is your granddaughter? Is it Ava?"

Glaring magenta is swirling through her irises. Need to cool my jets. Two secs before my outburst I was about to get back my land legs. Crap on toast.

"Still love me, Dionysus? Still claiming your heart cares one scintilla for this despicable excuse of a woman?"

"Yes!" Oddly. "I have more respect for you. You are willing to take chances on love, regardless of personal cost to yourself or others. As a god I can relate. We make irrational decisions all the time with total disregard for others. As a man I understand. I too, took the chance on love even though it backfired and blasted me out of my ozone, well, that was all you, but if I didn't, I never would have found…" I couldn't say her name. The final layer of ice enclosing my broken heart splintered. She's a child. She has her life to live, without undue influence from a grimy, old drunk.

Pandora gathered her hair and twisted it into a bun before grabbing the hankie from me and wiping tears from her cheeks. "Ava. You can say her name. Her mother was my beautiful girl. Epimetheus made me give her away as a baby since she was not his child. There has been a wall between us for years. Not a day has passed I don't regret doing so."

"Pandora, thank you." Did I honestly say that?

I had questions, so much more to say but the goddess of pandemonium swirled away from me, a giant sob caught in her throat. As she walked away, she looked back over her shoulder, her eyes still spilling tears. "No one, in my entire existence has ever said those words to me." While her feet carried her farther away from me, she took with her my last ounce of faith. I'd been left stranded once more.

If only I could hear the violins playing me a melancholy tune at least then I would know someone gave a rat's patootie about me other than me, myself and I. There are days I wonder about them.

Chapter Twenty-Seven

Cheek Pinching Time

Ava's nose twitched. Something smelled different and yet familiar at the same time. The scent slinked up her little nose triggering curiosity. The aroma didn't remind her of her mother's perfume or her father's cologne, but she knew somewhere she'd sniffed it before. From some distant buried memory Ava knew the scent clung to her mother. Musk with an untamed woodsy fragrance sifted around her the way the sun made you feel in the early morning hours when the birds were all out hunting for breakfast and the flowers blossomed to greet the day. She went to open her eyes, but the intense brightness instead had her shielding them. Between fingers she peeked out and noticed a few people—ah giants looming over her.

"I don't think I got to her in time," One of the giants said. "Dion will kill me."

"I'm alive," Ava proclaimed, her voice scratchy, her throat raw. She went to lick her lips, but her tongue felt foreign, thick and gross. Her lips cracked when she went to ask, "What happened?"

"She doesn't remember," a gorgeous lithe woman with braided snow-white hair remarked while she seamlessly sat at the end of the light blue velvet chaise lounge Ava lay sprawled across. The woman oozed the scent that Ava recalled.

"Stop that. Stop putting words in my mouth. I remember everything except this." Ava gave an agitated flash of her hands down the length of her supine body. "The last thing I recall is being on the elevator." Feeling something cool and wet lick her foot, Ava craned her neck and took in a three-headed dog, one head with its tongue lapping away at her foot, one asleep and the other with his head cocked sideways summing her up. The tongue tickled like crazy making her squirm. "Holy melted chocolate, that's Cerberus, isn't it?"

A tall, somber man with dark silk skin, and huge gorgeous green eyes stood tucked into the darkness of a corner. He appeared unapproachable until he gave a small wave and a smile that only the devil himself could own. "I'm Hades. The dog is very friendly. He gets a bad rap wherever he goes. People tend to be judge and jury before they've met him. They tend to forget that's my job." His voice came off even smoother than his skin looked.

"Wait! What? I ended up in Hell? Was it because I blamed Ayden for the frog in my parent's bed? Or because I switched out the sugar for salt on April's Fools Day? Come on, this can't be happening. Or because I put plastic wrap over the toilet bowl on April's Fools Day, and it made a really big puddle when dad peed?" Panic mixed with total disbelief covered Ava's face while she pat her chest.

"No dear, you are not. Yet!" Hades winked and simply left her in awe. "I am up here by request of my brother. I have some work to do. It was nice meeting you. Take care of my nephew or else!" With that, the gatekeeper of the underworld strode from the room, wearing a long black leather duster with heavy black combat boots, silver spurs included, clinking down the hall. The dog followed on his heels.

Teeth chattering Ava barely managed to ask, "Did that really just happen? Where's Zeus?"

"Right here, little twinkler." The great god answered walking in carrying a cup with steam pouring off the top. "For you." Zeus pointed to the woman with snow-white hair. "Athena, help her sit up."

"Athena? As in Atty, my pet owl?"

Athena placed her index finger to her lips and winked to quietly shush Ava. Ava found an abundance of energy stashed somewhere as she pushed herself up into a sitting position. "Oh my god, it's really you?"

Zeus tossed his hands in the air. "I'm right here."

Ava shoved at his chest. "Stop with that already. I was talking about her, Athena." She tried to smile only to have her lips split even wider. Her hand immediately covered the small wound. "Ouch! Not how I ever envisioned meeting you. Ever really!"

Zeus placed a gentle hand on Ava's shoulder. "Take it easy, little one. You really lost a lot of blood. And it looks like there's still a leaky spot, Apollo," Zeus raised his brusque voice. "Fix her up!"

"Apollo," came out engulfed with nervous giggles. Ava's eyes couldn't have grown wider. "You're real too?" She asked as the tall blond man approached. "Zeus, I truly might be dead because this sort of stuff doesn't happen to girls from an itty-bitty small western town. Maybe one of them falling stars conked me good."

One eyebrow on Zeus shot up while he gave Apollo an unblinking scowl. The god of light, healing, apothecary, and poisons reached behind him and brought out a rose-colored jar with what looked like petroleum jelly in it, but it smelled delicious enough to eat. The lanky god dipped his finger in the jar and bent forward to Ava.

"Pucker up, buttercup. This is lip balm. Do not lick it off. Give it a minute and the bleeding will stop. Then you may have whatever concoction father has brought you." Apollo looked at Zeus from under perturbed lids with a half-scowl. "I never got hot chocolate from you."

Athena laughed and slapped Apollo's thigh. "I did. All the time." She turned to Zeus wearing a puckish grin. "Thank you, Daddy."

Her head all but sinking into the cushion, Ava had disbelief plastered all over her better than the stuff Apollo was trying too slather over her. "What is in it? You all are funny, but Apollo has a reputation of poisoning people where I come from."

The blond god squared his shoulders and gave a gratified half smirk. "Ah, my reputation precedes me." Apollo lowered the jar so Ava could catch a glimpse of its contents. "Rose water, glycerin, a dash of olive oil, a smidgen of milk…" Apollo took a breath and whispered, "and a leaf or two of spinach, for its Vitamin K properties. Again, do not eat it."

"Why? You didn't have to whisper the spinach part. I'm one of the rare few who like it." Ava tried to grin, but her lip stung.

"Well aren't you an odd duck. You know who else loves spinach?"

"Shut up, Apollo," Zeus jumped in with a whack to the back of Apollo's head. "She could care less who loves spinach. Just heal the kid already."

"Killjoy father, which is what you are." Apollo

tapped the young girl's jaw shut, and as he was about to apply the balm Ava shot her hand between Apollo and her mouth and blurted, "Wait! Where are Jack and Tia?"

Apollo grabbed Ava's hand and entwined his fingers with hers, while he attempted to get the salve on her lips with his other hand. They wound up looking like boxers trying to outmaneuver each other's advances. "Dear god kid, hold still." Apollo shot Athena a look of exasperation. "A little help please."

"Ava," Athena persuaded, "Allow Apollo to treat your lips. Your hot cocoa grows cold in wait. Jack is safely tucked away."

"You mean he's still in the box. Did you find him?"

With a tender tap on Ava's head Zeus caught her attention. "Little one, I promise you shall see him when the time is right and not a second sooner."

Ava surmised, "So that's code for you don't know where he is either."

"She's smarter than Dion. I like her." Athena winked at Ava.

Apollo jumped on that. "Everyone's smarter than Dion."

"Except you!" Athena pointed at Apollo laughing.

"One last question and I'll sit still—how long was I asleep?"

"Roughly a week," Apollo answered dabbing the balm over her lip. The bleeding came to an almost immediate standstill.

Zeus held his hand to Ava. "One last bit of business to tend to, Ava. Please hold your hand out and place your fingers on this pad."

The pad held a soft, nonskid cover to it and the second Ava's fingers settled over the material patterns emerged. In Zeus's opposite hand he held a small tablet-like device.

Instinct's alert, Ava snatched her hand to her chest. "Why?"

"You ask an awful lot of questions, kid," Apollo butt in.

"I am making you a suitcase that will only open for your prints."

"You mean like secret agent stuff? Whoa!" Shoulders shrugged, Ava gave a genuine smile and thrust her hand out.

"You can take home whatever you collect here." Zeus answered in between coughing from Athena and choking from Apollo. "Drink up and meander about. Just stay away from the river." Zeus pointed his scepter then motioned his index finger to Athena and Apollo. "You two, with me." And with that decree the three of them left Ava on a cushy blue couch with her favorite drink to sink in while her surroundings sunk in too.

Cocoa gone and finally feeling like her old self, Ava glanced around at the magnificence of this room, her room. Zeus told Ava to make herself at home and get a feel for the place but to be back by dinner. This palace was her home away from home.

The fantasy was nice but that is all it was. Goddess in reality, she was not. If you're a god or goddess, chances are you're a celeb from the get-go. Treated like a diva from the second you popped out. Given a silver spoon, a tiara, more jewels, clothes… Fashionesta, Ava was not.

A quick disgruntled glance down at her ratty self, Ava currently wore stained shorts, a ripped tee shirt and mismatched holey socks under her galoshes, that felt like her feet had grown two sizes in the past week. Here and now she considered herself the kid next door; the one everyone acknowledged with a sideways glance because making eye contact had such an unpleasant settling effect, like walking past a homeless person and not dropping a dollar in the bucket and feeling guilty the rest of the day because you didn't help the person. Yup, she had so turned into *that kid*. Her grandpa nailed it.

Poking around, one thing utterly odd about this palace was not a mirror to be found. After Ava bathed, she needed to make certain she'd left her raga-muffin image on earth. She'd had a foolish notion Gods had complexes about well, everything, especially their appearances, and yet not one single mirror to be glanced in. Maybe vanity was the least of their worries. Maybe her mom was wrong about it, but she doubted it. Ava knew up here among all these otherworldly beings she would be the roughed up, tarnished penny someone found jammed into the crevasse in the street, and then tossed the spot of copper back down when they realized its worthlessness. Would Jack think of her as worthless? Especially after leaving him in the truck?

Heartstrings tugged until tears spilled down her cheeks. She missed him. Worried about him. Prayed for his safety. The trauma he endured, being locked away, being made invisible, basically stripped of his dignity would devastate him. It did her. She'd take special care of him on her return. Somehow she would make it up to him. Guilt already niggled her because on their first encounter he'd basically begged for freedom and she dismissed him. She'd treated him worse than a homeless man. She hoped he would forgive a child's ignorance.

Ava would make new memories for him. A new life.

A good life.

Until then, she swiped the last tears from her cheeks and marveled in her surroundings.

Ceiling to floor windows overlooked the Lethe River, with gem infused laced panels to capture the sun, trapping each ray in the room to form a glorious warm prism. She now knew what it would be like to live in a rainbow.

A spectacular glass floor gave a view of the water running directly beneath her room. Her room. She pinched her cheeks to make sure she hadn't been dreaming or wound up in a coma after slamming her noggin into the rocks the day of the tornado. The soft trickle of the water lulled her nerves. Once she tugged a huge arch-shaped wooden door open, she knew how Jack, not her Jack, but Beanstalk Jack, felt when he made it to the castle. Everything, everywhere she glanced held larger than life character.

Armored statues along one side of the main hallway led outside. Before her stood an abandoned army, each uniform unique. Some helmets were adorned with rigid combs that reminded Ava of the back of a Spinosaurus. Probably walk away with more than a paper cut if she were silly enough to run her fingers down it. After having to be healed by the ultimate god, Apollo, Ava moved on to the next suit, her hands clasped behind her back. An enormous helmet with a miniscule visor had bullhorns coming from the top, twisted up and away with three strands of iron-spiked flails. The heavy metal balls dangled like death from the end of a hangman's noose. If the person wearing the metal cap came swinging his head in anyone's direction and made contact—ouch! Razor wire covered the gauntlets or gloves. Forget punching someone in the face: What if the person wearing it had an itch? Not with any current need to scratch anything on her body, Ava picked up her pace. An uncanny feeling of being watched prickled the hairs on the back of her neck. She chalked up the eyes following her to an overactive imagination, but still it left her uneasy. Then a thought brushed her mind. What if ghosts were trapped inside the suits? From her point of view this didn't seem so outrageous. Look at Jack. Look at where she now stood. In the hall of dead soldiers of the home of Zeus.

I must have really conked my head good.

Once the doorman opened the massive steel door the sun and fresh scent of the flowers made her forget all her worries.

Something magical about the river piqued an unhealthy interest. Maybe all the brilliant crimson poppies lining the river's banks captivated her imagination, or their scent, but Ava knew she'd never seen anything like this, except in a painting of poppies, her mom owned that looked exactly like this. She wanted to run and jam her nose inside the blossoms and inhale the intoxicating scent, but recalling a movie with wizards, witches and flying monkeys she decided against this. With a quick survey of her surroundings possibly she already had sniffed the forbidden flowers. Gods, goddesses, Hades… a three-headed dog at the foot of her bed, tail wagging…

The sun—she couldn't get over its magnificence. Or away from it. Everyone always spoke about super moons being so well—super, but this sun? There would be no cows jumping over this mega ball of flames without having one heck of a barbeque in the end. The proximity she found too intense for her fair skin. Things happened so fast. Time here sped by so quickly it made the tornado she'd witnessed feel more like a gentle summer's breeze compared to the zooming clouds whipping past. Her flesh crisped already in her short stent outside. Sunburns, although fun to peel layers of flaky skin off someone else, they still hurt. Zeus also mentioned being this close to the sun people aged differently. Possibly it was the reason for his facial crinkles.

Following a sign along a path that read *Wine & Dine*, Ava hoped to see Jack's home, his sprawling hills displaying acres of grapes, vines, and magic, but instead she found utter ruin. He hadn't told her what happened his last day here but whatever it was, had a devastating aftereffect. The grove now resembled her version of Hell. Barren. The landscape had yet to sprout a single blade of grass. Everywhere she looked reminded her of all she'd lost at the farm. Charred. Broken. Dust-blown. Memories would be all he had left. Ava knelt down and rooted her fingers deeply into the soil and said one small prayer her mother had taught her, "Little seedlings grow strong and steady. Reach for your sun and soon you'll be ready. Do not wither, do not die, do not give up, you must try. Reach for the sky. Make Jack believe he planted a stalk. Give all others here a reason to balk. Make this garden green and lush, fill it with flowering brush, bring back the vines so Dionysus may make his wines." Bent over to the ground, Ava gave the ruinous dirt in front of her a quick kiss before she stood and brushed off her knees. Before her disbelieving eyes sprouts of green began to crawl out from the rich soil. "Holy crap, Dionysus." Then she realized this was the first time she'd ever called him by his given name.

And…it would be the last. She liked Jack. It suited him so much better.

Brokenhearted for him she made her way to the river where she followed an intricate stone path to the bridge. Her heart pummeled her ribs. Was it guilt because she'd been told not to venture off to the water's edge? Most likely. What was it about this place that revved up her fight or flight system as Jack had explained it to her? That conversation felt like eons past. Glancing around, taking in her surroundings there was no threat. There was no one here. Only Ava. With one strategically placed foot in front of the other she stood on the bridge and nearly fell in when her reflection glanced back to her. "Uhhh crap!"

Chapter Twenty-Eight

Father Time

The woman in the water was no longer the girl from small town U.S.A. Ava spilled onto a bench built into the bridge and practiced the breathing techniques taught to manage shortness of breath due to the Hemophilia. Only she was getting more lightheaded. Maybe someone, the woman Ava saw in the water, had fallen in. Needed rescuing.

Peeking over the bridge again to see the older Ava, she decided she needed rescuing.

Frantic screams echoed around the river and into the thick forest. No one rushed to her rescue this time. No Zeus. No dad. No grandpa. No Jack.

This line Zeus fed her about being so close to the sun aging people differently was absolutely the understatement of the century.

A flutter caught Ava's attention. Help, at last, was coming. From across the field of flowers a small, chunky, naked cherub swooped down and hovered in her face. Aghast, Ava pointed at him and closed her eyes and screamed again. Louder. "I am in Oz. Where are your clothes?"

Right here, right now, Ava knew she'd lost it when she worried more over *his* lack of clothes—one eye peeked... yes definitely a *boy*, than the fact she'd somehow skipped the prepubescent years, the need for pimple creams, braces, the dreaded teen years, all her school dances, her first boyfriend, her first kiss... Pointing at the winged chunky angel, a naked winged, chunky angel, she slapped her cheeks and rubbed her eyes. Barely able to mutter a word, she whispered, "You're an umm, an angel?" before uncontrolled giggles took over. It proved to be the insane type of laughter that when people hear it, they step backwards away from you because they know something is about to happen. Maybe she got too close to the flowers after all.

The pint-sized being straightened his crown of shells and feathers. "Cherub. Trust me, I'm no angel. When you catch your breath, we'll talk about me not being the only one naked."

"Huh?" Ava's neck snapped down and she gasped. The little being knocked her on her tush. Okay, maybe she fell on her own. Cherubs! Her mouth gaping wipe open, she tucked strands of hair behind her ears to get a clearer view. "Oh my god what happened to my clothes?" Her tee-shirt looked like it went through the dryer ten too many times. The seams were split open. A swatch could cover more skin. Her shorts resembled a thong. And the boots needed to come off immediately. Were her feet being bound? She barely squeaked out, "No! Please? Wait," while she frantically tugged off one boot and then the other. Ava needed answers. This second. "I need clothes! I can't go back to the palace like this!"

The cherub zipped around to her side and pat her shoulder. "Why not? People run around here in a lot less, especially after one of Dionysus's celebrations." With that he flit in a zigzag pattern into the thicket of the woods just beyond the water's edge, giggles echoing.

Ava thought about chasing after the putto, but four things stopped her. First, she didn't think her shaking legs were up to the chase and secondly, he was in his birthday suit with his junk swinging in the breeze. Ewh! Her mother would kill her for running off after an exhibitionist. Third, he looked better in his birthday suit than she did in her current state of public lewdness, and lastly, she needed to confirm she hadn't gone bonkers, which happened to be the easier of things to digest. Instead, she dragged her trembling body back up to the rail, craned her neck to the top of the support, counted to ten and peeked over the side of the bridge and glanced into the water. Same woman still there wearing the same scowl Ava knew was on her face, only the woman in the water looked amazingly perturbed. Frantic fingers began touching body parts, patting newly formed lumps, seeing a foreign image that somehow took over or occupied Ava. How? Was she possessed?

So much for the new lunch box for first grade. Maybe a new Louie V bag would do.

Now laughing uncontrollably.

Freaked out? The term inferred something plausible a person could digest in due time. This, her aging into a young woman over night was more like trying to win a hotdog eating contest. She gagged at the very notion.

Kids don't age twenty years over night unless they have the disease Progeria, and then they die because well, sadly it is Progeria, a fatal disease where you continue to age out. She'd learned the word from her stint at the hospital. A friend had it. And then she didn't.

Crap again. Did Zeus bring her here to die? Is this what they were going to discuss at dinner? Her stomach hurt. Her head pounded. And lastly her heart ached. She needed to get home to her grandparents. To Jack. To her normal mundane life feeding her horses, chasing chickens. Talking to Jack. Dressing Tia in doll cloths.

Yeah, totally normal!

Feeling like Tia did in heels for her first time…completely unsteady, Ava slowly made her way back to the palace, ducking behind trees, army-crawling in some instances so people wouldn't see her. From ground level, the vast stretch of open space to the palace would be the toughest. No well-placed trees or ice sculptures, or cloth's lines, or anything she could disappear behind should someone walk out and see the couture-less mess she'd become.

When something soft and furry brushed up against her ankle, Ava slowly turned to see who or what it was. She bit back a yelp and didn't move a muscle, take a breath or blink. Frozen in fear pretty much described her current standings as a long sleek black panther sniffed her, jabbed its pink wet nose into her side, licked her leg, pawed her hair and then plunked down beside her. "Now I'm catnip! Please don't eat me." The cat's thick tail swished playfully. Mischievous green eyes blazed. Long whiskers coiled out to the sides of the cat's head. Incisors hung over the kitty's lower jaw with the tip of its tongue slightly stuck out. From a jeweled collar dangled a nametag. Jill.

Jack and Jill. No one on earth would believe her.

And then she really laughed at that notion…on earth… Ava shook her head and held her hand out for the cat to sniff. The huge animal nudged her head beneath Ava's hand and angled her head just so, so the cat could get behind her ears scratched.

Together she and the panther slithered across the grounds to the entrance. Thank heavens the doorman said nothing as she approached, one hand trying to be a fig leaf covering her front, and the other arm square across her bosom, but his smirk... thank God there was no form of video communications up here.

That she knew of.

Scratch that, she heard the clicks of a camera and the doorman's snickers.

Charging full speed through the long, elegant corridor with the cat all but tripping her up, she managed to make it past all the creepy armored guys. Unfortunately, her imagination wasn't imagining anything earlier. The armored statues were watching her. The helmets creaked that toe-curling noise of metal–on–metal...the eye slits glared an eerie neon blue color and followed her as she sped by. The panther growled, its hackles sharper than the razor wire on the gauntlets of the soldiers. Ava continued running all out up three flights of stairs, down the wrong hallway, and busted into the wrong room. The panther sauntered in like it owned the place. It probably did.

To her chagrin it was Aphrodite's room she'd barged into. Absolutely no disputing it. This goddess had beautiful stamped on her forehead.

Not really, but she might as well have. But there was a flashing pink neon light that read, Love Shack, over her king-sized heart-shaped bed. Ava's breath caught in her throat. Pictures did not do justice to the woman.

The goddess smiled. "Hello. We had bets as to how long it would take you to get back."

The moment almost made Ava forget what she was about to say. "This is so cool," was not it, but it came out raspy regardless.

Aphrodite leaned over and ruffled Ava's hair and gently fingered a stray strand behind the girl's ear. Ava swallowed and then tried again to say, "Hi," and so much more, like 'Wow, you are all betting on me like I'm this week's entertainment,' but her voice caught in her throat and squeaked. Instead, jaw as far down as it would drop Ava planted her face in her hands. "This is not how I ever dreamt of meeting you."

"I'm teasing you child. You are beautiful. Come out from hiding. Let us get you proper attire for the evening. While I'm certain a few of the men would find your current wardrobe fascinating, there are a few who would find it scandalous. Hera for starters."

The first thing to hit Ava were Aphrodite's tempestuous eyes; they were stunning. Mesmerizing. Once she decided she was totally staring the goddess down she gave her the once over, a few times. To make things a little less awkward. A small snort, half giggle leaked out. Yeah, so much less awkward.

To be in the presence of this woman, this goddess, well it made her head spin. She wore a princess fitted ivory lace gown and had her thick auburn hair down in long soft curls. The rose-colored crown adorned with pink sapphires matched her lipstick perfectly. Ava couldn't match her socks. Nerves thrumming, Ava clasped her hands together, her fingers on her left hand tapping the fingers on the right hand in the 'make a church steeple' sort of pent-up energy. Back to breathing techniques… Toss in another snort or two because now the goddess looked like she was fighting back laughter. Ava wanted to die. Legs wobbly, Ava headed for the door.

Aphrodite murmured from a divinely soft, soothing voice, "Let us begin anew." And just like that, the panic button in Ava's gut switched off.

Did Aphrodite somehow know Ava thought about bolting to the edge of the cliff and leaping? She had no poker face skills, so most likely yes. Ava had been fast forwarded to a new chapter in her life. At the very least twenty years of her life vanished overnight. Zeus mumbled something in her ear on their ascent about time warps and whatnots, but this? She had freaking boobs. Boobs! Cupping the foreign lumps in each hand Ava gave Aphrodite a despairing wide-eyed gaze and a drawn out, "Ughhh! How? They. Are. Ridiculous."

The ethereal goddess approached Ava, seemingly floating with flawless poise across the floor. She made being so beautiful effortless in the manner Ava did looking like a crash test dummy going through a window.

"Breathe, Ava." Aphrodite coaxed the girl into a chair before she spilled onto the floor. "Yes, what you have witnessed is a shock, but it would have happened eventually in your home. Here things happen somewhat faster, on a grandeur scale. You get used to it. Nothing else about you has changed. Your quick mind remains as brilliant as the day you arrived. Your skills at acclimating your environment will catch up to your body within the next day or two. I've brought you a new wardrobe. Try the clothing on. If none is to your desires then we'll hit up Athena, although her taste in apparel is downright," Aphrodite scrunched her perfect little upturned nose before finishing, "dull. I love the woman don't get me wrong, but our tastes differ in everything. I will see you at dinner tonight. The green gown—wear it. It matches your eyes."

Ava made her way to an armoire that could've been on Fifth Avenue in NYC. She fingered through gowns, dresses, armor, negligees, some black leather straps with fur cuffs attached...

Aphrodite chuckled before saying, "Not those." Ava glanced over her shoulder to Aphrodite and the woman blushed as she rushed over and plucked them from Ava. "Too soon, kid."

A few nervous giggles left Ava. She bent over and picked up a pair of knee-high patent leather boots that showcased five-inch stiletto heels. "OMG, Tia and I can twin, not! I've worn sneakers and galoshes the last six years and barely managed to remain vertical in them. Do you have anything a little less deadly?"

Aphrodite gave a gentle shake of her head no. "I'll have Athena drop off a few pairs of shoes. The reflection glass is in the bath. Wave your hand after you've showered, and you will see the true you. If you have further need call Zeus. The god does love coming to the aid of damsels in distress."

An irked eyebrow shot upward on Ava. "Ah, hold up!" Her attitude finally made it up the last flight of stairs... "Is that what you think of me? A damsel in distress? I'm no such thing. Just a bit freaking overwhelmed." She couldn't help how many octaves her voice rose. "There's a difference. Five minutes ago, I was all about Disney princesses and now I'm like one?"

Aphrodite interrupted Ava, "—There's our girl. You'll be fine. Your new shape accentuates every inch of you."

Ava waved her hands in Aphrodite's face and pointed to her chest/breasts with what could only be described as sheer horror. "What do I do with the girls?"

A smile, genuine, favored the goddess's soft pink lips. She grabbed both of Ava's hands to still the trembling young woman. "They are what men refer to as voluptuous. Yours are a bit fuller than the rest of us up here. Must be the hormones, steroids, additives they put in cow's milk to feed babies. Take the afternoon to rest, get acquainted with the new you, and when you come to dinner, look more ravishing than the meal, all right? It'll help. Tonight, you'll meet Thor, Hermes, our gentle giant Hercules, my son, Eros, and Apollo will be there as well. Oh, and Hera, my dear ex-mother-in-law and my ex, Hephaestus. Once he's spoken, you'll understand the ex." Aphrodite closed her eyes and shook her head. "Watch your back."

Ava's lips thinned while she peeked up at the goddess. "What about Jack?"

"In your short time here, you've befriended a panther who hasn't given anyone other than your Jack, the time of day unless you were its dinner. Interesting. Until tonight, my little lady."

"Nice ditch on my question." Ava plopped down on the edge of the bed and gave an upward jaw thrust to the goddess hoping for a different outcome.

Aphrodite turned over Ava's hand and placed a slight kiss on her palm. With a sexy wink and demure nod, the goddess departed leaving Ava with a molehill of new clothes and a mountain of questions. Reveling in the moment, trying to make sense of things that were inconceivable Ava stood… slowly, and once somewhat steady, proceeded to rummage through Aphrodite's hand-me-downs. Forces greater than her brain took over the body's response; the shoulders hunched, the eyes clamped shut, the nose scrunched, the lips formed a huge grin, and the feet bounced. "Hand-me-freaking-down from the goddess herself. How I spent my summer vacation, definite A+." While Ava danced and jumped up and down the panther pounced into the center of the pile of dresses and rolled through them leaving black fur all over everything.

Cats! Doesn't matter what galaxy they strut around; they still believe the world is their playground.

Thinking ahead to her trip home, her grandparents would not recognize her when she returned. Heck, she barely recognized herself. Her strawberry blonde curls cascaded past her tush and held one white streak going down her left side. Then came the breasts. They weren't huge, but they were bordering on it, and they were uncomfortable. The stupid things bounced and jiggled with every step. The gowns Aphrodite gave her... well they accentuated, Aphrodite's word—not hers, the voluptuous things, again, Aphrodite's words.

Ava's baby-faced cheeks slimmed as well. Beneath all the pudge people used to pinch on her she found she had high cheekbones.

Freckles, apparently, they weren't going anywhere.

Her emerald eyes appeared greener, her lashes longer. Her legs now looked like a runway model; long, slender, strong, and so ridiculously fast maybe she could keep up with this panther, Jill, who now lay sprawled out across the bed, its huge head cushioned on a pillow, its thick black tail swooshing in a playful manner.

Ava crawled up next to the cat and lay beside her stroking the cat's velvety soft coat, scratching under her chin, prolonging the discussion she and Zeus needed to have. Adult things.

No kidding! Her turning into one being the main topic of conversation.

Speaking of adults…Jack. She wished he were here, showing her all this life had to offer, what he had to offer. She really missed him. How? It had only been a short time they'd known each other. He had somehow finagled his way into her heart, her life just when she needed him most and now, she needed him in her future even more. She felt it as easily as she breathed. His antics. His carefree attitude. He nailed charm, compassion, and sincerity while still able to poke fun at himself. She missed him so badly it hurt in places she didn't know she had until today. Made it hard to catch her breath, to sleep not knowing if he was safe. Were his feelings mutual?

Everything in this castle was larger than life, except Jack. How would he survive once he came home? How would she survive once he left her? Once he was his old self again? And he was old(er).

What had he asked of her in the first minute they met? *A simple kiss with a not-so-simple admission of love: Men, why are they so complicated?*

Would it be that easy to set him free? Would she forever be under his spell if she did those two things? Something inside her chest, centrally located around her heart flip-flopped. It might be harder holding the words back.

Trying desperately to stuff the girls into the skintight outfit Athena directed her to wear, Ava wondered who, other than her grandparents would believe her when she tried to tell them about her adventure.

Where did she begin? Boobs? In your face. How to explain them would be a riot. Being micro chipped for a suitcase? Zeus had a sly look on his stone-face the entire time she was being fingerprinted. A pixy? That fit perfectly in doll clothes? A trip to Mt. Olympus? Zeus? No one would believe this. And finally, her very own Jack in the box? Jack was the golden ring of the carnivals. Ava's new adult mind spun.

Sex flashed in the forefront of her mind more blaring than Aphrodite's neon light. Why now?

She had no idea, but the six-year-old Ava thought it, sex, sounded dreadful. It sounded painful when she'd overheard her parents on more than one occasion. All the 'Oh Gods!" that came from the room, she couldn't believe Zeus hadn't popped in thinking he was being summoned. The twenty-six-year-old Ava rather fancied the idea and needed a mentor to get her up to speed.

She needed Jack.

And she'd be mindful not to utter any, "Oh gods," aloud for privacy's sake.

A light tap on the door tugged Ava's attention away from her delightful fantasy of exploring Jack to finding out who stood on the opposite side of the door. Could it be him? Could he have freed himself?

Snug in Aphrodite's green ball gown with her hair done in a loose twist and sporting an emerald necklace defining her décolletage, Ava decided right here, right now, she could outdo any princess in the fashion department. She took a step towards the door and tripped, barely catching her balance before she took a header into the corner of a table. "Whoa!"

The grace part needed some serious work.

Handle on the knob, Ava creaked the door slightly ajar. The padding of paws and clicking of claws alerted Ava the panther came to her side. Jill brushed up against her thigh, and stuck her head out the door, placing her body protectively between whomever stood on the opposite side and Ava.

Outside stood Apollo. "Young lady, you need to come with me. Immediately."

The cat's pink nose twitched one split second before she leapt into action and headed down the hallway with her nose to the ground better than a cadaver dog on the trail of someone who had seen better days. "Jill! Wait up!" Ava hiked up the gown and gave chase while Apollo's long legs kept him beside her without breaking a sweat. "What is it? Have you found Jack?"

"Early seating at dinner." Apollo's deadpan face gave away nothing. Ava and the over-sized kitten continued down the stairs, past all the skeletal armor suits with blazing blue eyes.

Over her shoulder she hollered, "You have to explain to me why those suits creep me out."

With a quick break in his stride Apollo cranked his neck sideways to take in the abandoned army along the wall. Ava stopped long enough to notice his pupils dilate and then retract while one drop of sweat trickled down the side of his neck. He swiped it away and answered, "They must be haunted," as if it were an everyday occurrence to have anything haunted in a home, castle, palace.

"Perfect!" Ava grunted. "One more thing no one will believe."

They continued through the palace passing rooms adorned with paintings the small art shop in her hometown would kill to acquire. Lavish frames, some gold, some silver, intricate in detail. The rooms were excessive with furniture that bellowed obscene wealth and power. A gold table with elaborately carved legs held a floral arrangement that looked like someone stuffed an entire garden into it. Rose-colored sconces on each side of a walk-in fireplace flickered. A sofa made from deep purple velvet, adorned with cushions and throws sat directly in front of the fire. The room looked like something Ava's mother would have read a romance novel in. She had to admit it did look rather inviting.

"All right, little lady, in about two seconds your life is about to change—"

Ava cut Apollo off laughing. "—Surely you jest. I passed two seconds hours ago. Unless you can turn me back to the kid I was yesterday there isn't much that could surprise me right now."

"Never say never, Ava. By the way you look beautiful." Apollo's hand on the handle of the door, he placed his other hand on her shoulder. "You need to answer one question before you go in. Allow your heart to speak before thinking. Give a clear concise response to me."

Her head cocked to the side, Ava reached up and placed her hand atop of Apollo's. "Why so serious, Apollo? What is it?"

"Ava, just answer this: Do you love Dionysus?"

Her lips slightly parted, ready to answer him the door swung inward to startle both of them. Ava took in the room and had the eerie sensation a royal funeral was about to take place. Hers?

Chapter Twenty-Nine

Who's Your Daddy?

The running of the bulls accurately described Ava's stomach, a stampede of nerves all smashing into one another vying for freedom. The doorman gave a sweeping motion of his arm inward and announced, "Miss Ava," and then he nodded to Apollo, "Sunshine."

Shaking out his long blond ponytail, Apollo followed with, "I get no respect."

Ava found roots had seemingly sprouted from her feet. She didn't budge.

Gawking however? She nailed it. Chandeliers hovered over the tables the way icicles dangled from roofs waiting for the precise moment to spear some unsuspecting being walking beneath the deadly daggers. Candle's flames threw ghostly shadows across the walls. Everyone there wore black, but Ava.

Ava glared at Aphrodite and motioned a finger sweep down the length of her attire. "Wear the green gown! You're not funny." When the goddess gave a thumb's up, Ava choked down a scream. A table at the far center of the room had her stifling a second scream. Ava dropped her hand from Apollo, squared her bare shoulders, held her head up and smiled. Until it hurt.

From the head of a long table in the far end of the room Zeus waggled his long knobby finger to Ava. Black roses arranged in vases the length of the table added a brilliant fragrance of early autumn. Blood red crystal goblets were placed beside glistening black onyx plates. The starved raptors, eh deities, waited for her to enter. Zeus called out, "Come in little twinkler. Join us."

Gathering her courage, Ava bit her bottom lip and took in everyone hoping, praying, to see one familiar face. He wasn't there, but instead a suitcase with an encrypted code pad sat on the center of the table as a centerpiece.

Hands tossed out to her sides, palms up, her voice drowned in disbelief, she yelped, "You're kidding, right? Is that what I think it is? Is that why you needed my fingerprints? Haven't you advanced enough to use that CODIS system Earth has?"

"You have a brilliant mind, Ava." Zeus admitted.

Ava couldn't help but laugh. "Zeus, that night you and my dad were in handcuffs—"

"I'd have killed to see that, Father," Athena joked cutting Ava off.

Ava added, "The cops kept saying they couldn't find you in the system. I'm learning things the hard knocks way, like fingerprints." She took one well-placed step at a time, her legs shaking beneath the gown. Zeus crossed the room and greeted her with the infamous smile he'd secured her with on their first encounter in that dusky hallway not so very long ago. Right here it felt like an eternity past. That smile of his held knowledge, humor, cheekiness, and the ability to cut off someone's oxygen supply easier than unplugging a vent in a hospital. Right here and now she thought about wiping the smugness off his jubilant face. Ava's imagination went into overdrive. She'd read children's books about gods not liking their own kids. She needed to get out of the horror novel she was weaving in her mind and crawl back into a ridiculous happily ever after plot she so desperately needed.

"My little twinkler, one of things you need to learn about me is I never kid around, even when I'm kidding around. Life's lessons come in all forms, even death."

Ava stepped backwards. Zeus chuckled and held his hand to her. "By the end of supper, we will have answers."

"Not the last supper, I hope." Ava bat her eyelashes and smiled.

Zeus and all the other guests laughed, well everyone except Hera. Ava had seen all the portraits of the goddess. No disputing that sour mug. Power emanated from the woman the way swarms of killer bees converged on an innocent bystander... that would be Ava. The queen of goddesses remained seated, her beady eyes calculating. Ava's plan? To be seated as far from her as possible.

"Sit next to me child," Hera offered, with a hard pat to the vacant seat... the only vacant seat at the table beside her.

This can't be happening. Ava didn't budge.

"I don't bite." Hera's grin did nothing to offset her remark. She appeared gluttonous.

Laughter, whispers, words ciphered amidst choking throughout the room erupted. Ava picked out a plethora of cuss words, more than once. With a melodramatic tap of Zeus's scepter, the room fell silent.

"Play nicely, my queen." Zeus gave what Ava would call a reprimanding nod to his wife. Hera's nose twitched once before she took a sip of her wine and settled back in her chair. Jill gave a low growl. Ava rooted her fingers into the cat's pelt and gave her a loving stroke.

Splitting a glance between Hera and the panther it was difficult to see who would draw first blood. With trepid steps Ava made her way beside Hera.

"Ava," Athena pointed to everyone, "this is everyone. Everyone, this is Ava. Tonight, we will hold the suitcase reveal."

Not mincing words, Athena was all business. Athena crossed the room and placed her arm around Ava's shoulder and squeezed gently. "This is how it works. Up here fingerprints act like a paternity test. When born, the infant and their father's pinky have identical prints. That way there's no disputing who is or is not the father. Promiscuity is a way of life for some of the gods and goddesses here. Think Cinderella and her slipper with Prince Charming except we idiot-proofed the process."

"I am now the absolute loser on a reality show. How the heavens did this happen?" Ava plunked her bottom down in the chair beside Hera, put her elbows on the table and hid her face in her hands.

Athena ran her fingers through Ava's hair and smoothed out the locks. She finished, "Because someone showed your mother a heavenly grand time."

A loud groan crawled up from Ava's gut.

"It gets better, dear, trust me," Hera whispered in Ava's ear before a slight snicker slipped out. "I too have a surprise for you."

Ava's head popped back up, her head spinning in Hera's direction. "Gets better as in everything will be fine and dandy once I find out which one of these clowns donated sperm and rocketed back here even faster, or gets better for you finding out Zeus isn't my father?"

With his hand to his mouth making a circle like a foghorn, Apollo yelled down the length of the table, "I really like this kid. She is fearless."

"If you turn out to be her father it'll work out well for you, Apollo. One of you needs balls!" Athena flashed a mischievous grin. Laughter continued.

"Funny!" Apollo laughed too even though Ava saw through his humiliation.

Ava stood, the panther on her heels. Chin raised, her gaze bore into Zeus. Not even realizing it Ava had made her way directly in front of the god, her finger poking into his unforgiving chest. "You had no right to do this to me. I was a child. You stole twenty years from me. Why? Who do you think you are to go altering someone's life? My grandparents must be sick with worry. Why? And where's Jack?"

"Little twinkler, you will be my favorite daughter-in-law of all time."

When Ava chided, "Way too soon, Zeuster," the room went silent, all for one.

Apollo stood and pointed to Ava giving her a fist pump. "Like I said, fearless!"

Zeus gave a drained look at his son but continued "You are passionate, courageous, outspoken and for some reason not scared of me. All I did was take out the awkward dates, you scribbling gibberish in a diary as you cried yourself to sleep when some boy didn't call you back after you and he did the deed, and mean girlfriends you'd have endured. You and my son—"

Still not ready to hear all the truth Ava cut Zeus off, "—Well let's get this party started then." Ava pointed to the smallest man at the table donned in red tights and a tunic of white silk. Red patent leather shoes with a one inch or so heel had Ava biting her cheeks. A bow and set of arrows were draped over the back of his chair. "Cupid?"

In between more choking and snickers, Eros managed to answer, "Bite your tongue, young lady. Eros here. Pleasure was all mine until you called me Cupie."

"Sorry?" Ava's face scrunched in an apology.

Eros stood and walked to greet her. In front of her he kneeled, took her hand and placed a chaste kiss on her palm. "Accepted." He stood and went to the center table and placed his hand close to the grooves of the suitcase, catching his breath.

Ava interrupted, "Before you do this, I need to know how many of you—" Ava bowed her head, closed her eyes, and dropped her voice, "I can't even believe I'm asking this—knew my mother." Ava now felt the same humiliation Apollo had. It was one thing finding out your father isn't who you thought he was, but then, and she gasped when she looked up and took a head count of all the men claiming to have intimate knowledge of her mother; it was another to see a string of men all smiling.

Apollo posed, "Better question my lady, would be why did so many gravitate to such a lovely being?"

A dagger squarely landed beside Apollo's hand where he leaned on the table. His sideways glare towards his father said volumes.

Ava took in the faces of those surrounding her. "Now what?" she balked totally fed up with deities and their personal agendas. "Just tell me. How much worse can it get?"

Athena spoke up. "Your mother is the offspring of a very prominent angel. Hamied. Angel of white light. One from your planet. The light within your mom drew this wily mob. I fear child, you have the same brilliance within you."

Head shaking, finger aimed at the infamous baby daddy proclaimer Ava muttered, "Okay, let's do this. Grab the handle on the suitcase, Eros."

Once the case didn't condemn him to a child, Eros wiped beads of sweat from his brow. "Not sorry, kiddo." Eros snagged a glass of champagne and chugged it on the way back to his chair.

"Mature!" Zeus scorned.

An arrow went zipping past the god's head.

"Missed!" Zeus teased and laughed until the next arrow stopped one pubic hair from his personal royal scepter. "Still missed," Zeus roared.

Eros retaliated, "If the target weren't so small…"

"You have a death wish, don't you," Ava mouthed to the god of love. He laughed, but smartly kept his distance from Zeus.

"Next!" Zeus jabbed his scepter towards the hugest man Ava ever laid eyes on.

"Goliath?" She asked shyly as a giant with long brown hair, and thighs big enough to be mistaken for Red Oak Trees stomped to the table. The hideous mustache went without saying.

"He is long gone, girl. Hercules, here to save the day."

Aphrodite lifted her goblet to the hulk. "Really cheesy, big guy." The goddess turned to Ava. "The bigger they are the more there is deal with."

"I always thought—"

Aphrodite interrupted Ava. "—Wrong. You thought wrong. Fingers crossed the case remains locked for both your sakes." She tipped her goblet to Hercules and then chugged.

"You are cute kid, but not mine." Hercules gave Aphrodite a slap to the back of head in passing. "Slut!"

"You weren't complaining this morning." They both laughed.

Next in line Ava picked the man out and got his name correct. "Hermes?"

"No brainer, my lady. The shoes and helmet are a dead giveaway. Pleasure. Unless it isn't."

Before Ava could respond Hermes lifted off the ground, twisted into a horizontal pose, had flown to the case, did the fingerprint scan, said a few, "Hail Zeus's," when nothing happened, and was slumped back in his seat chugging down a glass of wine with a smile.

"Do you do everything that fast?" Ava asked feeling a little spryer, gaining confidence as she stood in a room full of stuff dreams and fairytales were made of.

All the women in the room chuckled. "Faster," Aphrodite answered. "If you're ever in a hurry—"

"Aphrodite," Hera cautioned, "She is but a child. This morning she went from liking dolls to men."

"I have never liked dolls," Ava added with chin nod.

Apollo again declared, "I really like her. Fingers crossed she's not mine."

Artemis added, "She may not be, but I bet ya pop's scepter her brother is."

"Not funny, my evil twin." Apollo chuckled.

"Wasn't joking, brother. We all know you went back to Earth trolling."

"Is nothing sacred?" Apollo gave a sweeping gaze left and right. To his chagrin all guests were bobbing their heads. Apollo shook it off and headed to the suitcase. Playfully he inched his hand towards the finger slots, then pulled away with a playful wink to Ava.

"Will you stop with the theatrics already, Apollo?" Athena shrieked.

The tall blond man turned to Ava with his green eyes glimmering. "Who's your daddy now?" He closed his eyes when his fingers connected with the case. "Did it pop?"

"You're off the hook," Ava answered.

Fist pump made, Apollo bolstered, "Sweet! Want to go out some time?"

One of Eros's arrows plunged squarely in Apollo's buttock. "Really, Eros?" One-second later Apollo lay face down on the floor.

"I had orders," Eros responded when greeted by a wealth of angry jeers. All those fuming faces turned to Zeus.

The god's shoulders shrugged. "Wasn't me, but wish I'd ordered it." Zeus then turned to Hera and rested the full weight of his fury on her. She said nothing. Gave nothing away, all for one small twitch of her lip.

Quick to make her way to Apollo, Ava bent down and ran her hand over his face. "Are you certain he will be okay?"

Eros finished with, "It won't last long. He has a really thick butt."

Ava stood, smoothed the skintight dress back into submission and glanced at the last man at the table, the quietest of all. "Hi," she offered. He looked like a muscle builder on steroids. His muscles had muscles. His long, wavy, blond hair looked like hers when she didn't condition it or comb it for a day. A disaster in the making. He had blue eyes, but nowhere near as spectacular as Jack's. His cape smelled like, well crap. Just because Ava grew up in a matter of seconds didn't mean she would start swearing because she could. Getting an uneasy sensation, she peeped around at everyone when she felt all eyes on her instead of the walking asteroid headed towards the suitcase. She had the distinct feeling when the guy smiled he was attempting to elicit a reaction from her. But what? And why was everyone watching her like she would morph into yet something else? Her change today would last a lifetime. "Who are you?" She pressed, squinting with her nose scrunched.

"The last man standing, sunshine. You don't know me?"

The hand went onto the cocked-out hip... and the twenty-six-year-old attitude evolved. "Obviously not."

"Thor."

Instantly the shoulders slumped, lips frowned, and a gusty sigh escaped. Ava grunted, "Honest?" unable to mask her disappointment, because the man didn't live up to the myth. "Really?" she asked again with one last desperate plea.

"I won this bet hands down," Hercules claimed with a fist to the table, goblets all teetering on the brink of toppling over and sending all the contents sloshing over the sides. Gold and silver nuggets that had been previously placed in a pile on the table, disappeared into the giant's pockets.

"Dion's going to be so upset he missed Ava's first reaction to you, Thor. And Hercules, you haven't won yet. Put it back big boy." Athena laughed, leaning over the table, resting on her elbows waiting with what some called bated breath. Anticipation filled the air better than the testosterone-laden odor emanating from the blond mastiff about to get fingerprinted. Grumbling filled the room as Hercules pulled out the chunks of precious metals and begrudgingly put them back.

Eros raised a glass to Thor. "Grab the case, Studly. I dare you. She doesn't find you the least attractive which only means one thing."

"The girl's got a brain," Aphrodite shouted.

"Not to worry Aphrodite, no one will ever accuse you of having one," Thor shot back.

"No, Thor, wait," Hera ordered just as Thor's hand slid into the grip. His fingers automatically splayed. "I too have a surprise for our guest." Hera stood and leaned over to grab a satchel she'd stashed beneath the table. She walked across the room, her black sheath of lace trailing behind her better the way the Grim Reaper's shadow skulked behind him. She kept her back to the crowd until she pulled three items from the bag and arranged them just so. When Hera turned and stepped aside her mock smile left Ava gasping.

On the table sat Jack's box. Next to the box, Tia pressed herself against the glass of a birdcage, looking like a ravaged wild being, and in Hera's grasp, an old-fashioned skeleton key. "Life is all about choices, Ava. You have a very important one now as well. You can save your beloved Jack, release the pixy that tried to kill your Jack the day of his wedding, or use this key to release your brother. Your choice." Hera dangled the key from her index finger and thumb.

"You have my bother?" exploded from Ava's lungs better than a sonic boom could counterbalance the horizon. The guests covered their ears. Ava took determined strides towards Hera, her face a stoic mask of unyielding will. Jill pushed past Ava and got between the two women. An awkward void hung silent as the two ladies sized one another up.

Slow to come around and a bit groggy, Apollo propped his body up into a sitting position. His voice still weak from the after-effects of the arrow Eros impaled him with, gruffly he pleaded, "Ava, wait!"

Impatient, Ava turned to him, her arm extended, her fingers about to grasp the key. "She has my brother, Apollo. What?"

"I heard." Apollo answered, his tone more somber than his appearance.

"She has Jack too. How did she get Jack?"

Apollo urged, "Answer the question I posed earlier, Ava. Answer it now. Life and death."

While Ava bickered with Apollo, Hera grabbed the pink jeweled box and bolted toward the back door.

"Seriously?" Ava screamed.

"Ava!" Almost to a standing position, Apollo repeated more urgently, "Now!"

"Yes," she yawped, "I love, Jack—"

"—Real name," Apollo demanded.

One hundred percent incensed, she bit out, "Dionysus. I love Dionysus. And my brother. And Tia. What does that have to do with anything right now?"

"Everything." Apollo shot a look of triumph Hera's way.

Hera went to grasp the door handle when a seismic rumbling had everyone swaying, hanging onto tables, spreading their legs apart for support, or groping the person next to them for balance.

"Hercules, so help me," Aphrodite yelped, "hands off!"

"You weren't saying that last night. I didn't want to fall on Eros and crush him."

"Don't drag me into this," Eros groused. "Can we focus please? She's trying to flee with the box."

Hera's menaced return sent metaphoric daggers into Ava's chest. The pink-jeweled box turned the color of embers in a roaring fire causing Hera to drop the box. The cage Tia sat in bounced off the table and shattered, freeing her. The pixy jet toward Ava's shoulder as Ava lunged after Hera again to get the key. Ava came up empty-handed, but none of them missed what came next. Another loud explosion rocked the room.

Chapter Thirty

Back In the Saddle

I've watched some strange things in my life. One is a kernel of corn exploding, taking on a new shape, a new entity, blossoming, cracking the outer casing with reckless abandonment, uncaring if the inside stuff survives.

See the popcorn. Feel the popcorn. Be the freaking popcorn.

I would have whined and screamed, "Help me," in the tragic voice, Seth Brundle's character bawled as he was reduced from human status to that of a germ-infested fly, but I remain true to nature, and quite honestly, I've already lived through the exact same experience. My dignity remains steadfast. I. Am. A. God.

"Ouch!"

And… my whining days are over.

Said no god ever!

A slow raspy groan whittled free. I am terrified to move. I open my eyes only to realize I am curled in fetal position, rocking on a cold unforgiving marble floor.

Butt naked thank you very much!

I move to unfurl my slinky skeleton and in doing so sounds emanate, like bones cracking under pressure. Pretty certain it is me, myself and I contorting back to the old body, or at least I pray the old body. I do recall my warthog having a rather nasty turn of events after she peeked inside Pandora's box. A quick peek at my hands shows no webbing. The nose remains a prominent fixture. My hand snaps to my head—the crown made it through the transition... I pause a moment to regain an ounce of clarity and wipe a few stray tears from my cheeks before anyone catches them. I look around to see a plethora of faces, family, friends, and one angelic face, that for the life of me, I do not recognize. I go to scan the crowd again, but I am immediately drawn back to this delicate creature. Pretty certain I am the syrup to her pancakes. Rather corny analogy but I am famished.

She is a goddess who I feel I've met in a different time, but I cannot recall her name. She looks familiar and yet as foreign as I now feel.

Thor's cape is instantly draped over me covering my eyes, along with, "You will dry clean this immediately."

Screw dry cleaning. I'll buy him a new one. It reeks of B.O. I yanked the heavy cloth from my face. As if he is balancing a bubble on his finger I wind up in the he-man's arms. I glance into his dreamy blue orbs and completely understand why lovesick damsels swoon beneath him. Clichéd, but I am that far gone. I clung to the mountain of muscles for my life, crying more efficiently than a babe, like I'd been trapped in solitary confinement for infinity rotting slowly as I wait for Thanatos to cart my carcass away... This happened to me years past. "You don't know how bad it is." Words hitched in my throat. Emotions controlled the heart. "I'd all but given up. I believed no one cared."

My friend responded, "Ah man, I thought the whining on your wedding day took the cake. Get a grip, Dionysus. We got your back. Always. You might want to look around at your surroundings."

The enchanting goddess approached us. Those eyes!

"Thor? Is it really Jack?"

"Ava? Thor, is this truly Ava?" I cranked my head from Thor to the young lady and more bones cracked. Not only did my neck ache but my chest. Be still my beating heart was so not the time for it to truly be still. I think I might have had a heart attack. I needed the broken muscle pumping at full capacity. "Ava?" I cried while I wormed my way from Thor's strong-armed grip and crashed back onto the floor with a thud.

The young woman dropped to my side, tears filling her warm, serene eyes. My heart started an erratic rhythm again. Some people can pinpoint an exact time in their life they knew their path would forever change. Those eyes of hers—the first time she cracked the box open on me and yelled something about a dumb kid's toy, I knew then we were destined to be together, but what I didn't know was the love I held for her would grow beyond anything I've ever experienced. Looking into the eyes of a child I knew I had to tread lightly, but now more than ever, looking into the eyes of a young lady, I needed to take this at a sloth's pace. Or slower. Is there such a thing?

"Ava? Is that really you? Are you okay?"

"Dionysus." Tia gave me a subtle nod just before she leapt from Ava's shoulder.

I knew my smile made it to my eyes seeing the grin the little queen reciprocated. "I'm glad you made it home, Tia," I added seeing her jet towards the highest chandelier out of range.

Ava placed both hands around my face, brushing my curls out of my eyes and giving the crown an adjustment.

"I am better," she added with a heartfelt grin. "I could ask the same thing. Is that really you?"

I nodded yes fearing if I said anything I'd come off as an idiot. Better to keep her guessing than knowing the truth for now. "How are they treating you?" I asked while I attempted to sit up and drag the edges of Thor's cape around me to cover up all the parts that so desperately needed manscaping. My eyes couldn't take her in fast enough. "You are beyond beautiful." Apparently, her eyes were busy soaking me in as well.

Ava's cheeks warmed to a delicate shade of pink. "Wow! You look—" Ava took another breath in as she gave me the once over focused on my groin, "—whole."

"You never quite say what I hope for."

Flustered, her attention climbed back to my face. She stammered, "I didn't… it just… It isn't what I wanted to say, but I'm so new to this grown-up crud… It was a compliment. Trust me."

The gorgeous woman winked at me.

"But I am pretty certain I got the words right a minute ago! Or you wouldn't be here." Her smile turned fast from delighted to one of *OMG what have I gotten myself into.*

My hand shot out and I slid my fingers beneath her jaw. "Ava breathe. I'll practice with you." I may have needed air more than her. "It is, or will be fine," I added for both our sakes. "I understand how you feel. You and I, we will go slowly, see where this takes us. So again, are you being treated like a goddess?"

Her eyes squinted, head cocked and bottom lip at a full pout she answered, "Thinking I am more like tonight's entertainment, Jack. There's this paternity test game, which if you think about it, is bogus and truly isn't a no-brainer because if everyone here has the same pinky prints then they all lead to Zeuster, so basically the only two who can rule themselves out are Eros and Thor. Jack, Hera has my brother."

"Father?" I went to stand and immediately was converged upon by Thor and Apollo helping me to my feet. Zeus did nothing other than point to the back door, now wide open as Hera fled the party.

"There's my boy." Dad did the chest tap and gave me a warm smile that literally melted the stone coldness I'd been encased in, then his paternal flip switched and he hissed, "Go get her and get your brother back, Ava."

Before I could say a word to get things in motion Ava stood and reached for Thor's two-ton clump of metal.

"Give me it now," Ava demanded of Thor.

Thor nearly buckled over in hysterics slapping his hands on his knees. "As if. It only responds to my commands."

"I wouldn't underestimate her, Thor," I offered knowing first-hand her will and determination.

Her arm extended, her fingers waggled, and she uttered one word, "Mine." The hammer rocketed into her grasp tossing her backwards a few steps before she caught her balance and sent my dear friend to linger in a puddle of confusion. It looked good on him. But then what didn't? This is Thor after all. With a giant heave and a toss, she flung the hunk of steel in Hera's direction.

Hercules voiced what everyone pretty much assumed, "I think the suitcase reveal is a done deal." He went back to scooping the coins from the table into his pockets.

"Ugh!" came from outside followed by the sound of

something crashing to the ground.

Zeus sprinted to the back door and turned giving two thumbs up. "Nice aim, little twinkler. Eros, go pop an arrow in her butt. I need her meddling out of the way for a bit."

Eros swooped into me, pat my shoulder, said a quick, "Welcome back," and flit off to do the one thing I'd always dreamt of, plugging the stepmonster.

"Two or three arrows, Eros… just in case," my words chased after him. Noting the suitcase center stage I teased, "Did I interrupt you, Thor?" I gave a playful shove forward to my friend.

"Dion, I was rather hoping for an eleventh hour save here. You owe me at least one."

"I've seen her in some situations I didn't think one of us could take on, let alone a small girl, so I need a definitive answer. The hammer could have been an anomaly. Go for it. Let us see who brought this gorgeous woman into my life."

Saying that, my panther rose from her haunches, her tail whooshing like a dog's when their best friend comes home. Jill pounced on me.

"Come here, baby," I said in a soft tone. "I'll get you later, Ava." I gave my half-grin eyebrow waggle to my lady. Her brows rose as did the color on her cheeks. Once the panther head butt me, received her welcome home kisses and attempts at a belly rub, too which I know better; Cats and belly rubs…it's a ploy to draw blood. I stood and met Ava, stopping only because if I didn't, I'd have bumped into her. She let out a soft sigh, with her head hung trying to hide her disappointment. I knew exactly how she felt. I didn't want to stop either, but she is so new to this, I will not scare her away, or harm her in any way.

Ava's hands went to my shoulders. Having her this close, touching me, eye level with me for the first time since that fateful day, and might I add in an adult body, I had a new lease on life. When she leaned in with her lips so close to my ear and whispered, "I had to physically touch you. Make certain this time you had stuff I could sink my fingers into, hold in my arms, play with…" and then finish with, "I truly missed you. I didn't mean to leave you…" I had to wonder if I had underestimated her too? She seems to have embraced her transition to a woman rather well. Out of nowhere tears filled her eyes. I brushed each drop away as it fell. "Shush! It's all right. I know what happened. We need to talk." She needs to know that she has a grandmother to meet. I'm still trying to wrap my brain around that one.

A gurgled yelp roared from Ava's lips. I may have said something wrong… Me?

"God, not you too? Seriously? Is this the only way you all know how to start a conversation? How about, 'Gee Ava, you haven't changed an ounce since I saw you last,' or nice boobs? Or I love you?'" Laughter, a wee bit on the cynical side, burbled from my young woman.

Okay, so possibly I gave her too much credit on accepting the transition. Thor sidestepped to get out of her way. I really wanted to make a comment on the boobs but for once in my life the brain kicked in.

"Any day, Mr. Thor." Ava added in a flippant tone as she prodded the man back towards her belongings. "Get it over with. Pop the case."

We will make one unstoppable team someday. Her flair for finesse, my ability to make a mess… heaven couldn't have matched a better pair.

She didn't wait around for Thor. Ava spun towards the back door, hiked up the green gown that gave the woman curves I haven't seen in a millennium and headed out, one bountiful, bouncy thump at a time, me on her heels, and a menagerie of inane family members following us like baby chicks waiting for one of us to regurgitate something. For the record, I've already done that. Let someone else toss cookies today.

Ava continued to plod her way from the castle, headed for the river. My gut started to rumble.

"Ava, no!" I pleaded, "Anywhere, but the river."

Chapter Thirty-One

Gold Dust Women

There seemed to be no slowing her down. I whipped around to see where everyone was. Thor carried the suitcase, not by the handle, but tucked beneath his arm, sweat teeming down his cheeks. Prolonging the inevitable to the very end. What a hot mess he'd turned into. Never pegged him as a coward. Aphrodite, Athena, Hercules, Eros, Apollo, and dear old dad trailed us, some in a slow jog, others at a quick pace while Hermes did crazy-eight loop-de-loops above us.

One blink later, my worst nightmare came to fruition. Hera lay on the bridge, most likely dropping in her quake from Eros's arrows. Ava went to grab the key when Hera sprang into action and maneuvered a headlock on her, her arm tight around my little goddess's neck.

"So much for the arrows, Eros."

Eros shrugged his shoulders at a loss. "I pegged her square."

With her eyes darting from myself to Zeus, her voice cracked when Hera yelled, "No one move. The crown for the kid, Dionysus. Hand it over."

"Why do you want the crown so badly, Hera?" Ava gasped as she struggled to get away.

"Because he'll die without it. The fool will die

without his crown. He's said it a million or more times. I want him deader than dead. And since the pixy didn't fulfill her end of the bargain her husband too shall perish."

"Dionysus," Tia swooped in front of me, "she has my king. Please forgive me for trying to send you to your death. She also has Pandora."

"Pixy!" Some moron broadcasted. "Grab the nuisance," Hephaestus screeched better than a girl, trust me, I know what I speak of since I've been dealing with this minor insecurity a bit now. Tia evaded Hephaestus's greedy phalanges easily. Red-faced, he bolted off for what one might consider the blink of an eye. He reappeared running all-out with… wait for it—you guessed it, a freaking pixy net.

History is in a serious rut. I believe someone approached me, pulled a metaphysical one-armed bandit and sent my eyes rolling backwards into my head. Three cherries didn't pop up. No one would win today.

The pixy carped, "Dionysus, isn't this how our last day here ended?" while she whizzed from one spot to the next trying to avoid capture. "Where is my army?" The tiny queen trumpeted while she spun mad circles around Hera's insolent appendage.

"They are mine." Hera sneered.

"I know where they are," Ava blurted. She wiggled enough to face Hera. "You enslaved them in the armor. Tia, the castle."

"Hephaestus, I have something for you…" Tia's voice dripped deception the way Hera did trying to be the goddess of children. Tia pulled her signature spin. One gaudy grunt preceded a paroxysm of purple glitter and down went the offspring. While Hera fought her emotions of either running to her boy, or keeping my lady in a death garrote, Tia vanished. Zeus pointed to Hercules.

"Son, show him door number three. You know, the one Minos went through." Hercules, with his giant smile as he trooped off with Hephaestus being dragged behind him and tossed over Heaven's Gate, I'll never forget. Hera didn't bat an eyelash. Yeah, I don't have a clue how she got mother of the year award time and time again. Polling machines must be rigged.

"Hera, stop this nonsense this instant," Zeus groaned. "Do not make me count to three."

Yes, even up here three is either a charm or a calamity.

Hera pulled Ava closer to her mouth, and growled, "Kid, you get me the crown and you can have the key, or your brother disappears in the cradles forever."

"The cradles?" A collective is echoed in disbelief.

"What are the cradles?" Ava asked looking at me with an expression one could only understand if you stood in the clutches of a mad queen with a chokehold on you teetering on the brink of the River Lethe.

Hera answered, "The cradles, dear child, are where my harpies bring my sacrifices. You may get an inside view if you do not give me what I want."

"My brother is so not a sacrifice. And harpies?"

"Harper, Ava—Harper was… is a harpy. It was one of the things I wanted to talk to you about. She showed her true form as her father and your young detective tried to arrest her. In all likelihood, she kidnapped your brother and brought him here as a bargaining tool for the release of her own kind."

"They are birdbrains, all of them," Hera snickered.

"Give me the crown, one of you." Hera's hold on Ava waxed, her knuckles now white.

"Give her the dumb crown, Jack. It won't—"

"—Fit her fat head!" I prayed for all we were worth Ava understood my intent. My tone came off harsh and it hit Ava as such. I hadn't meant to come off so brash, but if Hera knew I wouldn't croak without the crown, or that it sprouted beautiful flowers when Ava wore it, Hera would kill her on the spot.

"His head is too big," Ava added. "All muscle, no brain. And you, Goddess Hera, the only thing big and boisterous is your ridiculous butt!"

And so Ava caught on fast. No holds barred. I love this woman… woman! Still standing here in astonishment. It's honestly creeping me out.

"You are all fools," Hera glowered. "I sat in the tower watching all of you on earth fumble worse than a helpless newborn trying to hold its lolling head up."

My hands tossed in the air, I didn't care that a hefty wind caught the edges of the cape exposing me to all. I really didn't. An hour ago, I was invisible even to me. Gone to the place people don't usually come back from intact. Right here and now, I am drained of the proverbially give-a-you-know-what's. "Let Ava go. Release her and I will allow you to live."

Toe-curling satire wriggled from the depths of Hera's smoldering bowels.

"Mating call, Hera?" My cynical humor survived the change. Thor and Hercules did fist bumps. Athena and Aphrodite were more ladylike, both doubled over laughing hysterically.

Dear old dad even added, "I think she used the same cackle on me and I fell for it. Hera, this nonsense must end. Release her. She is innocent."

Seemingly unamused by us as we were by her, Hera held Ava out in front of her. "Husband, you have my permission to go jump off Heaven's Gate. Last chance or I count to three as well."

Apollo's snarkiness came out, "I don't believe you can count to two."

Apparently to prove Apollo wrong she counted. "One...two..." Before three hit the airwaves the river's edge and forest became illuminated with glowing eyes. All the armored suits in my father's castle trooped to both ends of the crossway blocking our escape with Tia leading the troops.

"My pixies and the elves are trapped within the steel." Tia's voice held abhorrence. Purple glittery flakes covered a circular patch of grass where she hoovered.

A dynamic black cloud flowed towards us in the way a torrential storm comes out of nowhere—one minute you are tiptoeing through the tulips basked in sunny delight and the next... cursing the weatherman for his inability to look out the darn window and do his job. I'm having a moment where I feel I've relived this black hole once and foolishly thought I'd escaped. Not without consequences mind you.

Emaciated harpies circled us as carrions do roadkill. One by one creatures plunged, talons extended aiming for the pixies and elves. I'd seen enough of the macabre. As for my little pixy queen, I had to keep her safe, no matter that she tried to kill me on my wedding day and never bothered to come clean about it. The guilt is hers to live with. Someday, should there be one, we will talk but until then, I have work to do. She tried her best on Earth to right her wrong. With what I can only call dumb luck I reached and snagged dear old dad's scepter, aimed with precision, and produced two lightning bolts each taking a different pathway. The wave of power swathed anything with wings, talons, or armor in an electrified citadel. Bully for me! The armored suits resembled zombie gnome-lawn pawns glowing deep red. Hope I didn't fry the little suckers in the process. I have a feeling by the death-by-glare in their gazes no one is thrilled with their current predicament.

Ask me if I care. Honey badger is back in business.

Whilst my family, friends and foe gawked at the light show, I stepped towards Ava. My hand in my pocket I'd found an interesting little object that later I would thank Thor for, but for now when I was within striking distance, I grabbed Ava in hopes of freeing her from the clutches of the stepmonster. "Here you go, Hera. All yours. Ava for the headpiece." I reached up and grabbed my crown and in what I can only describe as slow motion I watched as I tossed my crown, the one true possession I owned into the river without regret. The crown is not worth my little goddess's life. Nothing is.

Ava started to fidget and yell, "No, Jack! Why?" Then she started gurgling trying to say, "Ouch!"

"Ava?" I attempted to tug her away, but Hera jerked her body against hers tighter.

The most heinous sneer crept over Hera's obnoxious face, followed by a thin red line across Ava's neck. My stomach churned, my heart ached, and my breath turned to ash in my lungs. The red line widened then separated on Ava's neck. Something glistened. Stuff is not supposed to glisten on your throat unless it's diamonds or rubies or trapped moonbeams. Blood began to flow in streams down her chest and soak into the dress. Red is now considered the ugliest of colors in the cosmos. I couldn't move. Ava stood dying in front of me and I couldn't move a muscle. I'd become more helpless than when trapped in the pyxis. My heart went into a chaotic rhythm that I am positive spelled out my demise. Hera is about to get a two-for-one special. Ava's gorgeous head flopped backwards onto Hera's shoulder like they were best friends and Hera's intentions were comforting her. I screamed. I have no idea what I attempted to say but something guttural tore free. Ava's innocent green eyes filled with terror while her hands protectively went for her throat. I stared at Hera with disbelief. "You slit her throat!" It wasn't a question, but an accusation. Shock, I am in shock. I glanced at my family. We all looked identical.

Hera dragged Ava back a few steps away from me and before my muscles cooperated, Ava's limp body went over the side of the bridge into the water. My kitty, Jill leapt over the side of the bridge after Ava. This alone says more than words because my cat despises water. Jill reached Ava in seconds and struggled to keep Ava's head above water, swimming against the current.

My father's scepter still in my possession, I aimed at the treacherous lecher, with every grain of my altruistic fiber I shoved the weapon with the authority of a jouster into the devil's chest. The triumphant guise our evil queen wore splintered when she realized the scepter broke not only flesh but bone. Her iced glower widened. Her body cowered around the pole penetrating her chest, her hands frantic, she tried and failed to yank the weapon out. I added the juice the weapon stored with the flick of a finger. Her body lit up from the inside out. She'd turned into a light bulb: One about to blow. Her mouth gaped wide and one thundering cry pierced our universe.

I'd love to have claimed victory, to take a moment to bask in the knowledge I finally put the woman into oblivion whose hatred has plagued my entire existence, but there were more pressing matters.

Ava.

With a final thrust of the weapon, I shoved Hera over the side of the wall into the river. My next bounce landed me on the ledge of the bridge and once I spotted Ava and Jill I dove into the water, swimming as fast as I could before I couldn't recall why I'd dove in. Thor followed above me. Apollo ran along the side of the bank with my sisters. Spitting out water as I fought the current, I couldn't see my father anywhere along the river, but I did notice harpies floating past me, belly up. Jill was able to drag Ava's unconscious body up on a large rock allowing me the opportunity to reach her. Once in my arms, her cold, flaccid body crushed my will. I dragged her close and couldn't breathe. I didn't want to. We would sink together. Thor swooped down in front of us and extended his arm.

"Latch on now, Dion. Apollo waits for you."

My arm shot up from the frigid water allowing Thor to hoist us to drier grounds. As I dangled from his arm in the same manner someone does being rescued by a helicopter, I clung to Ava's body with my other arm for dear life, willing mine into hers as if my resolve alone could perform sheer miracles. This should never have happened to this beautiful child. What had we done to her? A loving human woman caught up in the ridiculous greed of deities that loved things more than others. We don't deserve these people, their love or friendship.

Apollo stood beneath us, his arms in receiving

position. When we were close enough, I relinquished what very well may have been the last time I held her.

"I have her, Dion," Apollo assured me as he caught Ava and carried her to a soft mossy patch, assessing her while his hands moved like lightning.

Stood on the embankment wooziness began to soak into my cognizance. Fearing I would pass out I bent at the waist and kept my head down struggling for strength and resolve. I seem to recall my tale of woe something reminiscent of this beginning. My cat came and stood beside me, shaking her thick coat out all over me, again proving cats can be idiots. But how I love this one. She saved my lady. I bent over and rubbed my face against hers and whispered, "Thank you."

Not certain if it was seeing Ava bleeding out, or me choking down a gallon of amnesia juice, or the stress of it all, but I now understand why people with vertigo or severe hangovers despise the world spinning around them. Eros took full advantage of the opportunity of my exposed state to dart my tush. Well, if getting poked in the butt didn't jerk me into a standing position in a jiff nothing would.

"You will feel better in a second, Dion," Eros yelled back at me flying in the opposite direction.

"What just happened?" I looked at Thor.

"You nearly found out the river is more potent than your wine. You good?"

I was no longer dizzy. "Is she?" I couldn't even finish the sentence.

His voice shaky, Thor answered, "I don't know. I can't force myself to look. Seeing the blood of enemies is one thing. Seeing it on…" Thor's voice trailed off and he tossed his arm on my soaking wet shoulder. The

341

suitcase lay at his feet, open. His body had a tremor to it. Can't imagine finding out you have a daughter and five minutes later possibly losing her. I threw my arm around him too and the two us stood there while Apollo performed his miracle. Aphrodite, Artemis, and Athena came up behind us, so the five of us stood huddled.

"Where's father?" I managed to ask without taking my eyes off Ava's lifeless body. I didn't want to see her die, but I wouldn't leave her. I had to be with her in her last minutes if this was to be good-bye. I would not abandon her.

"Spare a glance over your shoulder," Athena insisted.

I snapped my head to the right only to see suits of armor battling the remaining harpies. "How? I thought I put them all in a holding pattern?"

"When you released dad's scepter you basically killed the circuit," Athena answered.

We watched harpies dropping from the skies wingless. The pixies were sending pernachs into the flock that injured them to the point aerodynamics were no longer a part of the equation. The final blows came from the knights with their morning star clubs. Bloodshed blanketed the banks of the river red, more so than the poppies. Even the elves fought alongside the pixies.

I asked, "How do we free the pixies from the armor?" not really putting much thought behind the question. I think I was killing time, trying to keep from going insane while Apollo killed my patience saving Ava.

"Once Hera has been incapacitated the spell will be broken," Athena answered.

"It won't be long now. Look!" Artemis reached over my shoulder and pointed to the west. High in the sky two portentous clouds formed, each with two gold chains dangling. Harper hung suspended from one cloud, the spiked cuffs biting into her biceps. We could hear the teen cursing doom and gloom. I don't believe Zeus has any plans of her feet touching the ground ever again, unless she's being planted. Hera occupied the other cloud, her arms stretched far apart, bound in gold cuffs.

I looked away disgusted. "The gold is too good for her. Rusted iron would be my choice."

With a tick of her head sideways and brows arched, Athena smirked. "Dear brother, 'tis not gold, but the same dust your ex wore on her wedding day."

"There is a god after all," Thor added.

I elbowed Thor's side. "The man's head is already too big. Don't let him hear that."

This would be Hera's second stint hanging high in the sky. Father finds this torture rather amusing. Think crucifixion minus the feet being nailed to the stake. Deep down, for reasons I shall never understand my father loves the wench. He hasn't got it in him to kill her, but make her suffer the consequences of her actions? It is most likely a good thing we are extremely hard to kill and live basically forever because I foresee Hera spending the next century or two with her head in the clouds.

Impatience began to best me. I'd been through enough and seeing my Ava fighting for her life had to be the last straw. Apollo was taking too long. This should have been a quick fix. I've seen him save people drawn and quartered... me for starters. "Apollo?" I barked.

Aphrodite squeezed my shoulder. "Let him work,

Dion. Do not forget she has the blood disorder."

With a grim appearance Apollo turned and looked at me and then Thor. "She will need blood. Get over here."

Eros landed in front of the four of us with the key in his grasp. "Got it. Finding the right door might take some time. Hercules and I'll head over now and start. What I can't open he'll bust down." I reached out and grabbed Eros's arm and reeled him into me. "Thank you," was all I could muster without breaking down. I turned around and addressed Aphrodite, Athena and Thor too. "All of you. Family is everything. We may have our tiffs, but no outsiders allowed."

"To fighting for those we love and forgoing all others," Athena voiced.

The rest of us echoed the same sentiment, "Family!" And with that we all lined up to donate.

***

Hours passed while I sat with my back against a great roan tree, Ava nestled in my lap recuperating. I could no longer feel my feet or hands. I held her safe against me, her heartbeat matching mine thud for thud. The emotions I held so close to the surface were undeniable. One minute I had tears leaking from my soul and the next giddy laughter burbled out. Taking this gorgeous creature in, her freckled cheeks were rosy with color. Thank you, my dear Apollo. I love that man.

The branches of the tree above us supported vibrant, deep blue blooms reminding me of my family and the support they have always given me. I am truly one of the lucky ones. Today more than ever.

While I wait for Ava to awaken Athena, Artemis and Apollo had joined in searching the towers for Ayden. When Ava awakens, I want Ayden to be the second person she sees, although Thor has not left our side either so… Doesn't take a genius to figure out who the first person better be. Another vagrant tear slips past my stronghold. When one twinkling green eye popped open and half-scanned the area and then focused on my face the levy holding the rest of my tears gave way.

"Good evening." My voice might have cracked. I cleared my throat and Ava's other eye opened. This phenomenon was followed by a brilliant smile. Ava went to sit but I snuggled her in. "Before you move, take a deep breath, wiggle your toes and stretch your arms over your head. I don't want you passing out on me when you stand." When she reached up and ran her fingers up my throat and through the scruff growing on my jawline every tormented cell in my being took in a huge cleansing breath and chilled. The young woman's touch had a calming effect.

Her voice soft and angelic, she whispered, "I couldn't have dreamt of a better way to wake." Her smile warmed me better than Helios in all his glory ever did.

Or maybe Thor's hot breaths hitting us warmed us when his face got within inches of Ava.

"I could think of many, but we'll save them all for a day when your dad isn't so close at hand." Thor's hand cuffed the back of my head.

"This day shall never happen," Thor teased, or at least I think he's teasing.

A pinkish hue glowed over Ava's face. I'd made her blush.

"I can only imagine, Jack." Ava's gaze shifted to the mass of muscles with tears in his eyes. "Hi Thor."

"You can call me father."

A snort slipped past Ava's nose. "Let's take this

relationship one day at a time."

"Good, I'm glad to hear you act responsibly. Dion is my closest friend but—"

Ava cut Thor off, "—I wasn't referring to Jack, Thor. I meant you and I. There's a man on earth who I call dad who earned that title long ago and I really need to see him." Ava reached over and unknotted Thor's fist and held his hand. "I think you and I shall have fun with this arrangement. Do I have siblings?"

Both Thor and I stiffened, each of us looking down at the ground.

"Come on Thor, it isn't like I'm some distant princess vying for the throne. I need to let Ayden know who's off limits because he's most likely an adult now too. No kissing cousins or any other nonsense."

Thor cleared his voice. "You have two brothers, Modi and Magni, and a sister Thudr—" He looked at me with a smirk, before he confessed, "—that I am aware of."

Ava tilted her head back and tugged on my beard. "How many children do you have?"

My hands in a flurry of motions, I shrugged my shoulders thinking about it. "Can we have this discussion another day, say when you're older and might not pass out on me?"

"Now why would I pass out? That many kids?"

"Can we leave it at a lot? I'll round them up and let them meet you. We'll have a celebration where no one is trying to kill you."

"Kill me?"

She didn't know her throat had been slit? Do I tell her how close she came to death? No lies. "Hera tried to kill you. You lost an enormous amount of blood."

As if some deep seeded memory surfaced Ava's hands went protectively to her throat. "Apollo patch me up again?"

Still shaken by the thought of almost losing her, I nodded. I might be in worse shape now than she was earlier.

"How is it I recall everything but that?"

"Hera attempted the unthinkable and almost won."

"How did you miss that one, oh Swami? I thought you had foresight? I thought if you took a swim in the water, you lost your memory?"

"Ava, where you are concerned, I won't take anything for granted ever again. Nothing gets left to chance. We all carry the antidote to the river with us just in case. Thor gave me his vial and I poked you just as Hera attempted to kill you. You yelled ouch. I assumed the needle jab hurt."

"Assuming, Jack, is never a wise choice." Ava sat up a bit straighter and glanced around. "The needle never touched me. You probably hit Hera. I would have known if I got jabbed."

"So you kept your promise?"

Ava looked at me sideways with a smile holding our future. "Well, we did pinky swear! It's the real deal."

I ran my hand down her arm to her hand and brought it to my mouth. I gave that dainty little pinky a kiss.

She added, "You are impossible to forget, Jack. I won't forget about you. Ever. Where is everyone?"

"Searching the towers for Ayden. Gives us a minute or two alone." I shot Thor the one eyebrow arched glare.

"You two, I'll be right over there—" Thor pointed to the tower. "Don't do anything I wouldn't do, Dion."

"You mean would do, don't you, Thor?" I held back

347

laughter. He on the other didn't know whether to laugh or stomp off. Stomping won.

Ava lay back in the grass and pointed to all the stars making their debut for the evening.

She pat a spot next to her and smiled. Didn't take a genius to jump on that offer. I curled up beside her and laced my fingers through hers. She squeezed my fingers tightly, as in a grip her father could appreciate. "Ease up a bit, sunshine."

She turned her head to look at me and all I could hear was the blood thrumming through my veins.

"Do you ever lay here and try to make out shapes? I see a giant bear there." Ava pointed to a cluster of stars. "What do you see?"

"People who pissed off my father." I winked. It was the blatant truth.

Ava giggled. "Never again will I look at the stars the same way."

"No, seriously, I see our future up there, Ava. Brilliant. No boundaries. An adventure with each new dawn."

"Can I please ease into this adventure before we embark on any others?"

"This easing into arrangement you speak of, we will take it slowly." I brushed a soft kiss on the inside of her wrist.

"Not that slow," Ava teased me back with her own wink.

Dear lord. She shall be the death of me. And willingly I might add.

His voice teeming with excitement, Eros interrupted our moment and called to Ava, "I think we found someone you'll want to see."

"Seems Hera has hidden people in plain sight for centuries." I pointed to people being led outside by my family, some shielding their eyes from the midnight sun, while others fell to their knees. "We entrusted the towers to Hera a long time ago to keep our city and people safe."

Ava surmised, "Well, the age-old question on everyone's lips just got answered."

"What would that be?" I asked as I stood and held a hand to her.

"If gods really know it all. Seems you do not."

She held her hand out to me, and one slight tug, she stood beside me: my best friend. Someone who would hold my heart safely till the end of days.

Seeing Thor and Apollo carrying a young man out from the tower Ava's head swung in my direction and then back to them. "Ayden must be petrified. Holy cow, Jimmy Fields and Brady Wells are with Ayden."

"Go." Her gown clung to her better than caramel does apples. For the record, both are my favorites. The shoes were kicked off, the hem to the dress hoisted, and she headed to her brother.

When Ava looked down at the young man hugging his knees to his chest tears spilled down her cheeks. I'm rather certain she'd never been happier to see her baby brother even if he was no longer a baby. Dropping beside him, she reached for him and gathered him in her arms.

"Hi Ayden."

"Aves? Aves?" His voice hitched.

"Yes. Catch your breath a minute. You'll need it."

"Is it really you? What the hell happened to us? You look so much older."

Ava cupped her brother's cheeks gently. "Remember that day you laughed at my hair? And I told you that yours looked the same? Same deal, Ayden. So much has happened, Ayden. So much. Let me just hold you."

"Where are we? Who are all these people?"

"Before I answer that I need to know something. The star you found the night of my birthday, did you look at it?"

Ayden shook his head no. "Dad and Harper did. At first they were laughing, then crying. Dad grabbed my face and covered my eyes. Why?"

"Ever hear of Pandora's box?" Ayden shook his head no. "It's the real deal. The cursed gift changed our lives. And it's still down there, on earth."

"Earth? Aves?" Ayden's huge eyes grew enormous. "Where are we?"

"I just need to hold you for a minute, Ayden. Okay?" Ava planted one soft kiss on the top of his head then did just that, held onto him and sang him a little ditty. "I'm going to tell you a tale of a wayward star, a star that exploded from a sealed-up jar. On that fate filled night."

"You sound like Gilligan, Aves. And even though momma said you could sing, you can't."

Ava laughed and cried at the same time. "Ayden, when I'm done with this, you'll have a whole new outlook on fantasy, fiction and God. And if you think the frog trick was scary…"

While Ava and Ayden got reacquainted my father came to stand beside me. I looked him in the eyes and asked, "Why?"

He nudged me and shoved me off balance. "You are welcome," he replied with award-winning smugness.

"Not going to cut it this time, Father. Why?" I wasn't dropping the subject. I deserved an answer. I was steaming mad. Ava deserved the world.

"Because Dionysus. Because I know you better than you do yourself. Your impatience would not have lasted watching her grow into a woman in her world. And quite honestly you would have died waiting. I know you think you're invincible, but we all have expiration dates. And hers would have ended her on Earth. She needed to be healed."

My voice went up about one hundred octaves. "You had no right to bring Ava here. You stole her youth. I would have waited. You lost faith in me."

His voice toppled mine. He's such an alpha. "Yes, son I did. The moment you said, 'I do,' to Ariadne. You have always made the wrong choices, always done the opposite just to defy me. Ava would have died had I not brought her to Apollo. You are my son. I have every right to do whatever it takes to keep you breathing and happy. You have yet to grow up. Do it together." With that he smiled, dragged me into his arms and proclaimed, "I really love you, you dumb twit. Go enjoy your new life."

The hug…nothing in heaven ever felt so powerful. I shoved him away. "I'm going to need some time. You and I are different. I do things for love. You live for war."

"Son, I do not have the luxury of frivolities. I have many children to care for and will not pause or hesitate to ensure your or their happiness or safety anyway I see fit. You can hate me or love me, but my decisions will always stand. You need Ava. Ava needed help. I brought her here. At the end of the day, we won this battle." He hugged me before walking off. I waited to see if he would turn back and look my way. He was probably walking forward waiting for me to call his name. Neither happened.

As I approached, Apollo dropped beside Ava and her brother looking more exhausted than I felt coming out of the box. I crossed to the three of them and suggested, "You two talk. Ayden, this man and you have some catching up to do." I reached for Ava's hand.

The young man gave me a blank gaze. "Who are you?" He asked looking at Ava for answer.

"This is Jack." She inclined her head to my half-brother. "Apollo, meet Ayden. Ayden...meet your real father."

Ayden gave Apollo the once over and glanced at his sister. "Seriously? What? How do you know this?"

"It's more of a hunch. We'll do another suitcase reveal later and Apollo can sweat it out."

Ava and I started laughing. Apollo not so much, which made us laugh even more.

"Remember when I told you the tooth fairy wasn't real, Ayden?" Ava asked completely serious. "In hindsight, I might have been wrong. I'll be back in a few minutes." Ava leaned in and kissed her brother's cheek and then stood.

We walked quietly hands entwined until we reached Heaven's Gate. I wanted her to see how beautiful life is in my home. Instead, she pulled a fast one on me. With a subtle shift, Ava turned her head and planted those incredible green gems on me. My heart stammered. She is so breathtaking.

"Jack, I'm sorry about your crown."

It took me a moment to answer her. No lies between us. "I'll live, which shall infuriate Hera even more. She thought I'd keel over."

"I realized you'd be fine without it when I wore your crown the day Harper..." She drifted off in thought before she regrouped, "it didn't look the same. It had flowers blooming all over it. I thought Harper might try to steal your magic and use it against you. Oh, I tried to pluck one grape that afternoon too." Ava snuck in a shy smirk. "I couldn't get one single grape off the vine."

The old ticker flipped again.

"If I'd given the crown to Hera when she demanded it, she'd have found out you had some special powers too and she'd have hurt you. She hurt you regardless."

With a playful tone she poked fun at me. "Well then thank you for allowing me to get choked indefinitely, and throat slit before Hera tossed me over the bridge *anyway*." Ava shoved at my chest emphasizing the word anyway.

I was quick to snatch her hands and pull her into a warm embrace. Holding her this close I may have to really thank my father. "You wanna take the plunge with me and go back and see your grandparents? Take Ayden home? Get Tia's king back, and try to make sure the plague Pandora set free gets contained?"

"You sound more like Ayden, than Ayden. That's quite a list."

"So, is that a yes?"

"Absolutely." Ava ran her fingers along my neck and buried them in what was left of my curls. Everywhere her skin skimmed mine, cells roared to life. Electricity thrummed through my veins, or was it Ava bringing life back to a half-dead deity? I'm past the point of giddy and hearing the angels sing.

I broke free from our embrace laughing, "Shut up, Apollo."

"Never," Apollo answered, his voice now filling the grove with rich, warming melodies.

I stepped back from Ava and placed a hand between us. "When I said I needed to go slow, I meant it. Last week I was reading you bedtime stories to help you sleep. I can't flip the switch this easily."

Ava mouthed to Thor, "Earmuffs," as she pat her hands to her head before she leaned into my neck and whispered, "So, tonight we can make up a new story."

I am so screwed. Why now, after a millennia of stars have shone down upon me, why now do I have a conscience? "Ava! I'm an old man and you're—"

"A young woman with a new set of hormones that I have no idea what to do with."

"You are all that, but I can't do this. It feels wrong. Baby steps, ok?"

"Jack, I'm still the same person, just a bit more developed.

We both glanced at her bosom. "Developed is an understatement." We both laughed.

She continued, "I have hormones. Do you know what they do to a person? And get your glance up here to my eyes." Ava's hands were frantically pointing upward to her face.

"Ava what my dad did to you was wrong. He stole your youth. You'll never know what it feels like to go to a movie and have your date pretend to stretch his arms so he can place his arm around your shoulder and then try for first base."

She cut me off. "First base?"

Dear lord we needed to have the birds and bees talk…. I kept going. "You'll never experience butterflies in your belly telling you that this is the most exciting romantic thing in your life. You'll never have a young man walk you to the front door and try to steal a first kiss without your dad on the other side of the door waiting to pounce."

"Not to worry, Dion, I'll be right there," Thor bellowed.

Ava tried to ignore Thor but ended up chuckling. She squeezed my hand. "So, you can teach me. You can be my first everything."

I grabbed her arms and held her in front of me. "I want to be your last everything, Ava."

"I want that too, Jack."

We had a lot of ground to cover, and thank the gods, an eternity to do it.

Ava licked her lips and smiled at me. She mumbled, "Maybe there's hope I won't be the oldest virgin here after all."

"Sorry little one, you hold the record. I promise to teach you how to frolic on a grand scale."

Amusement glowed in her eyes. "Is it called frolicking up here?"

"Slow down, buddy," Thor cut in fighting laughter. He finished, "We will have fun with this."

Ava bat her long lashes at Thor. "Dad, can I see your sledgehammer for a second?"

"Awe, Ava, you called me dad. The answer is still no." Thor groused, "You'll never get it off the ground. The first time you had beginner's luck. You were boiling over with adrenaline. Only I"—Thor's next words were pounded down when Ava picked up the two-ton clump of steel and tossed it over the edge of the cliff. Thor's eyes almost popped out of his head before he leapt for the instrument. "You're grounded, Ava," came from somewhere south of the cliff.

Ava snaked her arm through mine. She joked, "He

can fly, right? Where were we?" Ava's attempts to break me in slowly were halted by a pair of pleather boots that landed in between Ava and I.

"Hey you guys, I'm back!" Tia squealed, "Kid, you clean up good as an adult. Here! Thought you might miss this ugly thing." Tia plunked my crown atop Ava's head.

Ava smiled. "I missed you."

"Same here, kid."

"I like you wearing my headpiece, lil goddess."

Tia swooshed and circled us and pointed. "Look, you two, Pandora is out of the cradles and look who is sat beside her."

"Oh god—no dad, not talking to you this time— Ava," I pointed to Pandora, "in a little bit I want you to meet your grandmother."

Both Ava and Tia said, "What?" together.

"That's the lady that put me in the box, Ava"

"Pandora's my grannie? And I thought my gram had a temper chopping off Harper's hand…"

"Both your grandmothers do. I will let her tell you all about her life later, but for now allow her and her husband some time."

Pandora and Epimetheus sat along the riverbank chatting, holding hands. There's a country song out there about finding love in all the wrong places, but just this once, I think Pandy has a shot at her happily ever after, especially since not a second after she leaned in and kissed her husband, he shoved her in the river and then jumped in after her.

Ava grabbed my hand and started to drag me toward her brother. "Let's go get Ayden and go home."

"Home sound divine." I put an arm around her shoulder and looked at my dad. I mouthed, "Thank you," to him. He tapped his chest three times and signed, "You dumb twit."

Love him.

As for me and my young lady, I'd wished for love, for someone to spend my life with, have a family to cherish, and in my wildest dreams, they'd all come true. Ariadne had deemed me the hopeless romantic. Nay, say I. I am forever the hopeful romantic. Some may call this our happily ever after. I beg to differ. I'm calling this our new beginning. Cheers!

A word about the author...

Jaclyn Tracey's life began in merry old England on an American Air Force Base, giving her dual citizenship to both beautiful countries.

She grew up in Saratoga Springs, NY, where she married her best friend and they were blessed with two beautiful children, and now four grandees who her world revolves around. And they know it.

Jaclyn is a Retired Registered Nurse, finding there is no such word as retirement. January 05', Jaclyn wrote, Eden's Black Rose, after the Boston Red Socks won the World Series. She figured if they could win the series, she could write a book. She's grateful it didn't take 86 years to get published! She has since written YA and Children's books to expand her library of paranormal romances.